For Ethan, with love always.

HOLY ISLAND

A DCI RYAN MYSTERY

LJ Ross

OTHER BOOKS BY LJ ROSS

Sycamore Gap

Heavenfield

Angel

High Force

'Here within these hills, in this space of ground, is all the world. All anger and vanity and covetousness and lust, yes, and all charity, goodness and sweetness of soul. God and the devil both walk in these fields.'

—Hugo Walpole

PROLOGUE

December 20ᵗʰ

Winter was an unforgiving time on Holy Island. Harsh winds from the North Sea whipped through the cobbled streets between the squat, stone cottages which huddled together as if for warmth. Above the village the Priory loomed, crippled but still standing after a thousand years.

Inside it, Lucy lay shivering, her skin exposed and helpless to temperatures which had fallen well below zero. Now and then her body jerked, a spasm of pain which racked her slim form as she rested beneath a sky that was littered with stars.

She thought her eyes were open but couldn't be sure. It was so dark.

She tried blinking, a monumental effort which exhausted her, but gradually she began to focus. The familiar outline of the Priory took shape, its walls towering around her like black fingers against the ink-blue sky.

The stones provided little shelter and even less comfort. She was shivering badly now, her body reacting to shock and hypothermia.

Why was she here? Her mind tried to penetrate the pain and confusion.

She had been drinking, she remembered suddenly. There was a lingering taste of red wine on her tongue alongside something more metallic. She swallowed and there was an immediate burning sensation in her throat. She found herself gasping for breath, mouth wide and searching as she drew in panting gulps of cold air. She tried to lift her hands, to ease the burn, but her arms were so heavy.

Why couldn't she move? Panic gripped her and her fingers began to fumble around for something, anything. The pads of her fingers brushed against solid rock and she tried to feel her way to the edge, the small movement making her nauseous.

"Help! Help me, please!" Her voice was no more than a breathless rasp. Tears began to leak from her eyes.

She listened for a moment to the sound of the waves crashing against the shore below, deafening against the hush of the evening. She strained to hear other sounds, hoping and praying that her pitiful call might be answered.

Miraculously, she heard the crunch of footsteps approaching.

"Here! I'm here! Please…" She bit her lip hard enough to draw blood. "Please."

The footsteps maintained their unhurried gait and followed their inevitable path.

A shadow fell above her, the face invisible against the darkness. But she heard the voice.

"I'm sorry, Lucy. You have to believe that."

Fear and disbelief stilled her restless body. She tried to move towards the sound, to seek out its source, but shook her head in frustration.

Sorry?

Her mind struggled to process the words, to believe her ears.

"You—you can't…" she whispered. She tried to open her mouth again but no further sound came out.

Protected by a blanket of darkness, he looked down at her for a long moment, memories swirling, mixed with regret. He raised trembling hands to her throat and felt the pulse beating wildly there. He paused, wondering if he had made a mistake in bringing her here.

Not this time. There would be no more mistakes.

Death did not come easily for Lucy, but in the lingering moments before the light was extinguished, she thought of home.

CHAPTER 1

December 21ˢᵗ

Hours later, hunched against the bite of the early morning December air, Liz Morgan dug in her heels and called her dog through the gate which led up to the ruins. She hurried, sensing that dawn was near. Only slightly out of breath, she weaved through the stones, feeling the peace amongst the ancient walls which seemed to sag slightly in their retirement. Much like herself, she mused, thinking not for the first time that her early morning dog walks no longer shifted the weight which seemed to have settled itself comfortably on her hips.

Rounding a corner, she prepared herself for the rush of cold air from the sea and was not disappointed. With the Priory at her back, she stood and watched the dawn rise, illuminating Bamburgh Castle against a wash of blue mist. It stood on its craggy mount on the mainland to the south and its warm, rust-coloured stone was beginning to burn with colour in the early light; a fitting tribute to a castle which was once home to long-forgotten kings of England. Her eyes watered against the breeze and she pushed back the hair which fell across them, greying at the temples. Absently, she ruffled the fur of the chocolate Labrador who was familiar with the routine and settled himself beside her while she paid her silent tribute.

Minutes passed comfortably before Liz turned away and strolled around the perimeter, with the vague intention of heading home for breakfast and a warm shower. The walls seemed to whisper as the wind howled through the cracks, watching her progress, silently waiting.

They didn't have to wait long.

With her breath clouding the chilly air, Liz huffed around the edge of the headland and followed the barking dog which ran ahead of her.

Then she shuddered to a standstill, her knees buckling.

"Bruno!"

Automatically, she called her dog back from its exploration of what lay ahead. Horror came next, with an acid flavour. Retching against the bile which flooded her throat, Liz stumbled backwards, her body unconsciously denying what her eyes could not. She struggled to breathe, to get past the first waves of shock. Eventually, she forced herself to look again.

The girl who had been Lucy Mathieson lay naked on a thick altar. Crumbled stone walls sheltered her from the worst of the wind and sea and brought a certain solemnity. Her body was arranged carefully, arms and legs spread-eagled to remove all vestiges of dignity, even in death. Ugly bruises smudged the lifeless skin on her throat and arms. Long dark hair lay fanned out behind her in a graceful arc, matted with blood at her temple and damp from the rain which had fallen overnight. Her eyes, which had once been a lively cornflower blue, were now filmed white and stared unseeingly towards the new dawn.

* * *

In a cottage on the other side of the village, Ryan knocked back his first cup of coffee and savoured the hit of caffeine as it swam through his veins. He'd spent another sleepless night listening to the waves slapping against the shore, wishing for oblivion. He moved to a window overlooking the causeway and rested his tall frame against the wooden sill. Eyes the same colour as the overcast sky watched the tide roll smoothly back towards the sea and he knew that, in another hour or so, the causeway road would be open from the island to the mainland. Lights flickered on the other side of the channel and provided small consolation that he was not the only soul awake at that hour. Another five minutes, he told himself, and he would go for that run he'd been putting off for weeks.

"Yeah, right," he muttered, watching a couple of two-man fishing boats heading back towards the harbour.

As a kestrel swooped low on the rocky beach outside his window, his thoughts turned to work.

You're not at work, came the sly reminder that his services would not be required by the Northumbria Police Constabulary in the immediate future. His lip curled and he dragged a hand through disordered, coal-black hair.

"Arseholes," was all he said, but he was more angry with himself. The department had suggested that he take a leave of absence for at least three months. As if they knew what was best for him.

As if they had given him a choice.

He rested his forehead against the cold glass of the window. Taking time away from the job could be the best thing he'd ever done. Only problem was, he had too much time on his hands. The quiet had a way of opening the door to memories best forgotten.

Heavy-lidded eyes drooped wearily then flew open again at the sound of a sharp bang. He had a brief moment to think that it could have been the sound of the brutal hangover rattling around his head, then the sound came again, more insistent this time. He pushed himself away from the window towards the door.

The banging grew louder.

"Yes—I'm coming!" The smooth accent became more clipped when he raised his voice. A leftover from his days spent in a boarding school where the Queen's English wasn't just expected, it was demanded, along with appropriate dress and manners. A smile tugged at the corners of his mouth as he caught his reflection in the hallway mirror.

Not exactly abiding by house rules, there, Ryan, he thought, noting the rumpled wool jumper and faded jeans, the stubble on his jaw.

Maxwell Charles Finley-Ryan. He preferred just 'Ryan'. Life was complicated enough without adding a series of ridiculous names into the mix.

He fiddled with the locks and eventually the door swung open. He struggled to place the woman who stood shivering in front of him. Mid-fifties, trim, with short, ash-blonde hair styled in a bob which was currently weather-blown and damp. Her hands clutched at the lapels of her anorak and shook slightly. A dark brown Labrador whimpered at her heels.

Dawn? Jeanette? He thought he had seen her working in one of the craft shops in the village.

"Ah…" he tried to remember the basic social graces but she cut across him, the words tumbling out of numb lips.

"I found her up at the Priory. You have to come with me."

Ryan lifted a brow but instinct was setting in. Her pupils were like pinpricks. Her hands shook and her breathing was unsteady.

"Okay, look…Liz," he remembered with a flash of insight that she had sold him a flowery scented candle he'd sent to his mother. "Come inside, out of the cold."

"No, no, you have to come *now*." Her body shuddered as he tried to take her arms in a gentle grip.

"I'm going to help you but first you need to come inside and sit down."

He led her through the little passageway to the sitting room with its cosy fireplace and worn leather sofa. He wished he had lit a fire. He had another moment's regret that he hadn't cleaned up the remnants of last night's bottle and a half of red wine, but by the look on the woman's face she wasn't aware of her surroundings. The dog sloped in after them, unwilling to leave her.

"Now," he eased her onto the sofa. "What's happened? Have you hurt yourself?"

"No, not me!" Her face was anguished. "It's Lucy—she's lying up there in the Priory."

He watched as fat tears began to run down her cheeks and a sick feeling rolled in his gut.

"What happened to Lucy?"

"I don't know, but she's dead." Her voice was hollow and hitched with deep, ragged breaths. "I used to babysit her when she was little. Her mother…oh God, Helen, how will I tell her?" Her eyes closed and when they opened again they were dark with grief. "She was just a baby. She was still just a baby." She began to weep; deep, heart-wrenching sobs which shuddered through her small frame.

Ryan's chest constricted. It seemed that, no matter what the department ordered, death followed him wherever he went.

"Are you sure?"

She managed a sharp nod. "She was gone."

He believed her.

"Wait here," he murmured, then moved quickly to the telephone in the hallway, looked up the number of the local coastguard and put the call through. There was no police force stationed on the island.

"Alex?" The phone was answered after a couple of rings and he knew the coastguard would have been up for an hour already on his present shift.

"Yeah?" The voice with its musical Northern lilt was friendly. "Got an emergency?"

"I need you to secure an area up at the Priory. No access to the general public, to anybody other than me at this point. "

"What? Look, you can't—"

"There's a girl lying dead up there."

There was a humming silence at the end of the line before Alex's voice came through again in hushed tones.

"Are you sure?"

Ryan thought of the woman in the room beyond. There was always hope that Liz had been wrong.

"Get hold of the local doctor and tell him to meet us at the entrance to the Priory. We'll find out for sure." He couldn't let the whole neighbourhood start helping themselves to a glimpse of the crime scene. "Nobody goes past the entrance, in or out, without my knowledge. Bring tape to cordon off the area and something to put over your feet and clothes—overalls if you have them."

Ryan paused to open the front door, sniffed at the air. "Bring some tarpaulin or plastic sheets too, it looks like rain. I'll meet you up there as soon as I can. Contact the police on the mainland. Ask the control room to refer it to Gregson and tell them to get a team over here."

Alex let out a long breath before answering. "My father's the doctor on the island, so I'll get in touch with him now. It's going to be another hour before the road will be clear for the police to cross, though. Ah, Ryan, are you going to…" He cleared his throat awkwardly. "Look, I've never done anything like this before." The coastguard on Lindisfarne held a special dispensation to act as an initial response team in case of emergencies, but so far that had involved breaking up a couple of half-hearted pub brawls and a squabble between two tourists about who had backed into the other's SUV. Murder definitely broke new ground.

"I'll walk you through it. Five minutes, Alex, ten max."

He replaced the receiver and moved back into the sitting room, pausing in the doorway for a moment. Liz sat huddled, seeming older and more fragile than before. Her face was pale, her eyes too dark and her hands still shaking.

"Liz," he said gently and watched her body jerk. "Is there somebody I can call? Can I get you something, a glass of water maybe?"

"I need Sean." She recited the number.

He called her husband and explained the situation. The immediate concern in the other man's voice told Ryan that he would not have to wait long before there was another knock on the door. It was good that she had somebody.

Ryan spent a few minutes taking down a brief statement, snatches of information from Liz before she broke down completely. Her husband arrived soon after and as Ryan watched them leave, he thought about how Liz's first instinct had been to run to him rather than to the husband she loved. Mouth grim, he grabbed his phone and the field kit he kept in the hallway cupboard.

It seemed like his three months' sabbatical was up.

* * *

Ryan vaulted over the visitor's gate at the entrance to the Priory, his long legs eating up the ground, shoes covered in plastic. He noticed the lack of deterrent to the public, which would need to be remedied immediately. Evidently, the coastguards had been slow to arrive. He pulled out a roll of police tape and didn't question the cynicism which had driven him to pack it when he moved to Lindisfarne. He rolled out the tape across the entrance and along the fence.

"Have to do for now," he grumbled.

He cast his eye around the vicinity. The place was secluded, the village accounting for ninety per cent of the structures on the island, with only a few scattered holiday homes by the beach or on the outskirts. Turning, he could see the edge of the village to his left and the harbour which spread out towards the fort with the coastguard hut at its base, to his right. No cars parked suggestively nearby, no people except for the girl who awaited him.

His eyes tracked as he walked carefully across the mossy grass which grew between the walls. He snapped pictures as he went—forensics would get it all, but you never knew what you might miss the first time around. No obvious footpath or footprints other than the well-worn path which led around the perimeter of the site, but he trod carefully to the side in any event. Without any obvious indication of where he would find the body, Ryan followed Liz's description and steeled himself, scenting that he was near as he wound through the high, arched walls and was met with an unmistakably sweet scent.

It wasn't the first time he had seen death. His system jumped but didn't revolt as it wanted to. A girl who had once been lovely was draped across a wide stone slab. Her legs were parted and only long experience allowed him to keep looking without feeling hideously voyeuristic. The animals had started to do their work, he noticed dully, but it led him to estimate that she had been dead only a few hours. Her body looked rigid but not as wooden as some he had seen. Rigor mortis might have set in, but only fairly recently if he was any judge. He snapped pictures from all angles and then panned out to take in the full scene.

He lowered his camera and frowned. The girl looked like she had been *arranged*. She lay there naked, palms both upwards, outstretched. Blood from the gash he could see matting the hair at her temple had been used to mark her forehead and palms, to sweep lines along her torso from chest to navel. Her hair seemed to have been combed out to frame her face. He sniffed the air. Amid the ripe scent of the beginnings of decay, there was definitely something else. Something herbal, which made him think inappropriately of curry. He filed the thought away and looked again. She hadn't died from the bump on her head, he thought. Treading carefully, leaving a wide berth around the body, he could see the mottled bruises on her slim throat and the signs of burst blood vessels under the skin on her face. Somebody with big hands had choked the life out of her.

Her clothes were missing.

"Careful, weren't you?" Ryan murmured.

Eyes tracking, always tracking, he moved back to the entrance to guard the scene until the coastguards arrived.

"Taking their sweet time," he said, checking his watch. *Nearly six-fifteen.*

It would be another forty minutes until police could get across to the island; calling out a helicopter from the RAF base on the mainland would take the same amount of time, as would trying to get a boat across.

There was a call he needed to make and he couldn't put it off any longer.

He slipped out his phone, keyed in the number and unconsciously squared his shoulders.

"Gregson." The familiar bark of the Detective Chief Superintendent, CID commander for Northumberland area, came down the line.

"It's Ryan, sir."

There was an infinitesimal pause.

"Good to hear from you. Is this a social call? If so, it's an unsociable hour."

Ryan ignored the question since he happened to know that Arthur Gregson arrived promptly at his desk at six sharp every morning, come rain or shine. Despite his rank, Gregson was still the first to arrive and the last to leave. He didn't appear to have been informed of the latest news, so Ryan came to the point.

"Sir, you're aware I've been spending some time on Lindisfarne. An incident was reported to me approximately fifteen minutes ago by one of the islanders, a local woman who was the first on the scene. In the absence of an attending officer, I took a preliminary statement from the witness and duly contacted the coastguard in the absence of a standing police presence on the island. I have advised them to contact the local authorities, referring the matter to your office."

"Incident?" Gregson was never a man to waste words.

"Yes, sir. I felt it prudent to attend the scene at the Priory ruins and will instruct the coastguards to cordon off any other access points at the earliest opportunity. First observation indicates the suspicious death of a local girl, approximately twenty years old." He thought of the body lying a few feet behind where he stood and spoke more firmly. "It looks like murder, with ritualistic overtones."

There was a barely audible sigh at the end of the line. "It sounds like you've done your duty, Ryan. I'll send Phillips or MacKenzie."

"Sir, requesting permission to return to duty and lead the investigation."

"Absolutely not."

Ryan gritted his teeth. It was no more than he had expected.

"I feel there has been a sufficient period of recovery since I was last on active duty." He couldn't bring himself to speak of it. When he continued, he made sure his voice was even.

"Respectfully, I would remind you that I have been an active member of the local community." He didn't blink at the lie but thought of all the hours spent lying in bed, staring out of windows. "I am acquainted with the island and its inhabitants. I am uniquely placed to interview and investigate."

At his desk at command headquarters, Arthur Gregson sat back in his wide leather desk chair—a present from his wife to ward off constant backache—and tapped broad, workmanlike fingers against the standard issue beech desk he kept neat as a pin. Ryan was one of the best he had. Until recently, he had been energetic, diligent and Gregson knew there was a razor sharp mind underneath that pretty exterior the girls seemed to love. Ryan had climbed the ladder quickly. A fancy education had helped get his foot in the door but it was no substitute for experience and he had to admit that Ryan had knuckled down and gone the rest of the way himself. Two years ago, he'd personally handed Ryan his promotion to Detective Chief Inspector.

Six months ago, Ryan had been in an impossible position and the personal cost had been high. The question was whether he was ready to get back on the horse. Gregson quickly considered the department's psychological report, the protocol and the paperwork.

"Have you been seeing that counsellor the department recommended? Had a check-up at the GP recently?"

The pause was just long enough to give Gregson his answer.

"I—"

"Christ, Ryan."

Ryan tried hard to swallow his pride, thinking again of the girl lying dead beside him. "I can address both of those matters."

In a tailored suit the same colour as his dress uniform, with a mop of steel-grey hair, Gregson was an imposing man who could play politics and give speeches with the best of them. Still, he wasn't so comfortable at the desk that he'd forgotten the time he'd spent on the beat, the years he had put in working CID before he took the helm. He was a cautious, meticulous man but he wasn't afraid to go with his gut.

"See that you do." Another pause. "I confirm the termination of your sabbatical period, subject to you contacting your GP, who will provide a written confirmation of your physical health. It would put my mind at ease if you were to find a counsellor."

"The report listed that as a recommendation, rather than a requirement, sir."

Gregson acknowledged the truth in that and tried not to worry about it.

"Return to duty, effective immediately." He hesitated, but took the risk anyway. "You're the SIO on this. Choose your own team."

Relief was palpable but Ryan's voice stayed level. "Thank you. I'll take Phillips for starters. I'll need a CSI team, couple of officers for sentry and house-to-house," he glanced around him and thought of the size of the area, the elements involved. "No real preference on the CSI, but Faulkner's good."

"I'll get onto Phillips myself and tell him to scare up forensics."

"I'd appreciate it if we could hold off on the media for as long as possible. I haven't had an opportunity to inform next of kin yet."

"Get a preliminary statement out by this afternoon otherwise these things have a habit of leaking on their own. I want regular progress reports. Don't disappoint me."

"Understood."

"Oh, and Ryan? Welcome back."

Ryan slipped the phone back into his pocket as he heard the sound of approaching feet, lowered voices. Part of him braced and adrenaline kicked in his system before he relaxed again. The customary red jackets of the coastguard station officer and his deputy rounded the corner. He nodded to both men, assessing. He recognised Alex, the senior, as a regular feature around the village. He was a little over six feet, around thirty years old, blonde and athletic with friendly features which made him popular with the ladies. He looked more like a surfer than a coastguard; Ryan had seen him jogging past his cottage in the early evenings and had almost worked up the motivation to head out and join him.

Pete, the deputy, had a young face. In fact, he looked like his voice had only recently broken but he'd worked up a bit of a goatee to try to offset it. He was around the same height as his superior but thinner, his limbs longer. He had messy light brown hair at odds with the rigidly sculpted beard, which told Ryan that he'd recently dragged himself out of bed.

Both men looked nervous.

"What the hell took you so long?"

"Ryan," Alex nodded to him, took off dark sunglasses and propped them in his abundant blonde hair while he extended a hand. "Sorry for the delay. We had some trouble chasing up plastic sheeting this time of the morning."

Ryan took the man's hand briefly, ignored the sarcasm and nodded to the silent Pete.

Ryan stood back, eyed them both and wished for a professional crime team but knew he had to make do with what he had.

"First thing I need you to do is cover your shoes and clothes. Did you bring overalls?"

"Ah—"

Ryan swore inwardly and rummaged in his rucksack. "Here," he barked, shoving a couple of plastic bin bags towards them and waiting while they tied the plastic around their boots and the bottom of their jeans. "Make do with this for now. I need you to haul up some plastic sheeting to protect the scene. It looks like rain to me."

Alex lifted dubious eyes to the sky, which was papered blue and washed with pale sunshine, but said nothing.

"Come on."

They headed up the visitor's trail, plastic buffeting in the breeze. As they turned into the Priory, Ryan watched their reactions. Pete was the first to buckle. Hand clutching his stomach, he turned away and puked up his breakfast without preamble.

Ryan couldn't blame him. It affected you, the first few times.

Alex slapped a manly hand on Pete's back but judging by the greenish tinge under his all-weather tan, it looked like he was only just holding up himself.

"Jesus…" He swiped the back of his hand across his mouth. "Jesus."

"Jesus had nothing to do with it," Ryan muttered, watching the other man. Alex wore a look he'd seen a hundred times before and recognised as a kind of horrified fascination. Eyes like saucers, he was staring at the body now, throat constricting. Ryan stepped in front of him, cut off the view and watched his eyes snap back.

"I need a tent set up in a perimeter around the body," he started, waiting for the other man's full attention. Ryan checked the sky, which was beginning to look overcast.

"Her name was Lucy," the other man interrupted, voice hard.

Ryan paused, confusion clouding his face before he nodded. "You're right. I need the area around *Lucy* protected—a ten metre perimeter around her body. Rain's coming in."

Together, they staked out a perimeter of plastic sheeting leaving a wide berth around Lucy's body and tacked a makeshift ceiling over it all. Ryan noticed that, by the end, both men were breathing heavily and he was glad they held it together without contaminating the scene. If they needed to throw up, they could do it elsewhere. Both men kept their eyes fixed on the task and said nothing until Pete's watery voice broke the silence.

"Can't you cover her up? I mean, why are you leaving her lying there naked?" Ryan turned and looked at the man, barely more than a boy, and saw sorrow in his eyes. He told himself to stay firm.

"This is a crime scene, Pete. You did your initial response training?"

"Yes, but—"

"Then you should know that the scene should not be interfered with in any way before the CSI team arrives."

"It's just…" Pete's eyes watered. "Nothing. Never mind."

The job finished, Pete walked out of the tent towards the far end of the church.

"It's hard on him," Alex began, watching his deputy struggle to maintain composure. "He went to school with Lucy. We all knew her, but they grew up together."

"Uh huh," was all Ryan said and stored the information away for later. There were more pressing matters to attend to.

"I need you to guard the visitor's entrance. Are there any other access points?"

Alex shook his head. "It's the only way up onto the headland. The monks built it defensively that way," he gestured to the sea through the gaps in the stonework, "only other way up here would be to scale those cliffs."

Ryan turned in the direction Alex indicated and saw the sheer drop towards the beach, protected by a wooden fence around the perimeter of the grounds. He nodded, satisfied for now.

"Send Pete to watch the gate, he needs to clear his head. I want names and times for everyone coming or going. Here," Ryan pulled a bottle of water out of the small rucksack he carried, "give him this."

Alex nodded thoughtfully, re-assessing the man he'd initially considered remote. He turned to dispatch Pete. Ryan watched the younger man nod eagerly, breathing through his teeth still. He turned and half ran back down the incline to the gate.

"Pete's a good kid," Alex defended his deputy. "Nothing like this has happened on the island for a long, long time. Not in my lifetime."

"People kill each other all over the world."

"Sure, but Lindisfarne—it's holy." Alex shook his head sadly. "It's like killing someone in church."

While Alex headed off to stand with Pete, Ryan turned back to Lucy and silently apologised. It was easier to work CID when you took a step back, tried to keep things impersonal. If he started thinking about Lucy with the brown hair and pretty blue eyes who had been home for the Christmas holidays, then about all the Christmases she wouldn't see, he wasn't sure he would be able to face it.

He stood frowning, a tall, unapproachable man who stood as still as the stones around him. This *was* personal. He may have only been on the island for a couple of months, but people like Liz trusted him to do his job. He'd told her that he would take care of Lucy and that was what he was going to do. Whether they knew it or not, the islanders had given him a home and a sanctuary when he had needed it. He owed them.

Besides, he thought as he rubbed his chilled hands together, they needed protecting from one of their own. He was damn sure the medics would find Lucy Mathieson was killed last night after the tide had rolled in and cut them off from the mainland, which meant somebody already on the island had her blood on their hands.

He checked the time again. Fifteen minutes until the causeway opened.

"Alex!" He called the man back from where he was hopping from one cold foot to the other. "I need you to send a couple of people down to the beach to man the road across. Set up a road block— nobody leaves or comes over the causeway unless they live or have business concerns on the island."

"Ryan, we can't do that. There's going to be a huge influx today, you know that." Alex's face looked pained. "Besides, we haven't got the manpower. I've got Pete on the visitor's gate and I—ah—haven't been able to get hold of Rob. He worked the night shift. Mark's on his way." He ran through his short list of coastguard volunteers.

"Why would today be so special?" Ryan shrugged. "Because it's almost Christmas?"

Alex looked at him as if he'd grown two heads. "Well, sure, Christmas is always busy on Lindisfarne, but it's the 21st today."

Ryan flipped through a mental calendar but came up blank.

"The winter solstice," Alex supplied with a look on his face which seemed to say, "stupid outsider."

Ryan wouldn't know a solstice from a cough remedy.

"Okay," he said, face blank.

Alex shifted his feet and adopted an authoritative tone. "It's the day of the year when all the neo-pagans gather round to celebrate shorter nights, longer days. Basically, everyone meets on the beach, they light a few fires, sing a few songs and eat barbeque."

Ryan didn't consider himself to be a religious man. He had seen too much of life and of what one person was capable of doing to another, to believe in a deity which could allow that to happen. Still, if people wanted to dance around a few pogo sticks and get drunk, there was no real harm in it. Unless one of them had decided to take symbolic sacrifice a step too far, he added, thinking of the girl lying on a cold slab behind him.

"What do the residents make of it?" he asked.

"The older population tends to be Christian but since most of them own the B&Bs and the gift shops, they just smile politely and turn a decent trade. The rest of us don't really give a shit," he shrugged eloquently.

Ryan considered this for a moment.

"What about the vicar?" His eyes fixed on the steeple of the island's church, just visible rising above the rooftops in the village beyond. The church graveyard backed directly onto the Priory grounds.

"Mike?" Alex laughed. "He loves it. Every year, it's an opportunity for him to spread the word, try to convert a few unbelievers."

Ryan paused to file it all away. Interesting, but it didn't change the fact that the last thing they needed was a hoard of tourists trampling all over the place.

"If there's going to be a swarm of visitors, that's precisely why they can't access the island. Think!" he cut across the other man's protest. "It had to be somebody who was already here, Alex."

Alex's expression darkened. "That puts a different complexion on matters. Still, the islanders won't like it."

"They're going to like the fact that one of their own has been brutally murdered a hell of a lot less." He wasn't prepared to be compromising. "Find Rob and Mark, drag them out of bed with your bare hands if you have to, but for God's sake get them down to the beach. I want names and licence plates for all cars approaching or leaving."

He paused, remembered Liz.

"Mark—is that Mark Bowers?"

Alex nodded. "He volunteers once or twice a week with the coastguard. The rest of the time, he manages the Heritage Centre and gift shop, does history tours."

"You need to tell him that the Centre will be closed for business today. There won't be any visitors coming up here. Tell him not to pester Liz Morgan, either. She won't be in for work at the gift shop."

His eyes sombre, Alex nodded and headed off.

Satisfied that the wheels were in motion, Ryan opted to ring Gregson's PA and leave a message. He knew it was cowardly but he could do without discussing the merits and demerits of closing off an entire island to the general public. It wasn't up for debate.

CHAPTER 2

Ryan was standing guard over Lucy's body when Detective Sergeant Frank Phillips arrived with two crime scene officers in tow. Ryan recognised them as Tom Faulkner and his assistant. The CSIs paused for a brief word before heading straight into the tent where Lucy waited. Ryan turned back to his sergeant. Phillips was a short barrel of a man with a boxer's physique and a weather-beaten face. He wore the dark grey suit badly but, oddly, the pale pink tie with yellow polka dots suited him.

"Ryan," he clasped a strong hand around Ryan's and pumped it enthusiastically, using the other to give him a clap on the shoulder. "Great to see you again."

Ryan didn't take offence at the lack of formality. He might have been the man's superior in rank, but he was a good fifteen years younger than Phillips and had been brought up to respect his elders. There had been times in the early days when he'd had to assert himself, but experience had worn down the prickly edges to leave a smooth friendship and an even smoother working relationship.

"You too, Frank." He realised he meant it.

"Wish it had been over a pint rather than picking over something like this," Phillips shook his head in disgust. "Dispatch gave me the basics. Never fails to amaze me what some bastards will do." His twinkling brown eyes were sharp as he took in the scene which was now protected by plastic that flapped in the wind.

Phillips looked back at the tall man in front of him and thought he looked tired and thinner than he had a few months ago. Still, there was a spark back in his eyes which was encouraging. "Heard from Gregson," he added, and watched Ryan's face turn slowly, expectantly. He admired the way Ryan's movements always seemed unhurried.

"He gave me the rundown, told me you're back on full duty."

Ryan remained silent, his eyes veiled.

Phillips chuckled slightly, reading him perfectly. "Glad you're back. Couldn't stand much more shit from MacKenzie."

Ryan nearly smiled. It was no secret that things were touchy between DS Phillips and Detective Inspector Denise MacKenzie. It didn't help that MacKenzie was a strong, attractive woman with a crown of glowing red hair and a temper to match her heritage. It was also no secret that Frank Phillips had been circling round asking her out for the full five years since his wife died.

"Gotta bite that bullet someday, Frank."

"Don't know what the hell you're on about." He scuffed a worn loafer against the moss and scowled.

Ryan's lips quirked but sobered instantly when he saw an older man weaving through the stones on the far side of the Priory graveyard, dressed for country weather in a dark green waxed jacket and well-worn boots. The small black case he carried with him was an unmistakable signal that he was the island's doctor. He watched the man pause amongst the gravestones to speak to Alex. Ryan could see the family resemblance between the older man and his son.

"Forensics will give us a better idea but I'm reckoning she's been dead no more than five hours," he said to Phillips.

"There was rain last night, though," Phillips watched the progress of the doctor as he lumbered up the slight incline. Both Phillips and Ryan knew that rain washed away all kinds of sins, as well as DNA evidence.

"I know, Frank. I'm hoping that we can preserve anything that's left." His face was grim.

"Gregson said it was a local girl," Phillips blew on his hands, wishing he had remembered to bring gloves.

"Young local girl, a pretty brunette called Lucy Mathieson. I recognised her vaguely; her family live on the island. Mother's a homemaker, father's a retired teacher. She'd been away at university in Newcastle. She came home for the holidays."

Ryan was amazed to find that he knew so much about the local people. To his knowledge, he had been no more than a passive participant in island life. Maybe his natural instinct to observe everyone and everything around him hadn't quite been extinguished after all.

Phillips shook his head again. "Picked a nice spot for it."

Ryan nodded, glancing briefly at the view out to sea, then back towards the altar. The crumbled stones indicated where walls once stood tall and firm to shelter the holy men from the worst of the elements. Columns of varying height ran down the centre of what he guessed must have been the main place of worship. He frowned, black brows drawing together as he looked at the scene afresh. Chunks of the stone and rock which had once been used to form clean, well-built lines were displaced and scattered in a roughly circular pattern a few feet wide of where the girl lay. At first glance, it looked like natural deterioration but he wondered.

"It looks," he paused to find the right word. "Ceremonial."

Phillips huffed out a sigh. "I hate these bloody ritual killings. Bad enough that they've snuffed someone out, they have to make a song and dance about it too. Adds insult to injury."

Ryan knew that Phillips needed the chatter. Everyone had their own way of coping with death, especially those who had to deal with it up close.

"It's the solstice today."

Phillips raised a bushy brown eyebrow. "Didn't realise you were into all that hocus pocus."

"I'm not. It never hurts to know what's going on around you, though."

Phillips chewed on his bottom lip. "In that case, you're going to have a hard job keeping people off the island."

"I know. I'm expecting a call from Gregson any minute now. I'll deal with it."

"The road block's bought us a bit of time," Phillips mused, "but this place is popular around Christmas, even without it being a special day of the year."

Ryan jammed impatient hands in his pockets. "Fucking tourists."

Phillips slanted him a look. "You're a tourist here yourself, boyo."

A ghost of a smile played on Ryan's lips. "Guess you've got me there."

Both men fell silent as the doctor finally approached, slightly out of breath. Ryan thought he looked very much like an older version of his son. Around sixty, but with an attractively lined face and a lean, lived-in frame coming in just under six feet. He boasted a full head of grey hair which still held glints of its previous blonde and the lively green eyes he'd passed onto his son flicked over the makeshift tent, before coming to rest soberly on Ryan's face.

"Ryan, isn't it?" He shifted his medical bag and held out a long, artistic hand. "Alex told me it was urgent."

"Thank you for coming so quickly, Dr Walker." Ryan took the hand, found it firm.

"Steve, please."

Ryan nodded, turned. "This is Detective Sergeant Frank Phillips. He'll be working on the investigation with me."

Ryan watched the older man's eyes register slight surprise and had a moment to think that he had obviously been the subject of some discussion on the island. At least the good doctor was forthright.

"I didn't realise you were visiting Lindisfarne in a professional capacity, Mr Ryan."

In other words, Ryan thought, word had spread that he had slunk across to Lindisfarne like a wounded animal. He wanted to resent the lack of privacy but the eyes which assessed him were kind.

"Seems I've had enough rest and relaxation, Dr Walker," he deliberately kept things formal, sending a telling glance at what lay behind him. "I'll be the Senior Investigating Officer in respect of the death of a girl who has been identified as Lucy Mathieson. Her body was found just under an hour ago. In the absence of a pathologist, we'd be grateful if you would confirm life extinct and provide us with any other preliminary medical observations."

The doctor followed his gaze.

"Lucy?" He shook his head sadly, his jaw sagged and tears burned his eyes. "I helped to bring that girl into the world."

Ryan and Phillips stayed silent. There was nothing they could say.

"Her parents will be devastated. There must have been a terrible accident…" his voice trailed off.

"No," Ryan returned flatly. "I doubt this was an accidental death but we would be grateful for your observations, as I say." He paused, considered. "If you feel that your prior knowledge of the deceased would prejudice your task...?"

The other man visibly pulled himself together but his eyes remained sad.

"No, I suppose I must see it as part of the cycle of life. God knows I've tried to understand why good people suffer the ravages of cancer and all manner of ailments over the course of my career but I've only ever had the misfortune to assess an unnatural death once before."

Ryan's ears pricked. "On the island?"

"No, no. Many years ago, when we lived in Newcastle. I worked as a police surgeon for the first few years of my tenure before deciding to become a general practitioner. You expect things like this to happen in a big city, but you just don't expect it on our little island community."

"I didn't realise you had been employed as a police surgeon."

"Yes, when I was young and thought it would be an exciting career choice," the older man shook his head, presumably at his younger self. "Then Yvonne and I were married and Alex was born. We decided we wanted a more peaceful life together, with more sociable working hours."

Ryan nodded and said nothing while he waited for the doctor to draw himself together.

"I'll head in now," Walker said quietly and nodded to both men. They watched him pick his way across the grass, head bent, to the CSI officers working the scene.

"Poor fella," Phillips commented. "It's not every day you have to sign the death certificate for someone you've helped birth."

"Yeah," Ryan felt his chest tighten again and deliberately exhaled slowly. A light rain started to fall and Ryan watched Phillips fiddle with a flimsy black umbrella.

"Go on inside and get a feel for the scene, speak to Walker. We'll let the lab boys do their work and see what we see. I need to set up an Incident Room but it's going to be difficult to do that back at HQ with the tides. Best to have the incident room here on the island, I'm thinking at my place. I've got office equipment there." He thought of the printer, fax machine and laptop gathering dust.

"It's not exactly protocol," Phillips said.

Ryan's mouth twisted. "Agreed, but the alternatives don't appeal, either. The base needs to be here on the island but I don't want to set it up in a communal area where anybody and their grandmother might have a spare key. Best to keep it in the family."

Phillips nodded approval.

"In the meantime," Ryan continued, "Contact the pathologist to confirm Walker's assessment when we have it and tell him to expect to receive the body by mid-morning." He thought a moment. "Mortuary at the hospital in Alnwick will be the closest, so tell him to get over there."

"Will do."

"I need you to oversee the coastguards, for now. I don't want them involved beyond crowd management."

Ryan didn't have to spell it out and, in any case, Phillips was a quick study.

"Everyone's a suspect?"

"You're damn right."

Phillips nodded slowly, popped a stick of gum in his mouth and offered some to Ryan. "Tide came in late last night, around what time?"

"Around eleven forty-five," Ryan answered easily, shaking his head to the offer of gum. He'd already checked the times the tide had rolled in and out again.

"Five hours dead, that takes us back to around one in the morning." Phillips looked past the walls of the Priory towards the village beyond. "At least you've got a pool of suspects."

"Oh yeah," Ryan laughed without mirth. "An entire island of them."

"Better get started, then."

Ryan watched his sergeant head towards the tarpaulin, square his stocky shoulders and dip inside. He felt his phone begin to vibrate and saw Gregson's number flash. He ignored the call, figuring he could buy another thirty minutes if he was lucky.

Besides, he had another call to make and this one needed to be made in person.

CHAPTER 3

Anna Taylor watched the clouds part high in the sky over Lindisfarne. Light streamed down on the island and she smiled from the relative comfort of her racing-green Mini. She could have sketched the view from memory, it was so familiar, but each time it stole her breath away.

It was an uneasy homecoming.

Slim fingers tapped an irritable rhythm on the steering wheel as she drove the car along the coastal road towards the causeway, sand dunes spreading out to her right. The phone call she'd received early that morning hadn't left her any choice but to drive up here. DCS Gregson from the Northumbria Police had contacted her through her position at the University. Apparently, he had read her latest work, *Pagan Northumberland* and her personal knowledge of the island was an added benefit. There had been a ritual murder and he wanted to enlist her as a civilian consultant.

Just like that, as if she consulted with the police on a daily basis.

She had to admire the man's style. He'd caught her half asleep and begging for caffeine, her brain not fully operational. Otherwise, there was no way in hell she would have agreed.

The fact was, he had told her a young girl had been killed and that hit a little too close to home. Right after speaking with Gregson, she had tried calling the old number she had for Megan but it had rung out, adding to her stress. Her sister had never been an easy person to pin down, she thought with a habitual sense of sadness. Still, she was the only family Anna had left.

She was clinging onto the fact that neither she nor Megan could be called 'girls' any more. Passing the threshold of late twenties and edging dangerously close to thirty put them well past girlhood and she was sure Gregson had said it was a girl who had been killed.

Hadn't he?

Still, she worried. Surely, he would have told her if the girl had been Megan. They had a duty to inform next of kin.

Didn't they?

Nearing the causeway entrance, she frowned at the line of cars standing stationary despite the clear road ahead across the channel. She wound her window down as a man she recognised as Rob Fowler headed towards her car with a clipboard.

"Morning, Miss. I just need to take some details before I can allow you to cross." He was using his official voice, Anna noted with a slight curve of full lips and she tipped down tinted aviators to meet his distracted gaze.

"Rob? Red suits you," she referred to the bright red coastguard volunteer jacket he wore on his broad shoulders. His name was embroidered in fancy gold lettering on the breast pocket.

Rob's tired face registered surprise before he flashed a broad, toothy grin which transformed him from an average-looking man to a downright attractive one.

"Anna! It's been a hell of a long time. Where have you been hiding yourself?" He greeted her like the old friend that she was and leaned in closer. Anyone who had shared a couple of sloppy teenage kisses and more than a few underage drinks could definitely be called an old friend.

"Durham," she answered. "I'm living there now, teaching at the university."

"I heard you'd done well for yourself. Should I be calling you Doctor Taylor now?" He wiggled his eyebrows, brown eyes twinkling.

"It'll always be Anna to you," she smiled. The reunion over, she jerked her head towards the island. "I heard there's been some trouble. Anyone I know?"

She kept her voice casual, but she held her breath.

"I doubt you'd know her, bit after your time. Young lass called Lucy found dead up at the Priory." He looked back towards the island, his face abruptly serious.

Anna let out the long, silent breath she'd been holding and felt relief surge because the girl wasn't Megan. Guilt followed quickly because she knew some other family would be suffering instead.

Rob cleared his throat and turned back to her. "I've been given instructions to take down name, number plate and purpose for being on the island before I can let you cross, Anna. So, ah…" he cleared his throat again awkwardly. "Are you visiting your sister?"

Anna watched sympathy pass briefly over his expressive face and chose not to feel embarrassed by it.

"No." She paused and strove for calm. "Mark's loaned me the cottage." She thought of her childhood home, now owned by an old friend. "I'm actually here on official business, Rob. I've been engaged by the police as a consultant."

"Right," Rob's eyes widened in blatant curiosity as he scribbled something down on his clipboard. "Guess we'll be seeing more of you, Anna."

"I guess so," she turned the ignition on again now the road was clear ahead, the cars having either u-turned back towards the mainland or driven on towards the island.

"Safe crossing, Anna." Rob gave an arm signal to his fellow traffic marshal to indicate she had been given the go-ahead.

As she passed, her smile widened and she slowed to wave to the marshal she recognised as Mark Bowers. As well as being the island's resident historian and part-time coastguard, he had been her teenage idol. He was an attractive, scholarly man who looked out of place in the sporty red jacket and khaki waterproofs. She remembered him in his usual garb of cream twill trousers and shirt, his forearms always tanned from long hours spent outdoors searching the land for clues to the past. He sent her a blank look before his lined face broke into a smile and she noticed then that he looked older than the man she remembered. Then again, she was older too. She gave a couple of short toots of the horn as she passed him and promised herself that she would pay a proper visit to her old mentor.

Even behind sunglasses, her eyes narrowed against the glare of the mid-morning sun. The shining water lapped on either side of the tarmacked road which had risen from the sea, as if by magic. The grey clouds of earlier had been swept away by the wind to leave sunny blue skies but the air still held the deep chill of winter.

She hadn't planned to be here, to be anywhere near Megan or the memories she would undoubtedly awaken, despite its being Christmas and the season of goodwill. She struggled to feel any kind of goodwill towards her sister. It had taken years to try to forgive and she had almost fooled herself that she had forgotten. Still, perhaps the serenity of the tiny island with its scattering of inhabitants could begin to soothe the ache. Tall reeds spread out and waved in the breeze to her right as she drove up the winding road towards the village. Seagulls circled and swooped above the water, their calls loud and comforting. As the first whitewashed cottages came into sight, she saw the trains of Christmas lights draped across the barren trees between the houses and knew they would be festive and cheerful come nightfall.

Anna drove through the village and recognised the Heritage Centre where she had spent every Saturday as a teenager, the gift shops and the tea rooms. Above all, she noticed the pub which sat in the centre, painted white with red trim and cheerfully named *The Jolly Anchor*. A six-foot plastic Santa stood outside the entrance, waving its mechanical hand and welcoming patrons with a jarringly loud, "Ho, ho, ho!"

Shaking her head, she swept through the village and was glad she hadn't seen anyone she knew. In fact, the streets had been surprisingly empty of their usual crowd. Though the island was sparse of people, they usually gathered in the village. She supposed that was the nature of the community—a community she had once been a part of.

The car meandered through the narrow streets towards Lindisfarne Castle, the scenic fort on the east of the island. At the foot of the mount was the coastguard's base. No bright red jeep stood on the driveway but both rescue boats were moored, indicating there had been no emergency at sea that morning. The drama had all been on land.

She pulled up in front of an attractive fisherman's cottage set in its own small garden. It held a faultless location; the fort stood to the east, the Priory to the west and Bamburgh Castle stood further down the coast to the south. The cottage held unspoilt views of all three and didn't have to share them with immediate neighbours. That suited her just fine, she thought, as she yanked out a battered black suitcase and dragged it across the gravel towards the house. After feeling around for the key Mark had left under the door mat, she pushed open the door and memories washed over her. The walls had been repainted, the floors freshly carpeted, but still she could remember the scent of her mother's perfume in the hallway.

She could remember when her father had taken the perfume bottle and hurled it down the stairs, claiming that her mother had worn it for another man. She remembered the ugly argument that followed and the sound of flesh hitting flesh.

Her skin crawled, icy tentacles snaking up her back as the line between past and present blurred for a painful moment.

Then her vision cleared. All that stood before her was a comfortable cottage with neutral furnishings. It was her canvas to paint however she chose.

* * *

Ryan's head throbbed painfully as the shiny red door to the Mathieson's home closed quietly behind him. Informing the family was always the worst, the very worst, part of the job. No amount of training or experience prepared you to withstand the abject grief of a mother and father who had lost their child. It was always an affront but, in these circumstances—practically on their doorstep—it must be almost unbearable.

He walked slowly to the other end of the street, hands thrust in his pockets, as he replayed the conversation.

The mother, Helen, had been completely unaware of who he was. That made it worse somehow, the open welcome she had been prepared to give him when she answered the door.

"Can I help you?" She had still been in her terrycloth dressing gown, pale pink and a bit faded. Her eyes had still been cloudy from sleep but they were the same colour as her daughter's.

"DCI Ryan, ma'am. Is your husband or another family member at home?" Those blue eyes had glazed in confusion when he told her he was from the police, flashed his ID. She had called out for Daniel, a tall, wiry man with long limbs and a slight stoop, who had answered her call with the same confused expression. She had asked Ryan inside, her voice trembling because underneath the social formality she had known why he was there. Instinct told her something was very wrong and she was drawing out the moment, denying the truth of it for as long as she could.

Ryan had followed them through to a tidy living room with a comfortable feel. The first things he had seen were the framed pictures of Lucy, her smiling image on the mantle and the window sill. Helen must have read something in his eyes because her hand instantly groped around for Daniel's and he grasped it. Ryan stood there and watched them shatter as he told them their daughter had been killed. He tried to keep his mind detached, his eyes watchful as he had given them the news that their lives would never be the same again. He had steeled himself while he watched Helen Mathieson clutch a hand to her womb, a heartbreaking reminder of what she had lost, before she collapsed onto the sofa.

He had watched the father, too. Lucy had been found nude and although he hoped otherwise, the manner of her death wouldn't rule out sexual assault. Daniel Mathieson had been on the island all night, he said, and Ryan recalled that most victims knew their killers and many lived under the same roof. Knowing that fact had not helped to ease the constriction in his chest while he had questioned a couple who displayed all the signs of complete emotional breakdown.

"Why, why has this happened? Who would do this?" Helen had moaned the words.

"I'm going to do my best to find those answers for you, Mrs Mathieson."

"No, no, no," Helen had begun to rock, her sobs guttural, still in denial. "It can't be Lucy," she shook her head vehemently, her eyes both pleading and angry. "You've made a mistake. It isn't Lucy."

"Shh, Helen," her husband tried to soothe a pain which he felt keenly himself.

"Your daughter has been identified, Mrs Mathieson."

Still she shook her head, angry jerks from side to side while her eyes burned into him. "I've *told* you it can't be. Lucy was out with friends last night and she's probably staying over at Rachel's house. I'll ring her now and then you'll see."

Helen surged upwards, her eyes frantic as she looked around for the phone. Her husband scrubbed both hands across his face before pushing himself wearily off the sofa to follow her.

"Come on, Helen, come on now."

Ryan watched their half-hearted tussle until Helen had simply sagged against her husband, emotionally exhausted and sobbing bitter, vicious tears which shook her body.

He waited patiently for the worst to subside. He knew that any normal person would have left them to their heartache, rather than spectating. He wasn't a normal person, though, and he had a job to do.

"I'm sorry to have to ask you this now," he began gently, waiting for them to raise their eyes to his face. He realised they had forgotten he was still there. "I need to ask you some important questions about Lucy, about where she was last night and about her life and her habits so that I can bring her killer to justice."

"How…how…" Helen couldn't bring herself to finish the sentence, but Ryan knew what she wanted to ask. They always wanted to know.

"We haven't determined that yet, Mrs Mathieson." He had a good idea, but until the pathologist confirmed cause of death, there was nothing he could tell her.

"You said 'killer'," Daniel spoke quietly. "How do you know there wasn't an accident of some kind?"

Always sticky, Ryan thought.

"The manner in which we found her doesn't indicate an accident, Mr Mathieson."

"Was there…" Helen drew in several deep breaths. "Was she hurt, you know, *that way?*" Her eyes pleaded with him, begged him to tell her that her baby girl had died quickly and without pain, without the terror of sexual assault. He wished that he could.

"I'm sorry, Mrs Mathieson, we don't know any of those details yet. We'll be working hard to find out."

Helen dissolved into fresh tears, the knuckles on her hands turned white as she gripped her husband's arm. Daniel Mathieson drew on some inner strength to face Ryan, to lift his head and meet his gaze squarely.

"We'll tell you anything we can." There was anger underneath the misery, Ryan could see. Beneath the mild-mannered man, there was a father, and beneath that there was a hard knot of impotent anger. He could give the man something to focus his anger on.

"Thank you, Mr Mathieson." He took out his notebook. "Let's begin with her movements last night. Can you tell me what Lucy did yesterday?"

"Lucy was with me," Helen whispered. "We drove over to Morpeth and had lunch, did some shopping." Tears coursed down the woman's ravaged face, which had aged visibly.

"Around what time was that, Mrs Mathieson?" Ryan kept his voice low and careful.

"We left at about quarter past ten, drove across to the mainland and we got to Morpeth at around eleven. We looked around the shops, I… I…" she covered her face with shaking hands and Ryan looked away.

Minutes passed until there was another break.

"Could you tell me what time you arrived back on the island after your shopping trip?" Ryan needed to know, had to piece together some sort of timeline.

"It was around four," Daniel answered for his wife. Ryan cocked his head towards Helen and waited.

"Yes, it was around then," she agreed. Only then did Ryan pick up his pen and write it down.

"After that?"

Helen Mathieson looked up and seemed to see Ryan properly for the first time. Her blue eyes cleared briefly to assess the man sitting in front of her. She saw a tall, good-looking thirty-something with a serious face and sad, striking grey eyes. Something about his intent expression gave her comfort enough to carry on.

"We had an early tea because Lucy wanted to get ready and head out to meet her friends. Rachel Finnigan and Ellie Holmes," Helen added, anticipating him. "They live on our street," she gestured out of the window, "Ellie's right across from us and Rachel's at number 34 at the end."

Ryan nodded. "Where were they meeting, and at what time?"

"Ellie came by around six to call for Lucy and the girls said they were planning to walk past Rachel's house and pick her up on the way to the pub. They both left here around ten past six." Ryan didn't need to ask which pub; there was only one on the island.

"Was that the last time you saw or spoke with your daughter?"

Helen could barely manage a nod.

"I have to ask," *another sticky question,* he thought, "could you please confirm your whereabouts during the hours of eleven-thirty last night and five this morning?"

He looked at both of them, tried to look apologetic although he knew this was a necessary question.

"We were both in bed, asleep," Daniel answered.

"I went up to bed around ten-thirty," Helen agreed.

"I came up half an hour later. I wanted to put the dishwasher on overnight, check the back door and that sort of thing. I like to leave the porch light on for Lucy," Daniel swallowed.

"Lucy usually let herself back in the house?"

"Yes," Helen nodded. "She'd done it a hundred times before." *Lucy's keys?* Ryan made a note and circled it twice.

31

"Did either of you hear anything or see anything else during the night?"

"No, nothing at all," Daniel said quietly.

Helen paused. "I went out like a light and slept pretty heavily. I always do, but sometime during the night, I thought I heard an engine backfire. It sounded like it was quite close by." She looked over at her husband. "Did you hear it?"

"No, I'm afraid I didn't."

Ryan looked between the two people in front of him and knew that there would be very little information he could get from them now. Shock had settled in. He rose, took out a card with details of a family liaison officer and set it on the coffee table in front of them. Neither of them moved from their huddle on the sofa.

"Thank you both. I'm very sorry for your loss," Ryan murmured. Then, to the father, he added that there would be an officer along to take a formal note of what they had just told him and ask some more questions. There would also be a CSI team along to do a standard sweep of the house. They would need to take fingerprints. To himself, he had added that he would need to take another good look at the people in Lucy's immediate circle; family, friends, lovers.

As he was leaving, he turned one last time. "One final thing," he said belatedly. "What was Lucy wearing when she left last night?"

"Wearing?" Helen shook her head as if to clear it. "Jeans and the new red top I'd bought her. Some black boots."

"Were the boots heeled?"

"Why...yes, they were, quite high."

"Thank you, Mrs Mathieson, Mr Mathieson. I'll leave you alone now."

* * *

Ryan found himself in the main square, standing beside a worn statue of Saint Cuthbert. He looked up at the carved stone and wondered what Cuthbert had seen as he stood vigil over the people of Lindisfarne.

CHAPTER 4

Anna knew her first priority should be to find the Senior Investigating Officer but her nerves fluttered at the thought. Ordinarily, she kept herself to herself and preferred not to become embroiled in other people's dramas. She understood that was the main attraction of a career as an academic historian, the erstwhile realm of middle-aged, balding men in tweed blazers. When you were looking at the history of a civilisation, speculating about the lives of others who had lived hundreds or thousands of years earlier, you could avoid thinking too hard or looking too closely at your own life in the present and there was no pressure to worry about the future.

She fished out the scrap of paper where she'd written the name and number of the person in charge. *Detective Chief Inspector Ryan.* Gregson had been vague on the details, come to think of it. He had just told her to report to Ryan, who would give her instructions. Apparently, Ryan was based on the island, but she didn't remember him. There wasn't a police presence on Lindisfarne that she knew about but her local knowledge was badly out of date. She fingered the piece of paper for a moment then shoved the scrap back in her pocket. Before she went against every instinct she had and stuck her oar into other people's business, it was time to face her own past.

Ten minutes later, bundled into a smart black woollen coat and jeans, Anna pushed open the door to the Jolly Anchor. She and the plastic Santa exchanged a long look and she took his jovial welcome as a good luck omen. Anna needed it. Inside, the pub was almost exactly as she remembered it when she'd last seen it eight years ago. Stretched along the wall to the right was a long wooden bar with stools taken by the regulars, the surface polished to gleaming. That was different, she thought. When it had been her father standing behind that bar, he hadn't often taken the trouble to polish the wood. As a child she remembered counting the tiny bar flies which used to gather around the beer spillages while she watched her father pull pints with his big hands.

Big, hard hands.

She blocked the thought and focused on the present, continuing to scan the room. There were old wooden tables scattered in nooks in the main area and each held a pretty carnation sitting in a miniature vase in preparation for the lunch crowd. The table tops had been polished too, their old scars covered over. It was the kind of thing her mother would have liked to do but the old clientele—made up mostly of gnarled fishermen and the disenchanted—wouldn't have appreciated it. A log fire blazed cheerfully in the huge fireplace which dominated the bar room and a couple lounged in comfortable leather chairs beside it, drinks in hand. A Christmas tree stood, fully decked, in the corner. All in all, it looked like a pleasant place to pass the time.

Anna moved out of the shadow of the doorway, her boots clicking softly on the slate floor. She scanned the room and headed for the bar. Bill Tilson, the landlord, spotted her immediately and let out a cheerful bellow in the Scottish brogue he had never quite lost.

"Anna!"

She smiled and tried to relax when he enveloped her in a bear hug. *Bear* being the operative word, she thought. The man was well over six feet and an easy two hundred and fifty pounds of red-faced charm. The last time she had seen him, he had been the sole bartender working beside her father, underpaid and underappreciated.

"Not a pickin' on you," he grumbled, setting her at arm's length and casting a critical eye over her. "Girl, you're so thin you could hide behind a lamp post."

Anna was lost for words, thinking that anyone would appear thin in comparison with his bulk, but she smiled cheerfully.

"I see you haven't changed, Billy," she murmured the old endearment and he smiled warmly in response.

"Well, you've done nothing except grow even prettier. Must have been breaking hearts all these years, that's why you haven't been back to visit us sooner."

She swallowed the bittersweet pain and tried to keep things light. "You know me, Bill. The folks at Durham University just call me the Heartbreak Kid."

He smiled, but the look in his eyes was a knowing one. He still remembered a cute little girl with soft dark hair he liked to ruffle and unhappy brown eyes.

Anna glanced uneasily around the bar. "Is she here?"

Bill ran an uncomfortable hand over his bushy hair and didn't need to ask who she meant. "Somewhere around here but God knows she comes and goes as she pleases. Ah," he shifted from foot to foot, "you want me to find her for you?"

Anna looked into his worried eyes and shook her head. "I'll just wait here awhile, grab a sandwich. I guess she'll be back soon enough."

Bill nodded, thinking that all hell would break loose.

* * *

In the square outside, Ryan found himself engaged in the second awkward conversation with his superintendent of the day. He suspected it wouldn't be the last.

"I'm not asking your permission, Ryan."

"Sir, I believe the appointment of a civilian consultant is premature at this time."

Ryan's teeth set with an audible snap.

Privately, Gregson agreed with him, but he wasn't willing to take any chances. The press would be all over this case like vultures as soon as they got a sniff. He could almost see the headline now: 'RITUAL KILLING DESPOILS HOLY ISLAND'. For his part, he wanted the investigation wrapped up quickly and quietly.

"Doctor Taylor is heading up to Lindisfarne today," was all he said.

Ryan knew the tone well enough to understand that further argument would be futile, so he said nothing. It burned, though. A few hours into the investigation and the boss had already decided he was incapable of hunting down some island crackpot who probably fancied himself as the Sun God.

Not only that, he raged inwardly, Gregson had gone *over his head* to appoint this Doctor Taylor—some university bigwig he imagined with frizzed grey hair and buck teeth. He smiled grimly and shook his head. If the DCS wanted to waste a chunk of his budget then that was his lookout. All he needed to do was shake hands, nod politely and give the professor some sort of useless research task. He would probably eat it up while Ryan got on with the real business of policing.

"Understood," he managed.

"Good. Now, about the road block you set up without requesting prior permission," Gregson said mildly.

Ryan could feel a headache developing at the base of his skull.

"Sir, as SIO and first attending officer, my main priority was to secure the crime scene," he began.

"The crime scene is at the Priory," Gregson interjected.

Ryan tried again. "With respect, the island has an eight-mile radius and a limited population, all of whom are currently being treated as suspects. The victim was killed during the five-hour period when the island was cut off from the mainland last night and early this morning. The implications of that are clear."

If Gregson were still working the beat he might agree, but the desk he occupied wouldn't allow him to be sympathetic when there were politics, media and budgeting to think about.

"It is not within your remit to close off access to an entire island, Ryan."

"Without the road block, the population would have increased exponentially this morning…" Ryan argued.

"I realise that," Gregson cut him off. "If it makes your job harder, then that's tough shit. Get it sorted."

After the call ended, Ryan swore loudly and to no-one in particular. He was under orders to lift the road block and what had he been thinking of, setting it up in the first place? Well, sir, he'd been thinking of investigating a little something he liked to call murder, but hey, sure, let the whole world come on down and trample on his crime scene. Why not let suspects and civilians mingle? That wouldn't make his job any harder, not at all.

"Chumps," he muttered, causing an elderly woman to pause on the pavement beside him and regard him with disapproval before wandering off again.

At least Gregson had agreed that the Incident Room should be at his cottage. Last thing Ryan needed was a bunch of well-meaning Sunday School grandmas barging into the Church Hall serving tea and cakes. Violent murder tended to kill your appetite for sugar.

Ryan paused to tick off his mental checklist. He'd planned the first briefing with his team at three, which gave him a couple of hours to set up the murder board and collate existing information, which he would do as soon as he got back to the cottage. Ideally, he would have wanted the briefing earlier in the day, but time and circumstance hadn't allowed it.

Lucy's body had already been transported off the island for post mortem after formal identification by her parents. The family liaison officer had been prompt arriving from the mainland and had held their hands through the ordeal. Elsewhere, the forensic team had nearly completed their work up at the Priory and Phillips was overseeing a small team who would comb the area in expanding circles on foot.

Everything had been photographed by the CSI team and the pictures were currently being developed. He had dispatched a two-man team of uniforms who were conducting house-to-house interviews at that very moment. He had the original traffic logs from the morning and he was in the process of obtaining records of all cars registered to the island, alongside a list of permanent residents. He'd ask Phillips to contact the hotels, inns and rental cottages to get a list of people who were guests on the island. As for the tourists, they were already flocking in their dozens.

He scowled at a family who had obviously just arrived and were climbing out of their people-carrier, cameras in hand. Well, they would find themselves disappointed if they planned to visit the Priory. That was, very firmly, closed for the foreseeable future. On that, he wouldn't budge. He had stationed two rookie officers from the mainland to guard the entrance. Happy to be working on a murder investigation, he was pretty sure they would have guarded the Priory standing on their heads if he'd asked them.

Ah, youth.

Frustrated by bureaucracy and a lack of physical evidence, Ryan's eyes fell on the pub across the square and he thought of Lucy's last movements. He stalked around Cuthbert's saintly effigy and made for the front door.

* * *

Inside the pub, Anna watched her sister enter the bar via the door to the outside courtyard which, she knew, led to an apartment upstairs. Apparently, Megan was still living above the pub, despite all her plans to leave and become an actress, or open her own beauty salon, or marry some rich banker. Those had been Megan's main goals in life the last time they had spoken but that had been years ago.

Things with Megan could have changed, Anna thought with a flash of optimism. From her vantage point, she studied her sister and tried to gauge the similarities between them. Megan was eighteen months older and would turn thirty next month. Once, their hair had been an almost identical shade of chestnut brown but Megan had darkened hers so that it fell in a dramatic black waterfall down her back. Her skin was always tanned, with a little help from a regular St Tropez spray tan. Like Anna, she was tall, but curvier around the hips and chest, something she had never failed to remind Anna of as they were growing up.

"Don't worry, Anna. One day you'll be able to fill your training bra," she'd say with a laugh.

Megan certainly had her assets on display today, Anna thought dispassionately, taking in the snug, low-cut top over skin-tight jeans which left little to the imagination. Under the harsh lighting of the bar, Megan was heavily made up, her eyes lined with thick black kohl, with long lashes and dark eye shadow. Her full mouth was a slash of red gloss. Anna watched her flirt with one of the regulars, leaning over the bar to give him just enough to think about.

Anna knew then that coming here had been a mistake. She gathered up her bag and was about to leave quietly, when Megan spotted her across the room.

"Well, well," her tinkling voice rang out loudly, causing several heads to turn. "Look who's come slumming."

Anna took a deep breath and stood as Megan rounded the bar, hips swaying in her direction, high heels clicking on the slate floor.

"Hello, Megan."

"If it isn't my prodigal little sister," Megan sneered, sharp brown eyes taking in the quietly expensive coat, the well-fitting jeans and suede boots, the classy haircut. It made her voice even harder as she played up for the meagre audience.

"Don't you look bookish," Megan jeered.

"You look well," Anna ventured in return, because she meant it. Underneath the veneer, Megan was a lovely-looking woman.

"Thank you," Megan said, running a hand through her mane of hair. She said nothing further, letting her expressive eyes do the talking for her as she raked them over Anna's less glamorous attire.

"Look, I can see that you're busy," Anna hurried on, "I only stopped in to say 'hello'. I can call back another time."

"No need to rush off when you've only just arrived. I might not see you again for another eight years," her laugh didn't quite mask the bitterness beneath it. Anna ignored the jibe and worked hard to keep her own resentment buried. If she'd stayed away, Megan knew the reason why.

Megan watched her younger sister's internal struggle and was frustrated when she chose not to rise to the bait. It would have been fun to have a showdown after all this time but maybe that could wait until there were more people around. If they were going to have it out, Megan thought, she might as well have her roots done.

At that moment, the door swung open and both women turned in reflex. Megan reacted first, recognising the tall, dark man who entered the pub instantly. In fact, she had been watching out for him whenever she could and had even taken to long walks around the village so that she could wander past his cottage whenever she thought he might be home. The curtains were usually always closed, the lights dim. He rarely came into the village and had only been in the pub once before. So far, she hadn't been able to pin him down, but it was only a matter of time.

"Well, hello handsome," she drawled, angling her body towards him so that he could see her figure to best advantage.

Ryan turned distractedly towards the sound of a female voice, and met the full force of Megan Taylor. He was man enough to admit that she wasn't hard on the eyes, with curves in all the right places and good features which she had taken the trouble to highlight. In fact, perhaps to over-cook, he thought belatedly, considering the over-made up face and dramatic fall of black hair which didn't look like it was the colour Mother Nature had given her. He found his eyes drawn instead to the woman who stood quietly beside her. This one had an entirely different demeanour but there were definite similarities between the two. Same height, but where the first was all buxom curves, the second had a willowy, bordering on fragile build. Dark, waving hair framed a fine-boned face with pale skin and full lips. Soft, dark eyes met his and held.

Anna could read nothing in the stranger's face as he greeted her sister with a polite nod. He was a good-looking man; almost cartoon-like with unruly black hair swept away artlessly from a symmetrical face with slashed cheekbones and striking grey eyes. She didn't think he would appreciate the description, she decided with a smile. For all its beauty, his face wore a serious expression, an intent watchfulness behind eyes which screamed intelligence. He returned her sister's greeting politely, but cast his gaze around the room while Megan spoke, a fact which she knew would irritate her sister who was used to undivided male attention.

Anna was so busy in her own quiet observation that it came as a serious shock when he suddenly turned and fixed those eyes on her. She felt the tiny hairs on the back of her neck stand to attention. His expression didn't change except for some small shift which caused him to frown at her. Still, he continued his silent assessment.

Eventually, he turned back and addressed her sister, who had been watching the exchange with interest.

"Megan, isn't it?" His voice was clipped and cool.

Megan preened, happy that he knew her name without having to ask. "That's right. Who's asking?" She smiled winningly, flashing pearly white teeth. Of course, she already knew who he was. She knew all about him; at least, everything she'd been able to find out after first seeing him drive up in the snazzy convertible he kept parked outside his cottage.

"DCI Ryan," he pulled out his warrant card and watched her eyes widen comically.

"I see," Megan whispered dramatically, moving further towards him so that she would have to tip her head up to look at him from under long lashes. "This must be about poor Lucy Mathieson." She crossed both hands over her chest in a display of concern, with the added benefit that it drew the eye unconsciously to her chest. Unfortunately, he missed the gesture as he took a wide survey of the bar, thinking that gossip was bound to travel like wildfire on an island this size. There were only a couple of hundred inhabitants and this was the only drinking hole. It was barely one in the afternoon but that was plenty of time for word to spread.

"That's right. I'm trying to piece together her movements last night. I understand that you work here, Ms…" he paused to fish out his notebook, struggling to remember her surname.

"Taylor," she purred.

Ryan's eyebrows rose slightly, thinking that was the second 'Taylor' he'd heard that day, but then he relaxed. Taylor was a common enough name.

"Ms Taylor…"

"*Miss* Taylor," she corrected him, eyes all innocence.

"Right," he battled frustration and carried on. He may have been hungover but he wasn't blind. He glanced again at the woman standing serenely to the right with a slight smile curving her lips. Disconcerted, he looked away again. "Perhaps it would be best if we sat down somewhere more private?"

Megan's eyes gleamed and he felt the urge to laugh. Funny how he had been more inclined to laugh in the short time he had been investigating a murder than the entire three months prior to it.

"So that I can ask you some questions pertaining to the investigation?" he supplied helpfully and watched Megan's pouting mouth turn sulky.

"That's fine," Megan was not a woman easily put off. "Why don't you follow me?" She started to sashay towards a corner booth at the far end of the bar.

"One moment," he held up a finger, turned back to Anna and fixed his gaze on her. "Do you work here as well?" Inquisitive eyes raced over her face again, leaving her feeling exposed. He couldn't remember seeing her before.

He was certain he would have remembered.

"No," Anna's voice came out sounding a bit breathless and she felt like an idiot. She cleared her throat and tried again. "No, I'm just visiting. Megan is my sister. In fact, I was going to look for you."

Ryan's eyebrows lifted fractionally. "Look for me?"

She held out one slender hand, "I'm Doctor Anna Taylor, I believe you're expecting me."

There was a pregnant pause.

"Pardon?" To his credit, Ryan's voice remained even.

She wavered and let her hand fall loosely to her side. "Anna Taylor?" She tried a friendly smile. "Mr—ah—DCS Gregson contacted me early this morning to engage my services as a civilian consultant," she spoke as if to a slow child.

"You're Doctor Taylor?" His face was still unreadable and Anna bristled.

"Yes."

"Bullshit," he drawled in calm, well-rounded tones and watched her mouth fall open.

CHAPTER 5

"Got any coffee?"

Phillips rummaged around the cupboards in Ryan's cottage and found them distressingly bare. He abandoned hope that there might be bacon and eggs and settled instead for a soft apple he found sitting lonely on the countertop.

"Got coffee, can't promise any milk. Jar's by the kettle."

Phillips wondered how people could stand to drink the stuff without a splash of full fat milk and a spoonful of sugar. Still, it was better than nothing.

"Need to fill the gaps in her timeline," Ryan muttered distractedly as he tacked up images on the makeshift murder board which was, in fact, one entire wall of the dining room. He'd taken down the artsy canvas with its seascape study to leave a bare magnolia surface which was already filling fast.

"Making good progress," Phillips countered and gingerly sipped at his coffee. It was almost three in the afternoon and the investigation had progressed like lightning, in his view. He'd seen veteran SIOs take double the time.

"Not good enough," Ryan said. He turned to pick up a thick black marker pen and Phillips watched him draw a long horizontal line on the clean magnolia wall. He wondered if it was permanent.

"You know, you don't have to do all of this manually. There's a computer program which helps you produce timelines, charts…" Phillips trailed off when Ryan simply looked at him balefully. "Hope you're on friendly terms with your landlady," he shook his head, wincing as the coffee slid down his throat like bitter mud.

Ryan mumbled something unintelligible as he marked up the details of Lucy's last movements. Five minutes later, he was joined by Faulkner, the Senior CSI, Detective Constable Jack Lowerson and some other uniforms. In other circumstances, he might have invited the coastguard to join the investigation team but he couldn't risk it.

Only the people in this room were completely unconnected to the island and therefore trustworthy.

It was imperative that he could trust his team.

He stood by the window and watched them pull up wooden chairs around the kitchen table facing the murder wall he'd set up. His eyes roamed their faces as he waited for the conversation to die down. When he was sure he had their attention, he opened his mouth to speak.

And was interrupted for the second time that day by a sharp bang on the front door.

Anna stood outside the pretty little cottage with ivy running up one side and tried to take deep breaths.

She was steaming.

After she had come all the way to Lindisfarne, ignoring her own misgivings in order to perform a public service…her *civic duty*, she thought primly, she had been met by the rudest, *the* most arrogant man. He had completely humiliated her at the pub. He had actually laughed in her face.

Oh, the nerve of the man.

She had tried to be reasonable, God knows.

"I'm happy to assist in any way I can," she had offered, albeit her voice probably frigid with offence.

"Look, sweetheart," he had drawled, *"I don't need a civilian consultant, but if I did, I would need one who looks like she's at least old enough to drive."*

Calling her 'sweetheart' had been enough to make her blood simmer. Insinuating that she was some naïve teenager had been enough to turn it up to boiling point.

He had effectively dismissed her. Thanked her for her offer, blah blah, but the message had been for her to run along. It hadn't helped that Megan had been there to witness the entire conversation, no doubt triumphing at her expense once again.

Anna had maintained what she liked to think was a quiet dignity, right until she had walked outside the pub, where she had sworn like a sailor and had very nearly kicked the plastic Santa, whose laughter had hit a little close to home. Now, she'd had time to cool off and come to the conclusion that DCI Ryan needed to hear some home truths. Well, she was just the person to let him have them.

Rich brown eyes glittered with barely suppressed temper as she rapped sharply on the oak door with its knocker in the shape of a leaping fox. She had raised her fist to bang louder when the door swung open.

"Yes?" His voice was clipped.

"I've got some things to say to you," she began.

"Save it," he said in bored tones, "I don't have time for temper tantrums." He started to close the door in her face but she thrust one small foot in the corner.

Ryan's eyebrows rose at the action and he cocked his head.

"Look…" he started.

"*You* look," she cut across him and jabbed a finger at his broad chest, encountering a surprising wall of muscle. She swallowed the distraction and carried on. "I didn't *ask* to be involved in this—I was perfectly happy where I was. Your *superior* contacted me personally to request my help and after some consideration I agreed."

"Well, now, don't do us any favours," he drawled, eyes narrowing pointedly at the finger which still prodded his solar plexus.

Anna clamped her teeth together and snatched her hand away. Her voice was rigidly formal when she spoke again.

"I am a leading authority on the Neolithic and Mesolithic periods, with specialist knowledge of religious practices during those eras, incorporating their modern denominations."

Ryan opened his mouth but she cut across him again.

"Part of that specialism includes knowledge of sacrificial practices, burial rites of those early religions as well as their more modern counterparts which people still practise today. Aside from that, I grew up on this island. I've read everything there is to read about it, Chief Inspector." That was no exaggeration; she had spent years studying the island and its history. Her voice calmed slightly and she added, "I don't need to do anybody any favours."

"Doctor Taylor…" he began.

"Oh, so now you believe that I'm a real doctor?" she said silkily, arms crossed over her chest.

Ryan folded his lips and sent up a prayer to a God he didn't believe in, to deliver him from angry women.

"*Doctor* Taylor," he repeated, "the department is grateful, *I'm* grateful, to you for agreeing to assist us in our investigation. The fact is, we don't know that the circumstances of the incident warrant such specialist knowledge at this time."

"Well," Anna pursed her lips, deflated. That seemed fair enough, she supposed. "I…"

Her voice trailed off and Ryan watched her colour drain slightly. He followed the line of her vision. In his hand, he clutched a swatch of photographs, freshly developed by the CSIs who had commandeered the resources of the only photographic studio on the island. The picture he held was a candid shot of Lucy as she had been laid out; lifeless, grey, her humanity taken from her.

He turned the image swiftly to the wall and watched Anna's eyes lift again. He had expected shock, which he saw, but he hadn't expected the quiet acceptance or the compassion swimming so near the surface. This woman was a constant surprise.

"I'm sorry that you had to see that," he said quietly.

Anna shook her head. "No," she said, "I'm not sorry. I'll leave you to your investigation, Mr Ryan, but here's where you can find me if you change your mind." She scribbled the address on the underside of a used envelope, thrust it in his hand and turned away without a backward glance.

From the image she had just seen, Anna was almost certain that he would need to know why anybody would arrange a body in so precise a formation, why anybody but a madman would mark the girl's body in such a particular red pattern.

She could give him those answers.

* * *

When her slight form had disappeared around the corner towards the village, Ryan moved from his stiff position in the doorway and stopped to consider why a young woman with all the appearance of fragility wouldn't balk at the sight of brutality in its extreme. He had an uncomfortable feeling that he would be seeking her out before long and an even more uncomfortable feeling that he might enjoy it.

When he walked back into the makeshift Incident Room, he cast his gaze over the people who occupied it. He had appointed Lowerson, an eager young detective constable, as the reader-receiver for the MIR. He had the unenviable task of looking over every bit of intelligence as it filtered through, giving it a log number before it was assessed for urgency and relevance. He'd spent the past three hours sitting at Ryan's kitchen table entering information onto the computer, reading documents then passing them on to one of the uniforms for cross-checking.

Ryan remembered the days when he'd been the reader-receiver and could sympathise. It was a rite of passage they all went through.

Phillips and one of the uniforms had made a good dent in the house-to-house calls, collecting witness statements from island residents. Nothing had popped up, except for one old woman who claimed to have been woken in the early hours by the sound of a boat engine. They would look into the harbour records to see if any boats had been logged during the early hours but from what Ryan had seen, almost every resident owned a boat and used it whenever they pleased without taking the trouble to inform the coastguard or harbourmaster, who happened to be one and the same.

Lindisfarne was a law unto itself.

Ryan moved to the front of the room and picked up his marker pen, scrawling a name at the top of the wall which read 'Operation Lindisfarne.' CID Command had named the investigation without an eye for originality before handing down their decree.

"Alright, settle down," he said, not bothering to raise his voice. Chairs scraped, voices died. Ryan watched them take in the details on the wall, note the smiling picture of the victim compared with how she had been found that morning.

"You all know each other," he said. He'd seen them go through the motions of hand-shaking and they had probably had a chance to talk over old times while he had been held up by an irate lady historian. He found himself wanting to smile at the memory, so he frowned instead to compensate.

"Let's get down to it. Victim is Lucy Jane Mathieson, aged twenty-one, arts student. You're all aware of the circumstances in which she was found."

There was murmured agreement.

"House-to-house interviews have been completed," he said, thinking that one of the few advantages of living on a small island was the reduced pool of people to interview. "Many of these were conducted early this morning, before the usual wave of tourists arrived. I thank those officers for their quick, focused work."

He nodded to the uniforms.

"DC Lowerson has been assessing the witness statements for relevance. In the interim, Lucy's parents have told us that she left last night to go to the pub with two of her friends just after six. The barmaid at the Jolly Anchor, Megan Taylor, has confirmed that they arrived around six-thirty and were there until just before closing at eleven forty-five."

"The friends—Ellie Holmes and Rachel Finnigan—confirm those times, sir." Lowerson piped up and received a nod of thanks.

"Initial indications suggest time of death would have been between midnight and one in the morning," Ryan tapped the timeline. "That means she was killed shortly after leaving her friends, within the space of an hour, two at most. As yet, we have no witnesses, except to say that she never returned home. No clothing has been located. The CSI team spent most of their morning up at the Priory and plan to conduct a routine search and sweep of the victim's home, where she lived with her parents on Church Lane, after this briefing. That includes taking fingerprints and swabs from her parents for the purposes of elimination. The Mathiesons have given their consent."

He closed a fist around the CSIs' preliminary forensic report of their findings at the Priory and held it against his chest possessively.

"As for the crime scene, why don't you give us an executive summary, Tom?" He eyed the Senior CSI, a man with twenty-five years' experience behind him, and hitched a hip on the window sill in the absence of a spare chair. Everything about Tom Faulkner could be described as average, from his height, to the mousy brown of his hair. Everything except his mind, which was finely honed tool.

Tom cleared his throat. Quiet, scientific men don't much like public speaking even in the close quarters of a kitchen-diner.

"I've just spoken to the pathologist, who has confirmed Doctor Walker's initial findings. Lucy had been deceased approximately five hours, no more than six, at the time of examination. Post mortem examination may narrow that down even further. We won't hear the results of that for another day, I would imagine."

"Does that estimate account for cold weather conditions?" Ryan cut through the spiel.

Tom nodded energetically. "Yes, the body would have been preserved to some degree overnight with weather conditions averaging at minus five Celsius. The estimate accounts for that."

"So, that puts her death somewhere between midnight and one in the morning, like we thought," Phillips grunted, chewing rhythmically on his last stick of gum.

Tom nodded, "Right."

"Cause of death?" Ryan needed it confirmed.

"It looks like straightforward asphyxiation by manual strangulation, sir, but we'll need to wait for the tox report to come back before that's final. A large gash on the victim's right temple indicates a blow to the head with sufficient force perhaps to stun or concuss but not to cause lasting injury and certainly not enough to kill. Blood clotting around the gash indicates that the blow was sustained ante-mortem."

"The bruising?"

"The pathologist's initial observations would suggest we are seeking a perpetrator with a hand span of approximately eight inches from thumb to index finger, judging from the pattern of bruising around the victim's neck. Couldn't get him to commit to anything more precise than that, not until he's had time to go over her properly."

"Likely to be male, then."

"Statistically that's the most likely probability," Faulkner agreed.

Ryan nodded, one quick jerk as he thought of Lucy Mathieson's pale neck.

"Carry on, Tom."

"Unfortunately, following a thorough sweep of the body including initial swabs, we have been unable to isolate any suspect DNA evidence aside from the victim's own blood, hair and so forth. The pathologist is reviewing Lucy's blood work and I have requested a rush on it, sir."

Faulkner's words hung in the air for one thick moment and Ryan's brows drew together ominously.

"No other bodily fluids, skin, hair, nails? Not a fucking thing?"

"Sir," Tom could sympathise with the frustration. He had felt it himself as he'd gone over that poor girl's body with a fine-toothed comb. "We were able to find various indications of herbal and man-made residue, which are currently being analysed and which I will venture to say are likely to come back as soap produce and some sort of body oil."

Ryan paused to digest that information.

"No defensive wounds? Hell, anything else at all?"

"He was extremely thorough, sir. The victim's nails had been cleaned and there was a trace sample of the disinfectant he used."

"Good. I want the name of it, when you have it. You never know," he said.

"Any sexual assault?"

Faulkner paused. "There were bruises on her upper arms to indicate she had been restrained, and a small tear to her lip, but otherwise no other evidence to suggest sexual intent, sir. Once again, pathologist to confirm, but swabs indicate that her mouth had also been cleaned with disinfectant. That's going to prove problematic for the pathologist in isolating any foreign DNA she may have taken on when sustaining the cut to her lip."

Ryan nodded for him to continue, his heart sinking by the minute.

"We found some other residue in the head gash, comprising of silicon dioxide quartz particles..."

"Silla-what?" Phillips pulled a face from the back of the room.

"Sand," Ryan supplied shortly. "You can give us the layman's version, Tom."

"Sorry," Faulkner laughed nervously. "Force of habit."

"Sand? That's not exactly a light bulb moment, considering that this whole island is surrounded by sand. The stuff could have been in her hair already," Phillips complained.

"The chemical compounds differ on each part of the island," Tom argued. "There was a sizeable sample found crusted with blood, which would suggest it was present at the time of injury. Give us enough time and if the sample is big enough we can cross-check against local geography to try to narrow the field."

"It all adds up," Ryan said quietly, "but it's speculative at this point." He got up to pace a few steps and then turned back.

"What time did it rain last night?"

"Locals reported rain around midnight," Phillips supplied. "Got a few witnesses from the pub saying that they had to run home to avoid the downpour after closing time."

"Heavy rain would likely have washed that sort of residue off the skin?"

"Even a light rain would have diluted it," Tom agreed. "If her body had been left out during the rainfall last night, there wouldn't be much to find on her."

"What about the underside of her body?"

"Same, sir. Nothing other than this residue."

It didn't take much for Ryan to follow the trail of bread crumbs.

"So, after the rain stopped, he washed her, oiled her skin?" His voice was remote. "Couldn't have done all that up at the Priory, he would have risked exposure. Where did he put her while it was raining? We need to find the kill site."

Tom agreed. "No residue was found on the ground, on or near the site where she was found, nor any residue around the body other than some small level of transference from skin to stone. That would be consistent with the assumption that the girl was cleaned elsewhere."

"You'll be sweeping the Mathiesons' car," Ryan said to Faulkner.

"We'll go over it," Faulkner nodded. "Same time as we go over the house this afternoon."

"No statements from anyone to say they heard a car at that time of night," Lowerson added. "Residents tend not to use their cars on the island, only if they're making a trip to the mainland. Everything is so close by, here."

"Okay." Ryan added that information to his mental file.

"What about floor markings?" Phillips' birdlike eyes were keen.

Tom swivelled to face him. "Some deep treads around the site where the victim was found and intermittent similar treads leading through the Priory. Took us most of the morning to try to trace his route," Tom addressed Ryan again. "He took the long route, skirted around the outside walls of the Priory. Still, the weather was on our side for that. Rain makes the ground soft, better for holding footprints."

"What are we looking at, then?"

"Likely male, again. Larger boot size, a nine or ten. Unfortunately, he stuck to the grass rather than giving us a nice, juicy print in the mud, so we don't have any casts for the sole. I can't give you any brands of boot to look for," Faulkner shrugged apologetically.

"Okay, thanks Tom, that's good, fast work. Our man took the long route, couldn't risk being seen," Ryan said. He glanced across at the map of Lindisfarne he had tacked on the wall and thought back to the buildings nearest to the Priory.

"Phillips, I want to know about any and all structures large enough to accommodate this son of a bitch, close enough to the Priory for him to transport a body without alerting the village. He needs enough space to clean her up. He might have needed access to water, so check on plumbing." He looked at his watch. "If there's no time after this briefing, start that tomorrow."

"On it," Phillips said and popped his gum.

"No other distinctive prints?" Ryan turned back to Faulkner.

"None other than the worn treads from what looks to be visitors from the previous day, sir."

Ryan thought of the high-heeled boots Lucy Mathieson had worn. She hadn't walked up to the Priory herself, it seemed.

"Even taking the circuitous route, he ran a hell of a risk dragging her up there. Surely would have been better to dump her body somewhere closer?"

"Who knows what these nut jobs think about?" Phillips chimed in.

Ryan ignored the comment. "What was his access point?"

"Similar markings indicate he climbed the fence further around from the visitor's gate," Faulkner continued, "then hiked up the steep side of the grass. If he was carrying her, it would have been heavy work."

"What about the fence?"

Tom smiled in an almost fatherly fashion. Ryan didn't miss a trick. "We found tiny traces of black polyester wool on the fence where the perp crossed over. That will take a day or so to analyse. We found trace skin samples on the fence and there were matching scratches on the victim's left flank and waist."

"From where he struggled to push her over the fence," Ryan surmised, imagining the actions of a desperate man.

"That would be my guess."

There was a moment's pause as the people whose profession it was to avenge the dead grieved for a girl none of them had known.

"And the return route?" Ryan broke the silence.

"More difficult to trace," Tom began. "We believe he returned by the same route, according to some shallower markings which follow the same path. He wasn't carrying such a heavy load, so we've been able to hazard a more educated guess as to his likely weight and height. Looks to be between five-nine and six-one, between one hundred and seventy to one hundred and ninety pounds."

Ryan took a long breath.

"So what you're saying is, he's a man of average height and average weight."

Tom nodded miserably.

"Any other possibilities?"

Faulkner sighed. "There are other fresh tracks leading around the perimeter heading towards the turnstiles. We've eliminated those which appear to have been made by Liz Morgan and her dog," he added. "We'll keep looking, but for now I'm minded to think that our perp left via the route he came."

"Okay, understood. What about phone data?"

"We haven't been able to recover her mobile phone, sir, although her family confirms she owns a black iPhone with a pink cover and her friends say she had it with her last night."

"There's one other thing," Phillips said cheerfully, after another brief pause. "There's no CCTV on the island apart from just outside the Heritage Centre, where they keep some relics and whatnot. I've requested the tape for last night, but nobody at the centre knows how to operate the system. I've asked one of the techies to come across from HQ tomorrow to help with it. Thought you'd want to know."

Ryan pinched the bridge of his nose to stop the pounding which had started there.

"Frank, we're going to need some more coffee."

* * *

Hours later, Ryan's head was heavy and his stomach was churning from too much caffeine. He watched from the top of the dunes overlooking the causeway as his team dispersed to cross over to the mainland, back to their ordinary lives and families. The sun rested low on the horizon and mist swirled above the water as the last tourist vehicles made their progress along the winding road. The cars moved like ants across the shadowed water, or rats deserting a sinking ship.

He watched them for a moment longer then turned to walk back towards the village, deep in thought. First, he would head back to the pub. The pub was the epicentre of the community. Perhaps some religious types would have disagreed with him but he knew plenty of people who said their prayers in church then headed down to the local drinking hole. His discussion with the Jolly Anchor's resident barmaid hadn't been especially helpful, he recalled, unless of course he counted the part where Megan tried to give him a palm reading or the part where she had brushed her leg against his in a move too practiced to be accidental.

When he sifted through the useless flirtation, he saw a dissatisfied woman stuck in a monotonous job without either the means or the motivation to better herself. Megan Taylor was a woman who lived by her looks, whether she was tending bar or rubbing up against murder detectives. He figured she would get a shock when she woke up one day, twenty years older and no further ahead.

Megan may have seemed like a bit of fluff, a pretty butterfly that enjoyed flitting from man to man seeking attention, but he had been trained to analyse behaviour. She was perceptive and she was observant. Megan had been on shift from five until midnight with a break from ten until ten-thirty and, in that time, she had seen who had come and gone. She could describe, in detail, what most of them had been wearing, what they had ordered and what they had spent, almost to the penny. She said she had seen Lucy come in around six-thirty with her friends, giggling and chatting. He was inclined to take her word for it.

Amid a host of transient visitors and regulars, Rob Fowler, the coastguard volunteer, had stopped in around seven-thirty for a couple of hours before leaving again in time for his night shift at eleven. Like a revolving door, Alex Walker had stopped by for a late drink at around eleven-fifteen after the end of his shift. Pete went straight home, according to the statement provided by his mother and the four guests staying at his family's inn. He was home by eleven-fifteen and tucked up in bed shortly after then. No doubt with a cup of warm milk and a bedtime story, Ryan thought with a smirk.

Lucy had stayed the whole night, eating, drinking and making merry during the festive season until she'd left around eleven forty-five to wander home alone. She hadn't worried for her safety; in fact, nobody had worried because nothing sinister ever happened on Lindisfarne.

Until now.

* * *

Elsewhere on the island, another man thought of Lucy as he stared at his reflection in the bathroom mirror. His hands shook as they clutched the porcelain rim of the sink, the knuckles turning white.

Just as they had turned white against her throat as he watched her struggle through a haze of confusion and fear. He had felt the awful power of it, the momentary arousal of invincibility.

He started to cry, tears rolling hotly down his face and he brought both hands up over his mouth to stifle the sound, rocking slightly. He dragged shaking fingers through his hair, pulling at it to try to ease the awful pressure in his head.

Lucy…Lucy. I didn't mean to do it. I would never have hurt you, if only you hadn't looked at me that way, if only you hadn't laughed. Please, Lucy. He whimpered softly under his breath.

He looked up again and a scream of terror welled up in his throat as he mistook a flash of red behind him for the red she had been wearing. He looked at his hands again and thought he saw her blood smeared across them. He groped for the soap and ceramic pots fell to the tiled floor, smashing into pieces. He ran the water to boiling and scrubbed desperately at his hands to cleanse his body before he could cleanse his spirit.

He had cleansed Lucy's spirit, offered her up to the Master on consecrated ground.

He had to believe it.

He fell to the floor, nicked his hands against the shards of ceramic and curled his body into the foetal position.

Eventually, he rose, calmer now. Methodically, he tidied the bathroom, washed and dressed himself.

He had work to do.

CHAPTER 6

"What did you tell him?"

The man's voice was deep, almost musical. It was one of the things Megan liked most about him. That and his bank balance. She turned from inspecting her make-up in the small mirror above the bureau in her cramped apartment and caught his eye in the reflection. Watching her, he remembered briefly what had attracted him to her in the first place. That look in her eye, the one she had now, held promises of dark pleasures. Even now, he felt himself grow hard.

"Tell me," he asked again and she rolled her eyes.

"Don't worry. I just gave him the basics; when I was on shift, when I took my break. I couldn't exactly lie about that, since Bill was there last night and could have told him the same thing."

"Did you tell him what you did in your break?"

Megan turned to him fully now and toyed with the buttons on her snug red top. Red was his favourite. She loved playing with him, could see the way his eyes followed the movement of her fingers and felt power course through her.

He would pay, they all did.

She flipped open a button, ran her tongue lightly over her full lips and watched his pupils dilate. Men were so easy.

"I told him I went back to my apartment all on my lonesome and watched some TV."

"That was stupid," he ground out. "He could have asked you what you watched."

She didn't care for his tone, not at all. Her eyes narrowed and she thought of the ways she would bleed him this time, but her voice stayed soft, breathy.

"Shh," she walked her red-tipped fingers up his chest, scraped them across the nipples through his shirt and felt his breath catch. "As a matter of fact, he did ask. Luckily for you, I'm not a complete idiot.

The same show always plays at ten on a Thursday night." She named a popular crime drama and he thought it was poetic.

"That's good, that's my clever girl." Relief rushed through him and his arms came around her, cradled her and then tightened as he felt her clever hands roam lower to curl around him.

Anticipation ran through his veins like a heady drug as he watched her walk away to crawl slowly over the bed with its cheap satin cover.

Megan widened her eyes and fluttered her lashes because it was expected.

"Honey," she purred, "we still haven't finished discussing that important matter we talked about last night."

A muscle in his jaw twitched and he felt his erection wane. She never knew when to stop, when to accept her limits.

"I've already answered you." His voice was hard.

"Well," her voice was abruptly hard too as she sat up again, yanked the top back down over her bare breasts. "Perhaps I didn't like your answer."

"Megan, I can't give you more than I have already." He thought of all the money he had poured into her waiting hands. For clothes to make herself pretty for him, she had said. For payment, that was the truth of it.

"I think you can give me plenty more," she said, the seduction over. "What happened to all your talk of love?"

He closed his eyes briefly and thought of his own stupidity. It was true, he had said those words, at the height of the crazy, all-consuming passion he had felt for her in those first few months. At times, she could still move him that way, but he knew that his obsession for her had passed and it was time to move on.

"Let me think about it," he said, but this time she wasn't buying.

"I think you've had plenty of time to think about it," she stalked towards him now, hands on hips. She cocked her head to one side, baiting him. "I know somebody else who would be interested to hear the tale I have to tell."

He stood silent, perfectly still.

"You won't be telling anyone anything."

Megan had a moment's concern at the odd note in his voice and then chose to ignore it. He was just a man and she could wrap him around her little finger. Still, he needed the stick before she gave him the carrot.

"I mean it," she said. "I'm sick of this dump." She gestured to the tiny apartment with its stick furniture, the cheap curtains and flaking paint. You told me months ago we would be married this summer. I'm sick of waiting."

"It's not that simple," he started.

"You're full of shit." She paced back to the bureau, lit a cigarette. She didn't usually indulge since she wanted to avoid the wrinkles in later life, but she needed the nicotine. After one long drag, she swung back around, black hair settling sleekly down her back.

"I'll tell you how simple it is. Either you marry me, or I'll fucking sky-write it. Oh yeah, imagine what the village would think if they found out about your little *weaknesses*." She paused, considered. "There is another option," she gestured with the cigarette in her hand. "Give me enough money to start again somewhere else and nobody needs to know a thing."

Megan's lips curved. That was a *much* better idea. If he was so attached to his reputation and this dead end community, then he could pay through the nose. That way, she didn't have to be saddled with him for the next however long and she could always tap him up again when the money started to run low. Perfect.

"You're trying to blackmail me?" There was that *note* in his voice again, she thought. Maybe she needed to sweeten him up a bit, get him back to where she wanted him.

She stubbed out the cigarette and let the side of her top edge down over the creamy swell of her breast.

"Sweetheart," she was all silky again, "don't be like that. I'm just talking about being fair. After all, I've been waiting for you all this time, expecting to be the new Mrs…"

He let out a short, mirthless laugh, cutting her off.

He would never have married her. It had been madness which had led him to even suggest it. Madness, some recreational drugs and her young, nubile body riding him like a stallion, making him feel like a man.

"You have to give me a day or so to think about it."

She swallowed, tears suddenly burning her eyes and she turned around again so that he wouldn't see them. She thought of all the men she had known. They had always wanted her, enjoyed her, but none had said they loved her and meant it. Oh, of course she had known that *he* hadn't meant it either. She had just half-fooled herself into believing that he *might* have. It didn't matter that she didn't love him. She would have been faithful…or tried to be.

Her face was composed again, her voice brittle with control when she turned back.

"That's fine. Only fair for you to consider your options, but remember, you've got until the end of the week."

"I understand what I have to do," was all he said.

"That's fine then." Her pretty face brightened and he realised she hadn't put as much make up on as usual. Looking at her in that moment, he thought she was beautiful, like a rare and exotic flower.

"Now," she continued, thinking it was time to sweeten the deal. "Why don't we pick up where we left off?" She draped herself over the bed, raised her arms above her head.

Like an offering.

"No," he said quietly, reaching for the bag he had brought. "We're going to play a different game tonight."

* * *

The Jolly Anchor had been decked out like a Christmas tree. Strings of multi-coloured lights were draped in uneven arcs along the edge of the roof. White lights edged each of the windows and the window panes had been sprayed with false snow. Judging from the chill in the air, it wouldn't be long before they had the real thing.

A mechanical Santa guarded the door but a real one waited inside.

"Bill?" There was only one man on the island who could possibly fill out that garish red suit without needing extra padding.

"Ho, ho, ho!" Bill's booming voice with the attractive Scottish lilt turned and greeted him.

Against his better judgment, Ryan's lips quirked.

"Playing dressy-up?"

Bill pulled down the elasticated white beard to reveal his ruddy red face underneath.

"I do the same every year," he puffed, wiping a hand over his brow. "I work at the grotto down by the harbour for the kids during the day and it tends to bring a smile to the big kids here too." He waved a hand at one merry-maker Ryan recognised as the local newsagent, who declared all he wanted for Christmas was a kiss from a girl called Faye. The girl sat across the bar and shook her head but there was a flirty look in her eye. Bill turned back with a smile. "I thought about whether I should tone things down...you know, after what happened to Lucy." Bill heaved out a sigh. "Hell, Ryan, life has to go on."

"You're doing a good trade tonight," Ryan looked Bill square in the eye and the big man acknowledged the hit, had the grace to look slightly abashed. It was Friday night and the bar area was full to bursting. Looking at the smiles, the merriment, you would think nothing had changed. Then again, most of the people in the room hadn't seen the wasted body of a young girl in the early hours of that same morning.

Ryan decided to let it go. He couldn't blame the man for making a living.

Several hands rose to greet him and he sent a nod in return.

"Looks like a good place to meet people," he turned to face Bill.

"Sure is," he agreed. "We're short on restaurants or fancy wine bars on Lindisfarne."

"Good for business at the Anchor. How long have you been here?"

"Crikey," Bill scratched under the white wig as he thought. "Fifteen years at least, the last eight as landlord."

"Oh?" Ryan's interest was piqued although he knew it wasn't particularly relevant.

"Andy Taylor used to own and run the place before me. I started out as the barman and all-round dogsbody when I was a lad. I bought the place when he died, got it for a song."

There was that name 'Taylor' again, Ryan thought.

"That would be Megan's father?" And Anna's too, he added silently.

Bill nodded. "Aye, that's right."

For an open, chatty sort of man, Bill seemed suddenly tight-lipped. Ryan wondered why.

"He died, you said? Wouldn't he have left the pub to his girls?"

Bill huffed out a breath and took a surreptitious look around the bar.

"Look, mate, it's a touchy subject around here. It was a bad business, a very bad business." Ryan tried to focus on the man's words and not on the ridiculous white moustache as it moved up and down.

"I'm the soul of discretion," he murmured.

Bill hooted out a laugh at that dry comment. "I believe you are," he nodded, thinking he'd never met a man with a better poker face. "Still, there are people who would still rather forget all about Andy."

"You're one of them?"

Bill paused for a moment and chose his words carefully. "Look, Andy gave me a job when I needed one, when I had nothing and nobody. Now, I got a nice home, a good business and decent friends." He paused before continuing. "I was grateful to him but, by God, he got his pound of flesh." Memories swirled in his eyes. "I wasn't the only one who paid a toll. He had a beautiful wife and two sweet girls. It wasn't enough for him to enjoy what he had."

Ryan didn't miss the past tense. He hadn't noticed a Mrs Taylor roaming around.

"What happened?"

"He made life hard for himself and he made life hard for others. Took too much of the drink," he supplied. "Spent too much on the horses and he had a nasty temper. By God, that's an understatement. More'n once I would see one of the girls with bruises, cuts here and there. Always said there had been an accident but I knew better. Never felt more useless in my life."

Old regrets, old fears swept across his round face and Ryan said nothing, waiting for him to finish. He knew the value of silence.

"They found Sara Taylor at the bottom of the stairs there," he jerked a shoulder towards the narrow flight of stone steps in the little courtyard outside that led up to the apartment Megan now occupied. "The flat was supposed to be empty—by that time I'd moved into my own place down on St Aidan's Road—but there was talk." He lowered his voice so that Ryan had to strain to hear him. "The flat was all made up, the bed slept in, candles all around. When Sara was found at the bottom of those stairs with her head smashed and her body broken, there was some who said Andy threw her down those stairs because he found out she'd been with another man."

"What do you think?"

"Depends which part. I think that if she had another fella, I wouldn't have blamed her. Delicate, she was, devoted to her girls. Anna's a lot like her, turned into a real beauty." Bill smiled proudly and Ryan found himself imagining an older version of Anna, a slender woman with striking features and a fall of rich brown hair.

"As for the other part," Bill continued with a frown, "much as I'd like to say otherwise, I think there's nothing Andy Taylor wouldn't have done back in those days. Like I said, when he was on the drink, he was past caring. Didn't know his own mind."

Ryan nodded. He knew the type, came across them almost daily. He didn't bother asking why Sara Taylor had stayed, why she hadn't taken her girls away. She had been too afraid.

"Anyway," Bill sighed, "Andy went and hurled himself off the bluff up at the castle. Found him lying at the bottom a few days later once the tide had bashed him around a bit. More forgiving types might say he was so overwhelmed with grief that he couldn't manage without her. Me, I say he hurled himself into the sea because he couldn't live with what he'd done."

Anger burned briefly in his friendly face but was quickly snuffed out when another patron called out to him. He snapped the beard back into place.

"Turned out he'd mortgaged the pub to the hilt. There were massive debts to clear, so they sold the old cottage to Mark Bowers. He rents it out to holiday-makers now. The girls were happy to sell the pub on to me with the proviso that Megan would have a job and use of the flat upstairs for as long as she wanted it." He shivered, "Don't know how she could stay there, after what happened, but it never seems to bother her. Always was a free spirit. Hope you'll keep what I've told you under your hat, Ryan," he said, "no sense in bringing the past back to life."

With that, he moved on to chat to the groups of people gathered around the tables, granting Christmas wishes.

Ryan found a semi-secluded spot at the bar and, since he was technically off-duty, ordered a glass of Lindisfarne Mead, the local fortified wine produced on the island. Ordinarily, he was more comfortable with a glass of smooth red, but sometimes it paid to blend in with the crowd.

"No Megan, tonight?" he asked the lad currently serving behind the bar. With a sharp double-take, he realised it was Pete.

"Nah," Pete spoke without turning from his task. "She called in this afternoon and told Bill she had the flu. She'll most likely be in tomorrow, though."

Ryan took a thoughtful sip of his drink, appreciated the flavour. He could add 'unreliable' to the list of Megan Taylor's traits. Pity; he had wanted to ask her some more questions. He might try knocking on her door later. He checked his watch.

Eight-thirty.

"Didn't realise you worked here, Pete," he spoke companionably, thinking that the younger man seemed to have some of his colour back after the drama of the morning.

"I only volunteer with the coastguards," he answered with a friendly smile in return. "I share shifts here with Megan when I'm not helping out at home."

"You were coast-guarding last night, then, instead of bartending."

Pete nodded while he mixed whisky and coke. "I came off shift around eleven, same time as Alex."

Ryan already knew Pete's movements last night. It was his business to know.

"You didn't fancy a drink?" Ryan knew that Alex had dropped by the pub after his shift, had flirted with a few of the women. He wanted to know why Pete hadn't.

Pete pulled a face. "I see enough of the place, to be honest. Don't mind a sociable pint every now and then, but mostly I'd rather chill out at home."

"Guess you would have been pretty tired after a long shift," Ryan nudged. "Anything happen on the high seas?"

Pete flashed that quick smile again as he handed out drinks, clunking ice into the glasses and once again Ryan thought he looked too young to be serving alcohol. However, he happened to know that Pete had graduated from the island's high school the same year as Lucy but, whereas she had left to study Art History at university, he had stayed to tend bar and be an everyday hero, not including the times when he helped his widowed mother run her bed and breakfast hotel. That put him at a youthful but respectable twenty-one.

"Nothing much happened yesterday evening, but sometimes that's worse—you know, the long hours on call without anything really to do." His face fell again. "Guess I shouldn't complain about that, considering what happened this morning."

Ryan watched shock flit across Pete's face and felt something like pity stir inside him, reminding him of his younger self.

"Don't worry about it, Pete. It won't change what happened to Lucy."

"No, it won't change that."

Ryan paused and then picked up the rhythm again. "It must have been hard on you this morning, since you knew Lucy so well."

Pete swallowed. "I've known Lucy most of my life, we grew up together. A bunch of us would hang out, you know?"

"Yeah, I know," Ryan had a flash memory of his own childhood, of long summer days playing in the fields around his parents' house.

"It was hard on Alex, too. They were sort of seeing each other."

After a delayed reaction, Ryan considered it a personal success that he didn't choke on his mouthful of wine.

"Alex Walker?" How in the hell had he missed that one, Ryan wondered frantically. More importantly, why hadn't Alex mentioned that little nugget of information when he'd given his statement?

"Sure," Pete nodded blandly. "She was a bit younger, but it didn't seem to bother either of them. I think he took her to the theatre in Newcastle a couple of times when he was over that way." Ryan thought of the old Theatre Royal in Newcastle, the region's major city further south. It was where Lucy Mathieson had attended university, an easy ninety-minute drive from the island.

"Did she tell you about this?"

"Uh huh," Pete nodded, resting his arms on the bar during a lull. "She told all of us, it wasn't exactly a secret. Anybody could see they liked each other."

"Did Lucy's parents know?"

"I reckon," he pulled a face, "on the other hand, I don't know how her dad would have felt about it. Alex is a good bloke, but he's nearly thirty and Lucy only turned twenty-one in September."

"I see," Ryan didn't see the full picture, but he intended to, and soon. First on his list of questions for Megan would be her observations of Lucy and Alex. For now, he shifted back to an easier gear.

"So what did you do after your shift? Head home for some shuteye?"

"Yeah." Ryan already knew that. The door-to-doors had confirmed Pete's whereabouts between the hours of eleven-thirty and five-thirty; he'd been sleeping like a baby in his room at the hotel. Still, never hurt to get a fuller picture about a person.

"Your mother runs the big bed and breakfast near the Heritage Centre, doesn't she?" The centre which stood near the visitor's entrance to the Priory, Ryan thought.

"That's right," Pete said cheerfully. "My parents ran it together and then my mum took over when my dad died. All in all, they've been running it for thirty years. My grandparents on my father's side ran it before then."

"Real family business, then."

"Uh huh," Pete let pride into his voice. It was a lovely old hotel and he worked hard to help keep it that way.

"You know," he turned to Ryan, "if you ever want to come over, have a meal, my mother hired a really good chef. She's trying to push the restaurant," he explained. "I bet she'd give you a discount as a new customer."

"That's kind of her," Ryan answered, thinking that he wouldn't be taking up any friendly offers. His eyes dropped to Pete's hands as he pulled a couple of pints. Long, thin fingers but the man himself was slight, almost girlish. He doubted he would have had the physical strength to transport Lucy's body. On the other hand, it took a fair amount of wiry strength to man a rescue boat.

He took another drink, measuring the man.

Pete, sensing the conversation was over, smiled again and moved off to serve a customer. Ryan turned to watch the people of Lindisfarne from his vantage point. In the corner, a group of teenagers started to get rowdy before Bill sent them a mild look from his perch at the other end of the bar. Ryan might have wondered whether their ID met the legal requirement to buy alcohol but he had a feeling Bill ran a tight ship.

He saw Alex and Rob sitting at a table in the centre of the room, red jackets slung over the back of their chairs and radios tucked inside the pockets. He guessed they were off-duty but you never knew in a place like this. Normal rules didn't apply. Alex seemed to be holding court with three women. His green eyes twinkled as he regaled them with some story, probably of his heroism at sea. He wondered how the man could sit and smile, down drinks and flirt when his girlfriend had been brutally murdered earlier that same day. It was time he found out.

CHAPTER 7

Alex took a drink of his pint and, glancing around the room, spotted Ryan standing in the corner. The man was watchful as a hawk, those cop eyes missing nothing. He had to admire that. He raised a hand in greeting, gestured him over.

"Ryan!"

Alex watched him weave through the tables with that unhurried, prowling gait of his. He noticed the women at his table eyeing Ryan too and smiled ruefully, toeing out a stool and shifting to make room.

Ryan didn't take up the offer of a chair. He turned to the others, "Ladies, Rob." He nodded politely, then rested a heavy hand on Alex's shoulder, tightened it slightly. "Alex."

The coastguard raised his eyebrows. He didn't have to be a detective to sense something was off. He could admit that being on the receiving end of this man's wrath was not on his list of priorities.

"Got a minute?" Ryan's polite question held just the right amount of menace.

Alex nodded, "Sure."

They went outside and, after a brief check to see that they were alone, Ryan rounded on him.

"Would you like to tell me why you felt it was a good idea to withhold information during a murder investigation?"

"I don't know what you mean." Alex's voice was calm, but since his eyes had been trained on the other man's face, Ryan saw it—that momentary flash of understanding. Alex knew exactly what he meant.

"Let's start again, shall we?" Ryan's voice was dangerously low and he took another step closer, boxing him in for good measure.

A pulse jumped in Alex's corded neck and he stuck his fingers in his pockets, jingling change.

"I don't know what you want from me," Alex said belligerently.

"Let's start with the truth. Want to tell me why you didn't mention your relationship with Lucy Mathieson?"

Alex paled.

"We never really…I wouldn't have called it a relationship."

"Really? That's interesting, because it seems like she told her friends a different tale, all about her boyfriend, Alex Walker."

"Okay, look," Alex pushed his hands through his hair and Ryan watched the action. He was another one with big hands—seemed like the island was full of them.

"Look," Alex started again. "Kim and I separated six months ago."

"Kim?"

"My wife."

"Oh, this just gets better and better."

"Don't start on me!" Alex ground out, hands fisting. "Things have been rough with us for a while. She was the one who wanted to end it. She moved back to her parents' house in Newcastle."

Ryan made a mental note that this mild-mannered ladies' man might have violent tendencies, if that simmering temper was anything to go by.

"That's when it happened. I was over in Newcastle to see Kim, to try and patch things up. She told me to go to hell."

"Tut, tut…" Ryan said, not giving an inch. "She catch you in the arms of another woman?"

Alex said nothing, looked away, back towards the bar.

Ryan snorted. "You get around, don't you?"

"Do you want to hear this or not?" Alex set his teeth.

"By all means," Ryan flicked his wrist in a gesture to continue.

"So I headed out, decided to hit a few bars. That's when I recognised Lucy. Or sort of recognised her; she looked a lot more grown up than I remembered her, to say the least," his lips quirked, remembering. "Nearly swallowed my tongue when I saw her in a skirt and heels." Unexpectedly, tears sheened his eyes and he fought a visible battle against them.

"What happened?" Ryan asked quietly.

"We got a little drunk; she told me how she'd had this crush on me for years. I was flattered," he looked back at Ryan now, met his eyes as he got the words out. "I'd just come from one woman who thought I was the fucking Antichrist, then this young, beautiful girl tells me I'm the man of her dreams. I'm only human," he shrugged.

Ryan nodded. He could see where this was going.

"So, I take it you never met the parents?"

Alex felt guilt tear at his insides as he shook his head.

"Well, I mean, I know the Mathiesons. Everybody knows everybody around here…" he caught the look in Ryan's eye and hastily carried on, "But no, I didn't meet them specially. She—Lucy—wanted to set that up, make things official. I'll tell you straight, Ryan, I put her off again and again. I told her to wait, not to tell her parents until we'd spent a little more time together. I would meet her in Newcastle, take her out a few times a month, that sort of thing. It's not that I didn't care about her, Ryan, I did, I just—"

"I get it, Alex. You were just using her." Ryan's voice was unforgiving.

"Right, because you're such a saint?" Alex turned on him. "You can stand there and tell me you've never done anything you're ashamed of?"

Ryan was silent for a long moment. No, he couldn't say that. There were things which haunted him, which kept him from sleeping night after night, but as long as he was fighting to find this girl's killer he could stop thinking about another girl he'd been too late to save.

"This isn't about me. I don't answer the questions, Alex, I ask them." His voice was flat.

Alex just carried on looking at him.

"So, you had an affair with Lucy," he began.

"You make it sound like something dirty," Alex muttered.

"Wasn't it? You weren't exactly desperate to join her parents for tea and scones, were you?"

"I didn't want to make her promises I couldn't keep. Besides, she knew I was still married."

"I bet you told her you were getting a divorce," Ryan put in. He knew none of this was admissible and no caution had been given, no statement taken. He just wanted to know what made this man tick.

"That's true! Kim filed the papers three months ago."

Ryan raised an eyebrow. That was something, but he pushed for more.

"Did you see Lucy last night at the pub?"

"You know I did," Alex answered wearily. He'd given his statement that morning, same as everyone else.

"What were you wearing?"

"What was I *wearing*?" Alex looked completely baffled by the question but Ryan's gaze was unmoving, so he answered. "Ah, coastguard jacket, khaki cargo trousers, brown boots, white t-shirt and…" he trailed off, looked awkward for a moment.

"And…?"

"A green Christmas jumper. Has a reindeer on the front with flashing antlers. Satisfied?" Alex shifted uncomfortably.

Ryan told himself not to be amused.

"So, you met Lucy at the pub. Was that planned?"

"No, it wasn't. I'd already spoken to her, told her we needed to cool off so that it didn't look bad for my divorce. I just ran into her at the pub, exchanged a couple of words. She was with her friends, anyway."

"You didn't make plans to meet after the pub, for old times' sake?"

"No, we didn't."

"See, from what I hear, Lucy was in pretty good spirits last night. Not consistent with a girl who'd just been dumped."

"I didn't exactly dump her."

"Oh, my mistake," Ryan held up a hand sarcastically. "You told her to cool off for appearances sake but still kept the stable door open in case you fancied riding that pony another time."

"There's no need to be crass."

"There's every need," Ryan bit out, eyes flashing. "You swan around like the island's resident Casanova, stringing Lucy along behind the scenes while you tie up loose ends with your wife. Then, less than twenty-four hours' after Lucy's found dead, you get your flirt on with the rest of the herd," he jerked his head towards the pub and the women at the table they had left behind. "What happened, Alex? Lucy got too demanding?"

"That's ridiculous."

"Don't think for a second," Ryan continued, "that I won't be looking at you, Alex, and looking hard. Your cottage isn't far from the Priory, is it?" He looked Alex directly in the eye. "Not difficult for you to arrange to leave the pub separately and then meet at your house later on. You're a fit guy, too. I've seen your morning runs along the beach and I bet you bench a decent weight. It wouldn't have been too hard for you to drag Lucy up to those ruins, after you'd finished with her."

Alex had turned sheet white.

"Have you got an alibi for last night, Alex? Where were you between the hours of midnight and five-thirty?"

"I was asleep, in my bed."

"Alone?"

Alex swallowed. "Yes, alone."

"How unfortunate for you," Ryan drawled.

Alex swallowed again, his Adam's apple bobbing. "I would never—I couldn't do what was done to Lucy."

"That remains to be seen," Ryan finished quietly. "Don't go anywhere, Alex, will you?"

He stood there for a while after the coastguard stumbled back inside. He watched the man walk with considerably less confidence towards the table he had left, retrieve his coat as if preparing to leave. Rob Fowler rose, put a hand on Walker's arm in a gesture of solidarity. Ryan had seen enough. He walked briskly around to the side of the pub, intending to call on Megan and clear a few things up.

As he rounded the corner of the wide stone building, he nearly collided with Anna. With instinctive timing, both pulled up short at the foot of the cobbled stone staircase which led to the apartment above the pub. A light burned dimly behind the single unwashed pane on the door at the top.

They stood, sizing each other up.

She saw a darkly attractive man with a face like thunder, wearing a thick navy parka jacket and worn jeans. She let her eyes wander over that sculpted face and caught herself wondering what his stubble would feel like against her skin. Horrified, she ordered herself to get a grip on her hormones and was glad it was dark so he couldn't see the pink flush working its way up her throat towards her face.

He saw a tall woman standing silhouetted in the light of the pub kitchens, dark hair peeping underneath a green woolly hat, framing pale skin and big brown eyes. He found himself smiling at her, wondering if she knew how much of her emotions showed on that expressive face of hers.

"Doctor Taylor," he said, "we really must stop meeting like this."

Anna scowled. The man seemed to spend his life trying to rile her. Worst part was that it was working.

She sniffed. "It's a small village."

"Indeed it is," he agreed. "Were you just visiting your sister?" He glanced up towards the apartment.

"No, I was on my way there." Anna's mouth turned down, her voice losing some of its natural warmth. He didn't think she was aware of it.

"I was on my way to see her, myself."

Anna's mouth flattened, her eyes became sharp.

"Don't let me interrupt you," she replied, turning to walk away.

He caught her arm and she automatically braced. He frowned and slowly took his hand away, palm upward. Bill had been right, he thought. This woman knew what it was like to be held by hard hands and he berated himself for putting that look in her eye, making her compare him with what had happened before.

"I'm sorry," he said simply and watched confusion wash over her. She nodded and crossed her arms over her chest defensively. Not for the first time around this woman, he felt frustration burn. He wanted to grab her, shake her...

He wanted to do a hell of a lot more than that, he admitted, but now was definitely not the time.

"I need to ask Megan some questions," he added.

Anna felt like a complete fool. Not only had she acted like a jealous fishwife, she had jumped like a startled rabbit when all he had done was put his hand on her arm. He must think she was some kind of idiot.

She stopped and reconsidered swiftly. Naturally, she hadn't been *jealous*. She'd been surprised, that was all.

Oh, hell with it. She hoped he would have better taste than her sister.

What kind of person did that make her? she thought guiltily.

"Why don't we just go up together?" His quiet voice with its smooth tone broke into her thoughts and she found herself nodding. Having him there might make things a bit easier between them, she thought. Megan could hardly rant and rave while a total stranger, who also happened to be a murder detective, stood between them.

"Ladies first," Ryan swept a hand towards the staircase.

Anna swallowed back the sudden fear, the shiver which raced across her skin as she stood at the foot of the stone steps. Her hand shook slightly as she gripped the rail because she knew she was standing exactly where they had found her mother eight years earlier.

Ryan watched her hesitate and wanted to say something but found himself uncharacteristically lost for words. Instead, he placed a hand gently on her arm.

"Slippery there," he said quietly, puncturing the silence of the evening. "Watch your step."

Anna turned grateful eyes towards him and found that he was closer than expected. Her face was nearly level with his as she hovered on the first step, clutching the old iron rail. She could smell the slight aroma of alcohol on his breath and could see the shape of his lips in the light of the solitary window.

"Thank you," she said eventually.

He said nothing, moved nothing as he waited for the heavy tension to pass.

When it did, she turned again and began to ascend, her head a jumbled mess. Ryan let out a breath and followed her, trying not to notice the fit of her jeans as she climbed the stairs ahead of him.

There was no answer when Anna rapped on the small wooden door and yet muffled sounds of a radio or television seeped through the cracks.

Anna shrugged and tried again, thinking that Megan could be in the bathroom.

Still no answer.

She tried telling herself that Megan could be ignoring visitors, unable to hear beyond the sound of the TV, or any number of other plausible reasons why she wasn't standing in the doorway in her filmy dressing gown telling her to piss off, as she had done earlier that day.

Anna rapped louder, her movements panicked now.

Ryan shouldered her gently to one side and gave a knock himself.

"Megan?" he called out. "It's DCI Ryan. I'd like to ask you a few more questions. Megan?"

A sick feeling began to roll in Ryan's gut; that sixth sense that all murder detectives were either born with or worked hard to develop. He supposed he'd always had it and, right now, it was telling him that Megan wouldn't be answering the door to anyone.

"Anna," he kept his voice deliberately light. "It looks like your sister isn't home. Why don't you head back? I'll hang around here, just in case she turns up."

Anna turned to face him directly.

"I appreciate what you're trying to do. I really do," she added. "But, I'm not a fool. If something's happened to Megan," she swallowed when her voice hitched, "then I should be here."

Ryan battled annoyance. Why wouldn't the woman just accept help when it was offered? Save herself the unhappiness for another few hours at least? But no, when he searched the serene, obstinate face looking up at him, he saw resolve and something else he would have called grit.

"If that's the way you want to play it, go down and get a key from Bill. If he asks any questions, tell him to keep a lid on it for now. I'll speak to him later."

She turned without a word.

CHAPTER 8

"Frank? I need you back on the island."
While Ryan instructed his sergeant to drive back to Lindisfarne with the team before the tides rolled in for the night, Anna sat shivering on the bottom step.

There had been so much blood. It covered the bedspread, dripped onto the worn grey carpet to dry in congealed clumps here and there. It sprayed over the wall behind and to the left of the bed in high arcs and spattered over the rickety dressing table, the perfume bottles and jewellery boxes.

Nobody could have survived blood loss on that scale, she thought logically, while her heart broke into quiet pieces.

When Ryan had opened the door, Anna tried to prepare herself and had moved to stand beside him, just inside the doorway. The devastation had been there for all to see, but in a room filled with the everyday items which were so very much a part of Megan, covered in what had to be her blood, there was no Megan.

"Where is she?" Ryan had asked himself, those grey eyes remote as they scanned the room. She had a feeling he had committed every detail to memory, down to the pile of the carpet.

"You have to find her," she had choked, before stumbling out into the night, gasping for air over the putrid stench of pints of wasted blood.

Ryan had indeed committed the scene to memory. He saw the drag marks from the bed across the floor towards the bathroom where he imagined Megan's body had been moved, presumably for cleaning. His eyes dismally tracked the direction of the blood spatter and he knew that an artery, or indeed arteries, had been severed here. Nothing else could cause the wash of blood which seemed to bathe the room and was made worse by the cheap red satin sheets and curtains. Red was everywhere.

Except the bathroom, he noticed. The spray had reached the tiny doorway off the main room which doubled as living area and bedroom, yet there were no spots on the white tile floor. He cast his eye around again, looking past the blood this time. The room was disordered and bordering on dirty. Clothes were draped over the single faded armchair and piled high on the mismatching two-seater sofa pushed against one wall. The coffee table was cluttered with magazines and other paraphernalia, and filmed with dust. The countertop in the small kitchen area and almost every other surface was either filmed with dust or other clutter. The few patchy areas of carpet which were not dosed in blood were stained or unkempt. Clearly, Megan was not house-proud, which led him to assume that her bathroom was sparkling clean due to the efforts of her killer.

There was no use pretending that they would find her wounded after a nasty accident. Turning away from his position in the doorway—he knew better than to walk around a crime scene—Ryan closed and locked the door behind him and left the radio playing. He needed a field kit, needed to orchestrate a search party once his team arrived. Had circumstances been different, he would have called on the coastguard, but circumstances weren't different.

He dragged a hand through his hair and wished for coffee. Better yet, something stronger. It had been a brutally long day and it was far from over yet.

Then he saw her, huddled and shaking at the bottom of the stairs. Quietly, so he wouldn't startle her, he moved to sit beside her. The fact that she didn't tense when he laid an arm around her worried him more; Doctor Taylor was habitually tense in his presence and ordinarily he found the fact amusing.

"Anna?"

She turned haunted eyes vaguely in his direction but had trouble focussing.

"I think we should get you inside." He started to move.

"No!" she realised her voice was nearly a shout and moderated it. "No, I can't face..." she waved a hand towards the bar, "everyone."

He looked at her then and saw the fear but also the weariness.

"I'll walk you home."

"I don't want to..."

"You need to go home, Anna." His voice was firm and more from fatigue than anything else, she found herself complying. He stood up and held out his hand to her. Anna had never held a man's hand in her life. Oh, she wasn't inexperienced, but nobody had offered her the simple gesture. Perhaps it was fairer to say that she had never welcomed it.

She took the hand which was offered now and, together, they walked quietly back along the main street towards the castle.

Minutes passed while they walked along the single track lane which led from the village and forked off towards the little cottage. All the while, she felt hazy, dream-like. Reality hadn't set in.

"I suppose you'll want to ask me some questions," Anna said as they approached the door to her cottage.

Ryan said nothing but continued to watch her with his enigmatic eyes.

"I understand that Megan is—I mean, she might be..." saying the words, or trying to, broke the flimsy barrier she had erected for herself. Hot tears flooded her eyes and Anna looked away furiously before she swiped a hand to brush them away. The sound of the sea lapping on the shore was a roar in her head and the cosy lights of the village were a harsh blur behind her as she stumbled unseeingly along the garden path, fumbling in her bag for the keys.

He simply held her there under the porch light, one hand cradling her head, the other banded around her waist as she let the emotion of the day wash out of her. Old regrets, old resentments churned through her and her fingers gripped and loosened rhythmically on his jacket as she battled against the guilt which threatened to overcome her. Grief was bitter. All these years, when she thought she had grieved for the loss of a family which never really existed, she had been wrong. This was real pain, this sharp, tearing sense of loss.

When her tears were spent, embarrassment started to creep in. She realised her face was nestled comfortably against his broad chest, her arms twined around him. His fingers gently massaged the nape of her neck and soothed the tension there. She drew in the earthy scent of him and wanted to burrow deeper but knew that this moment was given in sympathy.

"Thank you," she mumbled and tried to push away. "I'm sure it's not part of your job description to comfort hysterical relatives."

He looked down at her and thought that embarrassment only made her more attractive. He knew that he should let her go, move away now. He had already overstepped the professional mark. Hell, he had sailed over it with cheerful abandon.

And yet.

He lifted one tentative hand to cradle her face and watched her eyes darken. Another hand turned her, lifted her face to bestow the gentlest of kisses.

As her hands lifted to frame his face, tracing the rough stubble she found there, she felt his momentary shock and it made her reckless. Her fingers arrowed into his black hair to pull him closer, urging him to go on.

There was a battle waging inside him. Somewhere in the back of his mind, he felt the desperation in the kiss, could still taste the salty tears on her skin.

Her tears.

Sharply, he pulled away, held her away from him.

"I apologise," he said bluntly. "That should never have happened. I took advantage of a vulnerable moment and you would be well within your rights to report me."

Anna stood dumbfounded. Silently, she added 'prudish' and 'officious' to his list of attributes.

"Don't flatter yourself," she snapped out and was satisfied to note his surprise. "I may be upset, but I'm not the victim here."

She would never be a victim again. That was a promise she had made to herself a long time ago.

"I'm well aware of that. The timing only makes my actions more inappropriate." He began to turn away.

"It takes two to tango, Ryan. I wanted that as much as you did, if only for the comfort."

That brought his head around again, she thought triumphantly. Like a strung bow, he seemed to quiver for a moment before he melted away from her, back into the shadows.

"Lock your door," he said harshly, then turned and went in search of death.

* * *

"Bloody hell."

Phillips stood in the doorway of Megan's apartment and covered his nose with a handkerchief which had formerly been electric blue but was now greying after numerous washings.

"Quite." Ryan stood beside him whilst Faulkner and his team worked the room, covered in white overalls and hairnets. "Any word from MacKenzie?"

Ryan had braved the wrath of his sergeant and called in the services of DI MacKenzie and a troupe of additional uniforms, who had arrived on the island less than an hour ago, leaving their families and partners even at the late hour. He'd put them straight to work.

Phillips shook his head, feeling twin sensations of admiration and irritation as he thought of the detective with the siren-red hair currently overseeing the team of police constables scouring the island for a missing girl. "Nothing yet, boss."

Ryan swung out of the room and down the stairs and waited for Phillips to follow. The small courtyard had been cordoned off from the high street and was manned by two policemen who flanked the entrance like sentries. A small crowd of locals had gathered outside and were moved on.

"I want Bill Tilson, Pete Rigby and any other staff in the bar lounge in ten minutes," Ryan barked. "Keep them separated. I want their statements taken *now*. I don't give a fuck whether they're having the best wet dreams of their lives. Drag them out of bed and get them down here."

Phillips had heard the tone before and didn't bother to remark that it was highly unlikely any of them would be asleep. Instead, he looked around him. The stairs and a perimeter around the courtyard had been cordoned off as part of the crime scene. Large photographic lamps had been placed at intervals to provide stark light in jarring contrast with the night sky.

"Get a man on Alex Walker—I want a full statement of his movements for the day," Ryan was saying, looking down at his worn boots as he thought.

"Ah, technically we can't declare a crime..." Phillips snapped his mouth shut as Ryan turned on him.

"Then he can report us for harassment, can't he?" Ryan's voice was harsh.

Phillips pursed his lips, tugged at them with thumb and forefinger but said nothing.

"He's an arrogant bastard," Ryan said thoughtfully.

"Walker?"

"That goes without saying," Ryan huffed out a laugh. "But I was thinking more generally. Whoever he is, Frank, he's an arrogant son of a bitch."

Phillips grunted.

"He does two women in less than twenty-four hours and he does them in style. He doesn't care that the island was crawling with police today. Unbelievable."

"We don't know that Megan's dead," Phillips said half-heartedly.

Ryan didn't bother to turn his head.

"You know as well as I do, nobody survives that kind of blood bath."

Phillips knew and he wondered what had gone through Ryan's mind when he had walked into that nightmare.

"Each time it's a shock," was all he said.

Ryan drew himself up, tried to focus on the here and now.

"There'll be a body, Frank. He likes to leave them for us to find, he enjoys showing off his handiwork."

"Could be more than one of them," Phillips muttered.

"It's possible," Ryan considered, "but unlikely at this point. What would be the chances there are two of them on the loose? The island's full of well-meaning do-gooders."

"Always the quiet ones," Phillips said knowingly and Ryan couldn't help but smile.

"You may be right, Frank." Ryan stuck his hands in his pockets. "Let's concentrate on finding Megan. That should give us some answers."

Ryan wandered out past the police barrier, left the back-slapping and morale-boosting to Phillips. The main square faced him with its central figure of a long-dead saint. Lights still bloomed in the cottages facing the square despite it being well past midnight and he knew the inhabitants would be wondering and worrying. He moved to a wooden bench in the centre of the square and sat down for a moment's solitude, with the intention of clearing his mind. He watched the blanket of stars above him, felt his own insignificance and then dropped his gaze to the equally insignificant skyline of the island's settlement.

The pub was a long, low building with an odd sort of tower at one end, square with a weathervane on one side which seemed to be slanted at an unnatural angle.

He stood up slowly then moved quickly back across the square.

"Phillips." He broke through the other man's conversation with one of the CSIs.

"Still no word yet, Ryan."

"She's on the roof."

"Wha…?" Phillips took a moment to process and then swung his head around to look up. "How do you know? How the hell would he get her up there?"

"Just like he managed to drag Lucy Mathieson up the side of a steep rock face in the dead of night. Supernatural powers, clearly," his voice was dry and he looked up again. "Probably some sort of ladder up there. Tell MacKenzie to call off her search team. Megan's on the roof, I know it."

* * *

While men and women dressed in animal costumes danced their jigs around fires on the beach to celebrate the solstice, Ryan and Phillips stood guarding the dead, their faces forbidding and eyes bleak.

Megan Taylor had been dumped above her own home, her arms and legs clumsily balanced on top of a stack of old bricks, roof tiles and an assortment of punctured footballs and other rubbish which had found its way onto the roof. Her left leg lay heavily against the wiry foot of the copper weathervane, which had caused it to sag northwards.

"We might find our answers here," Ryan spoke into the heavy silence with a voice deliberately devoid of emotion.

"Looks like he used the bedspread to wrap her up, carry her here without trailing too much blood," Phillips said, eyeing the few spare drops leading up to the site.

Ryan could see it now. Most of the blood had been on the sheets, so maybe they'd kicked the duvet off the bed beforehand. He killed her on the bed, let her bleed out. The blood had seeped all the way through the mattress. After, he dragged her body to the bathroom, cleaned her up a bit, then wrapped her up in the duvet cover and took her up the fire escape. Probably used a fireman's lift to carry her.

Ryan paused, looked at the neck wound.

"Make a note for the pathologist," he said. "I want to know how long it would have taken for her to bleed out. It might affect our timings."

Phillips made a scribbled note.

"He wrapped her up in the duvet, carried her up the fire escape and dumped her on top of the stack of rubbish. Maybe he stopped to pile it all up, first, in a grotesque parody of an altar. He arranged her body, cocked her leg that way so that the weather vane pointed north, or maybe it had just fallen that way, then he went back downstairs and cleaned himself up.

"It's happening again," Ryan finished quietly.

Phillips looked up at the younger man with concern.

"It's not the same, Ryan."

"I know it isn't, Frank. Don't worry." Both men knew that they were comparing another death far away from here, at another time. "Let's try to do what we can for her."

Phillips nodded, his bright eyes dulled with pity.

"He really enjoyed himself," Ryan noted with disgust, wishing manners would allow him to spit out the foul flavour in his mouth.

"Sick bastard," Phillips managed, his jaw working.

Megan's body lay spread-eagled, her dark hair swept behind her. Blood red markings adorned her body, which had obviously been cleaned beforehand. Her skin bloomed an unnatural grey in the false glare of the photographic lights, providing her with the attention in death she had craved so much in life. The underside of her arms, legs and back were speckled reddish-brown where what blood she had remaining had succumbed to gravity. An angry, jagged line showed against her pale throat and tiny rivulets of dried blood crusted on each side in a delicate, web-like pattern. Brutal marks had been slashed into her torso and one of her eyes bulged unnaturally from its socket.

The other had fallen prey to the birds.

CHAPTER 9

When the CSI team had finally recovered all they could from the rooftop where Megan lay, Ryan told his team to pack up for the day. Or, more accurately, to pack up for the morning, since it was nearly four. They needed no further bidding and scattered across the island to various B&Bs in the early hours. Eyes burning and heart weary, he and Phillips oversaw the removal of Megan's body to the only secure cold storage on Lindisfarne: the huge ice hut by the harbour, where the fishermen stowed their catch before selling it. She would stay the night with the fish before she could be transported off the island. It seemed like one final insult.

Phillips knew better than to presume he would be offered a bed at Ryan's cottage. His SIO was an intensely private man, lacking in certain social graces, so Phillips had already secured himself a room at Pete's family inn.

"Keep your eyes and ears open," Ryan said and then scrubbed at his own eyes which burned from too many nights without sleep. "I want impressions; of Lucy, of Megan, anything you think may be of interest."

"I'll be everybody's best friend while I'm there," Phillips flashed a wicked grin which nearly managed to cheer them both up.

"Makes me think of the Bates Motel," Ryan said.

Phillips laughed nervously and hoped he wouldn't find any stuffed animals in his bedroom.

Their boots scuffed the tarmac road as they walked from the harbour back through the village. Ryan noticed a light burning in Anna's window as they passed her cottage and told himself not to worry. Purposefully, he carried on walking and then exchanged a quick handshake with Frank as they passed the Lindisfarne Inn, where Phillips took his leave. In a protective gesture, Ryan found himself waiting until Phillips was safely behind the solid oak door before continuing.

He walked towards his little sanctuary, which now housed a room devoted to murder; a shrine to the worst side of mankind. He walked slowly through the silent village, past the pub and the police tape and hoped that he would be able to banish what he had seen that day to the recesses of his mind, at least enough to enable him to sleep.

* * *

Sleep didn't come easily but when it did, it brought with it nightmares which were more memory than fiction. They replayed in his mind, tormenting him until the first tentative rays of sunshine broke through the sky.

He saw himself as he had been that night in June, dressed in jeans and shirtsleeves spotted with the blood of the girl he cradled in his lap. Her dark mop of hair was matted with her own blood which spilled in drying streams on either side of her mouth. A scream lodged in his throat as he watched her lifeless head turn in his hands and terror gripped him as she turned grey eyes which were so like his own.

"You did this to me," she said through bloodless lips, before her head fell away from her body. Ryan could feel the warm spray of torn arteries drenching his face, his hands, his clothes.

He scuttled away from her on all fours, breathing hard. He watched her broken body lift itself off the ground to crawl towards him, the torn clothes she wore hanging from her. Small animal sounds escaped him as he slept, imagining himself running until he found himself backed against a stone wall, plunged into darkness. He could smell the moss and something herbal as he scaled the wall blindly, trying to find an exit. He felt something wet on his hands and knew it was blood. The tinny scent filled his nostrils and he gagged, pushing away into the darkness.

Arms came up to steady him and he saw a young woman illuminated in the moonlight, the Priory at her back. He tried to make out what she said to him but the roar of the sea was deafening. Her hands turned to vices on his arms before they came up to his neck. He choked, gasping for air as her fingers tightened. Her eyes shone a bright, unmoving blue and when he looked down he realised his hands circled her throat and he could breathe again.

He dropped them in disgust, scrubbed his fingers frantically against his trousers.

"Be careful with me," she said softly, reaching out to him.

Again he ran, his bare feet skidding against the dewy ground as he tried to escape. He fell on the steep hillside leading to the village and landed heavily, hit his head on the hard ground beneath. He tried to lever himself up but found himself pinned by another soft body, sinewy limbs winding around his. His hands tangled in silky dark hair and full lips sought his. He relaxed, brushed a hand down the smooth skin of her thigh and found her naked. His breath hitched.

"Anna," he whispered, seeking her warmth but finding her ice cold. He brought his arms around her to warm her, tried to soothe her restless movements.

"Love me," she said breathlessly.

His hands froze against her skin and she threw her head back and laughed so that the moonlight shone against the serrated gash at her throat. Blood seeped in lines from the tear, over her rounded breasts.

Ryan shoved the woman away and awoke covered in a film of sweat, clawing at the duvet. Breathing erratically, he stumbled from the bed and into the tiny en-suite bathroom, yanked on the overhead light. When he saw the dark-haired man staring at him from shadowed, bloodshot eyes, Ryan almost didn't recognise himself. His cheeks were hollowed out, the bones in his face sharper than usual, the pallor of his skin telling tales of sleep deprivation and a poor diet. He touched a hand to his face to make sure he was truly awake and was shocked to find that he was shaking, his fingers trembling uncontrollably. He moved to the cabinet and fumbled about until he found what he was looking for.

Diazepam, the label read in clear, printed lettering.

The plastic safety catch was still intact on the unassuming white container he held in his hand. Ryan looked down at it for a long, long moment. He understood why he had been prescribed benzodiazepines. Logically, he knew that the capsules would enhance the effect of the neurotransmitter GABA in his brain, producing a sedative effect which would help to reduce the panic attacks and anxiety which had plagued him for months.

That was textbook, something he could read and understand.

Slowly, he returned the unopened container to the cabinet, shut the door with a steady hand.

* * *

While Ryan sought respite from his demons, another man slept soundly in his bed. Work complete, his mind wallowed in new-found contentment and was satisfied in a way he had never dreamed possible.

Earlier, while the blundering police had searched the island for Megan and the tourists had danced in a circle around a bonfire on the beach, the faithful had convened in the usual place. He had gone through the motions, swept a circle of symbolic fire with the little black-handled knife. As he had said the ritual words to consecrate the circle and held the knife aloft to draw a pentagram in the air, he had watched the faces of his followers as they knelt before him. Eyes unnaturally bright from the drugs, the people in the circle swayed as they watched the knife and repeated his words. He held the blade in his hand, he felt the power of it course through his arm to the rest of his body and he almost believed the words he was chanting. Remembering the potency of his arousal, the incredible strength he had felt as he had watched her eyes die, he felt like one of the gods he was praying to.

He felt like the supreme God; the giver and taker of life.

He called to the four elements and his voice grew strong. There was a well-timed break in the clouds and the moon shone through, as if he had conjured it.

The occupants of the circle watched their High Priest, nude but for the long animal pelt which he wore over his shoulders. They didn't know that the fur was fake and the 'pelt' had been purchased from a thrift shop in Newcastle. All of them felt his supremacy, none questioned it.

Except one, who shivered in the cold air and was afraid.

* * *

While the light was still thin, shining hesitantly on Lindisfarne and thawing the thin layer of frost which coated the windows, Ryan sat at the table in what had formerly been his dining room but was now firmly the Incident Room. A half-finished cup of cold coffee sat on the tabletop, lost amid a mass of papers which covered the surface in disarray. The murder wall faced him squarely with its black timeline and tacked-on photographs with arrows indicating potential links here and there. To his right, the wide window provided an unbroken view of the sea across to the mainland and Ryan could see a family of seals hunting for breakfast in the shallow waters as the tide gradually swept out.

Copies of statements taken from the islanders lay before him, alongside Lowerson's summary containing facts which were heavily peppered with gossip and innuendo about the deceased. Ryan went through the summary and then each statement, noting down times, gaps, possibilities. He was ready when the first of his team began to arrive at the door just before seven and he had even taken the trouble to shave.

"So," Phillips began without any pleasantries, slumping tiredly on one of the spindly wooden chairs. "We got a serial on our hands?"

"There hasn't been three," MacKenzie chimed in needlessly as she shrugged out of her coat, shook out the light rain which had dampened her copper hair. Every man and woman in the room recognised the official definition of a serial killer, but instinct went a long way in their business.

"I think we can presume that the two are linked, on which basis CID command has confirmed that the death of Megan Taylor should also fall under the remit of Operation Lindisfarne." Ryan paused, took a sip of coffee. "Presuming we are looking for the same person— which seems most likely at this point—whether or not we can call him a serial killer is immaterial in comparison with the fact that he is clearly escalating."

That dimmed the chatter.

Ryan pointed to a blown-up photograph of Lucy, taken by the CSIs after she had been found. It was a full frontal image, taken from a height a few steps above the ground to give a quasi-aerial shot.

"Here, she's been laid out, but carefully. Her arms and legs have been placed in position on an altar. Her body has been meticulously washed."

He tapped a finger to a similar image of Megan, taken from the same angle.

"Not so careful here," he commented. "Not so much arranged as deposited on the roof of the pub and her arms and legs are positioned at unnatural angles. This suggests one of several possibilities; he was short on time, he got lazy, he got carried away with the act. Maybe Lucy was his first, caught him by surprise but he also felt some remorse, hence the careful treatment. With Megan, he's started to get cocky."

There was general agreement.

"Strange mix of planned and unplanned," Phillips commented as he chugged down sugary coffee. "Strangulation is up close and personal, usually done in the heat of the moment."

"Agreed," Ryan nodded, interested.

"And going to all the trouble of transporting her up there, running the risk, it's all a bit amateurish," Phillips shrugged. "On the other hand, the cleaning, it's thorough. The ritual, special oils and stuff to put on her. That looks a bit more planned out."

There was momentary silence as the room thought it over. Ryan was in agreement. It was a perplexing mix.

"Notice anything else unusual?" He gestured to the room at large, interested to see if their observations matched his own.

"Both were cleaned up," Phillips carried on squinting at the images. "But is it part of a ritual or to cover his tracks?"

"Still waiting for the chemical analysis to come back on the disinfectant, sir," Faulkner chimed in. "But Phillips is right. Both women had undergone extensive cleaning, in every orifice as far as we can tell. Mouths, ears; we even found traces of the disinfectant in Megan's vagina last night."

Ryan's head whipped up like a bloodhound.

"But none in Lucy's?"

"No, sir."

"Fancied a bit of the other with Megan but not with Lucy?" Phillips offered in his usual forthright manner.

"For God's sake, Phillips," Faulkner protested.

"Look," Frank spread his hands in a conciliatory gesture. "I'm just saying it like it is. From what I hear, Megan put it about a bit. Maybe she'd been friendly with the bloke before he did her."

"It's not outside the realms of possibility that Megan knew her killer, since everybody knows everybody on Lindisfarne." Ryan responded.

"Aw, now, Guv…" Phillips pulled a face.

"What makes you think she 'put it about a bit'?" Ryan cut across him.

Phillips leaned forward, flipped open his notebook.

"I got chatting to some of the residents at breakfast this morning. Very decent breakfast, too," he added conversationally and Ryan snapped his teeth together to stop an expletive slipping out. "None of them had a bad word to say about Lucy Mathieson. Alison and Pete Rigby—they own the place—they were pretty torn up over it. Pete and Lucy used to play together as kids, went to the same school all the way through, their mums are good friends, that sort of thing. I guess we knew that already," he added as an afterthought.

"Never hurts to have it confirmed. Go on."

"Well, I didn't even need to ask before I heard the first bit of gossip about Megan. I was just sitting at the breakfast table and I hear Alison—that's Pete's mother—talking to one of the regulars, some old biddy who helps out at the church centre," he consulted his notebook, "Mrs Ivy Felton."

"What did they have to say?"

"Well, Mrs Rigby starts by saying what an awful tragedy it is and isn't it terrible to have two murders on the same day. They chatted for a while and both seemed a bit scared by it all, to be honest. Can't blame them, the old bird—Mrs Felton—said that she'd lived on Lindisfarne her entire life and there'd never been so much as a serious assault, never mind a murder. She looked to be in her seventies, too."

Ryan nodded.

"They talked for a while about Lucy and what a nice girl she'd been, both had a few tears. They sort of got conspiratorial when the chat turned to Megan, boss. Leaned in closer, lowered their voices like women do when they want to say something nasty…" he trailed off as he caught the eye of one of the female officers in the room and cleared his throat.

"Upshot is, these two seemed to think Megan had always been trouble. If she wasn't with one man, she was with another and the way she went around was asking for trouble. They reckon it was some sex maniac from the mainland who she spurned or some such."

"Was this all eavesdropping or did you manage to commit any of this to paper?" Ryan asked dryly.

"Got it all signed and sealed," Phillips grinned.

"Okay."

Ryan gripped the top of his chair and pushed away to pace. Megan's killer could conceivably have been from the mainland since she was murdered while the causeway was open. On the other hand, there were too many similarities between the murders and they were too close together to be coincidence.

He said none of this but gestured with his hand for Phillips to round it up.

"It gets better," Phillips puffed out his chest a bit, fiddled with the latest in the line of ridiculous ties he chose to wear. This one was blue with tiny red hearts.

"Christ, Frank, give me a break. Just spit it out."

"She was previously engaged to Alex Walker," Frank blurted out. "Word is that she stole him from her sister."

"From her sister?" Ryan's voice was dangerously quiet.

Phillips didn't pick up on the nuance.

"Yep," he confirmed cheerfully, pleased with his work that morning. "Anna Taylor and Alex had been an item since they were sweet sixteen. Turns out he preferred her older sister because apparently he upped and dumped Anna for Megan, right after Anna found them rolling around in the hay together, as it were."

Ryan dropped his head and gave himself a full thirty seconds until the red haze of anger cleared and he could see clearly again. It was none of his damn business who Doctor Taylor chose to shack up with.

Ryan made a show of flicking through the typed statements he had received from his officers last night, to give himself time to calm down. He pulled out Alex Walker's and skim read it again before lifting stormy grey eyes.

"Now, isn't it interesting that, when directly questioned as to his relationship with Megan Taylor, our lothario once again failed to mention his prior involvement. Bit unusual, don't you think?"

His team looked on, the light of battle beginning to shine.

"He says he spent yesterday morning assisting with the police investigation, after which he went to his parents' house to spend some time with the family. How touching," Ryan growled. "Then he decided to pop into the pub around seven-thirty and I can personally vouch for the fact that he was sitting in there playing up to a crowd of women at eight-thirty."

"Puts him in the vicinity," Phillips said eagerly.

"Pathologist confirmed time of death as roughly between four and seven yesterday afternoon," Faulkner added. "He'll have something more concrete by tomorrow, after the post-mortem."

"Have the Walkers confirmed that Alex was with them?" Ryan turned to one of the uniforms, who looked crestfallen.

LJ Ross

"Sir, we haven't been able to complete a house-to-house yet. Alex Walker was questioned late last night but there's been no time to conduct the remaining interviews. It's going to take the whole morning, if not the whole day, once we factor in transient visitors who were present on the island yesterday."

"Shit." Ryan tapped his fingers on the kitchen chair. "Get around to it as soon as you can, as a priority."

"Yes, sir."

Ryan turned back to the two photographs on the wall behind him.

"What else do you notice about these two?"

"The markings," said Lowerson, who had been acting as reader-receiver but didn't plan to for the rest of his career.

"Go on," Ryan said.

"They seem to be the same, sir." Lowerson carried on. "It seems to me that the lines are in the same place on each body."

"It seems that way to me too," Ryan said approvingly. A large, upside-down triangle had been drawn on Lucy's torso with her own blood, with a long vertical line cutting through it. A similar marking had been etched onto Megan's body, but this time it had been cut into her flesh. It was more aggressive.

"Any word on the murder weapon?"

Faulkner came to attention.

"We're most likely to be looking for a small, double-bladed knife, with a short handle I would think; it took quite an effort for him to saw down into Megan's throat and the line isn't neat, it's ragged. Nothing has been located, sir."

"Same implement used to mark the body?"

"The pathologist agrees that the incisions are consistent with that type of blade. The markings were made post-mortem, sir."

Ryan let that information sink in and found he was mildly surprised. The type of person capable of inflicting such pain would surely have relished drawing out the final kill while Megan was still alive to feel, to watch.

"The pathologist says he can give us his report on Lucy by the end of today but it's going to be tomorrow at the earliest before he can get to Megan," Faulkner continued. "Having said that, from my side of things I can tell you that there are a number of good print sets found around Megan's apartment, which we will run through the database on the off-chance."

That reminded Ryan to double-check whether any background checks had come back for people on the island.

"Presuming the islanders are clean and we don't already have prints on record, that leaves us with an open pool, doesn't it?"

"We would need consent to take fingerprints for a speculative search, sir," Faulkner commented. "We have a couple of footprints, smudged but suggestive of a male sized between eight and ten. Still, even if we limit fingerprinting to males resident on the island, that doesn't narrow down the pool much."

Ryan thought of the outcry it would cause amongst the islanders if he were to ask for the fingerprints for every male with an average-to-large shoe size. He was fairly sure that at least one of them would be savvy enough to make a complaint. Violation of human rights, or some crap.

He was more inclined to think that Megan's human rights overrode anything else.

"Wait until we have something more concrete from the pathologist, we can always come back to it later." Faulkner nodded his agreement. "Frank, what about that quadrant search? Buildings near the Priory?"

Phillips' eyes twinkled in his broad face as he smiled.

"Turns out the nearest buildings are the vicarage and St Peter's church, which is just beside the Priory. The garden backs onto the edge of the Priory graveyard."

Ryan thought back to the statements taken from the vicar and his wife. Both at home, tucked up in bed, at the time of Lucy's murder. Each corroborated the other's whereabouts.

"Then," Phillips continued, "you've got the tail end of Church Lane and the cottages there; both Alex Walker and the Mathiesons live there. Next lane along is St Aidan's Road and Bill Tilson has a house there. Slightly further along, just off the main square, you've got the Heritage Centre, the doctor's surgery and the Lindisfarne Inn. All three back onto the stretch of beach which runs past the Priory."

As Phillips ran through the possibilities, Ryan flicked through his recollection of the witness statements they had received. The Mathiesons had been at home in bed and Bill Tilson had been closing the pub with Megan. The Heritage Centre would be closed, as would the surgery. The surgery formed part of the Walkers' large home but both Yvonne and Steve Walker had been enjoying a late dinner and drinks with Alison Rigby over at the Lindisfarne Inn, which went on until the early hours. They were all accounted for, apart from Alex Walker, who claimed to be at home alone in bed at the time Lucy died.

"Doubling back over the other side of the Priory," Phillips continued, "there's just the beach, the lane leading to the castle and the coastguard station right at the end of the harbour. There's a few holiday cottages here and there. Anna Taylor's got one of them and the other three are empty at the moment. But," he said triumphantly, "there are a load of old upturned fishing boats sitting on the beach, practically at the foot of the Priory. People use them for storage or fishing sheds."

The two men exchanged a long look.

"Owners?"

"Local fishermen, mostly, but then there's Alex Walker. He owns the blue one nearest the Priory."

"MacKenzie," Ryan turned to the flame-haired detective with a charming smile. "Get me a search warrant, would you?"

CHAPTER 10

While MacKenzie pulled together the paperwork for a warrant and chased around for a local magistrate who would grant it, Ryan put two men on Walker. They would guard his movements because the last thing Ryan needed was his only real suspect rabbiting off the island and holing up somewhere. It would be inconvenient, to say the least.

He dispatched Faulkner to set a fire under the pathologist's arse so they could take a look at the blood and toxicology analysis on both women. Phillips was overseeing door-to-door interviews and talking to the group of students who had got drunk on the beach last night in the name of Mother Earth, or the Wicker Man, or whatever the hell. However much Phillips disliked doing the rounds, people found him easy to talk to and that made him the best person to go out gossip-mongering.

Maybe it was the ties he wore.

Ryan looked again at pictures of both women and swore. He knew what he had to do and he knew that he needed help to do it.

* * *

Anna had been up for hours, unable to sleep, thinking of everything and nothing. She had shed tears for the sister she had wanted to love but for Megan, love had been an elusive thing to be feared and coveted at the same time. Now, her tears dried up, she felt hollowed out.

Not especially religious, Anna surprised herself by walking through the quiet village to the little island church. The doors opened early and closed late, so she knew that there would be shelter there even just before six in the morning. Sure enough, the large curved doors were unlocked and rows of white candles burned inside.

She found the little church empty of sinners—clearly, it was too early in the day—but not silent. The strains of a requiem echoed around the stone walls from the organ in a recess beside the vestry and she followed the sound. Sitting in one of the church pews, she listened for a while, letting the music wash over her.

"Hello, Anna."

She looked up from her daydream and was pleased to find an old friend watching her.

"Reverend Ingles," she managed a half-smile for the Anglican vicar of Lindisfarne. Mike Ingles was well-matched to his profession, both in temperament and looks. He was reasonably tall and trim but with the slight paunch of a man who enjoyed being middle-aged. Salt and pepper grey hair was neatly combed and mild brown eyes peered at her from behind jazzy red glasses. A nod to fashion which contrasted with the bobbled olive green jumper he wore over his collar with brown chinos.

"May I join you?" He smiled kindly and she shuffled further along the pew, giving him room to sit down next to her.

He said nothing at first but together they enjoyed the play of morning sunshine as it broke through the large, stained glass window which dominated the vestibule wall and illuminated the church.

He let out a long sigh and then took one of her hands in his.

"It's a hard day for you, my dear."

Anna realised that she had come here with the subconscious need to talk to somebody. She had known this man all her life; she had been baptised by him when he had been a younger man. She remembered coming to church with her mother every Sunday morning to listen to his melodic voice as he spoke of forgiveness and love.

She had never agreed with those sermons. She remembered sitting beside her mother as the locals would gossip and point at the bruises marring Sara Taylor's pale skin, which she unsuccessfully tried to hide with make-up. Anna remembered the anger, the shame and the frustration of a child wishing she could fight back. Still, she went along every Sunday because that was one place Andy Taylor would never follow them.

"The loss of a loved one is one of the hardest burdens we face," Ingles was saying, his eyes crinkled with sympathy.

Anna took her time, tried to find the words.

"Megan and I had a difficult relationship."

Ingles liked to think he knew everything about island life and the people in his flock. He knew all about the young woman sitting beside him and more besides. He had married her parents and could remember Sara Taylor standing radiant before him as a bride next to the handsome devil she had married before God. He remembered the vows that both had taken and both had broken. His heart was heavy for the lives lost and damaged through that union but he drew strength from his faith and tried to give comfort.

"Your sister had a troubled soul, Anna. 'Forgive us our sins as we forgive those who sin against us'."

"I'm trying, Father."

"Your sister loved you, Anna, I'm sure of it."

She had thought there were no more tears to shed but in the quiet of the church, she found there were a few more.

"She hated me," Anna whispered.

"We hate that which we often fear," Ingles said quietly. Anna frowned, trying to remember which part of the Bible he had quoted from and then her brow cleared.

"Shakespeare," she murmured appreciatively.

Ingles patted her hand. "Megan was an unhappy child who became an unhappy woman. She didn't have the tools to find herself, to go out and get what she wanted from life, because she never realised that you have to build your own tools. Unfortunately, your sister envied your ability to move on with life towards happiness, or to put it another way, from darkness towards light."

Anna considered the words and tried to be honest.

"In many ways, I don't feel that I've truly moved on with my life. The work I do, it's all about the past, about other people's lives, never my own. I haven't had a relationship since Alex," she pulled a face.

"We all need time for healing, Anna. Perhaps you need to learn to forgive yourself as well as others."

There was truth in that. How long could she go on battling against the terrible rage inside her, the anger she felt against her father, her mother, even her sister?

"I tried to talk to her yesterday," she said, thinking of the day before. "I saw her in the morning," she thought back to the scene in the pub where she had first met Ryan.

"I took some time, cooled off a bit," *and then went to have a good rant at Ryan,* she added to herself, "but I decided to try again later. I went back over there around four. I don't know, but I could have been the last person to see her alive."

Ingles didn't bother to pretend that he didn't already know what had happened to Megan. His wife, Jennifer, had heard it all from Alison Rigby, who had heard it from Pete, who had been working at the pub last night. For a holy island, there was little that was sacred on it.

"How did your conversation go?" he asked.

"It was an unmitigated disaster." She thought back to the day before, tried to visualise the scene.

"I think I caught her at a bad time," she recalled. "When she answered the door, she was still in a bathrobe from the shower and she had laid out some nice underwear on the bed. It looked like she was getting ready to go out. She didn't invite me in, just left me standing outside in the cold." Anna paused, registering the hurt she had felt.

"I knew things hadn't worked out with Alex," Anna said slowly. "I heard that they broke up not long after I left the island but I was still surprised to find her living above the pub after all this time. She had such big plans."

The vicar nodded, understanding perfectly.

"We find comfort in familiar landscapes," he said quietly.

"There wasn't much comfort to be found in her apartment," Anna commented. "The place was a pigsty, paint peeling and everything. I even took it up with Bill afterwards but he said she wouldn't let him touch the place."

Ingles considered for a moment. "Perhaps she wanted to be in control of her own environment?" He thought of his wife and her obsessive stacking of scatter cushions around the vicarage. "Perhaps, in her own way, she was a meticulous woman."

"Perhaps," Anna agreed and then shook herself. "Anyway, I told her that I was on the island for a short time and that it would be nice to spend some time together. It was intended as an olive branch."

"Did she accept it?"

"I don't know why I offered it in the first place, Father. In all my life, I can't remember ever having wronged my sister and yet I found myself running to her. Why was that?" She turned baffled eyes to him and he smiled that kind smile again.

"Because you loved her and didn't want old hurts to separate you forever. You drew on a strength that Megan couldn't because she simply didn't have it."

Anna nodded. "I honestly forgave her for her betrayal with Alex," she said openly. "I stopped loving him a long time ago, if I ever really did. He was a port in a storm, in many ways. Perhaps he was the same for her.

"I said the same thing to her," she recalled. "Told her to put it behind us and that it didn't matter anymore. She laughed at me."

Ingles frowned.

"Yes," Anna nodded. "She told me that he had never mattered to her, that he was only ever useful as a means of hurting me."

Megan had used different words which she didn't care to repeat to the vicar. Anna could picture her sister as she'd stood in the doorway, her curves spilling through the ratty dressing gown she wore. Even without make-up, her face had been striking, all the more so as she spewed her venom.

Do you think I care about Alex? she had laughed. *He was a quick fuck, as far as I was concerned. A laugh between the sheets and it was all the sweeter for him because then he could say he'd had both sisters.*

Didn't you care about my feelings? Anna had asked.

Why should I? Megan scorned. *There's nothing you have that I couldn't take away from you.*

Those words seemed to convey a wealth of emotion and standing on the doorstep, cold and wet, Anna had known there was no shared feeling to draw on. She remembered all the years she had been tormented by this woman, all the little hurts and little lies which Megan had told.

I love you more than Anna does, Daddy, she would say as she crawled onto Andy Taylor's lap, desperately seeking his drunken affection and thinking it might save her from the blows he would later inflict.

Shaken, Anna pulled her hand away from the vicar's clasp.

"Thank you for listening, Father. I need to head back now."

Ingles stood and watched her as she stepped out of the hallowed walls into the world again.

When she left the church, morning had truly broken and the village was starting to come alive. Walking across the main square towards the road which led to the castle and her cottage, Anna saw the pitying looks and heard the whispered comments as she passed a group of local women. Back rigid, she carried on and didn't once look at the pub or the police tape as she passed it. Consequently, she didn't see the man who leaned idly against the stone wall, an ordinary fixture of the community. He watched her progress and wondered.

CHAPTER 11

He was waiting for her when she arrived back at the little white-washed cottage just before eight-thirty, as she had known he would be. She watched Ryan push away from where he had been leaning against the porch and allowed herself a moment to appreciate him. His dark hair whipped wildly around his face in the morning breeze and the ends brushed the collar of his navy jacket. He stood tall and sombre, with a cardboard file tucked under one arm, reminding her why he was there.

Those watchful eyes followed her progress up the path and she was annoyed to find that she was stalling, her steps slowing to prolong the moment before he would formally tell her that her sister was dead.

"Doctor Taylor." He took in the shadowed eyes and pale cheeks, the unmistakeable signs of a sleepless night.

"Hello, Chief Inspector," she responded politely. If he wanted to be aloof, that was fine with her. Head high, she moved past him to open the front door. Her fingers fumbled once with the keys.

She moved along the narrow hallway towards the kitchen at the back of the house and didn't wait to see if he followed. She could hear his quiet tread behind her.

"Do you want coffee?"

He always wanted coffee.

"Thanks, if you're making some for yourself." They waited a few moments in uncomfortable silence while he prowled around the room and she ground coffee beans. Eventually, she poured the fragrant liquid into cheerful spotted mugs.

Anna sat at one of the homely wicker chairs which had been placed by a set of French windows leading directly out onto the beach. There was a little bistro table and another chair, which she gestured for him to take.

He folded his long body into the chair, drank some of the coffee and let it burn his mouth before he looked at her again.

"I regret to inform you that your sister, Megan Taylor, was found dead late last night." He fell back on rigid formality.

She had known, Anna thought. She had seen the blood for herself, the police tape as she'd walked through the village. She had seen it in the sympathetic eyes of the vicar that morning and she had shed her tears through the long hours of the night and in the empty church pews. Still, the words cut through her defences and she had to look away, to stare out across the lonely stretch of sand.

"I'm very sorry for your loss," he carried on inadequately. He had never been any good at this part. He wanted to shove out of the chair, pace a bit. Instead, he stayed seated and watched her battle with unspoken feelings.

She almost smiled. "Got any more clichés you want to roll out, Ryan?"

He was glad that she could find humour even in her despair. Tenderness washed over him and he found himself reaching for her hand, rubbing his thumb over the soft skin of her palm.

She would pull her hand away, she thought. In another minute, she would tug it away and remember that he was a moody, arrogant son of a bitch who had left her without a second glance last night. Yet she let her hand stay where it was and enjoyed the sensation of comfort being given from one person to another.

"I'm sorry, Anna. The CSI team need to take some prints from you, as next of kin, and a swab."

Anna was surprised but couldn't quite work herself up to being bothered by the prospect.

"That's fine," she said and then asked the burning question. "Where did you find her?"

He sighed.

"She was on the roof of the pub, beside the weather vane."

Anna said nothing for long minutes.

"Why there?" she asked eventually.

He didn't have any answer to that but he planned to.

"I never really understood her," she found herself saying into the silence, her eyes looking far out to sea. "There were only eighteen months between us but it could have been a lifetime. I struggled for years to find things we could agree on, but never did."

"Siblings always argue," he said quietly, thinking of his own sister with affection, before he remembered. Unexpectedly, he felt another jab of emotion he recognised as homesickness. He pushed it to one side and focused on the woman in front of him, huddled into a thick cream knitted jumper which made her seem even smaller than she was.

"Not like this," she answered softly. "I never understood her, never liked her," she swallowed that painful truth, "and I'll live with the guilt for the rest of my life."

"It's not your fault she died, Anna." The words were easy but he knew that believing them was much harder.

"It depends what you mean," she answered. "I didn't kill her but I think that the Megan who was, or who might have been, died a long time ago. I did nothing to stop that."

She lost herself for a moment, thinking of when she had been very young. They had both escaped from the house her family used to own. Her father had stayed out all night, probably with another woman, she knew that now. Her parents had argued and then the violence had started. Self-preservation had forced the girls to run out of the back door down to the beach in their bare feet. Megan's legs held faded bruises just visible beneath the hem of her pinafore dress and Anna's back was a criss-cross of marks from the brown leather belt her father had used on her the previous day. She hid them underneath a thin t-shirt with scuffed shorts. To escape, they had played in the sand together, Megan directing her on how to build a proper sandcastle. Megan always liked to be in charge.

Anna had wandered off to play in the surf, dangling her toes in the cold water and collecting shells to make into a necklace. She went too far out, she remembered. Unknowingly, she had wandered along what was called the 'Pilgrim's Causeway'; a stretch of sand which lay parallel to the tarmacked road of the causeway and was only visible when the tide rolled out. Christian pilgrims had walked along the sandy route for centuries.

The water had risen deceptively, though, only in shallow pools at first and then a few inches above her ankles. The seven-year-old child had known real panic when she had looked around and seen her sister waving frantically for her to come back to the safety of the beach. Gripped with fear, she had dropped her shells and tried to wade through the water, which was rising fast. Over a hundred metres from the shore, she had tried to swim the rest of the way, thin arms and legs exhausted and struggling against the material of her clothes. Her head went under and she remembered that a fatalism had crept over her which made her stop flailing, almost allowing herself to drown.

That was when she had seen Megan, tired and desperate herself, swimming a ragged breaststroke. She had dragged her the rest of the way to shore and up out of the water. To this day, Anna didn't know how they had both survived the current; she only remembered Megan's words as they had spluttered on the beach.

"Don't you dare scare me like that again, Anna! We're sisters, we have to stay together."

Remembering those words, she found that she disagreed with Reverend Ingles. Her sister had had strength inside her. What was more, Megan had used it to save Anna, but she hadn't been able to do the same.

"Anna?"

Ryan watched the play of emotions and wondered what memories ran through her mind.

"How did she die, Ryan?" Anna fixed her gaze on him again and he knew that she didn't want soft platitudes or half-answers.

"Badly," he answered truthfully. "She had her throat cut, Anna."

Her face paled even more but her gaze didn't waver.

"You found her naked, washed, her body marked?"

Ryan frowned, dark brows drawing together. Those details had not been made public.

"Yes. How did you know?"

"I remembered the image of Lucy. I presume whoever killed her also killed my sister."

"We haven't determined that yet," he said. "Have you discussed your thoughts with anyone?"

"Of course not," she said wearily.

He paused for a few moments, considered how to begin.

"Best keep it that way. I need to ask you some questions, on record." He waited for her slight nod and went through the standard cautions before beginning. "When did you last see your sister, Anna?"

She had been expecting this, even welcomed the routine questions as a diversion from the relentless guilt.

"Around four, yesterday afternoon." She relayed the same information she had told the vicar and watched him make careful notes.

"You say she looked like she was going out?"

"Yes, she was still in a dressing gown, hair washed and blow-dried. There was nice underwear laid out on the bed and I think I remember seeing a pair of high-heels sitting at the foot of it. It seemed an odd time of day to get changed, unless she was planning to go out."

Ryan nodded. Megan had been found in the nude, as Lucy had, but this time there had been crumpled clothing strewn all around her flat. He was pretty sure he remembered a dressing gown on the CSI inventory but he would check. He thought back to the statements he had received from Bill and Pete. Megan had claimed she was ill in bed with a bout of the flu and, as far as they knew, she hadn't left her apartment that day. It didn't add up.

"Did you notice anything else unusual?"

Anna considered. "At first, I thought it was strange that she didn't invite me inside but afterwards I realised that could have been another way for her to keep me in my place, so to speak."

Ryan knew his next line of questioning would be hard, maybe for both of them.

"Your relationship with Megan was strained," he began. "Can you tell me why that was?"

"How long do you have?" she shrugged one shoulder, fingers fiddling with the mug of coffee she held in both hands. "As I said before, we were never close. You would think that, growing up in our household, it would have brought us closer together. That wasn't the case."

She paused, saw the understanding on his face and smiled. Of course he would know about her family history, he was a detective. Still, the invasion of her privacy stung. Away from the island, she was just Anna Taylor and she was free to tell or not tell whoever she liked about her past. More often than not, she chose to forget all about it. On the island, the choice was non-existent.

"My father wasn't a model citizen," she confirmed. "You could say that Megan and I both rebelled in our own ways."

"How so?" His voice was professional and somehow that helped her to talk.

"She went off in search of admiration and so did I, but in very different ways. She was never without a Friday night date," Anna remembered, not unkindly, "but unfortunately being popular with the guys can translate to being easy on an island this size. It didn't take long for her to get through the population of males under thirty."

Ryan nodded, understanding.

"And you?" his voice wanted to tighten but he deliberately kept it loose and unhurried.

"I was happy to watch from the sidelines. I spent most of my teens working weekends at the Heritage Centre, helping out on archaeological sites or visitors' tours." She paused, suddenly understanding where this was leading.

"You've heard about Alex," she said with a slight smile which seemed to mock him.

He tried to bank down the anger which was suddenly so near the surface and completely out of character.

"I'd like you to tell me about your sister's relationship with Alex Walker, yes."

Anna looked into his impassive face, schooled into a bland expression and would have been forgiven for thinking he was completely disinterested.

She took a deep breath.

"Alex is…was," she amended slowly, "the same age as Megan. We were all in the same class at school because on an island this size the school is tiny. They put the children of similar abilities together in the same class, so we three spent a lot of time together growing up.

"Alex was always just a friend, to both of us, for many years. He was a confidante; he must have seen how often we came to his father's surgery after 'falling down the stairs' and 'walking into doors'."

Ryan's jaw tightened, thinking of the girl she had been. Anna took a small sip of coffee and moistened dry lips before continuing.

"Anyway, I don't know, around the time I turned sixteen there was a lot going on. Megan was wild," she recalled sadly, thinking of the nights they had worried for her, "I was the opposite. I spent every waking moment hiding from my father, reading about the Dark Ages or getting under Mark's feet at the Heritage Centre."

"You said that you worked there?"

"It started off as a Saturday job but by the time I left for university I was doing shifts through the week too. I spent Sundays helping out on digs or preservation work."

He nodded, made a note.

"So," she picked up the story. "When I was around sixteen, things were getting pretty bad at home. Alex had always understood me, or so I thought. We started spending time together, first as friends but then I suppose he awakened something inside me which I hadn't wanted to see. He's an attractive man."

Ryan said nothing.

"He has the kind of confidence which comes from being brought up in a loving, secure family. His parents are wonderful," she spoke affectionately of Yvonne and Steve Walker. "For a while, they sort of adopted me."

She thought wistfully of the times she had been invited to the Walker household for family dinners, nights spent laughing in the warmth of their comfortable home.

"We became an 'item'. All very young, very sweet. He was my first," she said openly because somehow she felt he needed to know. "He was kind and more experienced. Oh," she laughed, "you know what he's like with women. Back then, he was only just beginning to hone his considerable charm."

He was amazed that she could smile with affection at the man who had used and discarded her. He waited for her to continue.

She caught the murderous look in his eye.

"You have to understand, Ryan," she spoke quietly. "I was young, emotionally needy. He offered me my first taste of love and stability and I wanted it so desperately that I think I overwhelmed him. He loved me, in his own way, but he was an eighteen-year-old boy. He wasn't ready for that kind of commitment."

"He was ready to commit to your sister," the words escaped his lips. He saw her swallow another shaky mouthful of coffee.

He stood up abruptly.

"Let's get some air," he opened the French windows without waiting for a reply but took her arm and led her outside onto the little deck area which overlooked the beach.

Anna allowed herself be led outside and stood beside him while the crisp breeze swept over her face. She waited until she was calm again before continuing.

"Megan dazzled him, as she dazzles a lot of men. Alex was a boy and in those days, believe it or not, Megan was vastly more experienced than he was. I don't think there was a thought process involved; she offered him escape of the sweetest kind, no strings attached. Consequently, because there was no pressure, he was happy to offer a kind of commitment."

Ryan considered the reasoning and understood, to a point.

"Weren't you angry?"

"I was immeasurably hurt, at the time. I felt betrayed, unattractive, all the things a woman feels. Once I had given myself some time, I found I could forgive Alex because he was a boy who wasn't yet a man. It took much longer to forgive Megan, because she was my sister."

"Did she love him?"

"No, not at all. She told me that only yesterday," she came back to the conversation they had before Megan died. "She told me outright that Alex had only been an exercise in proving her superiority as a woman. She did a good job of that one—I left the island two weeks later and never came back."

Anna looked down at the sand lodged in the cracks of the deck while Ryan wondered what kind of woman would set out to hurt her sibling in such a calculated way.

"Do you know if they maintained any kind of relationship more recently?"

Anna looked up again, her eyes troubled.

"I really have no idea," she said honestly, "but if you're asking me whether Alex is capable of killing Megan, or Lucy, or anyone for that matter, then the answer is no. He may be a philanderer but he's not vicious. He just doesn't have it in him."

Ryan reserved judgement.

"Do you know of any reason why he might not wish it to be known that he had a relationship with your sister?"

Anna's eyebrows raised but she thought carefully before answering.

"I suppose if he hadn't told his wife that might be a bit awkward for him. He could have been a bit embarrassed by it," she pondered.

Ryan was mollified to realise that Anna hadn't kept up to date with Alex Walker's life. She didn't, for example, appear to know that his wife had left him.

"When was the last time you saw or spoke with Alex?"

"Yesterday afternoon, at the pub. We exchanged a few pleasantries as I was leaving Megan's apartment."

His ears pricked up.

"Tell me about it."

"Must have been around twenty past four," she cast her mind back. "He was standing having a smoke in the courtyard as I left. I stopped, said 'hello', he said 'hello' back, asked how long I would be staying and that sort of thing."

Ryan could imagine just the sort of thing. He thought of the younger man swanning around like a young Robert Redford, charming Anna with his toothy grin.

He ordered himself to get a grip.

"You can't really suspect Alex," she said again. "The very thought of him committing murder is ridiculous. He loves women."

Ryan said nothing for a very long time. So long that she became restless. She angled towards him and was about to put a hand on his arm to shake him from his reverie when he spoke, his voice unexpectedly harsh.

"It isn't always about liking or disliking women, or at least not always. Sometimes it's about the sheer bloody hell of it, the power that comes from taking a life."

Anna stayed silent, waiting for him to continue.

Once he started, Ryan found he couldn't stop the words as they tumbled out of his mouth.

"I've chased killers who claimed they killed and battered women and men alike because the voices told them to; I've seen some who said it was because they had a crappy childhood. It's all bullshit, Anna," he turned to her and, for a moment, he thought of another dark-haired woman. "Some people kill and there isn't any reason for it other than for the pure fucking enjoyment of it."

She watched emotions too deep to fathom swirl in his eyes. She couldn't begin to understand the horrors he might have seen, or the pain he was feeling, but she felt herself drawn to him. She hesitated and then slid her arm around his waist. He stiffened and then seemed to relax, drawing her closer to him.

"I'm sorry," he said softly.

She shook her head. "You've no need. I understand what it's like to feel helpless."

He stared out at the sea and the clouds that were forming over the island, turning the sky from blue to an overcast grey. Funny, he thought, that she should understand how helpless he felt, when he hadn't fully understood it himself.

CHAPTER 12

"I need your help, Anna."

Ryan spoke the words and found them easier to say than he had imagined. He pulled away from her and walked back into the cottage, aware that things had already gone too far. He knew where it would end between them.

Anna thought that he needed her help in more ways than one. It was a novelty to feel needed by another person, even if the other person was a complex, inscrutable man with his own demons, who irritated her more often than not. On the other hand, she had seen signs of sensitivity and keen intelligence.

He wasn't hard to look at, either.

Disgusted at herself, she followed him back inside the cottage. How could she be so attracted to the detective investigating her sister's murder? Was she insane? Nervously, she cleared their cups away, the china clattering in the quiet space.

"How can I help you? I've told you everything I remember about yesterday." Her words were brusque as she scrubbed at the china with more force than was necessary.

"You may remember more, in time," he said, watching her tense movements. His timing had been way, way off on this one. He needed to spend more time focused on the two women who now lay in the mortuary and less time thinking about the woman currently standing with her back to him as she tried to scrub away her remorse.

Even as he told himself to stay professional, he was moving towards where she stood at the little sink.

"I'll let you know if I remember anything else, Ryan." She moved pointedly away from him and rubbed her arms to stave off a sudden chill.

He didn't follow her. The logical part of his mind agreed with her unspoken decision, he only wished his glands would catch up with his brain.

"You told me to contact you if the department needed your professional help," he began, watching her eyes widen in surprise. "Ordinarily, your appointment as a consultant would automatically be terminated owing to the fact that you are both a material witness and a relative of the de…Megan, that is."

"Go on," she leaned back against the counter and crossed her ankles. The movement drew his eyes to the floor and he realised she had been barefoot all this time. Her slender feet were lightly tanned and tipped with red polish. He forced his gaze upwards again.

"On the record, I'm going to terminate your appointment; there won't be a lot of paperwork since you haven't provided a formal consultation."

Anger simmered, balanced by an equally heavy weight of impotence, but she remained silent.

He blew out a breath and prepared to throw out the rule book.

"Off the record, I still want you to consult with us on this, if you're able to."

She tilted her head to one side, considering him. Clearly, he had no idea that she would have badgered him to let her help until he agreed. She had no intention of sitting on the sidelines any longer. If she could help find the monster who had butchered Megan, then she would.

Still, it wouldn't hurt to toy with him a while.

"You're asking me to break the rules?" she injected a note of shock into her voice.

He looked uncomfortable and she watched him fidget from one foot to the other and drum his fingers on the countertop.

"I realise it's not orthodox," he began in a bureaucratic tone and she tried hard not to laugh. Another minute and she would put him out of his misery.

"Orthodox?" she said with a sound of astonishment. "You're asking me to ignore police procedure, to consult with you without police approval. What would the professors at Durham University think? This from you, a man of the law; a sheriff of the people." She slapped a hand on her heart and wondered if she had laid it on thick enough.

He opened his mouth to speak again and then narrowed his gaze at her. The look in her eyes was altogether too innocent.

"You're making fun of me." He crossed his arms and huffed out a breath.

She did laugh then, a bright sound which he'd never heard from her before. It lit up her whole face and seemed to make her shine. That moment, when he saw her, truly saw her, etched itself onto his memory.

"Oh, Ryan," she said when the laughter died. "Do you really think you could have stopped me?" Her smile died too as reality returned. "I want to do everything in my power to help you find the man who did this."

"Thank you," he said, deeply grateful. "I'm asking a lot of you, Anna. Nobody would blame you for saying 'no'; the details and the circumstances are very close to home."

She moved around the counter to look out at the sea again and saw two little girls building sandcastles. She turned back with resolve.

"All through the night and this morning, I wept for my sister. She was never my enemy, but I became hers, I think…I don't know for sure," she shook her head, cleared it. "All I know is that I owe her a debt too large to repay. I left it too long to thank her and now she's been taken from me. If justice is all I can give her now, then I'll do everything I can to get it."

Ryan picked up the brown folder he'd left on the counter.

"I need you to look at some pictures and tell me what I'm not seeing."

She swallowed and rubbed sweaty palms on the back of her jeans but she took the folder to the table.

Before she could open it, he slapped a palm on the top.

"Are you sure about this?"

She nodded and he removed his hand, went to stand by the window in silence.

The folder contained close-up images of the markings found on both women. Anna closed her eyes automatically against the grotesque aberration of a woman's body, but she remembered her own words a moment earlier and opened them again to look.

Lucy's torso held the remains of what had been an upside-down triangle with a vertical line drawn through it. She assumed, correctly, that it had been drawn in Lucy's own blood. Otherwise, her body was scrupulously clean, her hair neat. She avoided looking at the girl's face. There were no secrets there.

Taking a shaky breath, she placed the image carefully to one side and braced herself for the next. With iron will, she blanked out her mind using every meditation technique she had learned over the years. Eventually, she looked down at the image and felt her stomach turn.

Here, there was more brutality than before. Her killer had not dipped his finger to draw his image on her body; he had carved the markings into her skin. The cuts weren't neat, either, she thought distractedly. The lines were torn with jagged, untidy edges. The symbol was similar and her body was likewise clean.

There was a third image, she realised and placed the clinical photograph of what had been her sister to one side. The third photo showed her back, mottled and dark red. Anna's vision wavered for a moment but she breathed through the fog and forced herself to look.

Carved into her sister's left shoulder was a tiny pentagram.

She set the photograph to one side and Ryan moved back to join her. He scanned her face and found her pale but steady.

"This," she began, pointing at the first image of Lucy, "is an ancient symbol normally associated with femininity and fertility."

Ryan took out his notebook. "A pagan symbol?"

Anna shuffled in her chair and shifted into work mode. "It depends what you mean by 'pagan'. In the dark ages, 'pagans' were simply people who believed that ceremonial prayers to the elements would ensure a good harvest."

"And now...?" he pressed.

She laughed. "You're asking me to condense an entire field of study into a sentence?" she shook her head. "I can't do that, but I can give you certain generalisations. When Christianity came along, 'paganism' became a derogatory word that people used to refer to peasants or the general underclass. Eventually, it was used to describe unbelievers, people whose beliefs were seen as ungodly and perhaps evil."

He set his jaw. "Look, I get that there's probably a lot to think about here."

"Oh, really?" her eyes widened.

His lips twitched but he carried on. "I need basic principles at this point. We can look into specifics later."

She rubbed at her eyes. "Okay, I understand. Let's start again. During the Palaeolithic period..."

She caught the pained look in his eye.

"Sorry. The first recorded findings of cave art date back to 12 or 13,000 BC. Drawings of male figures dancing, sometimes dressed as animals and so on." She paused to check that he was still with her. "Images like this," her finger hovered over the image of Lucy but didn't touch it, "were very common throughout Europe. It is generally accepted that the downward triangle is a pictorial representation of the female womb, particularly with the vertical line intersecting it."

"Does it have any other meaning?"

"Some historians have suggested that it could be an animal's claw," she admitted but didn't sound convinced. "Together with the fact that the image is drawn in blood, I would still lean towards the idea of femininity."

"Why is the blood relevant?" he thought aloud.

"It represents life force, particularly female menstruation. The colour red was generally important at that time."

"How so?"

"Red was symbolic in various ways," she explained. "People were buried in clothing that had been dyed red, bodies were sprinkled with red ochre…"

"But not blood?"

She raised her shoulders and let them fall again. "Red ochre isn't as easy to come by these days and he had a ready supply of blood to hand, didn't he?"

They both fell silent for a moment.

"Here," Anna gestured to the image of Megan, "the image is slightly different. The triangle is upward with a vertical line through it."

She frowned and rested her head on her hand, fingers kneading the tension there.

"I'm confused by the meaning," she confessed. "Normally, an upward triangle is recognised as the symbol of masculinity, but if that were the case, why draw the vertical line through it? That's contradictory."

Ryan absorbed the information.

"So, he made a mistake on the second marking?"

"Maybe," she murmured.

"Fair enough. Anything else?"

"Oh, yes," she brought her eyes to his and fear lurked in their depths. "There's a lot more to talk about."

CHAPTER 13

Alex stood on the beach outside his hut, flanked by two police officers. Phillips was lounging in the little doorway which had been cut into the upturned boat while the CSI team scoured the interior. He popped a stick of gum in his mouth and wished it was a cigarette. He had decided to give up the cigs after twenty years and it was certainly nothing to do with the fact that DI MacKenzie had let it be known around the station-house that she detested the smell of smoke.

Nothing to do with that at all.

Chewing resentfully, Phillips looked across at the pretty-boy coastguard standing on jittery legs in the sand.

"Sure you haven't got anything you want to tell us, son?"

Alex seemed to twitch and he lurched towards Phillips.

"You have to listen to me," he spoke quickly. "I didn't kill anyone. I've got nothing to do with this."

Phillips sighed.

"Look," Alex's voice grew firmer for a moment. "I'm not under arrest, am I?"

"Not at all," Phillips agreed reasonably. "You're simply exercising your right to be present while we search your hut."

And we're exercising our right to put the willies up you, lad, Phillips thought with a fierce grin as he eyed the two officers he'd deliberately placed either side of Alex to make the young man uncomfortable.

"You won't find anything," Alex said and for a minute, looking into his clear green eyes, Phillips believed him.

"We'll know for sure in a bit, won't we?"

Alex seemed to relax.

"That's right," he nodded, calmer now. "Once you've finished your search, you'll see there's nothing there."

Phillips already knew that nothing untoward had been found at Alex's cottage—except an interesting stash of porn and other sex paraphernalia which had been confiscated—but that didn't preclude the possibility of there being something in the little wooden hidey-hole behind him.

Phillips said nothing and continued to keep an eye on proceedings until he heard muffled sounds from the doorway. Faulkner emerged, covered in his overalls and goggles. With him, he carried a plastic evidence bag.

"Phillips, I think you'll want to have a look at this." His voice was muffled behind his face mask and light brown hair stuck out at odd angles beneath his plastic cap.

Phillips took the bag and opened it. Inside, there was a bundle of women's clothes, a pair of black high-heeled boots and a mobile phone with a pink cover. He looked up and caught the eye of the man standing shaking in his coastguard's jacket which the people of the island trusted as a symbol of protection. Something in Phillips' expression must have transmitted itself, because he watched the last vestiges of colour drain from Alex Walker's face.

Phillips spat out his gum.

"Can you explain where these clothes came from, Mr Walker?" Phillips added the standard caution about giving statements to the police.

Alex started to tremble.

"I have no idea."

Phillips took a step toward him, intending to ask him the same question again, when Walker panicked and shoved at one of the officers standing beside him, turning as if to run.

"Whoa there, lad, you need to calm down."

Walker was lightly restrained by the officers as he grew increasingly aggressive, shouting about the police planting false evidence. Phillips made a judgement call.

"Alexander Walker, you are under arrest on suspicion of the murder of Lucy Mathieson and Megan Taylor. You do not have to say anything, but it may harm your defence if you do not mention when questioned something which you later rely on in court. Anything you do say may be given in evidence." Phillips shook his head as one of the officers started to pull out his hand cuffs. Restraints wouldn't be necessary, Frank thought, since Walker had visibly slumped after his tantrum. The man looked as if he could be knocked over with a feather.

"Son, you're going to have to come with me."

* * *

While Alex Walker stood shivering on a cold Northumbrian beach, Anna basked in the warmth of a friend's hearth.

"It's so good to see you again," Doctor Mark Bowers settled himself opposite Anna in a worn leather wingback chair and sipped herbal tea.

Anna felt so much at home in the cluttered room with its floor to ceiling shelves stuffed full with books. Doctor Bowers was a leading historian in his field, having taught for years at the university in Durham before deciding to settle on Lindisfarne to complete his life's work: a history of Holy Island from the Dark Ages to the present day. He had been the one to write her recommendation for entry onto the History programme at the university, for which she would be forever grateful to him. When Mark wasn't writing his book or researching, he managed the Heritage Centre and the attached gift shop by the Priory gates. When he wasn't doing that, he was volunteering with the island coastguard, supervising archaeological digs or encouraging young people to develop an interest in history on one of the many visitors' tours.

She wondered how he found the time.

"It's good to be here," she said in return, enjoying the companionship. "Thanks again for letting me use the cottage. I'm sorry I haven't called in a while."

He brushed that away with one hand. "Never mind that."

"No, really. I don't know…I suppose it was just a bit easier to forget all about the island."

He took another sip of tea. "I was sorry to hear about your sister."

Anna appreciated the straightforward tone and nodded her thanks. She didn't want to discuss it, not yet.

"How are you finding it in Durham? Still the same as ever?"

Anna smiled and tucked her feet up onto the comfy leather.

"It probably hasn't changed much," she agreed. "Things are going well for me there, I'm enjoying lecturing and there are a few good students this term."

"But…?"

She smiled into his intelligent eyes and thought that he knew her too well.

"I'm restless, I suppose. Recently, I've been a bit distracted. When the call came from CID—"

"They called you?" he interjected sharply.

"Yes, to ask if I would help them develop an understanding of pagan ceremonial practices. I guess they wanted someone who didn't live on the island, otherwise they would have contacted you." She sipped her tea. "Anyway, when the call came, I suppose I was looking for an excuse to come back home."

She pulled a face and looked into the flames of the fire.

"I feel terrible saying that," she confessed. "Death is an awful reason to come back."

"You would have come back eventually," he said firmly. He was glad she had made herself at home, as she used to all those years ago. He could remember a young waif with a keen intelligence and unlimited potential. He had enjoyed nothing more than helping her to discover her talents and reveal the ambition beneath the shy exterior. Now, a cultured, beautiful woman sat before him.

Anna leaned her head back in the chair and looked around the cosy study. It was an eclectic mix of memorabilia Mark had collected on his travels abroad. African and Venetian masks vied for wall space with framed lithographs of Egyptian monuments. In a small glass cabinet there were pottery reproductions of Roman fertility goddesses and a polished wooden cabinet held various trinkets including spoons and bracelets. Amid the vast array of books, there was a mounted sword from the eighteenth century, which had been presented to him by English Heritage as a 'thank you' for all his years of loyal service.

She remembered the hours she had spent sitting in this room, or in the study area at the Heritage Centre, poring over textbooks and manuscripts to quench her thirst for knowledge about the past.

"You always did like this room," he said affectionately, watching her eyes roam over every surface.

"Who wouldn't? It's wonderfully eclectic; a testament to learning."

He mulled over her words and found he agreed with them.

"What's on your mind, Anna?"

"Aside from murder?" She turned sad eyes towards him and Mark wondered what she saw. An old man in faded corduroy trousers and a crumpled sweater with hair that was more grey than brown. He looked away from her into the bright flames.

"I met a man," she mumbled into her tea cup and felt like a teenager again. "He's difficult, complicated and utterly compelling. I don't want to like him but I do. The timing couldn't be worse."

In all his years spent as a bachelor, Mark had never known heartache or particularly wondered what it would feel like. He marvelled at his own naivety. Why hadn't he known that the pain would be exquisite, a shard through a heart which had been closed and comfortable for so long?

His unremarkable face remained affectionate and he swirled his tea before gulping it down whole.

"DCI Ryan," he said.

"How did you know?" She seemed genuinely surprised and his smile widened. Ah, still so very young.

"I have eyes in my head," he said shortly.

"I don't know what to do about it…or him," she admitted.

Bowers stood up and traced a finger along the edge of the mantle in front of the fire. Aromatic candles stood on the stone hearth and he contemplated lighting a few of them but decided to do it another time.

"You must do what your heart tells you," he said quietly, his profile shadowed except for the light which flickered from the fire. "You've spent too long using your head."

He wondered if he was talking to Anna or himself.

CHAPTER 14

L iving on Lindisfarne was a logistical nightmare, Ryan thought. There was no police station and since the tide had already rolled in, no way of transporting their suspect to the mainland. So, instead of spending a nice sweaty, sleepless night crying for his mother in one of Her Majesty's finest establishments, Alex Walker was currently sleeping off the stress of the day upstairs in Ryan's own spare room. At least the door and windows had locks, he thought, but it was hardly ideal.

His team milled around the dining area squawking about their success but Ryan wasn't convinced. The arrest, although justified, was a farce. Whoever heard of a suspect spending the night at the SIO's home?

His house phone rang again and he swore.

"No comment," he barked down the line after listening for a few seconds. Reporters had been hounding him all day, having finally got a whiff of two juicy, ritual murders on a secluded island. Those vultures would be circling as soon as the causeway opened.

Phillips cleared his throat meaningfully.

"What?" Ryan redirected his wrath.

"Had Gregson on the line earlier," Phillips said. "Said we were to be cooperative with the media otherwise we would have a circus on our hands."

Ryan leaned back in his chair with a face like granite.

"I don't give a flying fuck about what Gregson wants. He's denied our application for funds to requisition a helicopter to transport Mr Lover-Lover off the island for formal questioning, which will potentially compromise us later on if and when this thing goes to court."

As Phillips opened his mouth to speak, there was a sharp rap on the front door.

Ryan turned disbelieving eyes heavenward. One of the rookies opened the door and directed their visitor into Ryan's front room. It wouldn't do to have members of the general public getting an eyeful of the murder wall.

After confiscating Phillips' coffee, he gestured the other man to come with him. Together, they found Dr Walker tramping muddy boots angrily across the living room floor. He looked furious.

"Dr Walker, what can I do for you?"

The older man stepped towards him and, although Walker was a good few inches shorter, Ryan almost felt that he was looking up to him.

"You have my son in custody. I would like to talk to him."

"I'm sorry but I can't allow that before questioning."

A muscle twitched in the other man's face. "He may be in need of medical assistance."

The man was tenacious, Ryan thought.

"Phillips? Would you please ask one of the attending officers to check that Mr Walker doesn't require any medical aid at this time?"

"Will do," the other man nodded and stepped out into the hall.

"Alex is also entitled to a solicitor," Walker said through gritted teeth and Ryan had a moment to admire family loyalty and the automatic support of a father for his son.

The situation was definitely tricky.

"Indeed he is, Doctor. Since we are unable to leave the island presently and likewise nobody is able to cross without a great deal of trouble, rest assured we won't be questioning your son until the morning. He will be able to exercise his legal rights then."

The doctor nodded but was nowhere near mollified.

"I will contact our family solicitor in the morning. In the meantime, I speak for our whole family when I say that this arrest is wholly without foundation." His voice lowered in appeal, "I know my son, Chief Inspector. He wouldn't have the heart to kill a bug, let alone commit the atrocities we have seen over the past two days."

Ryan watched Walker's face and thought that he truly believed what he was saying. However, just because his family had blind faith in him, didn't mean that Walker Jr. hadn't upped and decided to go on a killing spree.

"I understand you're in a difficult position, Dr Walker. I want you to know that we appreciate your cooperation with our investigation and we will conduct ourselves in line with the departmental code of conduct at all times in our dealings with your son."

Walker's face grew sad, the lines around his eyes no longer seeming to enhance his features. "I expect nothing less," he said quietly. After a pause during which he scrubbed a hand over his face and through the cap of blonde-grey hair, he turned to Ryan again.

"I don't understand what has led you to arrest him. I heard there was a search of Alex's home and his storage hut on the beach?"

Ryan had no intention of discussing any details pertinent to the investigation but he could understand the father's need to know how the nightmare had come about.

"Evidence and information has come to light which, we believe, provide us with reasonable grounds to suspect your son of these offences, added to which he appeared to be on the verge of absconding when questioned informally. I'm not at liberty to discuss anything further with you, Dr Walker. I am sure that things will become clearer in the light of day."

Steve Walker stood quietly for a moment, dreading the walk home to tell his wife her son wouldn't be coming back tonight. Not to mention the chatter of the village once this got around. He supposed it couldn't be helped. He handed over the small bag of fresh clothes Yvonne had sent for her son.

"I'll be in touch in the morning. Please tell Alex that his family have faith in him." With that, he pulled the hood of his anorak over his head and stepped out into the rain.

Phillips stood in the hallway behind Ryan and, like his superior, was impressed with the solidarity displayed by the Walker family.

Once again, the hour was late, heading towards nine-thirty by the time Ryan called his team together for their final briefing of the day. As he looked around the room, he saw the clear signs of fatigue but also of renewed energy which came from the belief that they had their culprit in custody.

"Alright, settle down," he didn't need to raise his voice; the tone of command was enough to quieten the din of chin-wagging police officers.

"Firstly, let's tie up some loose ends. Harbourmaster and coastguard logs confirm that no vessel was logged entering or leaving the harbour in the early hours of December 21st, which tells us one of two things: either no boats came in or out, or there *was* a boat and it simply wasn't logged. Neither option would surprise me. No cars were sighted and the witnesses don't think they heard a car engine, in any case. We've re-interviewed locals to see if anyone else heard an engine sound and a couple have added their recollection of a low rumbling sound but can't be sure of the time. Let's keep our ears open, there's not much more we can do for now." Ryan picked up his coffee and held it but didn't drink.

"The CSIs conducted their search of the Mathieson house and car last night and came up nil on suspicious evidence, correct?" Ryan gestured to Faulkner.

"Right, sir. There were, of course, prints and DNA all over the house and prints on the inside of the car but nothing which gave us any cause for concern. No blood, no fluids, nothing in the boot of the car. The bathrooms were clean but not spotless and contained DNA samples from all three inhabitants. We took samples from the parents and have retained them but in summary, sir, everything looked normal."

"On that note," Ryan pointed a finger at Faulkner again and, remarkably, the other man blushed under the scrutiny. "Tom, I want a round-up of where we are with forensics and pathology."

Faulkner shuffled some papers and faced his superior.

"Pinter has really come through for us, sir," he started, referring to Jeffrey Pinter, the senior police pathologist.

"He should," Ryan drawled. "He was paid double-time to work through the night."

"Well, the incentive seems to have worked. He's come back with reports on Lucy and Megan, ahead of schedule. Beginning with Lucy Mathieson, he confirms the cause of death as strangulation. The toxicology report has come back negative of narcotics but her blood alcohol level was 0.19, which is pretty high."

Ryan thought back to Megan's witness statement, Bill Tilson's too.

"None of the staff reported her drunk or disorderly," he observed.

"No, it's more likely that she would have appeared merry. At that level, the alcohol would have made her more emotional, perhaps with some slurred speech, impaired motor function and so forth."

"So, we can safely assume that she wasn't operating at full capacity which would have affected her ability to defend herself against an aggressor."

"True, sir, but there are still no defensive marks on the victim's body; no skin or fibres under the victim's nails."

"We're already working on the assumption that she knew her killer."

"That's the safest bet," Faulkner commented, then consulted his paperwork again. "As we suspected, there was no foreign DNA found on Lucy's body and nothing further of interest in her blood work."

"Hell," Ryan muttered.

"On the flip side, whilst we found minimal alcohol levels, we did find a reasonable quantity of lysergic acid amide in Megan Taylor's blood."

Phillips groaned at the back of the room. "Tom, you're killing me here."

Faulkner laughed shortly. "It's a hallucinogenic drug known as LSA. It's closely associated with the more common LSD, but it's fifty or a hundred times less potent."

"Effects?" Ryan asked.

Faulkner blew out a breath. "Well, although there are some similarities to LSD, it's a lot less stimulating, as I say. If the dose was too high, it would be more likely to act as a sedative. On the other hand, ingesting the right amount would bring about a psychedelic state where she would have been floating."

"So are we looking for some sort of compound?" Phillips' voice came from the back of the room again.

"No," Faulkner shook his head. "LSA occurs naturally; you can find it in the seeds of certain plants. It's much easier and more cost-effective to just grind down and eat or drink the seeds rather than trying to extract the active alkaloids."

For the sake of his own sanity, Phillips decided to ignore the last part of the sentence and focus on the first.

"Street sales aren't high on LSA, otherwise we would know more about it," Ryan noted, flipping through his knowledge of narcotics. "Where would Megan come by LSA seeds?"

"Well, you can find it in the ipomoea violacea plant, for example," Faulkner said knowledgeably.

There was a collective silence.

"That's Morning Glory," Faulkner supplied and watched some of the furrowed brows clear.

"We need to isolate potential supply," Ryan said. "There may be a cottage drugs industry on the island but frankly I'm sceptical. More likely that she would bring it over from the mainland. Lowerson?"

The young officer sat bolt upright in his chair.

"Sir?"

"You want a more active role in this investigation?" Ryan hadn't missed the enthusiasm, the diligent hours and detailed reporting.

"Yes, sir."

"I want you to shake down known sources in the area. Start by contacting the narcotics team in Newcastle. This is our baby," he wanted that to be clear from the start, "but they may be able to point you in the right direction."

"Understood, sir," Lowerson was practically chomping at the bit.

"I need the information fast," Ryan added and was pleased to see the junior detective's head bob up and down like a yo-yo. Still, privately, he would ask Phillips to keep an eye on his progress. He was all for advancement but he couldn't afford mistakes either.

He turned back to Faulkner. "Carry on, Tom."

"Back to Megan, then. Pinter confirms cause of death as asphyxiation following a severed jugular artery. Judging from the pattern of wounds, he considers it most likely that the throat was slashed left to right, first," Faulkner gestured in the air with a sharp movement of hands.

"Likely to be right-handed, then?"

Faulkner nodded. "He followed up the initial action with a deeper slice, which cut deep into the throat, more than halfway through." Faulkner paused again, swallowing. "Pinter's set out the technical details in his report, for anyone who's interested to know."

There were nods of understanding. Unless it was relevant to the case, none of them had a burning desire to know just how many specific veins and tendons had been severed.

"Pathologist estimates at least an hour for Megan's body to bleed out, which would be consistent with the volume of blood found in her apartment, particularly on and around the bed," Faulkner continued.

"We have a statement from her sister, Dr Taylor, confirming Megan was alive and well until around four-twenty yesterday afternoon," Ryan said. "The pathologist has given an estimated time of death between then and six-thirty. That gives us a window to focus on." There were nods around the room.

"That's all the useful info we can take from the pathologist for now, sir," Faulkner concluded.

"Good," Ryan shifted mental gears again. "What was the analysis of the sand residue found on Lucy's body?"

Faulkner held out a hand to one of his minions for the chemical report.

"The results have been interesting," he began. "Firstly, the sand found in Lucy Mathieson's head wound has been isolated as building sand, rather than the expected marine by-product."

"Go on," Ryan urged.

"Building sand is quarried and tends to be quite soft, unlike the sharper marine quartz sand found on the beach by the Priory, for example." Faulkner paused to ensure he still had his audience. "The sample in this case was reddish in colour, consistent with this part of the country. It wouldn't be found on the island without quarrying deep into the rock."

"You said building sand," Phillips spoke up again, leaning forward in his chair. "What sort of building?"

"Good question," Faulkner nodded approvingly. "This type of sand tends to be used in connection with mortars, rather than, for example, paving a driveway or something like that."

"So," Ryan took the information and ran with it, "our next question is whether there was any sand of that type, or recent building work, on or near Walker's properties?" He turned expectantly to Denise MacKenzie.

MacKenzie ran through the inventory list and description of Alex Walker's properties. "None, sir," she said eventually, disappointed.

"Check again tomorrow," Ryan ordered. "Walk the access route from his hut to the Priory and make sure."

MacKenzie nodded her assent.

"Meantime, we're looking out for any recent building work." He spoke to the room at large. "Be observant. Lucy may have been killed elsewhere, or fallen on her way to the fishing hut."

There were nods, less eager than before. He couldn't blame them: if the sand in Lucy's wound hadn't come from a beach, and there were no building works or materials around Walker's properties, then where the hell had she hurt her head and subsequently been killed? Was there another site, another person serving as Walker's accomplice?

"What about the oil and soap residue found on Lucy?"

"Again, interesting," Faulkner said, revelling in his subject. "Nowadays, most people opt for a body wash or shower gel rather than good old-fashioned soap but this wasn't the case here, otherwise we would never have known the difference. Body wash or shower gel has a petroleum rather than a fat base, which means that it doesn't leave much mineral residue on the skin after use."

Ryan nodded. "The perp used good old-fashioned soap."

"Yes," Tom agreed. "There was a mineral layer found on the victim's skin consistent with saponified produce…"

Ryan slanted him a look.

"The, ah, long and short of it is, a traditional soap product with added shea butter was used, the chemical properties of which match these known labels but could also have been reproduced elsewhere." He took out a typed list of soap manufacturers and handed it to Ryan.

Ryan glanced at the list of well-known brands. At least there were only five to choose from but those five could have been found in almost every household in Britain.

"There is one final point regarding the soap," Faulkner added. "The interesting thing is that the fragrance compound added to the soap matches synthetic sandalwood."

"Sandalwood?"

"Yes, sir, which suggests that the soap was designed to be used by a man."

It all added up, Ryan thought.

"I want a list of stockists on the island, to start with. What about the oil residue?"

"Well, now, that's more unusual." Faulkner's eyes lit up again. "There was no known match to mass-produced body oil. Instead, we found large traces of camphor mixed with household turpentine."

"Camphor?"

"It's a white, sort of waxy aromatic substance found in the bark of certain evergreen trees."

"Used for what, exactly?"

"Religious and spiritual ceremonies, mostly; sometimes in Indian cooking, owing to its aroma."

That explained the odd scent of cooking he had smelled when he had first seen Lucy's body.

"Any physiological effects?"

"Actually, since it can be easily absorbed by the skin, camphor can be potentially dangerous but in this case the oil was applied post-mortem. No trace found in Lucy Mathieson's blood stream, sir."

"So, most likely he used it for some spiritual or religious purpose?" The question was rhetorical. "I want to know if there's a shop anywhere on the island or mainland within a hundred miles that sells camphor. Phillips?"

"On it," the other man was scribbling on his notepad with a chewed pencil.

"Any soap or oil on Megan?"

"Although her body was cleaned, we found no soap or oil residue of sufficient sample to analyse, sir."

That brought Ryan up short.

"What about disinfectant?"

"Yes, there's plenty of that but he didn't take the trouble to treat her skin to soap or oil after he'd removed traces of himself," Faulkner supplied. "However, we're hopeful that we'll be able to recover some DNA samples from the plugholes in her bathroom, perhaps some hair or skin samples from the rest of the flat."

"That's something," Ryan acknowledged.

"It's painstaking work," Tom added with a note of apology. "We're mostly working around the clock but I'll need another couple of CSIs brought in."

"Understood," Ryan said. "I'll find the resources for it."

"We've lifted several prints, as I said yesterday. Unfortunately, none of them match any on the database. We were able to eliminate her sister's prints, one set of which were found on the doorframe to the apartment and we had one other match. The prints taken from Alex Walker when he was arrested match several sets around the doorframe, the railing leading up to her apartment and on the coffee table. I can't give any indication of how fresh those prints are, though."

Ryan considered the man in the bedroom upstairs and weighed up the options.

"We need to eliminate more people." Ryan turned to MacKenzie. "I need prints from Bill Tilson and Pete Rigby, since they both work in the vicinity. They might provide them without any hassle. Realistically, they're the only two we can ask at the moment."

"I'll see to it," MacKenzie said.

"The bathroom was spotless," Faulkner remarked. "No prints or other samples anywhere to be found, although we'll look at the plugholes and drainage system tomorrow morning since it's likely the perp cleaned up in there. The entire room was drenched in bleach, sir."

"She didn't strike me as being a conscientious housekeeper, so we can assume he brought the bleach with him," Ryan commented.

"There were no bottles found on the premises," Faulkner confirmed.

"Okay," Ryan nodded, picturing the scene in his mind. "He must have brought a change of clothes, too. No way did he come out of there without blood covering him, otherwise."

"Could have been naked," Phillips said, causing several heads to turn.

"Just thinking outside the box," he muttered defensively and folded his arms.

"Frank's right," Ryan nodded. "Let's hope he's left something of himself down the plughole, since he's neglected to leave any helpful clues anywhere else."

* * *

Later, after he dismissed his team to their beds for the night, Ryan sat in the quiet kitchen and felt doubt cloud his mind. There were too many inconsistencies here, he thought. Ritual killers followed just that: ritual. They tended not to deviate from a general pattern, preferred to follow their own internal code. With Megan, there had been escalation, brutality and what looked like ritual, but without the same tools or methodology that had been displayed with Lucy. Aside from that, the setting was all wrong. With Lucy, the man had been willing to break his back carrying her up to the Priory, risking exposure, presumably so that she would be found on religious ground.

With Megan, the killer had been lazy. He may have carried her but only up the short fire escape they had found leading from her apartment to the roof. He had dumped her there, on top of a pile of rubbish that hardly passed for an altar. They hadn't found anything except a few lipstick-covered cigarette butts, which had been Megan's guilty pleasure. No sacred setting, Ryan thought, but it still made a statement. Maybe that was the point of it all: to capture their attention and awe.

One girl found on sacred ground, one atop a rubbish pile. Was it supposed to be symbolic?

Or perhaps his quarry had decided to deviate from his chosen course, which made him infinitely more unpredictable and dangerous.

Ryan got up and looked out of the window into the darkness. The sky was black, except for a few flickering lights across the channel and the flare of a bonfire somewhere on the beach.

Ryan looked up towards the ceiling to where Alex Walker slept and wondered.

* * *

While Ryan had been preparing to brief his team, two men sat a comfortable distance apart in the main square as twilight began to fall. Just two members of the island community, passing the time of day.

"Father," one began reverently, "there are some things on my mind I need to talk to you about."

"By all means," the other said in a rich baritone, waving a cheerful hand to one of their number who passed them on his way from the corner shop to St Peter's Church for the evening service. They would show their faces there later, for appearances' sake, but first there were matters to discuss.

The other man felt his throat dry up.

"Tell me what troubles you," the High Priest said, breaking open a packet of mints and reclining further on the bench beneath St Cuthbert's statue. On the previous evening, Ryan had sat in the same spot and contemplated the stars.

"I feel uncomfortable with what I've seen, Father. I feel—I feel that things have changed…"

"Do you question my authority, or the natural course of events set out by the Gods of Nature?"

The other felt his chest tighten.

"No, Father. Never. It's just…our ceremonies are changing."

"All of Nature is change," the other said softly, but his tone brooked no argument.

"But it used to be that we would just meet and pray. Now there's been Lucy…and Megan—"

"If one of our number has seen fit to make sacrifices to the Master, who shall in turn rain fortune upon all of us, you should be thanking him," the High Priest snapped, then quickly controlled his voice. It wouldn't do for passers-by to notice anything untoward.

The other man balked at the tone, everything in him wanted to obey, not to question.

Yet, conscience demanded that he speak.

"Father, I believe I saw who killed Lucy," he whispered.

" 'Killed'?" the other snarled. "You blaspheme. Surely 'offered' would be a better way to describe it."

"Very well. I believe I saw who…who *offered* Lucy to the Master."

"Indeed?" The High Priest was curious to know.

"It was one of our number," the other said softly and described how he had watched a shadowed figure haul Lucy over the fence leading up the hilly side of the Priory, how he had heard the muffled curses and gasping breaths as the man had struggled under her weight.

"If all is as you say, then he has performed the ultimate sacrifice; he has given of himself so that we all might reap the rewards."

They both paused as one of the locals came over to greet them and exchange a few words. They all agreed that Lucy and Megan's deaths were a terrible tragedy and bade their neighbour farewell.

After a few moments, their hushed conversation began again.

"Alex has been arrested on suspicion of their mur… their deaths," the man said urgently.

"Naturally, I'm aware of that," the High Priest said.

"O—Of course you are. But, he shouldn't have to pay for another man's actions," the first said vehemently.

"Keep your voice down," the High Priest ordered and was pleased when the other man shrank away, like a whipped dog.

He thought for a moment about the predicament they were in. He weighed the pros and cons and made his decision.

"Rob," he murmured, never raising his voice. "There is a way that we may see justice done. It will require your help."

"Anything, Father," the other agreed quickly, pleased not to have angered his High Priest.

They agreed a time and place to meet, finalised their plans and then bade friendly farewells audible for those around them.

The High Priest watched the young coastguard volunteer walk swiftly away towards the church, meeting others as he went on his way. Anger coursed through him, causing his hands to tremble violently.

He *dared* to question their worship? His *authority*?

However, the boy was right. Alex did not deserve to rot in prison for the crimes of another man. Despite everything he had said, underneath the pomp and ceremony he was fully aware they were crimes, not sacrifices. It amused him, really, to think of how easily his followers had wanted to believe their fortunes could be turned by uttering a few prayers to nature, singing songs around a fire.

He paused, reconsidering.

Perhaps there was something in it, after all. He had thought himself lucky to go unobserved as he had entered and left Megan's pitiful apartment but had it been luck? Perhaps it had been ordained.

Power, the heady feeling of it, overwhelmed him and he remained a little longer sitting in the quiet square savouring the feeling. He had not intended Megan as a sacrifice, or at least not in any religious sense, but perhaps he hadn't appreciated the full import of his actions.

Only now did it occur to him that Megan had been his offering and the beauty of it almost brought tears to eyes which shone with madness and renewed purpose.

The Master always demanded more.

CHAPTER 15

December 23rd

DS Frank Phillips was up with the tides. His dark grey suit was freshly dry-cleaned courtesy of the merry widow who was his present landlady, Mrs Rigby. He ummed and ahhed a moment over his tie selection and eventually settled on one decorated in varying shades of neon. He had acquired it from a museum of modern art and so he liked to think it lent him an air of cultured sophistication.

Today would be interesting, he thought as he nodded a cheerful goodbye to Pete, who had taken the trouble to get out of bed at that unsociable hour to provide a hard-working officer of the law with a bacon sandwich and a cup of sugary tea. He hadn't seen MacKenzie, which meant that she was either running late or—and he suspected this was the case—running *ahead* of schedule and was already sitting at Ryan's table drinking his questionable coffee.

He tried not to feel bothered by it, or her.

The island was quite a sight in the grey-blue hues of a winter morning, he thought as he shrugged into his long overcoat and headed towards the centre of the village. In a spontaneous departure from his usual path, Frank found himself practically skipping down the flight of wooden stairs which led to the sandy beach which ran along the base of the cliff on which the Priory stood. It curved east towards the castle and the harbour and west towards the causeway and Ryan's place.

He headed west, not minding the sand which stuck to the sides of his polished work shoes, or the fact that the scenic route would take him twice as long.

He was whistling a show tune from *Oklahoma* which proclaimed the start of a beautiful morning—though he would have strenuously denied it—when he saw the vicar running towards him. Phillips envied the man's discipline; they were of a similar age but rather than jogging off his middle-aged paunch like the good vicar, he was already regretting the hefty sandwich that sat heavily in his stomach.

He raised a hand in greeting, then lowered it when he realised that Ingles wasn't so much jogging as sprinting full pelt. Looking closer, he could see the man's expression was one of profound dismay.

"Detective, thank goodness," the man huffed as he grew closer, his face a mottled mixture of pale skin drawn with shock and pink spots from his exertion.

"Reverend Ingles. What's happened, man?" Phillips wanted to give him a bracing slap on the shoulder but thought it would be improper.

"B...b...back there," Ingles started to shiver and seemed to have trouble getting his words out as he tried to catch his breath.

"What's back there?"

Phillips glanced over the taller man's shoulder and could see nothing except more sand and dunes.

"Two, three hundred yards back that way," Ingles shuddered. "I was jogging." Phillips mentally counted to ten.

"Pull yourself together, Ingles. What's back there?"

"I'm sorry," the reverend said. "There's an inlet in the dunes. There's a big stack of wood left over from a bonfire the other night and in the middle of it...in the middle..." he doubled over and braced his hands on his knees before taking a couple of deep breaths. "There's a body."

Phillips' jaw fell. If there was another body, Alex Walker would have to be Houdini to have pulled that one off.

"Who is it?"

The vicar's face contorted.

"I could hardly stand to look but," he took several more deep breaths, "there wasn't any face left. I couldn't make out who it was."

Phillips looked heavenward and gave the other man a rap on the shoulder after all.

"Go on back to the vicarage. Mind you don't speak to anyone about this, give as few details to Mrs Ingles as possible. There'll be an officer along to take a full statement."

Phillips watched the vicar run back along the beach towards the village as if the hounds of hell were after him. At another time, he might have laughed. Instead, he walked slowly onward, eyes tracking for footprints in the sand. After a few minutes tracing the outline of the dunes, he turned a corner and for the first time in over twenty years on the force, threw up his breakfast.

* * *

When the call came through from Phillips, Ryan told the team already milling around his cottage to stand by. The causeway would open in thirty minutes; he had his prime suspect eating cornflakes in the spare room and a crowd of baying reporters ready to pounce.

Could life get any more complicated?

Actually, it could.

He had Gregson breathing down his neck for a progress report and he strongly suspected he was developing *feelings*—he frowned at the word—for his unofficial civilian consultant, which not only stretched professional but his own personal boundaries.

Not to mention the small matter of a homicidal maniac running loose on the island.

Oh yes, he thought irritably. If Alex Walker had managed to escape and re-enter the house during the night with the sole intention of committing another bloody murder to add to his existing tally, then Ryan would sprout wings and fly.

"Faulkner, bring your team. You're with me."

When they stepped outside, the wind hit them like a slap in the face. Ryan took a moment to gather his wits before striding towards the dunes.

As Ryan looked upon the grisly remains of another poor soul, he reflected that he had seen cruelty before. As recently as yesterday, he had seen the destruction of two women who had only really just started to live. But today, the perpetrator had outdone himself.

The remains of what must have been a rudimentary funeral pyre lay scattered in a charred wooden heap in a sheltered inlet of the dunes overlooking the causeway. Amid the pyre lay the unrecognisable body of what once had been a man, burnt and battered, skin flayed black. Stepping closer, Ryan wrinkled his nose against the lingering smell of burnt flesh and forced himself to look closer. The arms and legs had been tied down with wire at the ankles and wrists to a large wooden structure, now vastly reduced. The jaw was closed, indicating some sort of restraint across the mouth.

Otherwise, they would surely have heard his screams.

Ryan realised that this had been the bonfire he had seen on the beach the night before. Eyes darkened with fury, he stepped back again and recognised the shape of the wood as something he had seen before in one of the books Anna had shown him.

It was a pentagram.

"Who is he?" Ryan asked Phillips, who hovered a few metres away, still shaken by his earlier loss of control.

Phillips was fairly sure Ryan was referring to the victim. He stepped forward with a plastic evidence bag.

"Found these folded over there," he pointed to a spot a few metres back from the pyre, currently sporting a bright yellow marker left by the CSIs. "Have a look at the coat."

Ryan exchanged a look with Phillips and opened the bag with latex-covered hands. Inside, there was a red coastguard jacket embroidered in fine gold lettering. It said 'Rob Fowler'.

Ryan thrust the bag back at Phillips and paced away to look out towards the mainland, fists bunched in his pockets. Another life pointlessly taken, he thought angrily. Another family devastated.

Why? he thought. *Where was the pattern?*

When he turned back, all vestiges of anger were gone. His eyes were hard and his voice was unyielding.

"Faulkner," he watched the other man's head snap up. "Report."

Tom scratched at his chin beneath the tight overalls and passed his long-suffering gaze over the remains.

"Preliminary observations indicate male, around six feet tall. Poor bloke died a long, painful death. We didn't call out Dr Walker to pronounce death, this time, given his relationship to Alex."

"Good call. The pathologist can sign off the formalities when we transport the body over to Alnwick. He died from the burns, you reckon?"

"Sure, that would have contributed, but the fire here looks like it was quite intense. He could have died from the carbon monoxide generated by the flames. Otherwise, it would be a case of eventually capitulating to heatstroke, thermal decomposition of internal organs or simple blood loss. We won't know for sure until we get the blood and tox report back, post-mortem results." Faulkner lifted a shoulder and looked back at the crumbled remains with a pitying eye. "Even then, it depends on whether we have enough of a sample. We'll get him across to the pathologist within the hour."

Ryan nodded, lips tight.

"I want a full tent erected. The press will be swarming the island today and they've got long-range lenses. I want this scene protected." He paused, eyed one of the younger CSIs. "You," Ryan jabbed a finger in his direction. "If I find any leaked pictures of this poor bastard in the evening paper, I'll know where to start looking for a rat. Understand?"

The man's head bobbed up and down. He wondered how the SIO had been able to read his mind.

Ryan eyed him for a moment longer to ensure the message had been received loud and clear and then spoke to the wider group.

"Expect the press to be creative," he said. "They're not above hiring a boat to come and get a close-up from the water. Phillips, I want a barrier spanning the dunes from there," he pointed to a spot twenty metres further down the sand, "cutting across to there," he traced his finger over to the wooden steps used to access the beach.

Phillips nodded. "Aye, I'll see to it."

"I want two men on the tent at all times," Ryan couldn't spare any more than that and the lack of resources irritated him.

"Got it," Phillips nodded again.

"No, Frank. Get someone to handle all that. I want you with me in interview."

Ryan checked his watch and swore softly. The water had all but melted away and he saw the first eager cars speed across the far side of the mainland, ready to get a scoop. Amongst them would be Alex Walker's solicitor.

"Let's get a move on," he said.

"You can't be looking at Walker now, can you?" Phillips asked as they walked briskly back to the cottage that was their temporary base.

Ryan stopped, turned to him and his black hair flew around his face in the wind.

"Walker has no alibi, he's lied in his statements to the police and we found material evidence on his property. I'm looking at every fucking thing, Frank. Then I'm looking at it again and again until we find the person responsible." His eyes were fierce. "Don't think that just because Walker was under lock and key last night, he didn't kill those women."

* * *

When Ryan and Phillips got back to the cottage, they saw two unfamiliar cars in the driveway. Both were German, expensive and polished to a high sheen. Letting himself in, Ryan could sense the charged atmosphere and prepared himself for further drama.

"You'll do as you are commanded by a superior officer." Gregson's unmistakable voice boomed out, filling the four walls of the house.

"Sir," MacKenzie replied, "I am under strict instructions not to discuss anything further until DCI Ryan's return."

Ryan took a moment to appreciate the loyalty of his staff and then stepped into the room.

"Sir." He nodded respectfully to Gregson. "Is there a problem?"

Gregson sent a fulminating glare towards Detective MacKenzie. "Just insubordination."

Ryan tried not to smile. Looking at Denise MacKenzie, he could almost see the Irish curses hovering over her head.

"DI MacKenzie is operating under my command and therefore any complaint can be laid at my door."

Gregson rolled his eyes but secretly approved of his DCI's calm approach under fire. MacKenzie took her cue and melted away.

"For God's sake," Gregson ground out. "All I want is a status report."

"Sir, I appreciate that and I will be happy to provide you with one. Unfortunately, another incident, likely murder, was reported forty minutes ago. Prior to that—"

"Walker's solicitor is conferring with his client upstairs," Gregson interjected. "Are you going to tell me he was arrested without cause?"

"No, sir, I'm not telling you that." Ryan took a breath and leapt in. "At the time of his arrest yesterday evening, Alex Walker had made certain false statements to the police and we found material evidence on his property following a search which was warranted through the appropriate channels. He has been unable to provide an alibi for the murders of both women and has been unable to provide an explanation for the items we found—Lucy Mathieson's missing clothes and mobile phone," he added.

Gregson nodded. "By the book?"

"Everything has been done according to relevant protocols, sir. The suspect has been provided with food and water, comfortable facilities and access to medical care. The unusual geography of the island has prevented us from questioning Walker before now but if his solicitor has arrived I will proceed with questioning."

"Good," Gregson took a drink of his coffee and frowned. "This coffee tastes like shit. Get yourself a machine."

"Yes, sir."

"Has he got previous?"

"No, sir," Ryan replied. The standard background check had not disclosed any criminal record.

"I had Walker Senior on the phone to me late last night," Gregson said irritably. "Complained that he had been refused access to see his son."

Ryan raised an eyebrow.

"Doctor Walker was refused access, rightly in my opinion, owing to his previous involvement assisting our investigation. Furthermore, I felt it was in the best interests of the investigation for Alex Walker not to discuss his story with anyone except ourselves, sir."

Gregson smiled in a somewhat fatherly fashion.

"Good lad." He thrust the mug of coffee at Ryan. "I'll handle the press, give them nothing but the basics. We've set up the conference for eleven-thirty in the main square."

Ryan felt a cowardly relief. He hated nothing more than talking to reporters.

Gregson watched Ryan closely. A dazed expression came into the man's eyes for a moment and his skin looked clammy.

"Ryan," he said firmly and waited for him to snap out of his daydream.

"Sir."

"I never got that GP's report, did I?"

Ryan's teeth snapped together. In the space of forty-eight hours, there had been a body down on the beach, two more in the morgue and Gregson was worried about a bit of paper?

Gregson read his thoughts effortlessly.

"It can wait," he decided. "But tie this up now, Ryan, and do it fast."

CHAPTER 16

Ryan and Phillips cleared out the Incident Room and set up a folding table and four chairs with a tape recorder in the middle alongside a jug of water. Walker and his solicitor seated themselves on one side of the table, Phillips on the other.

Ryan preferred to stand.

He looked at Walker, who was sitting confidently with his arms folded and hair gelled. He realised that it was probably his own gel which had been sitting in the upstairs bathroom which currently graced the blonde head. Walker's solicitor was a trim woman in her mid-forties with neat brown hair and a classy navy suit. Her small hands were folded calmly. All of which told him that neither the man nor his counsel were particularly concerned by Walker's predicament.

Ryan would change that.

He turned on a small recorder and stated the date and time as well as the names of those present. He repeated the standard caution.

"Are you aware of your rights?"

Walker glanced at his solicitor.

"Yes," he answered and Ryan smiled cheerfully.

"Good, let's get started then."

"Chief Inspector, my client would like to state for the record that the manner of his detention is not consistent with the requirements set out in the Police and Criminal Evidence Act."

So, they wanted to play around? That was fine, Ryan thought.

"In what way?"

"He has not been held in an appropriate place of detention."

"This building has been properly authorised as a place of detention."

"By whom?"

"The Commanding Officer of CID, Detective Chief Superintendent Arthur Gregson." He recited Gregson's departmental reference number and held out a copy of the signed paperwork faxed through by Gregson's office the night before.

"This should have been included in standard pre-interview disclosure."

"No," Ryan said calmly. "We are required to inform you of the lines of questioning we are likely to pursue, along with the evidence held against your client which led to his arrest. At no time did we intend to discuss the manner of his detention; that was your decision."

The solicitor shoved the paper in her folder.

"Do you intend to waste any more time or can we get down to business?" Ryan braced his hands on the back of a chair and leaned forward slightly. He pinned her with his stare and watched a blush creep up her skin.

"The custody officer should have made a determination about whether to charge my client long before now. Failing that, he should have been released on bail."

"There were reasonable grounds for believing it was necessary to detain your client," he eyed the man sitting next to her, who looked significantly less confident as the minutes wore on, "without bail or charge in order to secure evidence or obtain it during questioning. Our reasoning is detailed on the requisite form, a copy of which you were provided with on your arrival this morning."

"Well…"

"Stop wasting all of our time," he said quietly. "The sooner we can ask our questions, the better for your client."

She folded her arms mutinously.

"Now, let's start again," Ryan folded his long body into a chair now. He placed one hand on the folder laid out in front of him and stared into the bold green eyes of Alex Walker.

"In your statement of 21st December," Ryan retrieved a copy of it, although he knew the words by heart. "You state that you knew Lucy Mathieson only as another member of the island community. To be precise, 'as a girl you'd seen around the island' and 'hardly knew'. Is that correct?"

Walker swallowed and nodded.

"Please speak up for the record," Ryan said.

"Yes, that's correct," Walker said with an edge to his voice.

"Good. Later on that same day, around eight-thirty outside the Jolly Anchor you held a discussion with myself as the Senior Investigating Officer where you retracted those statements. Is that correct?"

"My client had not been made aware of his rights and obligations before making any such statements," his solicitor swooped in.

Ryan was unperturbed. He leaned back in his chair and carried on looking at Walker.

"You are aware of those rights now, as we've already established. Let's go over it one more time, then, for the record this time. Do you deny that you had a personal, intimate relationship with Lucy Mathieson?"

Walker was the first to look away.

"No."

"Fine then," Ryan smiled his cheerful smile. "Can you explain why you did not include the fact in your original statement?"

"I forgot."

Ryan had to laugh but he took out another bundle of documents.

"Here, I have copies of sworn statements provided by staff members of the Theatre Royal in Newcastle, at the Union Bar at Newcastle University, at the Golden Dragon restaurant..." He flipped through the sheaf of papers faxed through from officers working CID in Newcastle. "They all confirm they saw you with Lucy Mathieson on separate dates through the summer. Did you forget all that?"

"It must have slipped my mind."

Ryan removed one of the statements.

"This statement was provided to us by a well-known member of the Lindisfarne community. It states that they observed you in an intimate exchange with the deceased here on the island very recently. Does that jog your memory?"

Walker struggled to swallow.

"I have a busy life, I meet a lot of people. I don't remember meeting Lucy recently."

"How long have you lived on Lindisfarne, Alex?"

"What is the relevance of that question, Chief Inspector?" the solicitor chirped up.

He didn't bother to look at her. "Pertains to the line of questioning. Answer me, Alex."

He looked nervously at his solicitor and his chin wobbled.

"I've lived here my whole life."

"I'm sorry, I didn't quite catch that."

"My whole life!" he burst out, then closed his mouth quickly.

"Thank you. Ms Mathieson was also born and raised on Lindisfarne. Are you aware of the population of the island?"

"No." He *was* aware.

"Just over two hundred," Ryan supplied helpfully. "Do you agree that your position as coastguard on the island makes you a recognisable figure, even amongst such a small population?"

"How should I know?"

Ryan let the silence hang.

"All right—yes!"

Ryan smiled inwardly. The golden boy was soft as a peach.

"Do you also agree that, as such a recognisable figure, within a small population and a close-knit community, an islander would be unlikely to mistake you for someone else?"

"Could have seen the red jacket and mistaken me for someone else," Alex thought with a flash of inspiration.

"Indeed, they could," Ryan said agreeably, "except that, in this case, they saw you without a jacket. In fact," he looked up the relevant passage and quoted from it, "our witness states that they saw you, 'in the buff, around the back of the lighthouse, going at it like rabbits'."

Ryan thought momentarily of his love for northerners and their unique turn of phrase but his face was neutral. Walker looked worried now and turned to his solicitor.

"My client would like a moment to confer."

"No problem," Ryan said and stopped the recording after reciting the time. "Five minutes," he said to both of them before he and Phillips left the room.

Outside, Phillips turned to him.

"I don't understand why he's drawing this all out." Phillips tugged at his tie to loosen it. "Why not just admit that he banged the girl before she died and move on?"

"He's scared."

* * *

Five minutes later, they re-entered the kitchen-diner and took their seats.

"Ready to proceed?" Ryan asked politely.

"My client would like to make a statement regarding his relationship with Lucy Mathieson," the solicitor said primly.

"We're all ears," Ryan said, before switching on the tape recorder and turning to Walker with an expectant look on his face.

The other man shuffled in his chair before he eventually reiterated what he had told Ryan outside the pub the previous night.

"Thank you," Ryan nodded. "Can you tell me why you have been so uncooperative in confirming those simple facts? Please be aware that inferences can be made from a refusal to answer when questioned."

Walker paled again.

"I had my reasons," he muttered.

"You're going to need to share those with us, son," Phillips interjected in his conversational way. "So far, you've told us that you went straight home alone after the pub on the 20th and nobody saw you after then until you re-joined the coastguard with Pete at 5am the following morning of the 21st and came along to help guard the scene at the Priory."

"Then, you can't tell us where you were between 4.30pm and 7pm on the 21st, which coincides with the time period when Megan Taylor lost her life. It doesn't look good, does it?"

Ryan couldn't have put it better himself and so he merely cocked his head at Alex and waited for a response. Walker was looking distinctly uncomfortable and his styled hair was sagging already.

"I've told you, I was at home a…a…asleep in bed when Lucy was killed," his voice wobbled. "The first I heard of it was when you rang me in the morning." He turned appealing eyes towards Ryan.

"My client has already confirmed his whereabouts that night, any further badgering on that topic will constitute harassment," the dutiful solicitor said.

"Thanks for your input," Ryan said mildly, thinking that they both knew there were no grounds whatsoever for any suggestion of harassment. He turned back to Alex.

"I was at the pub yesterday afternoon," Alex offered. "Remember? You saw me there," once again his eyes appealed to Ryan for confirmation.

"Sure," Ryan shrugged his shoulders. "I saw you around eight-thirty. We have confirmation that you were there from around seven. What we don't know is where you were before then, Alex."

"I visited my family," he said desperately.

"I know that's what you claim, however when one of our officers questioned your mother," he glanced at his papers briefly, "Yvonne Walker, she could not confirm. In fact, she said she hadn't seen you all day."

Walker swallowed and said nothing.

"You really should talk to your parents before trying to incriminate them in false statements made to the police," Phillips tutted.

Walker's hands clutched at the table.

"My dad—it was him I saw. I meant to say that I saw him."

Ryan just shook his head. "Doctor Walker was out doing his rounds all afternoon, which has been confirmed by several members of the island community."

"I didn't kill anybody, ok?" Walker's voice started to rise in panic.

"Where were you, Alex?"

Walker dropped his head in his hands.

"I can't...I can't tell you. You'd never believe me."

"Try me," Ryan offered, leaning forward to create a sense of confidence.

When Alex raised his head again, his face was miserable.

"Please...you can't tell anybody. Please."

"I can't make that promise, Alex, but I will treat the information you give me with respect."

"I was with Rob," he whispered in a voice that was almost inaudible.

Phillips and Ryan exchanged a quick look and a sharp shake of heads to confirm that the man was, as yet, unaware of Rob Fowler's death. Ryan treaded carefully, interested to hear what Alex would say.

"By 'Rob', you are referring to Robert Fowler, the coastguard volunteer?"

"Yes."

"So, you were with Rob. Doing what?" Phillips asked innocently.

Three heads turned to look at him. After a moment, Phillips' baffled expression changed to embarrassment.

"Ah..." He shuffled papers and looked like he wished the ground would swallow him up. The gay porn they'd found in Walker's house made a lot more sense now.

Ryan took the helm again.

"You were with Rob Fowler, intimately, on the dates and times in question?"

"Yes." Walker looked beaten and Ryan began to feel sorry for him, before remembering he had a job to do.

"How long were you and Mr Fowler in a relationship?" Ryan wondered if the other man would pick up on the past tense.

"On and off, around six years." Walker didn't notice any subtleties.

Ryan's eyebrows rose.

"Throughout your marriage and whilst you were 'seeing' Lucy Mathieson?"

"Yes," Walker admitted in the same monotone.

"Would you describe yourself as bisexual?"

"Yes," Alex nodded tiredly.

"Mr Fowler was comfortable with this?" Past tense, again.

Alex shuffled. "No, not really. He tolerates it because he knows I'm no good with commitment. Rob's never, you know, been with a woman. Kissed a few but he realised pretty early on that he wasn't interested. I'm different, I suppose. I never really had a preference. He finds that hard to accept."

Ryan flipped through his folder and retrieved Rob Fowler's statement of events from the evening of 20th December and early 21st. He skim read for a few moments and then raised cool grey eyes again.

"Mr Fowler states that he was on duty throughout the early hours of the 21st."

"Technically, he was. He started his shift when mine ended, around eleven. He did an hour or so down at the station. I had a couple of pints in the pub and then went to see him. We had the place to ourselves."

"What time did you head home?"

"Must have been after one," Alex said vaguely.

"Your route home would have taken you past the Priory," Phillips commented, beating Ryan to it.

"Yeah, it did."

"You didn't see anyone en route?" Ryan listened closely to the next answer. At around one in the morning, their killer would likely have been killing or transporting Lucy's body.

Walker screwed up his face in concentration, which caused his mop of blonde hair to rise and fall like a comedy wig. Ryan tried not to notice.

"I don't remember seeing anyone but to be completely honest with you, Ryan, I was tired and still a bit drunk. It was dark, too. They don't spring for streetlights here." He paused. "I think I remember hearing a boat or a car somewhere over the other side of the Priory—the hilly side—but that's about it."

"What makes you think it was a boat?"

"Sounded like an engine spluttering," Walker said.

That made three people commenting on a boat or car engine around that time and near the access point the CSIs had located. Ryan filed it away.

"Why would Mr Fowler omit to tell us that he spent part of his evening with you?"

"Because I asked him to keep our relationship private and, I suppose, because he was in violation of his duty." Walker took a deep breath before speaking. "I've never been comfortable with that side to my sexuality."

Ryan sighed. This wasn't a chat show and he wasn't Oprah.

"What about yesterday afternoon?"

"I had been helping out manning the Priory entrance during the morning, actually until around lunchtime. Rob had been working the traffic block with Mark. You know all that. I met up with Rob around quarter to five and we went back to my place. We both went for a drink down at the pub around seven."

"Are your parents aware of your relationship with Mr Fowler?"

"No. They'd never understand. They're just outdated," he explained. "My parents are good people, Ryan, but the reason they live so well on Lindisfarne is because old-fashioned values agree with them. I'm all they have and I've already let them down by not becoming a doctor." He ran a hand through his hair. "I was never any good at science and I feel queasy at the sight of blood."

Walker looked up and let out a half-laugh.

"You don't have to believe me," he shrugged it off, tired all of a sudden. "The only other thing my parents always wanted was for me to find a nice girl and settle down. They loved Anna, so naturally I pushed her away. They hated Megan, which made it easy for me not to settle down," his smile became slightly lopsided. "In the end, I hated her too. She knew about Rob," he added.

His solicitor, who had been listening avidly much in the same way she enjoyed watching her favourite evening soap opera, stirred herself enough to put a warning hand on her client's arm.

"No," he shrugged her off. "I want to tell them." He turned back. "You're the only people I've ever told."

"You've just said that Megan Taylor knew of your relationship with Rob," Phillips prompted.

"She walked in on us one night," he admitted. "She called us names, terrible names, and said I disgusted her." Walker stopped to take a shaky sip of his water. "We weren't...that is to say *I* wasn't ready for people to know. I had to pay her to keep quiet about it."

"Ms Taylor blackmailed you?"

"Bled me dry," Alex muttered, then raised horrified eyes at his unfortunate choice of words. "That is—"

Ryan just looked at him. "Did you stop by Megan's place on the 22nd?" He already had Anna's statement of events which told him that Walker had been there around four-thirty but he wanted to hear it from the man himself.

Alex let out a breath. "Yes, I did. Around four-fifteen, maybe a bit after, I went over there to try reasoning with her, like I did every time a payment was due," he said bitterly.

"What did she say?"

"Same old," Alex lifted a shoulder and let it fall. "She liked to say that the money I paid her was a kind of compensation for all the pain and suffering I caused her. Load of crap," he added with feeling.

"Did you notice anything unusual?"

"Not really. I thought she would be at work but she was lounging around her flat. She didn't seem unwell or anything. She looked like she was primping," he said.

"Primping?" Phillips queried.

"Yeah, she was covered in perfume, fancy red underwear was lying on the bed, that sort of thing," Alex supplied.

"You think she was going out?"

Alex's mouth flattened. "Megan didn't always have to be going out to get dolled up like that."

Phillips and Ryan nodded, understanding.

"Did you run into anyone else around that time?" Ryan asked casually.

Alex looked confused for a moment and then his face cleared.

"Yeah, I did actually. Bill was changing the barrels, so he was in and out of the courtyard around then. We said 'hello' and that," he took another sip of water. "I ran into Anna. I saw her up at the top of the stairs chatting with her sister, around half past four, so I thought I'd wait until she'd finished. I didn't want her knowing I was on my way up there."

Ryan nodded and felt a wave of relief. Megan had been alive when Anna had left her, at least. He didn't want to add Anna's name to his list of suspects.

"Do you remember what was said between you?"

"Sure," Alex nodded. "Anna ran into me having a cig in the courtyard. Could use one now," he added hopefully, but his plea fell on deaf ears. He continued, "It was a bit awkward, to be honest."

"How so?" This was pure curiosity, Ryan admitted to himself.

"She and I used to be together, years ago when we were kids."

"Uh huh," Ryan nodded. "Until you slept with her sister."

Alex had the grace to look abashed.

"Gotta get me some of your aftershave, son," Phillips remarked with a grin, quickly extinguished.

"It was for the best," Alex said in his defence. "I could never have made Anna happy."

It was on the tip of Ryan's tongue to agree with him but he managed to control himself.

"You didn't have many reasons to like Megan Taylor," Ryan said instead, thinking that he would run a check on Megan Taylor's bank accounts at the earliest opportunity. If she had been fleecing Walker, who was to say she hadn't been squeezing a few other people?

Alex took the meaning straight away. "Look, she was vindictive," he said, leaning forward again. "I've told you, I ended up hating her for it, but I didn't kill her. Rob can tell you I was with him from around quarter to five until around seven, when we stopped in at the pub again."

Ryan thought that Alex could still have killed Megan Taylor around four-thirty, just after Anna left her sister, but it would have been a push. He took pity on him in more ways than one. The time had come to put their cards on the table.

"I'm afraid Mr Fowler will be unable to confirm your whereabouts on either occasion, Alex. I regret to inform you that Robert Fowler was found dead earlier this morning."

Every ounce of blood drained from the other man's face.

"You're...you're lying!" he thrust upwards, over the table, to grab at Ryan's shirt. Ryan put a restraining hand on each of the man's arms but that was all. He had seen the grief, the terror and disbelief.

"I'm sorry."

Alex fell back into his chair and Ryan watched him fall apart. Gone was the cocky look in those twinkling cat eyes, replaced with a deep sorrow which was only really beginning. Walker hugged himself to fend off the chill in an otherwise heated room. Tears fell openly down his face, unchecked.

Several minutes passed, during which time the tape was stopped and refreshment was offered along with a few moments' privacy.

In that time, Ryan had also decided that Alex Walker was not his man. The evidence they had found reeked of a plant.

"Did anyone else know of your relationship with Mr Fowler?"

"No...that is, Kim does. It's the reason she's divorcing me." Ryan held off commenting that, given the man's record on infidelity, Rob Fowler was probably the least of his wife's worries. Instead, he made a note to contact Kim Walker for confirmation of Alex and Rob's relationship. It added weight to the growing belief that Walker wasn't their man.

"Megan does. *Did* know about us," Walker continued, dragging a hand over his eyes which were red and swollen.

"Would she have told anyone?"

"I was paying her not to. I don't know if she would have kept her word but since I never heard any gossip about us, I assume she did."

"What about your parents, Alex?" Ryan's voice was almost gentle. He knew a broken man when he saw one.

"No, I never told them."

"Why?"

"I told you before, they're conservative people. They have a certain idea about me, about marriage and grandkids one day. I think," he scrubbed at his eyes again. "I think I married Kim to keep them quiet. I've never seen my mother so happy. Rob was my best man." Tears started to fall again and his body shuddered.

"Do you know of anyone who would wish Mr Fowler harm?"

Alex shook his head. "No, never. He was so gentle. Nobody would ever want to hurt him." Walker smiled into the distance, remembering.

"Are there any individuals on the island who have spoken out against homosexuality?"

Walker started to shake his head again and then reconsidered.

"You might get a few comments from the kids. You know, 'that's gay', 'you're gay'." Alex shrugged it off. "Mostly, it's harmless chat from a bunch of kids who haven't lived enough of life to know any better."

He paused again, thinking back.

"There was one thing. I remember Rob was upset about it." Tears threatened again but were held back by willpower alone. "It was a couple of months ago. We went along to the Sunday church service—separately—with our families. Reverend Ingles said a few things which cut a bit close to the bone."

"What did he say?"

"Managed to include some long-winded quotes about man not lying with another man. Leviticus, I think. He more or less said he was pleased the island wasn't 'plagued' with mortal sinners but the few who were out there would be forgiven by God."

"Do you know if he was referring to anyone in particular?"

"No idea. We just hoped it wasn't us." Walker looked away, through the window out across the sea, before he turned back to them.

Ryan changed track.

"Who else would have access to your fishing hut, Alex?"

The other man appeared to think for a few minutes and Ryan was on the verge of asking his question again, when Walker finally spoke.

"You don't understand the way this island works, Ryan. Everybody knows everybody; people know where you'll be, what's yours and where you live." He turned to them. "Practically everybody would know which one's my hut and that I never padlock it. A twelve-year-old could unpick the lock on that thing."

Ryan said nothing but angled his head.

"One other thing, Alex," he fixed the man with a stare and watched for any ticks. "What was Lucy wearing the night she died?"

Alex screwed his face in concentration.

"What relevance does this have, Chief Inspector?" the solicitor roused herself from her slumber.

Ryan merely held up one finger, telling her to wait. She bristled.

"God, I..." Walker scrubbed his eyes. "I can't remember. Maybe jeans and a bright top?" He looked up hopefully.

"What colour?"

Alex shook his head desperately. "I really don't remember."

Ryan nodded and looked down at his paperwork.

"Tell me how he died." Alex said quietly.

Ryan turned off the recorder, stood and put a hand on the man's shoulder for support.

"Don't ask me that, Walker. Do yourself a favour and get some rest. We'll be releasing you without charge."

* * *

After Walker left with his parents and all the paperwork was done, Phillips turned to his superior with some surprise.

"I know it's a sorry tale of Brokeback Mountain romance but just because he shed a few tears over Fowler doesn't mean he didn't do those women. He admitted Megan Taylor was blackmailing him and he might have wanted to pop Lucy off because she was starting to get clingy."

Ryan smiled grimly.

"That's why I've assigned two men to watch him. This way, he's relaxed. He thinks the worst is over."

Phillips shook his head, partly in admiration and partly fearing the shard of ice lodged somewhere in the heart of the tall man standing next to him.

"Still doesn't explain Fowler."

"No, Frank, it doesn't."

CHAPTER 17

At eleven-thirty, Anna stood amongst the crowd that had gathered in the main square, listening to DCS Gregson giving a statement to the press. A small platform had been raised just in front of the statue of St Cuthbert and a crowd of local and national reporters fired out questions while their cameras rolled. Roads were blocked from the village to the causeway by vans and cars. Local hotels that hadn't already reached capacity with police guests were now overflowing with cameramen and reporters. For once, the tourists fought to gain entry.

Amid the spectacle, the Priory stood, unchanging and unmoving as before.

"The Northumbria Police Constabulary is working hard to bring justice to the families of those who have lost their loved ones in these tragic and senseless crimes. We want to assure those families that we have our best men and women investigating. We are sparing no resource in our hunt for the person or persons responsible." Gregson was authoritative, a man of the people who had a habit of command. Every intonation in his voice was designed to build trust in those who listened.

"Is it true these are ritual murders?" a reporter shouted out.

"We cannot confirm or deny anything that may prejudice our investigation." Gregson favoured the short woman from the local television studio with a hard stare.

"Is it true there has been a third murder?" She didn't relent.

"I can confirm that a third person identified as Robert Fowler, a local man who worked as a volunteer coastguard and fisherman, was found dead this morning. We are investigating and our condolences go out to his family."

Several voices shouted out at once.

"Is it true that a suspect has been released without charge? Do you have any other suspects?"

"The investigative team can and will question individuals where appropriate."

"Is it true that the police have no other leads?"

"The CID team are pursuing all leads and will continue to work quickly to bring the person or persons responsible to justice," Gregson reiterated firmly.

"Are the three murders connected?"

"The CID team are treating these crimes as linked," Gregson confirmed shortly. They would know that already.

"Is it true that DCI Ryan is heading the investigation?" one smart-mouthed little weasel shouted out and was pleased to see the consternation on Gregson's face. "Do you really feel he is competent to lead, given the events following the *Hacker*?"

Away from the platform, Ryan felt his stomach sink. Gregson turned to him with a question in his eyes and Ryan nodded. His hands were sweaty and his knees wanted to shake but when he stepped up to the platform to face the cameras and the questions, he was in control.

In charge of himself and his team.

Gregson moved smoothly away from the microphone as Ryan stepped forward.

There was an unusual hush. Many of the reporters recognised him instantly as the tall, handsome detective who had taken over the *Hacker* case earlier that summer. The aptly-named '*Hacker*' made a habit of slashing his victims, cutting them apart with surgical precision. At the beginning of the investigation, the press had seen Ryan at the top of his game, appearing before them in sharp suits, speaking to them in his usual articulate but concise manner. He had brought fresh energy and sparked new confidence in an investigation that had dragged on for months without any apparent leads.

By the end of it, they had seen him battered, broken and bloodied. Ryan had brought the *Hacker* to justice but only after he had stalked and killed Ryan's own sister. Although the national papers had been offered paparazzi photographs of Ryan as he'd been carried out of the house where Natalie had been found, along with her killer, they had chosen not to print them.

Even the toughest hacks had a heart.

Now, they saw a harder man, a colder one perhaps, but the light in his eyes had returned. If they had questions, he would answer them.

"Good afternoon," Ryan began in his velvet-smooth voice. "I can confirm that I have returned to full duty after a period of voluntary sabbatical leave."

Everything inside him screamed and the faces of the crowd blurred for a moment, then his gaze locked with Anna's. She was near the back of the crowd but she stood out. In that instant, he noticed everything about her. The rich fall of hair rippling over one shoulder beneath her woolly hat. The bloom in her cheeks and pink tinge to her nose, which had reacted to the cold weather. The unswerving, forthright look in her dark eyes which seemed to demand that he say whatever he had to say.

"As many of you will be aware, the *Hacker* investigation closed six months ago. I will always grieve for my sister," he said honestly, feeling the truth of it burn through his system. "However, life must move on. That being the case, I would remind you that I have over fifteen years on the force, firstly working with the Metropolitan Police and the last twelve years in Newcastle and Northumbria. I have worked on numerous serious crime investigations and was appointed Chief Inspector two years ago. In that short time and with the help of an excellent team of staff and colleagues, we have closed fifty-seven cases with successful prosecutions."

It was an excellent statistic and he knew it. If they were going to question his competence, then the press should know it too.

"With that record, I am confident that our investigative team, comprised of some of the force's finest men and women, will conduct itself with all expedition to bring justice to the families of those who have been robbed of their loved ones."

His eyes moved away from Anna's and scanned the crowd, passed over a number of people he recognised. It crossed his mind that the perpetrator was likely to be one of them.

He looked squarely into the crowd, as if speaking to the killer. "To the person responsible, I say this: we can and will find you. There is nowhere safe for you now. We will continue to hunt you until there won't be a corner of this island or this country that can shelter you. That's it."

Ryan left the words hanging and stepped down. Reporters and cameramen surged forward to get a picture of him shaking hands with Gregson, to get a few more soundbites for the evening news. Anna turned away and began to walk back through the crowd. Several pairs of eyes watched her progress.

* * *

Among the crush of people, a man shivered and huddled further into his coat.

They knew, he thought frantically, eyes darting from side to side.

They were watching him.

His fevered mind saw police officers in full uniform around every corner. He caught the eyes of some of them.

We know it was you, they seemed to say.

His hands began to shake. Why hadn't they charged Walker? They must have found Lucy's clothes by now. Why hadn't they charged him?

His eyes fell on the tall figure of the Chief Inspector, who stood solemnly on the platform looking like an avenging angel with his black hair blowing around his face. He shivered again as Ryan's words rang out into the crowd.

We will hunt you…there is nowhere to shelter you…

The woman hanging on his arm began to rub his fingers, mistaking fear for cold. He smiled down into her expectant face but sweat ran cold and clammy down his back.

* * *

Another man watched the proceedings from the edge of the crowd, his face carefully schooled into a grave mask. He nodded politely to his friends and neighbours. Earlier, he had offered a heartfelt embrace to the woman who had lost her only son that morning and had sat and consoled with another family who had lost their only daughter.

He had felt invincible, divine.

He listened to the words of the Superintendent and nearly smiled. He had to remind himself to keep his face blank but oh, how he wanted to laugh. He wanted to soar, high and far above the little people who stood around him wittering like the idiots they were.

They thought they could hunt him.

They knew nothing.

His gaze passed briefly over DCI Ryan and he felt the anger building inside him, rising and ready to erupt.

Ignorant, arrogant fool, he thought while his fists clenched.

Grasping for control, he looked away again and felt his blood cool. He met the eyes of the woman standing beside him, pretty as a picture in her navy winter coat and he smiled.

He was still smiling when he turned back to meet the eyes of his hunter.

* * *

"Ryan? With me," Arthur Gregson barked out the order and moved swiftly through the crowd to his vehicle. He ushered Ryan inside before the cameramen could follow.

The car moved off slowly but the department had sprung for blacked-out windows, so Ryan could feel reasonably comfortable that the flashes of cameras wouldn't have much effect. He resented the fact that he was forced to hide while a murderer roamed free.

"Stop brooding," Gregson said forcibly and, without a thought for social proprieties, lit a fat cigar. He took a couple of long puffs to soothe his nerves. Even he wasn't immune to the pressures of the media. "You did well out there. Came across strong, met the criticism head-on. Especially liked your monologue to the killer," Gregson puffed his cigar and let out a wheeze.

"Thank you, sir." His hand had been forced, Ryan thought. He hadn't had time to tell Anna about any of it personally, but now she knew.

"He's got us on the run," Gregson carried on, his eyes narrowed. "That has to change."

"We're doing everything we can, sir."

Gregson waved that away. "Am I blind? It isn't me that you have to convince, it's them." He jerked an angry thumb back towards the reporters they had left behind.

"There's hardly any physical evidence, which is a major obstacle," Ryan admitted. "CSIs are due to come back with more detailed reports today. There were prints and potential DNA evidence at Megan's crime scene. I've forwarded the report to your desk, sir. As for the ritual element, we're trying to get a handle on it."

"You know that you can't use Doctor Taylor anymore," Gregson interjected.

"Of course," Ryan agreed smoothly, his face carefully neutral.

Gregson watched his chief inspector through a haze of cigar smoke and his eyes gleamed.

"I'm glad we understand one another," he said, equally smoothly. "One of the few things in our favour is the fact that all three victims were young and good-looking. Rightly or wrongly, that will capture the public imagination a lot more than it would if it were the other way around. People always sympathise more when it's about attractive people."

Ryan may not like it, but he couldn't argue with the truth of that. How often did the press keep up with an investigation when the perpetrators or victims were old or ugly or perceived as defective in some other way?

Rarely.

"I want to get my head around this sooner rather than later. Our perp has been on a spree, but now it's time to call in the debt."

"Nicely put."

"Thank you, sir."

* * *

In her bid to escape the gaggle of people crowding the main square, Anna headed for one of the little cobbled alleyways. Sensing freedom was near, her heart jumped into her throat when a strong hand grasped her arm and pulled her back.

"Psst," said the familiar female voice. "Let's escape this way."

Anna looked back and down into Yvonne Walker's face. She was in her fifties but had the slim, well-kept build of a much younger woman. Her hair, which had been a light brown years ago, had since been darkened and stylishly cut. Her face held few lines and was flushed with good health.

"Mrs Walker? You look wonderful."

The other woman blushed with pleasure and instinctively touched a hand to her hair.

"Do you like it? I suppose I just got bored with myself," she chuckled.

Unexpected tears burned the back of Anna's throat. Yvonne Walker had been a long-time friend of her mother's and even now, Yvonne's new hair colour was a fresh reminder of a woman who was long gone.

"Darling, have I upset you?" Instantly concerned, Yvonne took Anna's hand in a motherly grip and held her close.

"No, no. It's nothing."

"Come on then," Yvonne tugged her hand and they made for one of the side roads. Anna knew the route so well she could have made the journey blindfolded.

Eventually, they came upon the large, stone-built property which housed the doctor's surgery and the Walker family home.

"Um, Mrs Walker, I don't know if Alex will really want to see me just now," she began hesitantly.

Yvonne sent her a knowing look.

"He would always like to see you, Anna. He may have made his mistakes in the past," it was always hard for a mother to admit them, Yvonne thought, "but he's grown up a lot since then. This recent *experience* will have been a shock to him as well."

"Still, I don't know—"

"You needn't worry. Alex has his own cottage nowadays."

Anna relaxed a bit and stepped into the old house. It was still lovely, she thought with a wave of nostalgia. Built in a Georgian style, the floors were wooden and polished to gleaming. Expensive, worn rugs were scattered over the floors. Family photographs covered the surfaces and tasteful art adorned the walls, which were muted, restful shades. House plants added bloom and colour to the rooms and a sense of peace.

Anna had always felt peaceful here.

"It's just as I remember," she murmured.

"Of course it is," Yvonne said briskly, shrugging out of her coat. "Let's get a cup of tea and catch up."

Five minutes later, Anna found herself seated in the slouchy sofa which stood in one of the smaller sitting rooms. A fire had been lit and was just starting to blaze. In one hand, she balanced a small plate which held an enormous slab of cake. Her other hand was occupied in trying to keep the family cat, Tennyson, from devouring that cake.

Realising that he was not in luck, the cat eventually abandoned any hope of an afternoon snack and turned to curl up at the far end of the sofa, favouring her with the view of his ginger backside.

The animal didn't need to talk for Anna to understand his meaning.

"You look marvellous," Yvonne started, after she'd kicked off her brown boots and wiggled her toes. "What have you been doing all this time?"

"Ah," Anna struggled to know where to begin. "I finished my PhD and managed to get a teaching post at the university."

"Oh, that's wonderful," Yvonne smiled warmly. "But then, we never had any doubt that you would do well."

Anna didn't know what to say. She hadn't realised that so many people had faith in her. She'd only ever had faith in herself.

"What about you and Doctor Walker?" She shaved off a slither of cake and savoured it.

Yvonne smiled. "Darling, you don't need to call him 'Doctor Walker' these days, you're a grown woman. It's just Steve and Yvonne to you."

Anna shook her head. "It feels so strange. Sometimes, I forget that I've grown up. Perhaps it's because I'm so far behind the other women my age, in many ways."

"Nonsense," Yvonne was quick to defend the girl she thought of as one of her own chicks. "You're just taking your time, being choosy, that's all."

Anna smiled down into her tea.

"Aha!" Yvonne pointed a manicured nail in her direction. "I know that look, I had it myself when I met a certain young blonde doctor, all those years ago. Spill it."

Anna lifted a shoulder and tried not to look smug.

"It's nothing to speak of, really. Just a sort of…a connection, I suppose." She frowned suddenly, thinking that she had simply assumed that he felt it too.

What if he didn't?

"That's always a good start," Yvonne commented. "Dare I ask who the lucky man is?"

"DCI Ryan," Anna was almost afraid to speak his name aloud.

"Maxwell?" Yvonne smiled and her pretty face lit up with approval.

Anna nearly choked on her cake. Were they talking about the same person?

"I mean the Chief Inspector, who's staying on the island. He's handling the investigation," she added and wondered if Yvonne might be offended that she was considering a romance with the man who had put her only son under house arrest.

"I know who you mean, sweetheart," Yvonne said. "Didn't you know his name was Maxwell? I badgered it out of him, when he first moved here."

Anna opened her mouth and then closed it again. She supposed she had never asked. She rolled the word around in her mind.

Maxwell.

Max?

"I like it," she decided after a moment. "But I think 'Ryan' suits him better."

Yvonne licked icing sugar from her lips and adopted a motherly expression.

"I want you to know three things, Anna," she began seriously, fixing the young woman with a stare. Anna sat up straighter to listen. "The first is that I love my husband."

"Of course—"

"The second," Yvonne cut across her smoothly, "is that I was *extremely disappointed* when your young man took my son into custody."

Anna swallowed, but liked the way she referred to Ryan as her 'young man'.

"And the third," Yvonne said primly, "is that I am not over the hill yet. That being the case, I will say that Maxwell Ryan has to be one of the most fabulous-looking men I have ever seen and if you don't jump on him, I might."

Her speech complete, Yvonne took a big bite of cake and grinned over the top of it. Anna had to laugh.

"Cut me off a piece of *that*," she thought she heard Yvonne mumble as she polished off the crumbs. Anna chuckled again and looked across at the woman who had, in many ways, been like a mother to her when her own had been taken from her.

"I've missed you, Yvonne. More than I realised," she admitted.

"I've missed you too," was the tender reply. "We're all proud of everything you've achieved. Your mother would have been so proud too," she added softly.

Anna swallowed the lump in her throat and turned tear-glazed eyes towards the fire.

"There now," Yvonne said, "there's no need to get upset."

"I'm not," Anna sniffled. "I'm just overwrought, that's all."

"It's been a terrible few days for you," Yvonne shook her head sadly and thought that it had been more like a terrible few years. She had been so lucky that her own little family had never known tragedy like the Taylors. Now there was only one of them left, she thought with a stab of pity.

Anna pulled herself together. "I just wish that Megan and I could have parted as friends."

Yvonne sighed.

"You were always so different," she said carefully. Blood ran thicker than water after all and she didn't want to cause offence. "Things which should have brought you closer together only pulled you apart."

Anna nodded. It was the truth.

"You've always done your best by her," Yvonne added. "Even when she hurt you so much."

Anna looked down and set the cake back on the coffee table beside her. She should have done more for Megan and she knew it.

"I forgave her for what happened," she said quietly. "And I never blamed Alex, not really."

"Well, I did!" Yvonne surprised her by saying. "I'm his mother and God knows, I love him to distraction, but he was never a great judge of character."

"He was only young. So was I," Anna said.

"I know," Yvonne calmed down and sent a smile to the girl sitting across from her. "But a mother has her dreams, you know. You were…you still *are* everything a mother would wish for her only son."

Anna felt tears clog her throat again but swallowed them back.

"Thank you," she said.

"We were happy when Alex found Kim, even if it was a bit sudden," Yvonne continued. "It's a shame that hasn't worked out, but to be quite honest with you, they were never very happy together. They rushed into things and regretted it almost immediately. At least there aren't any children to be hurt by the divorce," Yvonne's lips turned down on the last word and she looked troubled.

"Alex still won't tell me where he was when these killings took place." She looked across at the fire and her fingers twisted the hem of her skirt. She caught Anna's eye and spoke quickly. "Oh, I'd never think he had anything to do with what happened to Lucy and Megan. He's always been gentle. It's just that I can't understand why he's suddenly so secretive. I thought we were so close."

Anna didn't know what to say.

"The police obviously have no concerns," she managed feebly. "Otherwise they wouldn't have, ah—"

"Let him go? Yes, I suppose you're right." Yvonne paused before she spoke again. "The police came by, you know, to take a statement. To ask what I'd been doing and who I'd seen the other day. I told them the truth; that I'd been at home for most of the day and that Steve had been out helping the police in the morning, then doing his rounds in the afternoon. I had no idea that Alex had told them he'd been here with me when he hadn't."

"Why would he do that?" Anna wondered.

"This is what concerns me," Yvonne said earnestly. "Why would he tell lies to the police? It's not like him."

That was true, Anna thought. In all the time she'd known him, Alex had always been up front about himself, even when his behaviour had been less than perfect.

"Why don't you try asking him again?" she thought aloud.

"He's shut himself away in his cottage," Yvonne said miserably. "I can't seem to get through to him. I know that this experience with the police might have been a shock but surely he knows how much we all support him?"

Yvonne turned baffled eyes to Anna.

"Would you like me to speak to him?" she offered half-heartedly.

"Would you? I know you feel a bit awkward around each other but really once you get to know each other again I just know you'll be the best of friends."

Anna looked into Yvonne's hopeful face and knew when she was beaten.

CHAPTER 18

Anna hesitated outside the door to Alex's little cottage. The curtains were shut, despite the sunshine. She should never have agreed to this, she thought. Would she never learn?

She raised her knuckles to rap on the door. If there was no answer, she would just leave him to it and head back home. Or, rather, back to her temporary home, if you could call it that.

There was no answer and she shifted to peek through the window. The lounge was in darkness, papers and magazines strewn across the coffee table along with the remains of a half-eaten pizza.

She rapped again and called out Alex's name but there was still no answer. She turned to walk away and then swore quietly. She would only worry about him if she didn't try one last time.

She jogged to the end of the street where there was a long alleyway leading to the back gardens of the row of terraced cottages. She tried the gate and found it open—people didn't lock their doors on Lindisfarne—so she pushed through. After some tugging, she managed to yank open the smaller gate to Alex's garden and didn't stop to worry that she might not be welcome. She had come this far, after all.

His lawn could do with cutting, she thought idly as her boots trod across the thick green grass towards the back door. She stepped up to the door and peered through the single window pane. She saw him slumped at the kitchen table.

Fear gripped her for an instant before she saw his shoulders rise and fall.

Thank God, she thought and after another moment spent wondering if she should leave him to his solitude, she tapped on the window.

Alex's head sprang up and he looked around in confusion before his bloodshot eyes came to rest on hers. His mouth turned downwards and Anna watched him as his ingrained manners battled with his desire to be alone. Eventually, manners won out and he pushed back from his chair wearily to let her in.

"Anna," he said. "I'm not really in the mood for visitors."

She looked at him closely. His hair, normally styled to within an inch of its life, was matted and messy. His face was unshaven and his eyes deeply shadowed. His shirt looked like it had seen a couple of days' wear.

Stepping inside, she found herself reaching for his arm in a friendly gesture.

"Alex? Your mother asked me to stop by."

He let out a husky laugh.

"Of course she did," he said quietly. "You didn't have to."

"I'm glad I did," she said slowly, watching him. She had expected him to be a bit shocked, perhaps, after his experience with the police. She had expected him to be upset, as they all were, about the loss of one of their friends. But she hadn't expected to see the black depression which seemed to cloak him now.

He looked broken.

"The police were only doing their job," she began.

"I know that," he agreed. "I don't care about the police, Anna."

"Your parents love you so much," she tried again. "They don't care about what's happened, although I think your mum is a bit concerned about why you would lie about where you were the other night."

Tears sprang into his eyes again and he swung away from her to rest both hands on the edge of the sink.

"I've got nothing to say to her."

"Alex," she moved towards him and put a gentle hand on his arm. "Something is obviously upsetting you. I know you must be sorry...we're all sorry about Rob. It was a terrible thing," she swallowed.

His body shuddered and she realised that he was crying. She had never, in twenty-eight years, seen him cry. Her hand moved in rhythmic, calming circles over his back and he sobbed, turned towards her and held on tightly.

"I can't...I just can't..." he mumbled into her shoulder.

"You can't what?" she soothed.

"You'd hate me, if I told you," he whispered, tears clogging his throat.

Fear clutched briefly again, but when she eased him away from her and looked into his tear-drenched eyes, she remembered the man she had grown up with.

"I could never hate you," she said with certainty.

He looked at her pale face and wished he could have loved her more, could have been more to her. It was one more thing to add to his list of disappointments. Yet, when he looked, he saw forgiveness and understanding. It gave him strength.

"I loved him."

He spoke the words and felt a kind of release, like a bird being set free.

"Who? Rob?" Anna felt surprise but not as much as she would have thought.

"Yes," he nodded, wanting to turn away and hide, but he stood firm and told himself that he would brave whatever words she had to throw at him. She was entitled.

"For how long?"

"Years," he said briefly. "We began a relationship not long after you and I broke up. I was with Megan, but..." he shrugged, thinking it was pointless to elaborate.

Anna nodded slowly, searching herself to find the right words. She understood now why he had seemed so restless and unfulfilled. She understood why he looked broken and beaten; he was a man struggling with the grief of losing the person he had loved.

"I'm so sorry, Alex. I wish that I had known sooner," the compassion in her voice nearly undid him again.

Alex stood still for a moment, until he could be sure that his legs would hold him. He hadn't expected her immediate understanding or concern but perhaps he should have.

"Thank you," his voice was hoarse with emotion. "You can't know what it means to me, to hear you say that."

Anna was baffled.

"What else would I say, Alex? It's the greatest tragedy there is, to have a loved one snatched away from you. I only wish that you could have—that you both could have—lived together openly."

"So do I," he agreed shortly. "It was my fault that we didn't. I was too concerned about what people might think." And now he would hate himself for it, always.

"Lindisfarne is a small place, sometimes too small," Anna agreed, thinking that there was no point giving him empty platitudes or pretending that it wouldn't have been difficult. There were people on the island who would still rather be living in the Dark Ages.

He looked at her again. What he had to say, she deserved to hear.

"I want you to know, Anna, that what I felt for you wasn't a lie. It isn't simple, with me. It was, for Rob," he added. "I've always been more confused. I always thought—still think—you're one of the most beautiful women I've ever known. Your forgiveness only makes that more true." He looked away briefly. "I just thought you should know that. I've lied to people and I've cheated, but I've never regretted anything more than the mistakes I made with you. I'll always love you, Anna."

She wanted to cry but told herself that she wouldn't. It was kind of him, she thought, to give her that much.

"I understand, Alex, don't worry. I'll always love you too. I've missed your friendship and, really, that's all we should ever have had."

A ghost of his former self swept across his jewel-like eyes, lending him a rakish air.

"I don't regret what we *did* have," he murmured. "For me, it will always be special."

"For me, too, Alex," she agreed quietly, sealing the door to the past with a gentle click.

They held hands side-by-side in the kitchen and he let himself lean on an old friend, one who would never judge him lacking, or judge him at all. It made him stronger, just knowing that.

He wetted lips which were bone dry.

"What you said, Anna, about the people of Lindisfarne living in the past."

"Mmm?" She gazed out of the kitchen window and watched a robin perch on the little wooden nest Alex had built.

"It's even truer than you imagine," he said.

She turned to him again and he almost lost courage under the force of those serene brown eyes.

"What do you mean?"

"There are the people that you see," he said slowly, thinking of the men and women of the village. "Then the people you don't." He still thought of the same people, but this time they wore masks and danced naked in the moonlight, their faces alive with false cheer.

"You're talking in riddles, Alex," she complained.

"I'm scared, Anna," he said quietly, thinking of Rob and the punishment he had endured. "There are people who believe in a sort of code. If you deviate from that code, or rebel against it, there are consequences. Sometimes, those consequences are terrible, too terrible to imagine."

Anna struggled to follow him.

"Code? Do you mean the religious element on the island? There's a bit of homophobia around…"

"There's that," he agreed, thinking of the island's vicar. He turned to face her and his eyes were bleak. "But there's more, Anna, so much more."

He swung around to face the garden again and he thought he saw eyes in the bushes, watching them, watching him.

"You have to go now," he said abruptly.

"Go? But Alex—"

"Please, Anna," he pasted on a friendly smile. "Thank you for everything you've done today. It's meant a lot to me and, I promise, I'll go and talk to my mother soon. I'm working up to it."

Anna nodded slowly.

"Alright," she said eventually and, after giving him a chaste kiss on the cheek, she let herself out the way she had come.

When she glanced back, Alex watched her from the kitchen window and raised a hand in farewell.

* * *

A couple of hours later, when the sun was high in the sky, Ryan walked up the little path leading to Anna's cottage. As he grew closer, he heard the music as it soared through the cracks in the doors and windows. He didn't know what he had expected of her taste, he thought with some bafflement. Perhaps something classical, along the lines of Puccini.

He hadn't expected nineties skate punk.

Not that there was anything wrong with that, he amended quickly, or indeed with eighties power ballads, he thought with a slight wince as the music changed.

There was no answer after a couple of raps on the door and fear clutched at his throat like an iron fist. He tried the handle but it was locked.

"Christ," he muttered, shoving at it again with his shoulder.

He didn't stop to worry or wonder about his actions. He kicked the door in without a second thought and burst into the hallway.

Although she hadn't been able to hear him knocking, Anna certainly heard the sound of a door splintering and she felt her own share of fear as she stepped out of the shower room. Grabbing the nearest thing to hand, which happened to be a large porcelain figurine from the mantelpiece in her bedroom, she padded onto the landing.

"I've called the police!" she shouted down the stairs.

At the sound of her voice, Ryan let out a distinctly shaky breath. He tried to tell himself he was just pleased there wasn't another fatality, but he knew this went deeper. He gave himself a moment to collect his thoughts.

"No need," he called out dryly. "They're already here."

Her head peeped out over the top of the landing and he looked up into big brown eyes that were wide with alarm.

"Oh, it's only you," she let out a shaky breath, her face softening. Then she looked at the door and flew down the stairs. "What have you done?"

He looked back at the damage and felt like a prize moron.

"I knocked, there was no answer," he said defensively.

"Didn't you hear the music?" she asked.

"I *did* hear the music," he said sarcastically, as Bonnie Tyler bellowed that she was planning to hold out for a hero.

His lips twitched as Anna practically flew across the hall to turn the music off.

"Yes, well," she said when she turned back.

"Well," he agreed and then moved to pick up the broken door and stand it against the gaping hole in the wall.

"Cup of tea?" she asked as he turned back to her. She tried to gauge his mood, wondered if he wanted to talk about what had happened at the press conference.

He shook his head, to both offers, and then looked at her properly. She was lovely, he thought, with her face unadorned and flushed from the shower and her skin wrapped in an emerald green towel.

It made him want to unwrap her, he realised, and felt his body respond. He told himself to think of other things. But how could he?

Her hair was damp from the shower and curled slightly at her temples. Then, he noticed that she still clutched the figurine of a couple dancing and he grinned.

"Were you planning on bludgeoning me with that?" he asked.

She looked down at the figure in her hand. "I…well, it was either that or my hairbrush. I thought this would do more damage."

He wanted to laugh but her instincts had been good.

"It's a good idea to keep on your guard, Anna," he said quietly. "I would feel better knowing you were staying somewhere in town, at one of the inns."

"They're all full," she said without thinking. She had already checked. "I like my privacy, anyway."

The matter wasn't over, he thought, not by a long shot.

Looking at her, he forgot the reasons he had come, the distress and carnage he had left behind and reached for her instead. Her eyes widened for a moment as his hands framed her face and then her fingers speared into his thick hair, tugging him towards her.

"I can't seem to stop," he muttered into her neck.

"I don't want you to stop," she replied and felt his arms tighten around her, lifting her.

Grey eyes met brown for a long moment.

"Which way?" he asked.

"Top of the stairs, on the left," she answered.

* * *

He lay face down on the bed, one heavy arm draped across her stomach and one long leg tangled with hers.

"I need water," she croaked happily, eyes closed.

He grunted.

"I think I may be dying," she added for good measure.

He grunted again but managed to turn his head to look at her through the black hair which fell across his eyes.

She was beautiful. All long, slender curves and smooth skin. Her face was a curious mix of angles which worked together harmoniously but it was the eyes which grabbed him and held him.

He levered up and kissed her. When he eventually released her mouth, he brushed the hair back from her temple and saw mild confusion on her face.

"You ok?" she asked quietly, bringing one hand to his cheek.

"Never better," he said with complete honesty. He couldn't remember feeling so happy in his life, which was completely at odds with the reality that awaited him outside her bedroom.

Thinking of it, remembering it, he rolled off the bed and away from her to start pulling on his clothes. As she watched him, gloriously naked in the afternoon sunlight, she thought again that he was an excellent male specimen.

She blushed furiously and was glad he wasn't facing her.

"We need to talk," he said and she knew his thoughts had turned back to the investigation.

"Give me ten minutes," she agreed. "Oh, *Maxwell*?"

She beamed a smile when he spun around.

"Where did you hear that?"

She chuckled. "Should I call you 'Maxwell'? Or how about 'Max'?"

He looked at her, sitting in the middle of the wide bed, her long legs drawn up to her chest and smiled wolfishly. He padded towards her again and watched her eyes widen fractionally when his face hovered a few inches above her own.

"Ryan," he growled. "Ryan will do."

* * *

Downstairs at the little bistro table overlooking the sea, they faced one another again. There was a new knowledge, a new understanding between them, but the wariness remained. For her, she supposed it came from never trusting men, or from never finding a man whom she could trust.

For him, it was more complicated.

"Do you want to...?" she began.

"Not now, Anna," he answered her unspoken question. He couldn't think of Natalie now.

"Okay," she said softly. There it was again, he thought. That quiet understanding. The automatic comprehension of his feelings, without him having to explain them to her. Was that one of her many skills?

"I need to find the pattern," he said baldly, looking her in the eye. "There were pentagrams on Megan's body and Rob had been tied down to a few big bits of driftwood in the rough shape of a pentagram. Why didn't we find one on Lucy? The girls' bodies had been washed, taken care of in some way, whereas Rob's had been burned."

Ryan let out a hissing breath between his teeth which she knew was all frustration.

"I've got the CSIs going over the scenes again, which is a big ask. I've got the pathologist going over his own findings and reassessing the bodies for anything he missed the first time. I've drafted in another police pathologist from Teesside," he referred to a county further south, "to provide his own views. The reports are due this evening. I don't think I'll be at the top of anyone's Christmas card list, but it has to be done."

Anna let him talk because he needed to.

"I'm sorry," he added belatedly. "The delay will mean you won't be able to hold the funeral for another few days."

She nodded her acceptance. Better to lay her sister to rest peacefully knowing that her killer had been brought to justice.

"About Megan," he began, reading her mood and finding her sturdy enough to question.

"What about her?" Anna felt her brief post-coital euphoria drain away completely.

"Do you know if she was seeing anyone in particular?" He thought back to what Alex Walker had told him and added, "Anyone who might have wanted to keep their relationship secret?"

Anna let out a breath and pulled a face. "Ryan, it's hard to have to speak ill of the dead, especially my own sister." She rubbed at cold arms and compressed her lips. "You have to understand that Megan needed love and admiration, almost desperately."

Ryan understood that it would be hard for her. The guilt, the grief, all weighed heavily. But he needed to know.

"I'm not here to judge her, Anna. It may help to find her killer if we can put together a list of people who she knew. Especially intimately," he added. "People she would have let into her apartment without a second thought."

Anna nodded.

"You already know about Alex," she said evenly. "That's just the tip of the iceberg." Anna kneaded her temples where a brutal tension headache was starting. "There was always the odd fling with a passing tourist. Young lads on holiday with their parents, sometimes the fathers too," Anna's voice lowered sadly as she went through the tally. "It wouldn't surprise me if the same applied to people already on the island. She used to keep a diary of her conquests."

"Do you know if she still has it?"

"Ryan," she turned to him in apology, "I hadn't spoken to my sister in eight years. I haven't got a clue whether she kept that old diary. I can only tell you that it was green with a gold wraparound thread. She saved up and got it from the gift shop when she was sixteen."

"Okay," he said, thinking that nothing matching that description had been found or listed on the inventory of Megan's belongings.

"I knew that she had been with older men," Anna said, picking up the conversation. "It was a source of pride for her, another way to make me feel gauche and inexperienced."

"It was nothing more than a cheap way to bolster her self-esteem," he said succinctly, annoyed at the remembered hurt he saw reflected in her eyes once more.

"I know that," she nodded. "As a grown woman, I understand what she did and why she did it. I didn't envy her then and I don't envy her now. The point is, she bragged about knowing what made a man tick and she liked to show off the little trinkets they bought her, but she never told me who these men were. I always assumed they were married or figments of her imagination."

"Where did she keep her trinkets?" he asked.

Anna shrugged. "She had all kinds of hidey-holes. Our father used to enjoy smashing up the things we valued, so we both learned never to put our keepsakes on display." She thought back. "When we lived at home, she hollowed out a chunk of the mattress and used to keep her bits and bobs in there, between the springs."

Ryan knew the first place he would check.

"Other than that, I couldn't tell you," Anna finished with regret.

"You've been very helpful," Ryan took her hand and gave it a reassuring squeeze. "Really."

Her face brightened slightly and her fingers curved into his.

"The problem is, there's hardly any DNA evidence," he said unexpectedly and let go of her hand. "He's done a professional job on them and he's laughing at us."

He's laughing at me.

Ryan wasn't used to losing, he had been fortunate in his life in many ways and a combination of skill and luck had ensured that things mostly went in his direction. Recent times had put paid to that assumption of endless good fortune. He had lost too many people, too quickly. He had to ask himself whether it was because he had lost his edge.

He looked up into Anna's patient eyes and felt twin emotions of passion and peace. He wanted to tell her then, to pour out the demons that haunted him at night, but he couldn't bring himself to do it.

"I want to know what I'm missing," he said instead. "I've got a profiler drumming up a report on this whacko's psychology, but I can tell you that it's going to say we're looking for a white male between the ages of eighteen and forty, megalomaniacal tendencies, poor relationships with women. It's always the same."

"It's not all about women, though, is it? What about Rob?" Anna asked quietly, thinking of the boy she had grown up with. It was awful to realise that the more people who died, the more numbed she became.

"Exactly," Ryan jabbed a hand out to capture her thought. "This guy isn't particular. He does two young women in a similar way, so we start to think he has issues with the opposite sex. Then, he throws us a curve with Rob Fowler."

Ryan tapped his fingers on the table.

"Does it have to be only one person?" Anna thought aloud.

Ryan turned to look into her quiet, intelligent face.

"No, it doesn't."

They both fell silent, considering the implications of that.

"You think definitely male?" she asked.

He nodded. "The physicality alone suggests a male killer. The first two women were moved from the place where they died, although we're still searching for the site where Lucy was murdered. As for Rob, we have to work on the presumption that he went to the beach of his own accord and was overpowered once he was there. The manner in which all three victims were killed would suggest a male killer; statistically, women are more likely to use different methods."

"Oh?" she asked, intrigued.

"Yep, poison, for example, requires less physical strength."

"I'll bear that in mind," she said with a smile and he flashed a quick smile in return. Another shared moment.

"These murders," he said thoughtfully, "they follow similar threads, but they're different in so many ways."

"Was Rob strangled or did he have his throat cut?" Anna forced herself to ask the question and blanked her mind of thoughts of Megan for the moment.

Ryan saw her as one of his team. As such, he had no hesitation telling her what had happened, but he did regret causing her pain.

"He was burned, not quite at a stake, but in a similar fashion. He was strapped to a wooden pentagram and placed on top of a pyre."

Anna closed her eyes for a moment against the image in her mind.

"The fire would have burned all his skin off," she said.

"Yes," he nodded, frowning slightly.

"The manner of Rob's death could have been inspired by a number of different historical practices," she began, switching smoothly to professional mode. "Celtic Druids used to build wicker figures which they filled with people and then burned alive."

"Like in the *Wicker Man*," Ryan commented.

"Yes, like in the film," she nodded. "It was a form of capital punishment for all manner of sinners, from those seen as sexual deviants to traitors and rebels, although archeologically-speaking, the Roman sources have largely been discredited."

He had to smile. She was nothing if not a stickler when it came to her work, but then he supposed the same could be said of him. His ears pricked up at the idea of the fire as a form of punishment. What had been Rob Fowler's crime? His sexuality?

"Then, there were the Carthaginians," Anna continued.

"The Carthaginians?" He raised a brow.

"Carthage was a city in what is now modern-day Tunisia," she supplied. "In antiquity, the people who came from there are said to have practised child sacrifice. Obviously, we're not dealing with children here, but it's said that the children were sacrificed at Tophet, which means 'roasting place'."

"A fire?" he asked.

"Yes, simply put."

The removal of skin could also be significant," she added quietly, resting her head on her hand. "Aztec ritual sacrifices were made to

Xipe Totec, otherwise known as 'the Flayed One', a sort of life, death and rebirth deity who commanded the seasons and the harvest."

"Victims had their skin flayed?"

"Yes," she said. "The skin was flayed and then the priest in charge of the ritual would use the skin for his own ends."

Ryan studied the skin on his hands and thought of how Rob Fowler's body had looked lying there on the beach.

"What's the point of it all?"

"Depends what you're asking, Ryan," Anna lifted one shoulder. "I'll leave the motivations of the killer or killers to you. As for the point of ritual sacrifice, it's an ancient practice, dating all the way back to Neolithic times. It was believed to bring good fortune, or to pacify the gods."

"Good fortune?"

"In harvests or hunting, mostly. In those times, people were often nomadic. They followed the migration of large herds of animals. It could be that you have someone making his—or her—sacrifices in the name of good fortune." She paused, thinking of the Priory. "Sometimes, sacrifices were made to dedicate a temple which had just been built. It's rumoured that there are thousands of people entombed in the Great Wall of China," she mused. "Could be that you have a religious fanatic who believes in making sacrifices to dedicate to his temples."

Ryan had heard that before. When he'd walked a stretch of that Great Wall a few years earlier, it had felt eerily like he was walking on somebody's grave.

He snapped back to the present.

"What about Anna and Megan? The ritual is different."

"The ritual cleansing is an old burial ritual," Anna supplied. "It exists amongst some neo-pagans, even today. They consecrate an area and thoroughly clean the body using special soaps and oils..."

"Oils?" Ryan interjected.

"Yes, they can be very specific. Usually, the oil contains an element of camphor, which is..."

"I know what camphor is," Ryan interrupted. "We found it on Lucy's body."

"But not on Megan's?" she queried, a small line of grief marring her face.

He shook his head, sorry to hurt her.

"Okay," she mused, swallowing the lump of pain in her throat. "Perhaps he didn't have time with Megan. Either way, the cleansing usually signifies some sort of respect, usually for a loved one or ancestor. But this," she gestured to the folder on the table, "this isn't about respect."

Ryan was quiet for another minute. "Lucy's body was treated more carefully in general. Her hair was brushed around her face and every inch of her body was taken care of. You could say that was just the actions of a guilty man wanting to remove all traces," he said bitterly, "but it's bothering me that he didn't take the trouble with Megan, other than to serve the purpose of removing evidence."

"Yes, I see what you mean," Anna agreed. "It's unusual for a person who believes in the ritual enough to practise it initially, not to be consistent."

Ryan nodded. "Exactly. Why was Megan's body dumped on the proverbial rubbish heap whereas Lucy was transported to hallowed ground? What I need to find out is what made Megan and Lucy so different, aside from the obvious. They were chosen for a reason."

His face was stony as he considered the motivations of a killer and Anna felt the same kind of faith in him Helen Mathieson had felt two days earlier. This was a man who would never stop looking, never stop chasing until he had his answers.

"So, we're looking for someone who believes he's making sacrifices to the gods, for whatever good fortune he's hoping for?" Ryan asked.

"Although the rituals are confused among the three victims, I think it's safe to say you're not looking for someone who is dedicating a sacrifice to a god, or at least not one that we would think of," she thought of the pentagram on the bodies and turned back to him. "The pentagrams were inverted."

He thought of what she had told him the previous day.

"The sign of Satan?"

"Yes," she nodded and searched for a pen. She came back to the table and drew a five pointed star. "An ordinary pentagram drawn as a five-pointed star like this is an ancient Christian symbol of the five senses, or the five wounds of Christ."

"And the reverse pentagram?"

She drew a star with two points of the star facing upwards, circled twice. "This is a well-known symbol of satanic worship. I think it even has a patent," she added sadly.

"It symbolises a goat—Baphomet—with the horns at the top, ears on both sides and beard at the bottom."

Ryan's mouth flattened into a hard line.

"There was a lot of that kicking around twenty years ago, mostly in America," he thought aloud.

"Yes, moral panic, I think they called it."

"There was supposed to be satanic worship around every corner, from the highest to the lowest echelons of society."

Anna rubbed her hands across her knees and got up again.

"I don't think it's as simple as some Satanic cult," she said.

"Why?"

She didn't answer him but moved to the kitchen, where she opened a drawer and pulled out a small item wrapped in paper.

"I found this on my doorstep this morning," she said, handing him the package.

He met her eyes, saw the slight fear and took out a pair of gloves from his inner pocket.

Inside the newspaper wrapping was a small, polished stone with an intricate design of the figure of a man standing in front of a crude stick building, with one word carved underneath: 'JOHN'.

"What does it mean?" He looked up at her and tried to remember if there were any men named 'John' resident on the island.

"I believe the building is the Priory and the man standing in front of it is Saint John."

Ryan had never felt particularly stupid in his entire life but spending time with a woman like Anna reminded him there was always more to learn.

"Explain, please," he said simply.

She picked up the stone and felt its weight. She didn't notice his frown at the lack of gloves.

"Traditionally, small copies of the Gospel of Saint John were used as protective amulets, to ward off harm."

"From the Lindisfarne Gospels?"

Anna nodded, pleased that he knew the history of the Gospels which had made the little island famous. The manuscript of gospels produced by the monks on the island hundreds of years ago was one of the finest examples of artistic script in the world.

"The original Gospel was placed inside the tomb of St Cuthbert, who was Prior of Lindisfarne around 664 AD. He was sainted after his death," she added. "Anyway, it was said that the gospel could heal the sick. People used to gather around his tomb and pray for healing because the book was buried with him."

Anna looked at the stone again and then back into his fathomless grey eyes.

"I think whoever you're looking for is very confused. He uses Christian symbols alongside Pagan ones, then mixes in a bit of devil-worship by using the inverted pentagram."

Ryan nodded. "Whichever way you look at it, somebody believes that you need protection." He gestured to the stone.

"Apparently so," she agreed and felt her stomach jitter.

"That settles it," he said.

"Settles what?"

"You're coming to stay with me," he said abruptly, thinking of the complications that would arise having her stay in a house that had been authorised as a police designated area.

He would look forward to that conversation with Gregson.

CHAPTER 19

She had argued until she was blue in the face. She had protested while he dragged her upstairs to pack a bag. There had been a brief respite when they became entangled among the bedclothes, during which time she thought he would have forgotten his hare-brained idea that she would be moving in with him.

He hadn't.

In fact, the exertion had lent a certain smugness to his handsome face, making him more determined.

Since reasoning with him and shouting at him hadn't made a difference, Anna had resorted to silence while he grabbed her car keys and drove them along the road to his cottage.

She had seen the curious looks of the vicar's wife and Mrs Rigby as they had watched their progress from the pavement on the high street. She could only imagine the wild rumours that would fly.

"As far as anyone is concerned, I'm bringing you into protective custody," he said into the silence.

If possible, she grew even angrier.

"This is ridiculous!" she burst out, rapping a fist on the plastic dashboard and regretting it when pain sang through her wrist.

"What is ridiculous is your juvenile behaviour," he said cuttingly.

"My…" she had to take several deep breaths while her skin flushed dark red.

"How *dare* you speak to me like that?"

"I dare, because it's the truth."

"Just because we slept together, it doesn't give you the right to manhandle me or bully me whenever you like," she said.

He turned to look at her then and his eyes were cold.

"This has nothing to do with what we shared earlier and if you think that it does, then that's more of a reflection on your own attitude, isn't it?" With that, he unfolded his long body from the confines of the mini and slammed the door behind him.

Innate manners forced him to walk around to her side of the car and open the door for her. He stood in silence waiting for her to get out, his entire body vibrating with anger.

She dared to look at him and realised that she had made him very, very angry. Looking closer, she thought she saw something like hurt and felt instantly ashamed. She had lashed out at him because she didn't trust...couldn't trust a man, any man.

She wanted to, desperately.

"I'm sorry," she mumbled.

"I beg your pardon?" he said in the same coolly polite tone.

"You heard me the first time. I apologise for the accusation that you would misuse our earlier intimacy. I still say you bullied me here," she added vehemently.

He cocked his head. He could accept all that, because he *had* essentially bullied her. It was also true that their relationship had everything to do with it. He wanted to protect her with every fibre of his being.

He wouldn't see another woman he cared for end up dead in his arms.

He managed to work up a smile.

"Forget it," he took her hand to help her out of the car. As they walked up to the front door, he paused. "Next time, we'll take my car. That mini nearly broke my back."

She had a smile on her face when she walked through the door.

* * *

"Look, guv, I can't blame you for wanting to protect the girl. Very nice looking lady," Phillips added.

Ryan smiled as they walked towards the centre of town.

"I won't lie to you, Frank, the lines are blurred for me but what is crystal clear is the fact that someone has singled her out."

"Aye, true enough."

"The stone looks like protection, but this guy is fucked up. Could be someone with multiple personality; or a copycat..." Ryan shook his head. "Either way, I'm not handing her to him on a plate like a prize turkey."

"Well, you know what you're doing," Phillips stuck his hands in his pockets. "Got Faulkner's team looking at the stone. He should be able to tell us if there's anything to it," he said.

"Yeah," Ryan nodded. "We'll be lucky if there are any prints on it; Anna handled it before she showed it to me. Easy mistake to make."

Phillips clucked his tongue.

"Still…" Ryan trailed off as they passed the Heritage Gift Shop. He stopped dead and looked in the window where, nestled amongst the candles and figures of St Cuthbert, there lay stones of all shapes and sizes engraved with Christian symbols.

"Bingo," Frank said, reading his SIO's mind.

They stepped through a tinkling door hung with wind chimes. Ryan recognised Liz Morgan working behind the counter. She was looking a little more like herself but alarm lingered around the eyes as she rang up orders.

"Liz," Ryan stepped forward when her last customer left.

"Mr Ryan," she said and came around the counter. He tried not to feel awkward when she took his hands. "I want to thank you for the way you helped me the other day. I was in such a state."

"Anyone would have done the same," he said, thinking that he had been a cold bastard, questioning her facts and motives only minutes after coming across what would likely be the most traumatising sight she would ever see in her life.

She patted his hand and stepped back. Her eyes were drawn to the garish colours on Phillips' tie but she remembered it was rude to stare.

"How can I help you?"

"We saw some unusual stones in the window," Ryan began, moving to point at the display. "I'm looking for one in particular; polished black with a white engraving of the Gospel of Saint John on the front of it."

"Well, let me see," Liz moved back to the counter and pulled out a large stock book with pictures. She flipped through the pages for a moment then gestured him closer.

"Like this one?"

Ryan moved to stand beside her and looked down at a picture of a stone, an identical copy of which he had seen earlier that day.

"That's the one."

"The stone is onyx," Liz supplied. "Local artists do the engraving with a specialist chisel then paint over the engraving in white enamel."

Phillips tried to look over Ryan's shoulder, but the man was a good six inches taller, so he mumbled his agreement instead.

"How many of these have you sold recently?"

Liz whooshed out a breath. "I would have to check the records, I'm afraid. We sell so many of those little stones."

"Okay," Ryan nodded and favoured her with one of his best smiles. Liz may have been nearly twice his age, but she still recognised a fine man when she saw one. She banked down a giggle and offered him a matronly smile in return.

"I'd be grateful if you could do that as soon as you can," Ryan said. "It could be very important."

Phillips looked over from his inspection of pocket handkerchiefs decorated in Celtic symbols. "Does anywhere else sell those stones?"

"The craft shop across the square might," Liz answered, "but I couldn't say for sure."

"What about the artists? Do they work on the island?"

"No, actually we cheat a bit and bring them over from an artist in Morpeth," she confessed.

"Just one other thing," Ryan smiled again. "Do you sell any soap with sandalwood extract?"

"Why, yes we do!" Liz reverted to sales mode, misunderstanding him. She bustled around the counter and picked up a block of elegantly wrapped soap with a dark blue tie and a sticker which explained its hand-made origins. "This one is lovely and it's made locally."

"Really?" he took the block she offered and studied the list of ingredients written on the back in an elegant dark blue script. Sandalwood and shea butter were both on the list.

"There's a body wash and an aftershave in the same range," she gushed.

"I'll take the set," Ryan said, not wanting to burst her bubble. He waited while she wrapped them up.

"Where did you say they were made?"

"Oh, we get them from a wholesaler in Berwick." Ryan thought of the old town sitting on the border of England and Scotland, further up the coast from where they currently stood. He took down the name of the manufacturer.

"Thanks, Liz. Have a good day."

Both men nodded politely and left, Phillips with one last longing look at a silk handkerchief in fuchsia pink.

They took the trouble to check at the craft shop but their job was made easier by the fact that they didn't stock anything like the stone Anna had been given.

"What now?" Phillips said and almost reached for the emergency cigarette he had squirreled away in his breast pocket.

Ryan thought back to the meeting they'd held earlier that day.

"Faulkner's got his work cut out for him but he's going over the forensics again with a fine tooth comb. He says he'll have another report on Lucy and Megan by this evening. We'll have to make do with preliminaries for Rob. I don't think Faulkner will discover anything new, he tends to be at the top of his game."

"MacKenzie's team has gone over the island, contacted local builders merchants and she's come up with a list of people who've done a bit of DIY recently," Phillips chimed in.

"Good," Ryan nodded, pleased. "Tell her to cross-check with any individuals whose statements we've already taken and to have the list ready when we get back." He stopped to check his watch. "Let's say around six."

Phillips nodded and pulled out his phone, made the call, spread the word for a briefing at six.

Ryan looked down at the little bag he held and Phillips noticed the action. "I've seen miniature packets of that soap in my room at the Inn. Never realised; I should have made the connection."

"Not necessarily," Ryan shook his head. "Problem is that it opens the field even more. We don't know this is a match for the product used on Lucy, but if it is, anyone could have had access."

Ryan switched the bag to his other hand while he thought.

"Go back," he said. "Tell Liz that, as well as a list of stone sales, I want a list of people who have bought these soap products from her shop in the past month, for starters. Then, I need you to contact the manufacturer in Berwick, get a list of outlets they sell to. Afterwards, I'll meet you at the pub."

Phillips' face perked up and Ryan almost laughed.

"I want to have a word with Bill," he added and watched the other man's face fall again.

"Can't we stop for a bite?" Phillips asked hopefully.

"Don't whine," Ryan said mildly and then relented since his own stomach was grumbling. "A quick sandwich and that's it."

"Gotcha."

Ryan watched Phillips walk off with a slight spring in his step. Keeping the morale of his team high was important at a time like this.

A sandwich wasn't too much to ask, after all.

* * *

As Phillips walked back to the gift shop, Ryan found himself a spot on his favourite bench in the main square. Christmas lanterns hung from the centre of St Cuthbert's head in the middle and outward to the four corners in a delicate arrangement. They were not yet lit but he knew when dusk fell they would illuminate, bringing much needed levity.

He took out his phone and called Gregson.

"Ryan?"

"Yes, sir. I have an important matter to bring to your attention." He proceeded to set out his concerns for Anna following the amulet she had been given.

"An observant man would ask why you were having a cosy chinwag at Doctor Taylor's house. I'm an observant man," Gregson added with a touch of menace.

"I was in the process of informing Doctor Taylor that, given her connection to one of the victims, it would be unethical for the department to employ her as a civilian consultant at this time."

"I bet you were happy about that," Gregson harrumphed.

Ryan's lips quirked. For once, his Superintendent had misread the situation. There was nothing Ryan enjoyed more than spending time with Doctor Taylor, in a professional capacity or not.

Perhaps he had crowed too soon, Ryan thought, when the next question came down the line.

"What does this Doctor Taylor look like, Ryan?"

"I hardly feel that's relevant, sir," he prevaricated.

"On the contrary, I believe it could be very relevant," Gregson replied.

"Doctor Taylor is twenty-eight, I believe. She is approximately five feet eight inches tall, with dark brown hair and eyes."

"I hear she's a looker."

Ryan vowed to tie Phillips' wagging tongue around his neck the next time he saw him.

"Doctor Taylor is attractive, yes."

"Uh huh," Gregson drawled. "Just make sure you keep the blood flowing to your brain, Ryan. We can't afford sloppy mistakes at a time like this."

"Understood, sir."

"I'm on the road to Newcastle, got a press conference down there. Don't want the media running away with themselves any more than they have already. Did you see the afternoon papers?"

Ryan had seen them online.

"They've come up with some novel nicknames."

"They can call the bastard whatever they like," Gregson snapped, but thought that giving the killer titles ranging from 'The Butcher of Lindisfarne' to 'The Lindisfarne Loony', depending on the standard of paper one chose to read, was both unhelpful and predictable.

"It will feed his ego," Ryan said.

"Yes, it will," Gregson agreed. "Another thing he'll be enjoying is the bloody slow job we're making of this investigation. Did you see the headlines?"

Ryan's lips firmed.

"Yes, sir." He could hardly have overlooked the pages plastered with editorial theories on the killings, their damning reports on the police investigation so far or the fact that they had raked over all the old ground relating to Natalie's murder and his involvement.

" 'POLICE STUMBLE OVER FLAT FEET WHILE KILLER ROAMS HOLY ISLAND', was my personal favourite," Gregson said.

Ryan knew it was no use going over the hours of work or the dedication of his staff. Gregson was letting off steam; that was the chain of command in action. As he held the phone to his ear, he spotted Phillips heading back towards him and smiled thinly.

CHAPTER 20

Bill Tilson looked distinctly harassed when Phillips and Ryan walked into the Jolly Anchor. The lunch crowd had been particularly busy, catering to the swollen numbers on the island. He'd fended off dozens of questions about Lucy, Megan and Rob from reporters frantic for a scoop.

Now, he cleared away the debris in a mechanical fashion, his wide bulk moving smoothly between the tables collecting empties. The Santa costume hung limply from a peg behind the bar.

"Afternoon, Bill."

Ryan watched the man swing his head round, the light of battle still in his eyes in anticipation of more reporters having chosen to darken his door. The look faded and was replaced by a mix of curiosity and wariness when he saw who had come to visit.

"Gents," he nodded to both of them. "Get you something?" He jerked a shoulder towards the bar, his hands filled with empty dishes.

"You still serving food?" Phillips' eyes rested greedily on a bar menu.

"Aye, no problem. Let me know what you're after."

The selections made, Ryan gestured them all to a quiet table in the corner with a wide view of the room. After a quick scan, he saw that the place had cleared out except for a few regulars dotted around the room.

"Bad business," Bill said deeply, when they were settled.

"Agreed," Ryan said, taking a sip of his lemonade and wishing it were something stronger. "We need to ask you a few more questions, Bill."

"Fire away," the other man said, but felt his stomach jitter.

Ryan paused to recall the information he needed. Around the time of Lucy and Megan's death, Bill Tilson had been in full view of the community, pulling pints. Likewise, he'd been calling last orders the previous night when Rob Fowler was dying on the beach. Still, that didn't necessarily prevent the man from dipping out of the pub for a few minutes now and then.

Especially if it was just to nip upstairs to visit a pretty woman.

"You've already told me you've known Megan and Anna since they were girls," he began.

"Aye, that's right."

"Could you tell me again how Megan came to be staying in the apartment upstairs?" Ryan watched surprise flit across the other man's face.

"Well, I don't know how that's important, but if it makes any difference to you…"

"It might," Ryan confirmed in a mild tone.

"Well, it's like I already told you. Andy Taylor had mortgaged the pub to the hilt. I'd managed to save a few pennies here and there and so I could afford to buy the place from the girls." He shuffled in his seat. "They lost their home because the bank repossessed that straight away. Anna didn't want to stay; she left the island soon as she could. Megan asked if she could take over the apartment upstairs."

"What was the rent?" Ryan picked up his pencil, as if ready to make a note of the answer. A red flush began to seep into the other man's skin.

"She didn't pay me any rent."

"Oh?" Ryan smiled with apparent understanding. "I suppose she worked some hours for free, instead?"

"No," Bill said with a tinge of irritation marring his usually cheerful demeanour.

Ryan put his pencil down and steepled his fingers.

"How come you didn't charge her any rent?"

Phillips grinned into his sandwich. There was nothing like watching his SIO squeeze facts from a witness.

Bill shifted in his chair again, clearly uncomfortable.

"Look, I felt sorry for both the girls. Megan needed a start in life and I said she could stay there for free while she got on her feet. My way of saying 'thank you' to her parents for the start they gave me."

"That was very generous of you," Ryan gushed, not believing him for a second. "Eight years is a pretty generous start, isn't it? I guess you didn't mind her having gentleman callers, either?"

Watching Bill Tilson's face, Ryan caught the moment when jealousy sparked behind his mild brown eyes and thought, *there we go.*

"She didn't have any callers," Bill said, his jaw tense.

"Sure, she did," Ryan said affably, sweeping the other man's denial aside. "The whole village knows about her rep. Don't get me wrong, I'm sure she was a nice girl, but she did the rounds, didn't she?"

He watched as Tilson visibly tried to keep his temper under control. Ryan almost smiled, thinking that the big man looked like he could happily shove a fist in his face. Gone was the merry Santa Claus.

"That was all in the past," Bill ground out, breathing harder.

"That's not what I hear," Phillips piped up, wiping his mouth with a napkin.

"Who's been talking about her?" Bill turned on him. "They're filthy liars, whoever they are."

"Why didn't you tell us you had a thing for her, Bill?" Ryan said quietly and watched the other man's eyes close.

"I just cared about her, that's all."

"Nothing more?"

There was a hesitation before Bill spoke. "Nothing more."

"I don't think you're telling us the full truth, Bill." Ryan said with disappointment. "We found your fingerprints all over her apartment," he added.

"Well, so what?" Bill said with some heat. "I own the place, I check it every now and then."

"That wasn't the only thing you were 'checking', was it?" Phillips smirked and earned himself a glare from Ryan.

"Shut your mouth," Bill gritted, temper sparking again.

"Bill, we'll find out eventually, you know we will. Make it easy on yourself," Ryan advised.

Tilson clasped both hands on the table and they shook slightly.

"We were never..." he took a breath. "She didn't want people knowing about us. Said that I was like her older brother or an uncle and how it was wrong for me to have feelings for her."

"Go on," Ryan nodded.

"I honestly never expected anything from her," Tilson said. "Things just sort of happened one night."

"You slept together."

"Yes," he nodded. "This was years ago. She told me that we could carry on just like that, but she would be keeping her independence because she didn't want to be tied down."

"And you never charged her rent, in return," Ryan finished in a monotone.

Bill's lips wobbled. "I know how it sounds."

"Really? Because it sounds like you were paying her for services rendered."

Bill looked murderous, Ryan thought.

"You have no right to talk about her that way," he said.

"Did you give her any expensive presents, petty cash?" Phillips asked. "We can check the records," he added.

Bill warred with himself.

"I gave her a few bits and pieces." Bill listed some jewellery and clothes he had gifted to her over the years. "She…I suppose she used to help herself to a bit of cash from the till now and then."

Ryan and Phillips both held off making any obvious comments. Their earlier baiting had served its purpose now.

"Making false statements to the police is a serious matter," Ryan said quietly, pinning Tilson with a stare. "I have to ask myself why you would do that."

"I was embarrassed," Bill mumbled. "I felt like a fool every day I was with her. You think I didn't see how she went on with other men?" he turned blazing eyes on them. "I saw."

"Made you angry, didn't it?" Ryan kept his voice gentle.

"Bloody right, it did!" Bill said without thinking. "She knew how I felt about her."

"Angry enough to kill her?"

Pure shock entered the other man's face. Shock mingled with something else, Ryan thought.

"I could never have done that. I loved her."

Ryan was silent. Sometimes that was best.

"Megan spent years looking for someone who would love her, spoil her. I spent years trying to do that and all I got in exchange were a few tumbles in the hay and the odd kind word." Bill's voice was flat. "Still, I would have settled for that rather than nothing at all."

He turned back to them and said simply, "I would give anything to bring her back, but I can't."

* * *

At precisely the same moment as Ryan and Phillips found a blood-stained green and gold diary hidden in the mattress at Megan's apartment, Anna was sneaking out of Ryan's cottage like a thief in the night.

She'd had enough of being held prisoner and wanted a taste of freedom. She didn't think too much harm could come from a walk in the middle of the afternoon through a village teeming with people.

She snuck along the road, expecting to bump into Ryan at any moment. Guiltily, she took the back alleys through the village, skirting around the edge rather than taking the more direct route through the centre. She didn't see the young police officer a few hundred yards behind her, hurrying to keep up.

The Heritage Centre came into view and she trotted over to slip through the automatic doors. Letting out a sigh of pure guilt, she found herself smiling at the familiar sights and sounds. How many times had she led visitors around the displays? Too many to count.

"Lindisfarne Priory is the site of the earliest known Anglo-Saxon Christian monastery. Irish monks settled here in 635 AD following an invitation from Oswald, the Northumbrian king who has been the inspiration for characters such as Aragorn in *Lord of the Rings*," Bowers' voice rang out clearly as he brought history to life for a group of children from the local school on the island. "Northumbria was the largest kingdom in Britain at that time, so it was very powerful."

Mark caught her eye above the heads of the children and smiled, gave her a gesture to say he would be five minutes.

Anna smiled in return and settled back against the wall of the visitor's centre to listen. She had heard it all before but she never grew tired of hearing about the island's past.

"A monk called Cuthbert came to the island around 670 AD. He became Prior of Lindisfarne and was eventually made a bishop. Eleven years after he died, his body was exhumed and they found that it looked just the same," Mark paused for effect, watching the avid faces of the young teens listening to the tale. "Which was said to be a miracle and a sure sign of his saintliness."

He pointed to a painting which showed the body being exhumed from its coffin and smiled when a few of the boys made the obligatory gagging noises to attract attention.

"Miracles were reported at St Cuthbert's shrine," he continued. "People started to make the pilgrimage to Lindisfarne which also meant that the Priory grew in power and wealth, because the important people of the land made donations and gifts."

He moved along to the next viewing screen, where a portion of the Lindisfarne Gospels was displayed in an airtight cabinet.

"Another thing to remember is that Lindisfarne was a great centre of Christian learning and scholarship. Most importantly, there was the Lindisfarne Gospels, a beautiful example of early Mediaeval art made around 710 AD. Here's a bit of it," he gestured to the case and several eager faces moved closer, pressing their noses against the polished glass.

Anna smiled as she watched him enthral the next generation of young minds. She remembered when she had come here as a child, wanting to know more about her heritage. He had been as patient then as he was now, she thought.

"Didn't the Vikings come?" one of the children asked, thinking of long-ships and horned helmets.

"They did, young man," Mark nodded. "They raided Lindisfarne in 793 AD. The Pagans desecrated the Priory."

"What's a Pagan?" the same child asked.

"It was a word used, mostly by Christians, to describe unbelievers of any kind. In this case, the Vikings."

Anna raised her eyebrows at the response but said nothing. She hadn't realised Mark took such a sympathetic approach to interpretation.

"What happened to the miracles?" another child asked.

"Well, they were still said to happen," Mark answered, "but they had to move St Cuthbert's relics to the cathedral in Durham for safekeeping."

"Didn't he miss being on Lindisfarne?"

"I'm sure he did," Mark answered, looking at Anna. "But he was brought back, years later, during the Norman Conquest."

That wrapped up the lecture for the day and Anna watched the children file out. Funny, but Mark was right, she thought. Like Cuthbert, she had come back to her home after a period of unrest.

Mark waved the children off and turned back to where Anna stood, tall and serene in the dim room offset by the subtle lighting of the display cabinets.

"Missing me already?" he said, only half-joking.

"Always," she agreed with a smile but she was already turning away to look at the old coins and relics resting carefully on their cushioned beds.

Mark walked over to join her.

"How is the investigation progressing?" he asked after a few moments' companionable silence.

She shrugged. "Hard to tell. They're tireless and dedicated but I think frustrated because they can't find any DNA evidence." That was no more than most of the islanders already knew.

"I understood that you were on the island to assist with the police," he said quietly, then added, "terrible news about Rob."

"Yes," she agreed, thinking of her childhood friend but mindful of the agreement she had made with Ryan. "I can't help them officially because I'm related to one of the victims."

Mark looked at her with one of his enigmatic smiles.

"Officially."

"Exactly," she said.

They were both silent for another moment.

"But they asked for you in the first place," Mark circled around to the point. "I suppose that means that you have relevant expertise. Pagan rituals?"

She sighed. She could never hide the truth from her mentor and besides, he had a sharp mind.

"Yes, they believed I could help them with matters of pagan ritual and history."

"Is that what we're dealing with?"

"Hard to say," she muttered, not wanting to give away too much but feeling conflicted. "There are distinct overtones."

"Such as?"

"Mark, look, I…"

"Never mind, forget I asked." He held up his hands.

"It isn't that I don't want to discuss it with you. I wish that I could," she said with feeling. "I just don't want to break any rules."

"Don't you mean any *more* rules?" he said mildly.

Anna said nothing.

"Let's talk of other things," he murmured, leading her away.

* * *

Ryan and Phillips found the vicar of Lindisfarne bundled in his outdoor gear, wrestling with the door of his greenhouse.

"Reverend Ingles, we'd like a moment of your time, please." Both men walked across the lawn and watched the vicar jam the door shut with an almighty heave.

"Looks like that door hinge could do with oiling," Phillips commented.

"Oh, it's the weather," Ingles said. "Always freezes the joints."

Ryan followed the line of an electric cable leading all the way from the vicarage to the greenhouse.

"What's the cable for?" he asked.

"That's for the heater," Ingles replied. "To keep my tomatoes warm."

Ryan glanced at the fat red tomatoes sitting cosily inside the greenhouse and was reminded of his mother's blooming garden.

"That's pretty fancy," he said with some admiration. "It must take dedication and a hefty electricity bill to keep the tomatoes ripe at this time of year."

"That and a touch of madness to even try to harvest tomatoes in winter," Ingles agreed with a smile. "Shall we?" He gestured them across the lawn towards the vicarage.

Inside, the vicarage was comfortably furnished with quality antiques and expensive materials. Obviously, Ryan thought, the Anglican Church was doing well on Lindisfarne. They took a seat on a squishy pale pink sofa heaped with cushions of varying shades of the same colour.

Mrs Ingles, small and bird-like in a simple navy wool dress hurried into the room with a tray of tea and biscuits which reminded Ryan of afternoon teas at his grandmother's house.

Phillips eyed the expensive china cups cautiously but took the offered tea. Ryan watched him sip delicately.

"Thank you, Mrs Ingles," Ryan said politely, with a charming smile. There was no answering smile, however, merely a nod from the pinched face of a woman who was clearly old before her time. She left the room without another word.

Interesting.

"Now, detectives," Ingles settled himself in a winged chair opposite them and took his own cup. "How can I help you? I presume I don't need a solicitor present?"

Ryan took in the pleasant room with its fussy, feminine décor that didn't match the mistress of the house or its master, for that matter. Ingles still sat comfortably enough in one of the flowered chairs, one thin leg crossed over the other, Ryan noted. Phillips had related the tale of the morning to him, starting with Ingles finding the body on the beach. The job made you cynical, Ryan thought, but Ingles could easily have been revisiting the scene of his crime when Phillips stumbled across him.

He'd spent some time considering the setting of Rob's body, too. It was possible that the pentagram on which the young man rested could have been dislodged as the bonfire blazed, which meant that it could have been the right way up all along rather than inverted.

That made it a Christian symbol after all.

He hadn't forgotten what Alex Walker had told him, either, as he watched the harmless-looking man sitting quietly opposite.

"No need for a solicitor, Mr Ingles. We're merely following up on the details you've already given in your statement. You have a lovely home," he began genially.

"Thank you, Chief Inspector."

Privately, Ryan thought it looked like a show home. "I hope you've recovered somewhat from your ordeal of the morning," Ryan continued, turning to the vicar with a sympathetic look in his eye. He thought that the man looked the very picture of contentment.

"Indeed, yes," Ingles said gravely, his face changing slightly to reflect sadness. "It was a great shock, one that I won't forget any time soon, but the Lord works in ways we may sometimes find hard to understand."

"That's putting it mildly," Phillips said quietly.

"Quite," Ryan said. "I'm not a religious man," he confessed and saw disapproval pass across Ingles' face. "So I have to say that I do find it difficult to understand why anyone would wish to hurt Rob Fowler in that manner."

"Why indeed?" Ingles sighed deeply and shook his head. "Such a nice young man."

"How long had you known him?"

"He and his family have been members of my congregation since he was born," Ingles said.

"Would you say that you knew him well?"

"I like to think that I know my entire congregation well, detective," he said. "A shepherd should know his flock."

Much more of this God-speak was going to start pissing him off, Ryan thought, but his face was placid when he spoke.

"Do you find that people come to you in confession, Reverend?"

"Well, now, formal confession is a facet of the Catholic faith," Ingles said with a chuckle, "but of course, people feel that they can talk to me."

"Did Rob come and talk to you about anything that was bothering him?"

Ryan watched mild discomfort pass across Ingles' face.

"Not especially," he said.

"You're sure?" Ryan said with puzzlement. "I understood that Rob had such a high regard for your counsel."

Ryan understood no such thing but what he did know was that Mike Ingles was a man who responded to flattery. He could see it.

Sure enough, the other man's chest puffed out slightly.

"That's very comforting to know," he said. "As I say, I do my best to make all welcome in God's house."

"Yes," Ryan agreed, then leaned forward as if to conspire. "Of course, it must be hard when you're faced with, well, *undesirable* people." Ryan let a trace of distaste into his voice.

"Undesirable?" Ingles enquired.

"You know," Ryan lifted a hand, "let's just say people who don't follow the word of God," he said meaningfully.

Ingles' face cleared and he leaned forward, mirroring Ryan's stance.

"I think I understand you, Chief Inspector." He sighed again, as if tormented. "Sometimes, individuals do come to me to confess that they have had...we'll say *improper* thoughts."

"Mmm," Ryan nodded knowingly.

"I do my best to counsel them towards the path of righteousness," Ingles carried on, stirring his tea thoughtfully.

"Was Rob one such person?" Phillips interjected.

Ingles looked pained. "Gentlemen, I feel a sense of duty towards that young man. If he told me anything, confessed anything, you might say, it was in confidence."

"Of course," Ryan and Phillips said in unison.

Ingles looked between them.

"He *might* have come to me a few months ago," he confirmed slowly, drawing it out. "I seem to remember that he was struggling with his own urges at the time."

"Urges?" Ryan's face was deliberately blank.

"Towards members of the same sex," Ingles said in hushed tones, as if to speak it aloud would bring the wrath of God upon him.

Ryan's mouth formed an 'o' of surprise and Phillips nearly snorted into his teacup.

"That must have been difficult for you," Ryan said.

"Indeed it was," Ingles recalled. "Of course, I immediately referred him to the words of the Bible. 'You shall not lie with a man as a woman, that is an abomination.' Leviticus, chapter 18, verse 22."

"Hmm," Ryan mused, putting the tea cup down. "Of course, other passages in the Bible forbid all manner of practices which are acceptable today. One could say that those lines reflect outdated cultural values, Reverend."

Ryan's placid voice fell like a hammer in the silent drawing room. Ingles watched him for a few quiet seconds before his hand picked up the rhythmic stirring of his tea again.

"I always welcome theological debate with intelligent people such as yourself, Chief Inspector. However, in this case, I really think that the words of our Lord were unambiguous."

"And how did you approach the matter when Rob Fowler told you he was gay?"

Ingles mouth twisted.

"I told him the same as I have told you, Chief Inspector. I advised him to study the words of the Bible and find healing in them."

"Healing?" Ryan's voice was incredulous.

"Quite so, Chief Inspector."

Ryan looked at the man responsible for the spiritual guidance of an island.

"Do you believe that his death was motivated by intolerance toward his sexuality?"

"I couldn't say," Ingles commented mildly.

"To your knowledge, is there an anti-gay movement on the island?"

Ingles looked shocked. "Our little island is inhabited by loving people who embrace God's word and His forgiveness. As such, it is likely that our congregation adheres to the words of our Lord in all things, including the subject of homosexuality. However, that does not mean that there would be a witch hunt, Chief Inspector."

"How did you feel when you found Rob Fowler, Mike?" Ryan deliberately dropped any respect for formality. The gesture did not go unnoticed.

"Horrified, of course."

"Did you feel that God's work had been done?"

Ingles was silent, his face a mask of anger.

"I would like you to leave my house," he said eventually, replacing his cup and saucer with a clatter.

Ryan and Phillips stood, looking down on the man sunk against his chair before they walked out into the crisp air. Apparently, they had outstayed this shepherd's welcome.

* * *

When Ryan turned back to look at the house they had just left, he saw Jennifer Ingles peering out of one of the bedroom windows and felt a chill. If man was supposed to take a wife, he felt sorry for the reverend in his choice.

"What did you make of that?" he asked Phillips as they walked back through the village.

"Narrow-minded old coot," Phillips said with a sunny smile.

"Enough to get rid of one of his congregation?"

"Don't know if he's got the balls for it," Frank said. "You didn't see the state of him this morning."

"I saw the state of you this morning," Ryan couldn't resist saying.

Phillips merely grunted.

"Let's get back to the cop shop and see about wrapping this damn thing up."

CHAPTER 21

Ryan's cottage was a hive of activity. The log-burning fires, which invited a man to sit with a glass of Bordeaux and a decent book, were stone cold with disuse. The hallway was littered with boots of all shapes and sizes, mostly caked with mud. Faulkner's team had appropriated the smaller sitting room, where he and his gofers pored over chemical data and lurid shots of the crime scenes in an attempt to revisit their initial findings.

MacKenzie and her team sprawled in the Incident Room, which was conveniently located near to the fridge. Some thoughtful person had stocked it with sugary drinks and snacks but it certainly hadn't been him.

As Ryan and Phillips shrugged out of their coats, the noise level told them that Gregson wasn't on site. If he had been, they certainly wouldn't have heard the sound of grown men and women arguing over whether Santa Claus really existed.

Ryan was gratified to see his staff come to attention as he moved through the hall but he didn't see Anna.

"Lowerson," he pointed a finger at the young detective currently swallowing an over-large bite of thick chocolate in the shape of a reindeer. "You've got a woman in protective custody upstairs. She still up there?"

An odd flush crept up the young man's skin and Ryan's eyes darkened.

"Please tell me that when I go upstairs, I will find Doctor Taylor sitting comfortably at the writing desk in my spare bedroom."

"Ah…" Lowerson's chin wobbled dangerously. "The thing is, sir, we couldn't hold her against her will."

Ryan took several deep breaths.

"Where is she?"

"In the village, sir."

"Send one of the rookies after her."

"Already done. He's been keeping an eye on her all afternoon."

With a face like thunder, Ryan dismissed him and headed through to the Incident Room. It was a marvel, really, how easily Anna could annoy him. Did she think that they had endless resources so that he could just send an officer to trot after her while she went for an afternoon stroll around the island?

Did the woman have any idea of the kind of danger she could be in?

Ten minutes later, the team crammed in, covering every available inch of space.

Ryan had separated the murder wall into three sections with three different timelines to indicate the last known movements of each victim. Any more deaths, he thought, and they would run out of wall space.

"I want to go through what we have on each victim, one by one," he said. Best to keep things logical, when the volume of information was building rapidly and threatened to swamp them.

"So, beginning with Lucy Mathieson," he pointed to a picture of Lucy as she had been in life, smiling out at them from her high school graduation picture. "We already know that a particular soap product was used to cleanse her body, containing, amongst other things, sandalwood and shea butter." Ryan picked up the bag from the gift shop and handed it to Faulkner. "I need the analysis expedited. I have a feeling that it's going to match what we found on Lucy's body but I want to be sure. Phillips will get onto the manufacturer for a list of known outlets first thing in the morning, in case it was purchased off-island. Meanwhile, I have a list here of the number of times that item was sold at the Heritage Gift Shop and the credit card numbers for each." Liz had come through, he thought with a smile.

"It's a big leap, but say we hit lucky and this is the soap, which he bought on the island. He could have paid cash, which means we're at a dead end. On the other hand," he smoothed out the list from Liz, "he could have been sloppy. Phillips, get me the matching names for these card numbers."

Phillips took the list in his stubby fingers.

"While you're at it, I want to know where the camphor was purchased."

"Already got that," Phillips flipped open a dog-eared notebook. "Only two places you can buy it within a hundred miles. One of them is a health shop in Newcastle," he said matter-of-factly, "and the other one's the health food, jingle-jangle, crafty-type shop on the main square."

Ryan smiled slowly.

"Naturally, you checked the shop in Newcastle first," he said, tongue-in-cheek.

"Naturally, guv, but as it happens, camphor isn't one of their top sellers. Hadn't had a sale for months," he shook his head in sympathy. "On the other hand, the craft shop here on the island reported a sale only two weeks' ago."

"To whom?"

"Lucy Mathieson," Phillips returned flatly.

There was silence in the room for a full minute while various options ran through their collective mind.

"She didn't have it on her when she was found," Ryan said aloud and received a nod from Faulkner. "It was mixed with turpentine, in any event, wasn't it?"

"Yes," Faulkner confirmed.

"What reason would she have to buy camphor?" Ryan thought aloud.

"Could ask Pete or one of her friends in the morning?" MacKenzie suggested.

"Good idea," Ryan nodded and moved to the window to look out across the sea. The wind was starting to howl, he thought, watching the waves roll and crash against the sand.

"MacKenzie," he turned back. "What about building works on the island?"

"Sir," she nodded and flipped open her pad. Phillips tried not to notice the way her red hair glimmered in the warm light of the room. "We covered the entire eight-mile radius in a quadrant search. Some properties are unoccupied - mostly holiday homes - and we were unable to gain access to certain homes without a warrant, a list of which I have compiled." She leaned over and handed him the list.

"What about the rest?"

"Most people were happy to give us permission to look around. There were various bits and pieces," she said. "Lots of paved driveways, new tarmacking, a couple of house extensions. I've listed the details on here," she handed him another piece of paper. "In essence, sir, nothing popped up at first glance."

"What about purchases?"

MacKenzie turned to another page in her book. "There are five builders' merchants in the vicinity, sir. We've contacted all of them for details of purchases of quarried building sand of the relevant type and weight. We are in the process of analysing the card purchases and have requested copies of the CCTV footage from each establishment for the past month. They're couriering it over at first tide tomorrow."

Ryan nodded. It was good work but just not fast enough.

"What about Lucy's phone?" He turned to Tom Faulkner and watched his unremarkable face come alive under the scrutiny.

"Recent text messages wiped, as with outgoing calls, but we contacted the phone provider and they've sent through a spreadsheet of recent calls and texts. Seems she had six missed calls from her father between ten and midnight on 20th," Faulkner said. "She also had a further four text messages asking when she would be coming home."

"Concerned father?"

"Looks that way," Faulkner agreed. "One outgoing message back saying that she was on her way home at eleven thirty-two."

Ryan couldn't remember Daniel Mathieson mentioning in his statement that he had heard from his daughter via text.

"Anything else?"

"Quite a few messages outgoing to Alex Walker," Faulkner said. "All flirtatious," he coloured a bit as his eyes scanned the transcripts. "A bit, er, suggestive, sir."

Ryan decided not to torment the man, so held out a hand for the paperwork. He scanned the transcript and hitched a hip on the edge of the table while he did.

"She wasn't shy," he commented but thought that the messages seemed so...*young*. "Only one reply from Walker, saying he was busy, that he might see her in the pub."

"Innocuous enough," Phillips said.

Ryan nodded, reading Phillips like a book. Why would the messages need to be wiped if they didn't contain anything suspicious?

"Nothing else jumping out here," he said, placing the paper in his folder. But a feeling was starting to spread in his gut. He told himself they would check things out thoroughly, first, because without the rest of the data they had nothing on which to build a case.

Perhaps there was another way, he thought after a moment.

"Phillips," he murmured. "I need you to contact the Mathiesons. Tell them I need one of them to make a statement to the press tomorrow morning, an appeal for Lucy's killer."

"Just one of them?" Frank queried. "Don't you want to contact Gregson for approval first?"

"We won't need it," Ryan replied, face poker-straight. Phillips sat back and clasped his fingers over his stomach, mulling it over.

"Let's move on to Megan Taylor," Ryan said, once again gesturing to an image of Megan tacked to the wall. It was of her leaning against the side of the pub, slim, curvy and gorgeous while blowing a kiss to the camera. Bill had given up this photograph from his personal collection.

"Lowerson," he turned to the younger man, who was still feeling chastened from his SIO's earlier disapproval.

"Sir."

"I want your report on the narcotics." Ryan sat back expectantly.

Lowerson cleared his throat and battled with nerves but won. "I contacted the narcotics team in Newcastle and Morpeth, sir. Both units report that known incidents of LSA abuse have generally been low for the past ten years. However, there's always a spike around June and December."

"Why?"

"They are at a loss, sir, except to say that recreational drug use spikes over the summer months alongside better weather and outdoor activities or as an accompaniment to the holiday festivities." Lowerson looked up and swallowed. "However, following our present line of investigation, I considered any ritualistic element that could be relevant. As you're aware, Lucy was killed in the early hours of the winter solstice. The summer solstice falls in June, sir."

"You think the drugs spike coincides with these festivals?"

"Yes, sir. The drug is primarily used for its hallucinogenic properties, which seems to fit the bill."

"That's good thinking, detective," Ryan approved, "but we don't have any proof. Never hurts to have a working theory, but tell me some facts."

"Well," Lowerson consulted his notes, although he had committed the information to memory. "Around fifteen years ago, the only known local operation was shut down in Morpeth where large amounts of Morning Glory were harvested for the purpose of onward sale."

"Who was the operator?"

"Well, that's the funny thing, sir. The house and garden were owned by a woman living alone, who seemed to run the whole thing herself. House was registered to her. She got five years in Durham prison after a prosecution back in '99."

"Where is she now?"

"Seems to have dropped off the face of the earth," Lowerson complained. "Changed her name. The house is still sitting there unused. No family still living."

"Physical description?"

"Back then, she was five-five, around 110 pounds, light brown hair and brown eyes. Unremarkable, by all accounts. She would be fifty-two now. I've asked the department to hunt out a picture of her, sir."

"Good work, Lowerson. Let me know the minute it comes through."

Lowerson barely held off a grin.

"Any ideas about where current supply is coming from?"

"No known operations, which indicates a private supply, sir."

"On the island, or near it," Ryan muttered.

"Seems most likely," Lowerson agreed.

Ryan thought of all the pretty gardens and the large nature reserve with its acres of wild flowers. He wondered if their mystery woman had moved to Lindisfarne and set up business again.

"Have to do a search," he decided. "Get a picture of what we're looking for and do a house-to-house search where the owner gives permission. Too flimsy to ask for a warrant for every house on the island, but we can shake a few places down." He paused and turned back with a fierce look on his face. "Start with the vicarage."

Lowerson's eyebrows shot up but he was not in the habit of questioning his superior. "Yes, sir."

"Where are we with Megan's financials?"

MacKenzie sat forward again, slid a folder across to him.

"Bank faxed through copies earlier this afternoon, sir, but they've blanked out the names of any named accounts other than Megan's. Data protection," she explained, with a twist of her lips. "At first glance, there appear to be a number of regular payments into her account via standing order, as well as a number of regular cash deposits."

Ryan hummed and glanced through the numbers.

"The first of the month indicates her regular salary from the pub, but the other payments at other dates in the month are unaccounted for," MacKenzie added.

"One of these standing orders will be from Walker," Ryan said. "You'll probably find some of these cash payments are also from Bill Tilson. I want to know where the others are coming from."

"We're looking into it now, sir," MacKenzie said with a slightly harried air. "The bank is being very uncooperative."

"Tell them to get the stick out of their arse," he muttered.

"I may use different terminology," Denise said primly, but her eyes gleamed with amusement. Phillips folded his arms and tried not to resent the easy camaraderie or the fact that his SIO would always have a smooth way with women.

"DS Phillips and I found a journal of sorts in Megan's apartment earlier this afternoon," Ryan continued, thinking of the green and gold diary currently secured in a plastic evidence bag. "Faulkner gave it the once-over, but there's only one set of prints on it—hers. If there's anything tasty in it, her killer would have confiscated or destroyed it since he's such a meticulous man. I'm betting he had no idea it was there."

He thought of Anna and the help she had given him that afternoon, without which they may never have found the diary. As if he had conjured her up by thought alone, he saw with some amusement that she was sneaking around the back of the house like a guilty teenager. His lips quirked as he watched her through the window, battling against the wind and the rain to find the handle on the back door. Clearly, she hadn't seen the roomful of police officers waiting behind the door.

He strolled over and unlocked it, watched her trip and practically fall into his arms.

"Well," he purred, looking at her pink cheeks and mutinous eyes, "look what I've found."

Anna glanced around her in mortification. Stupidly, she had thought the back door would be a better bet than the front if she wanted to make an unobtrusive entrance. Now, she looked into the faces of a roomful of expectant police staff.

"Ah…" she twisted her hands together.

Before she had time to say anything further, a cold and harassed-looking young man stomped through the door behind her and nodded to his superior.

"Evening, sir," he mumbled, shaking off the rain and heading towards his comrades.

Anna looked on with undisguised shock and then turned on Ryan without a thought for the audience.

"You had me *followed?*"

Ryan's lips compressed. Now was not the time for histrionics.

"Actually, my loyal staff organised for you to be followed for your own protection. Clearly, you have no sense of self-preservation, so you should consider yourself fortunate that there are people willing and able to safeguard your wellbeing."

Anna was vibrating with anger.

"If, by 'safeguard', you mean 'keep under house arrest in your spare room'," she said, "then excuse me if I struggle to be grateful. I know the island, I know the people on it. I was perfectly safe."

His temper snapped and he grabbed her arm in a firm grip, frogmarched her from the room and the prying eyes of his team. Once in the hallway, he rounded on her.

"For an intelligent woman, *doctor*, you can be incredibly stupid." His eyes were a swirl of emotion and she almost stepped away but pride kept her where she was.

Anna had been called many things, but 'stupid' was never one of them.

"Listen," she said, "I didn't ask you to play the hero and kidnap me to your cottage to be babysat."

"You don't get it, do you?" he said disbelievingly. "You're in danger, Anna. Listen to me," he said sharply, when she started to speak. "Someone who is seriously disturbed is telling you that you need protection. We don't know who, or whether they believe you need protecting from them or from someone else but what I do know is that I'm not letting them get their bloody paws on you. Understand?"

Anna swallowed and realised there wasn't just anger under the hard words, there was real concern.

"I'm sorry," she said quietly. "I was feeling claustrophobic."

"I understand that," he said in a gentler tone. "But help me out here, will you? I can't get this done if I'm constantly worrying about you."

Her lips twitched.

"You worry about me?"

His eyes were gentle pools now. "Yes, Anna, I do."

He lowered his mouth to hers in the briefest of kisses, a brush of lips only, before releasing her again.

"I'll stay here until you catch your killer," Anna found herself saying.

"Thank you," he replied and watched her walk up the stairs. At the top, she paused and looked down.

"I'm ordering a take-away," she said gruffly. "Your hospitality stinks, Ryan."

He was smiling as he walked back into the incident room.

"Alright, show's over," he said, noting that several members of his team were sporting knowing smiles.

"We don't have a murder weapon for Megan," Phillips started.

"Right you are," Ryan agreed, grateful that Frank had dived straight back into business. "Faulkner has already given us an idea of the sort of implement we're looking for," he nodded to Tom and then reached for a picture Anna had printed for him earlier. "This might help us, too."

He turned and fixed the image onto the wall behind him. It was a diagram of various different types of ceremonial knives.

"This diagram was found in a grimoire known as the Key of Solomon," he began.

"What the hell is a 'grimoire'?" Phillips complained. Why couldn't people just use normal words for things?

"It's a sort of textbook of magic," Ryan said. "Like an instruction manual for ceremonial religions or covens."

Phillips didn't bother asking where his SIO had found that out.

"Some modern pagans use a grimoire known as the Book of Shadows," Ryan continued. "We don't know that our perp is following any of this, but since we're already pissing in the dark, why don't we carry on?"

There were a few sniggers.

"As you can see, there are various types of knife drawn here," he looked at the assortment of daggers. "The most appropriate in this case would be the 'athame'," he flicked a finger over a drawing of a ceremonial dagger with a double edged blade and a black ornate handle.

"Blade would be consistent with the wound," Faulkner nodded.

"There's a lot of symbolism attached to it," Ryan shrugged, thinking that he was tired of trying to understand what went through the mind of a mental defective. "It's supposed to represent fire."

"Four weapons of Celtic significance," Phillips said knowledgeably and shrugged at his SIO's stare. "What? I can read," he added defensively, catching MacKenzie's eye.

"Tell me more," Ryan invited.

"Earth, air, fire and water," Phillips barked out. "When people want to fanny about in the woods calling up spirits and God knows, they use four things to represent each element. A sword or a dagger means fire, a wand represents air, a cup is for water and a pentacle is for the earth." Phillips wouldn't admit he had no idea what a pentacle was. "You can save yourself time and just watch *Angels and Demons*. Tom Hanks spends his time chasing around a Catholic killer and finds the victims by reference to the four primordial elements which make out the geographical shape of a cross in Rome."

Phillips wondered idly whether there was any resemblance between himself and Tom Hanks but was forced to admit that he looked a lot younger than Hanks.

"Anyhow," Frank tugged at his ear. "Then they purify the circle with the rest of the elements—for air, they use incense, for water, they use salt water and for the earth, they use good old-fashioned salt. The athame is more of an individual tool, whereas the sword would be used in a gathering by a high priest or whoever's walking around wearing the bat cape. They cast a circle using the sword and it's supposed to be like a ring of fire," Phillips added. "Makes me think of Johnny Cash."

"Where did you get all this?" MacKenzie asked him.

"I got chatting to Liz down at the gift shop," Phillips answered casually, inspecting his nails.

MacKenzie's lips flattened and she looked away with a sniff.

Ryan grinned.

"Full marks for research," he said dryly. "We can bear it in mind, but the setting of Megan's body seems far too opportunistic for us to assume that our perp has put that much thought into it."

"Rob was found burned," Phillips persisted.

"But neither Megan nor Lucy were found doused in salt water, or salt for that matter. None of them were found drowned, were they? Lucy was covered in oil, but you could hardly call it 'incense'."

Frank was stumped.

"On the other hand, our perp seems to like dipping in and out of existing rituals," Ryan carried on, "so we may be looking for a ceremonial knife like this athame. I want a list of places where somebody could get one. Lowerson, that's your next project along with the narcotics."

"Yes, sir," he bobbed his head and started scribbling frantically. Ryan tried to remember being that eager at any point in his life, but failed.

"Faulkner, where are we at with forensics?"

"Sir, we found trace blood samples in the drainage pipes leading from the shower in Megan's bathroom and they're being analysed as we speak. I'm hopeful that we'll get those results by noon tomorrow."

"Good," Ryan nodded.

"We recovered a number of hairs and fibres, which are also being analysed. We'll find a lot of these belonged to Megan, since they're long, dark and appear to be porous which is consistent with coloured hair," Faulkner added. "Still, we might find a few strays among them."

"Anything else we can use?"

"Nothing further, sir. We have fingerprint matches for Bill Tilson but none for any other sets we have taken from the islanders. Do you want me to seek further prints?"

Ryan considered. Already on file, they had prints from the Mathiesons, Bill Tilson, Pete Rigby (after much argument from his concerned mother, Alison), Alex Walker and Anna. The only matches so far had been from Anna, Alex and Bill, none of which were in sufficient number or placement to be of concern.

"It's worth a try, Tom. Go on and ask the men of the island for their fingerprints, voluntarily. What's the worst that can happen?"

"They'll complain to Gregson? Shout about victimisation?" Phillips supplied helpfully.

"Thank you, Frank."

"No bother," he returned cheerfully.

"Getting back to it," Faulkner said with an owlish smile, "we have some fingerprints; the boot prints and the samples are in for analysis."

"Let me know when the results come back," Ryan said and then thought of loose ends. "Did we hear back about the CCTV outside the Heritage Centre?"

"Yep," Phillips said. "Got precisely zero activity outside the Centre or the Gift Shop at the time of Lucy's murder."

"Well." Ryan blew out a breath. "It was worth checking. Frank, when we've isolated names on soap sales from the Gift Shop, go back and ask the technician to cross-check for those times and dates. That will take a lot longer and it's working on the presumption that they've kept the tapes from weeks ago, but it all adds up."

"Aye," was all Phillips said.

"I'm going to go through Megan's journal tonight," Ryan continued. "We'll wait for the results of the financials and see if we can cross them with any names I find in there. Meantime, I want to find the stash of morning glory kicking around on the island. First thing," he nodded to Lowerson and received his nod in return.

"Consider it done," he murmured.

"Now," Ryan poured himself a cup of lukewarm coffee and tried not to gag. "Robert Fowler."

* * *

Another hour later, empty pizza boxes lay strewn around the kitchen from where Ryan's team had attacked them like a pack of hungry lions. He'd barely managed to nab a slice of double pepperoni with his hand intact but he was grateful to Anna for thinking of fuel for his team.

The toxicology results had confirmed the same use of LSA on Rob Fowler but in a massively increased dosage, indicating that Fowler would have been in a mild coma when he was tied down and thrown on the fire. There was some comfort in knowing that he would have been unaware of what was happening to him, at least for a while. Fishing wire had cut into his wrists and ankles, holding him in place while the fire had been lit. They were looking into the type of wire and where it could have been purchased.

From what had been left of Rob, the CSIs had been able to discern some slight abrasions on the inside of his mouth, indicating that it had been forced open. Presumably, so that the seeds could be shoved down his throat. Ryan thought of Rob Fowler, of the well-built young man in his prime of life and doubted that one person alone could have taken him down. The pathologist had commented that, since the body had been so badly burned, it was nearly impossible for him to discern whether Rob had suffered any head trauma, or other wounds, before he was trussed up. It was therefore possible that he was immobilised by one person, who could have taken him by surprise with a blow to the head.

That was something to think about.

The fire had burned away most of the skin, removing any need to ritually cleanse the body as with the previous two. Ryan had to wonder whether the funeral pyre had been a premeditated act or an expedient one.

Door-to-doors had revealed that many of the islanders had been in their homes, alone or with their partner or spouses, at the time Rob had died. Without links to the other murders, they weren't going to chase down anyone in particular.

He had requested the call logs from the coastguard base, where Rob had been on duty the previous evening. There was nothing of interest on his personal mobile, which had been found in the pocket of his red jacket, so perhaps there would be something on the main line.

* * *

A few miles south of Ryan's cottage, in a wine bar in the pretty little coastal town of Alnmouth, four men sat together, smartly dressed and affluent.

"Apparently, Megan kept a diary," one murmured as he enjoyed the rich merlot with a hunk of expensive cheese. "They've found it."

One of the men jerked forward in his chair, sloshed wine in his glass.

"*What*? What did she say? Does she name anyone?"

"Calm yourself," the third man said in mellow tones, casting a subtle glance around the room.

"I don't know what it says, Ryan's keeping it under lock and key while he goes through it but if anything comes to light, rest assured we will take the necessary action."

"It was opportunistic, offering Megan without consulting with us first," the quiet man said.

"It is not for you to question your High Priest," the other snapped defensively, while the first stuffed more cheese in his mouth. "The Master demanded she be offered up to him."

Considering the matter closed, he turned to the fourth man, sitting silently in his chair, unable to eat.

"Your actions have endangered all of us," he said in whiplash tones which caused the other man to shiver. "Offering Lucy was selfish and unnecessary. Added to which, you had no *right* to take it upon yourself to implicate another."

"I'm sorry, I…I wasn't thinking."

"It is not for you to take such decisions," the High Priest said.

All three men watched the fourth in condemnation.

"It is fortunate for you that we were able to turn your actions to our advantage," the High Priest continued after a significant pause.

The fourth man darted looks around the table.

"What—what do you mean?"

"The circle is indebted to you, despite your disobedience," the first man sipped more wine. "There is a way for you to redeem yourself."

The fourth man swallowed tears of relief. He knew what usually happened to the disobedient.

"H—how?"

The High Priest sat back in his chair, satisfied. Their thoughts turned to the future.

CHAPTER 22

Psychopaths are goal-oriented. Basic criminology training gave you the facts on paper, written in fat textbooks in clear, black-and-white print. Experience taught you that it was true.

Ryan settled himself to read. He wasn't dealing with a disordered, unstructured individual who reacted without thought or planning. These crimes were premeditated, with some ritual added in for flavour. Underneath it all, you had someone entirely lacking in moral compass, capable of destroying life without conscience. It was interesting, Ryan thought, that the man had tried to create a moral code for himself where one did not exist, by surrounding himself in ceremony.

He didn't know which was worse; hunting a killer who acted without moral boundaries, almost at whim, or hunting one who acted under false pretences.

Digesting that, Ryan reached for a blue folder that contained a fat sheaf of papers listing the criminal background checks for many of the islanders; men, women and juveniles alike. For the most part, it made for uninteresting reading.

Alex Walker had a few speeding fines and had nearly lost his licence because of it a few years back. Ryan chalked that up to being a classic boy racer. His father, Walker Senior, had a clean sheet, as did his mother Yvonne.

It amused him to read that Liz Morgan had been prosecuted for a public order offence thirty years ago, for demonstrating against animal cruelty. He moved her into the 'harmless activist' category.

It came as a twin shock to find that Megan Taylor had a squeaky clean sheet, whereas her scholastic sister had received a formal caution for public indecency.

Public indecency?

His mind boggled and he wondered if there had been some sort of mix-up in the records office. He checked the name at the top and, sure enough, it read 'Anna Marie Taylor'.

The description detailed finding her intoxicated and partially nude, frolicking on the beach which, the statement read, was not a designated nudist beach. His lips quirked as he thought of Anna, maybe wearing those secretary glasses he'd noticed sitting on top of her laptop upstairs. He almost gave in to the desire to shove the paperwork to one side and head upstairs to bed and to her.

He picked up the next piece of paper and took a long swig of wine.

* * *

Upstairs, Anna spent a few hours working on her laptop until she could stand the solitude no more. Following the soft strains of bluesy music, she padded downstairs and found Ryan sitting against the backdrop of a crackling fire, surrounded by paperwork. He had stripped down to jeans and a thin black sweater the same colour as his hair. His feet were bare and for the life of her she didn't know why she found that so attractive.

"Why didn't you come and find me?" she asked, stepping into the room.

He looked up, face shadowed but his hair gleaming blue-black against the firelight.

"I'm sorry, I didn't realise the time," he said, rising to meet her and arching his back to ease out the kinks.

"Is there anything I can help you with?" she waved a hand at the papers and tried not to look at the photographs just visible underneath.

"No, not just now," he said quietly, drawing her towards him.

He started to sway her in time to the music. With a gentle hand in the small of her back, he urged her closer against him until their bodies locked together; her head nestled under his chin.

"You didn't tell me you had a criminal past," he said softly, smiling over her head when she tensed.

"What do you mean?" she said defensively, trying to pull away.

"Just that I never knew you were so...liberal, until I read about your antics on the beach a few years ago."

Anna didn't know what to say.

"I'm sorry, I forgot all about it," she began stiffly. "I was going through a bit of a funny phase back then—"

"Anna," he interjected, "It makes you more human and, if possible, more attractive."

"It does?" This man was a mystery, she thought.

"Sure, it does. I don't want an effigy, Anna, a porcelain doll who looks angelic. I'd much rather know the real woman." He lowered his lips to her ear and added, "Perhaps, one day, we can re-live the moment together."

"Oh, well then…" she trailed off, thinking that he had a knack for jumbling her brain so that she couldn't think clearly. She would still rather he hadn't known that she had once danced naked on the beach. "I didn't realise you'd been snooping into my past."

He detected a slight huffiness to her tone and was even more amused.

"It's my job, Anna."

She said nothing for a while, but didn't pull away.

"Who reported you?" he asked.

"What do you mean?" her brow furrowed.

"There's no police on the island. Somebody would need to make a report to the station at Budle or somewhere close. Who ratted you out?"

Amazingly, she had never thought of it, never wondered to ask.

"I have no idea," she said honestly. "If I had to guess—and it hurts me to say it—I would have to say it's exactly the kind of thing Megan would have done. Back then, especially, she would have done anything to cause trouble for me. If she had her sights on Alex, then she had to know that getting in trouble with the police would upset his family. There's nothing more important to Alex than his family," she added.

"What about your place at university?"

"Mark rang the Dean," she remembered. "He explained that the whole thing had been blown up, gave me a glowing reference."

"That was good of him," Ryan said.

"He's been like a father to me," she said with affection.

Ryan smiled, but thought that, for an intelligent woman, she had no idea of the effect she had on the opposite sex. Perhaps that was the source of her charm. Either way, he would be adding Mark Bowers to his mental list of people to look at. It wouldn't be the first time an older man had developed feelings for a much younger woman.

"What are you thinking?" he murmured against her hair.

"That there's more to you than meets the eye," came her muffled answer.

"It doesn't seem to bother you," he commented after ordering his body not to tense.

"Why should it? I'm not afraid of you, Ryan. We all have secrets." But she wondered if she should be worried by the fact that, already, she felt so safe in his arms. She hardly knew him.

"I don't have any secrets," he said simply.

"You keep most of yourself hidden," she argued.

Perhaps that was true, he acknowledged. In that moment, with the house empty of people but for himself and the woman he held, the past didn't feel half as terrifying as it had only a few days earlier.

"There was a woman," he found himself saying quietly.

"There always is," she replied lightly, preparing herself to hear about the trail of broken hearts he had left behind. She had known there would have been other women; he was a grown man, it was only natural. It was childish to expect otherwise, but still she felt an uncomfortable stab of jealousy for the other women he might have held in his arms, as he held her now.

Over her head, his lips twisted and he gently tugged her back to him. He knew her so well, after only a collection of hours spent together.

"It's not what you think," he said after a moment. Her head lifted from his chest and she looked up at where he stood, face still shadowed. When his eyes lowered to face her, she saw sadness hidden there.

"Tell me about it," she said and led him to the sofa, drew him down into the circle of her arms.

He had never done this, he realised. He had never purged himself of the bleakness which filled him and the guilt which consumed him. He had turned away from family and friends. Although he had tried to say that the job had abandoned him, perhaps on reflection it had been the opposite.

"Six months ago, I was working on a long-running case. You heard me mention it the other day—the *Hacker.*"

"Yes, it was covered in the papers over the summer," she nodded, trying to remember the details.

"Well, the *Hacker* wasn't a computer geek. He hacked his victims to pieces, bit by bit, over a number of days. He kept them alive by administering a mix of adrenaline and antibiotic. He had a ready supply, being a doctor working on the A & E department down at the RVI." He referred to the largest hospital in the region.

"I remember," Anna nodded, thinking back to the horrific stories reported across the local and national papers. "There were five victims."

"It was my fault there were five."

"How could it have been your fault?" She covered his hands with hers.

"Oh, I know that, logically-speaking, I couldn't have stopped the first few. The case had been assigned to a different DCI, down in Newcastle. CID transferred it to me after the third. Still."

He took a breath, letting the past come back.

"The man was careful and there wasn't a pattern. He was snatching women from all over. The work spanned three separate CID divisions, took a shed-load of paperwork and bureaucracy."

"I understand administrative crap better than most, working in a university," she smiled.

"I bet," he nodded. "Well, at first the only linking factor was physical type. They were all pretty young brunettes."

He looked at her with a sad smile. "Yes, I know. Like Lucy, like Megan. Like you," he said softly.

"It must have been so hard for you to see it happening again," she said, feeling cold in the warm room.

He saw her shiver and drew her against him. He was pleased when she didn't pull away or tense in his arms. Maybe he could get through the rest of it.

"Their bodies…" he swallowed. "I'd never seen anything like the destruction, Anna. I didn't think somebody would be capable of doing that to another human being but I was wrong. He wasn't a person; he was an animal."

Anna closed her eyes briefly, felt his pain.

"The families were distraught; the press were ravenous for a story. They spread panic like wildfire, binned the department and all the man hours we had spent. I'm telling you, I saw every man and woman in CID work double shifts back-to-back over those months to try to close the case.

"What I didn't account for was that he was tracking me." Another pause before he could get out the rest. "Around that time, I had my sister staying with me."

Anna felt her breath hitch in her chest and tears spring into her eyes because she already knew the next part.

"He killed her and I couldn't stop him," Ryan said flatly. "Natalie was five years younger than me. She was beautiful."

He was quiet for several minutes and Anna didn't interrupt him. She thought of a young woman with black hair and silvery eyes.

"She had only been with me for a few days. She was planning on spending a couple of weeks with me because, as it turned out, my mother was worried that I was working too hard and needed company." His voice threatened to break. "If she had stayed with our parents, it would never have happened."

"You couldn't have known that," Anna said quietly.

"He was picking victims at random," Ryan said. "He didn't stalk them but he made an exception for Natalie. I should have considered the possibility."

Anna opened her mouth to argue with him but he carried on.

"I came home after a long day," Ryan remembered. "It must have been one or two in the morning. He had left pieces of her for me to find: two of her fingers were propped on the coffee table with instructions to catch him if I could."

"You did catch him."

"I was too late." All the anger and grief spilled out with those four words. "He left his fingerprints all over, so he wanted to be found. I think he wanted to go out with a bang; maybe he expected that I would kill him and put him out of his fucking misery."

"You didn't," she said softly.

"I would have killed him," he corrected her. "Phillips dragged me off, but only after I'd smashed his face and broken three of his ribs. I had my hands around his neck when Frank came through the door."

"Self-defence," Anna said with a touch of desperation.

"That was what the department argued," he agreed. "But he had put down his weapons. He killed her in front of me and then told me to take my revenge. I saw red, just a haze of red in front of my eyes, Anna. I would have killed him."

"He murdered your sister," Anna didn't try to pretend that she understood how he must have felt. She had lost her own sister in a brutal murder but not in front of her eyes. She couldn't say what she might have done if it had been.

"Yes. I tried to block the knife," he remembered, fingering the long scar which ran along his upper arm. "He sprayed me with some sort of chemical, blinded me for long enough to smash a hammer into my knee. I went down, couldn't get up again. He slashed her throat in the meantime."

He remembered the hot gush of blood as it had rained down on him.

She had waited for Ryan to open up about this but nothing could have truly prepared her. Anna grasped his hand, linked her fingers with his.

"It wasn't your fault," she repeated and her voice was thick with emotion.

His body shuddered, once.

"So many people have said that," he said, calmer now. "But I'll never believe it."

"Where are your family?" she asked. Why weren't they here, to help him?

"I don't want them," he said flatly, discouraging any further discussion on the matter.

"It's Christmas," she said.

"Do you think my mother wants to visit an island where girls like my sister are being killed off like flies? Do you think she wants to see the son who failed her?" He pushed away from the sofa and walked over to stand in front of the fireplace, rested a hand on the mantle for support.

Such a well of pain, Anna thought, her heart breaking for him. How he could face the investigation each day, she had no idea. The emotional cost must be enormous.

She walked over to him and tentatively wrapped her arms around his waist, rested her cheek against his back.

"Thank you for telling me," was all she said.

"You needed to know," he replied, staring into the flames. "I needed you to know."

There was a long pause while both of them were lost in thought.

"I think you should leave the island, Anna," he said eventually.

"I'm not leaving."

He turned back to her and his face was hard.

"You're in danger. I'm ordering you to leave the island, first thing tomorrow."

"I'm not yours to order around. If I tell you I'm staying, then that's what I'm going to do."

"You *are* mine, Anna. I want you safe."

She understood that, tonight, something had snapped inside him. He needed the comfort that she could give him; that they could give each other. She looked into dark grey eyes which were slightly wild.

"I'm not leaving you," she said quietly, then lifted her arms and let him strip the thin sweater from her body.

Much later, when Anna slept soundly in the curve of his arm, Ryan lay awake staring up at the ceiling. The demons had chased sleep away again but instead of awaking alone, he felt her warm body resting against him. He heard her even breathing and saw her hand resting against his heart.

Amazing, he thought. He hadn't known that he had anything left inside him to share or to give but she had proven him wrong. His mind wanted to think of murder, of whether somebody else would lose their life that night, but fate was kind to him.

He turned into her and, for the first time in months, slept peacefully until morning.

* * *

Elsewhere on the island, the circle met again. Its members were shaky with nerves without the benefit of the drugs they had come to expect. In hushed voices, they whispered about the risk they took and skirted around their unspoken fear that one of their own had committed the island murders. Their leader tried not to sneer. How weak they were, he thought with disgust. How pathetic.

He nodded to one of them, who drew out a small velvet bag filled with the seeds they seemed to need. He watched each of them take a handful and swallow greedily.

He raised the sword and cast the circle, enjoying the theatre of it all. At his signal, they started to say the usual words, each of them wishing for his own share of good fortune.

Cernunnos, we call to You.

Horned One, Dark One, Receiver of the Dead, Granter of Rest, we call to You.

Hunter and Hunted, we call to You.

He held up a hand so the circle stuttered and fell silent. Beneath the animal masks, each of them darted confused glances to each other. He tried not to laugh. They would understand soon enough.

Tonight, their chant would be different. His voice rang out clear and true into the darkened night with words none of them had heard before.

Emperor Lucifer, master of all the rebel spirits,

We beg you to favour us in the call that we make to you.

O, Count Astarot!

Be favourable to us and make it so this night you appear to us in human form.

Accord to us, by the pact that we make with you, all the riches we need.

Ave Satani!

His eyes glowed through the holes in his mask, as if the edifice of a horned goat had come to life. Those around him swayed, no longer frightened but mellow now. He was no longer a man, he realised. He was the bringer of life and death, more than the feeble Horned God their pagan circle had worshipped.

He channelled the power, had made his sacrifices and had become a God.

One by one, they chanted, but one of them scattered their handful of seeds on the ground and watched his High Priest with a clear mind.

CHAPTER 23

Christmas Eve dawned on a misty, grey day. The fog rolled thickly across the sea in a slow chug until it settled heavily over the island. It crowded the walls of the Priory and poured through the streets of the village until visibility was so poor that it was impossible to see beyond a few metres.

At first light, Ryan left Anna sleeping peacefully in his bed. He felt the uncomfortable ache of a man growing used to having a warm and willing woman nearby.

It was more than that, he thought. This woman was under his skin, in his thoughts. How else could he explain how he found himself humming Bonnie Tyler in the shower? It was bizarre. Shaking his head, he headed downstairs to finish reading Megan's diary and gulp down his customary gallon of coffee. Last night's cathartic outburst seemed to have cleared his mind and lifted his spirits. Another thing he had to thank Anna for.

Clearing out the emotional junk had been a lightbulb moment, he realised. Although it was an integral part of the investigation to understand the motivations behind three ritual murders, it had become so that he couldn't see the wood for the trees. At the heart of it, their killer was using ritual and ceremony to provide himself with a reason for killing, when he was really no better than your average murderer. Ryan had seen men and women like that before and had put them in a cell. That made life much simpler.

He sat down with the green and gold journal, filled with renewed purpose.

The diary made for poignant reading, Ryan thought with a twinge of sadness. He knew Megan had been unhappy, but there was nothing more intrusive than reading through the private thoughts of an embittered and disillusioned woman. It was a fat book, filled with small, neat writing. Some of the earlier pages were yellowing with age, but Ryan opted to read the most recent entries and work backwards.

December 21ˢᵗ

Anna came back today. She looked so capable and untouchable in her expensive clothes. I was so angry; I could feel it welling up inside me. I wanted to upset her, to make her shout and scream so that we could make up like we used to. I wanted to tell her I was sorry about Ken, but I said the usual crap instead. I don't know why I did it.

It had taken him a moment but Ryan worked out that 'Ken' was the nickname Megan attributed to Alex Walker. He had to laugh; the Ken doll was a spitting image of the island's coastguard. He read a few more paragraphs where she'd described, in excruciating detail, the love-hate relationship she had with her sister. He thought he understood that already, so he skipped ahead until he found Lucy's name.

Little Lucy was found dead this morning. Lucy was harmless, but she was getting herself in too deep. She shouldn't have poked around or prodded into things she didn't understand.

Ryan looked at the words and wished fervently that he knew what Lucy had been getting herself into and why Megan hadn't disclosed what she knew about it. Frustrated, he carried on. The day before, Megan had written about the mundane quality of her life, about a jacket she had liked, and of her landlord:

December 20ᵗʰ

Billy told me he loved me again today and for some reason I wanted to cry. He's a nice man, but I could never love someone who stands in the same spot my father did, day after day.

Ryan wondered if it was meaningful that, although she had mocked all those around her by replacing their real names with nicknames he had yet to decode, she had always referred to Bill Tilson by name. Perhaps she had cared more than she realised.

December 9ᵗʰ

Greenfinger harassed me again today. I said I wasn't interested in doing any more business and to back off, otherwise D would hear about it.

So, Ryan thought, the unfortunately-named 'Greenfinger' enjoyed doing business with her. What kind of business? And what the hell did she mean by 'D'?

He read on.

<u>*October 15th*</u>

Skinny-P asked me out tonight. I told him to find someone his own age, although it might have been fun to bounce around and teach him a few tricks. His next girlfriend would thank me.

Ryan was disposed to think that the hapless suitor was their own Pete Rigby, the innocent-looking bartender-cum-deputy coastguard.

<u>*September 2nd*</u>

The God Squad tried to convert me again today. A group of them cornered me and started mouthing off about eternities spent in Hell. I told them to have their hair done and they might feel better. But I was thinking that I had fucked their husbands, every last fucking one of them. I had seen them panting with their trousers round their ankles. It made me laugh to think that maybe the wives couldn't afford a decent dye job because their husbands had already spent the petty cash.

This was the darker side to Megan, Ryan thought. The woman slept with a group of married men, for profit. She must have known what that made her. Was this the 'business' she referred to?

At the back of the diary, Megan had inserted a loose table of monthly figures, entered by hand alongside the various nicknames. Ryan bet that these characters exchanged money for Megan's favours and that the sums would be tidily arranged as deposits to her account. No cash had been found in her apartment, which either meant her killer had decided to help himself to her stash, or she was a careful woman who didn't keep cash lying around. He would have to find out.

If they were anywhere else in England, Ryan would have been intrigued by the mention of a 'God Squad'. Unfortunately, on an island that was aptly named 'Holy' and its population ninety per cent Christian, that could be a reference to almost anyone.

Ryan found himself embarrassed by one of the entries she had written about him:

August 31^{*st*}

August 31st

TDH arrived on the island today in a dark grey Merc. Don't know if he's coming or going, but I would love to have a taste of that one. Never had a policeman on the island and I think it's a shame he doesn't wear a uniform, but maybe he'll wear one just for me once we get to know each other a little better. That's one I wouldn't mind doing for free.

After a puzzled moment, Ryan had worked out that 'TDH' meant 'tall, dark and handsome.' He took another hasty drink of coffee and tried not to think about the fact that her sister was sleeping upstairs. His eyebrows shot up when Megan described regularly wandering by his cottage in order to try to catch him. He'd never even felt her pursuit, he realised with some awe. If he had, he didn't know what frame of mind she would have found him in. Perhaps he would have succumbed to her charms, like the rest of her tally of men. Where would that have left him with Anna?

He made a copy of a series of passages which interested him the most, all describing the enigmatic 'D'.

June 21st

D invited me to the circle today. I've never felt so powerful, so included. We were one and I felt whole. It was amazing. He was amazing.

July 1st

Met D in the usual place. He was desperate today. It was funny, really, seeing him reduced to that. Not quite so powerful, or in command when he was begging me to do him harder. What a joke.

July 8th

D came over mid-afternoon, unexpectedly. Told him he needed to make an appointment. He didn't like that and said that I was his property, not to be shared. I told him I needed an incentive. He took his watch right off his wrist and told me it was mine. Should make a healthy dent in my credit card bill for this month, which will do for now.

Circle met again today. Slightly awkward seeing so many of them naked and recognising each of them despite their faces being covered. I wonder if D knows. He said he loved me last night and I think he's on the verge of making a big commitment. Won't that be a shock to the island's elite?

Ryan sat back and re-read the notes he had taken. So, 'D' was an elite member of the island's community and there had been meetings at or with a 'circle', consisting of some or all of the men she had already known. That confirmed an element of ritual existed that wasn't confined to one person acting alone.

He noticed too how easily Megan's feelings towards 'D' had changed from admiration to contempt, as the months had rolled from mid-summer to mid-winter. Where she had once described him as 'amazing', soon enough she referred to him as a pathetic old man, outstaying his welcome in her life. Even more pertinent was Megan's intention to deliver the man with an ultimatum. Had he been married? Ryan wondered. It was a definite possibility.

He thought once again of Lucy Mathieson and started to plan the rest of his morning.

* * *

Ryan was ready when the first members of his team began to filter in, groggy and bleary-eyed after a short night's sleep. MacKenzie and Phillips were both staying at the Lindisfarne Inn and so filed in together, already arguing despite the fact it was just shy of seven-thirty.

"It should have been obvious, even to you, that the bathroom is a shared one," Denise was saying as she unwound her poppy-red wool scarf.

"Bloody hell, woman, how was I to know there was a door on the other side?" Frank's face was set into hard lines, which Ryan recognised as acute embarrassment. He didn't have to be a genius to work out what had happened.

"Now, now, children," he said with a gleam in his eye.

"Tell *him*," MacKenzie jerked a thumb behind her. "He's the one who got an eyeful this morning and then just…just *stood there!*"

Phillips went an even deeper shade of puce.

"Minding my own business, heading for a shower, that's all I was doing. Wasn't my fault you didn't lock the door," he grumbled.

"You could have turned around," she said with one hand on her hip. Frank would have endured all manner of torture before he'd admit that he couldn't have moved a muscle that morning. Not after seeing Denise MacKenzie in full, glorious technicolour.

"Could have happened to anyone," was all he said, looking away.

"Always seems to happen to you, doesn't it?" She brushed past him haughtily and helped herself to a coffee.

Ryan sidled up to his friend and clucked his tongue sympathetically.

"Got a temper on her, that one," he said under his breath.

"You can say that again," Phillips said heatedly.

"A temper and, if you don't mind me saying, an excellent arse."

"You can say that…" Phillips cleared his throat and brushed some lint from his jacket. "I couldn't possibly comment. Like a perfect gent, I averted my eyes."

"Like hell you did," Ryan said.

Phillips warred with himself for a nanosecond.

"Mighty fine arse," he said gruffly. "Shame she's got a tongue like a poisoned dagger."

"Aw, now, you don't really think that," Ryan slapped a hand on Phillips' broad back.

"Doesn't matter what I think, she never looks twice," Phillips grumbled.

"Hmm," Ryan stroked a thoughtful hand across his chin and realised he'd forgotten to shave again. "Don't remember her getting so riled up before, do you? Makes me wonder if you've got under her skin."

Phillips slanted him a look.

"Just because you're feeling fresh as a daisy this morning—and three guesses why that is—doesn't mean the rest of us will be so lucky."

"I'm a closet romantic," Ryan grinned.

"Humph," was all Frank said.

"By the way," Ryan said as he moved towards the table, "nice tie."

Phillips looked down and was devastated to find that, amid the drama of the morning, he'd forgotten to wear one. That was definitely MacKenzie's fault, he decided.

He slunk after his SIO, feeling half-naked.

* * *

It was astonishing, Ryan thought, what could be accomplished after a good night's sleep. In one hand, he held a list of the names of people who had purchased sandalwood soap from the Heritage Gift Shop within the last month. In the other, he held CCTV footage from a particular builders' merchant in Budle, the little town farther down the coast. Not only did MacKenzie have an excellent arse, he decided, she had an excellent eye for detail. She had spent the early hours of the morning looking through the tapes for a face they might recognise.

And she had found one.

Interestingly, the name of that person was also listed as having purchased a bulk load of sandalwood soap, only two weeks' earlier. It could just be a coincidence but Ryan didn't believe in them.

That was why he had ordered Phillips to requisition the CCTV footage from the Heritage Centre on the date the soap had been purchased.

While he stewed over that, Lowerson would be firing through a list of specialist blade smiths with a description of the type of athame dagger they were looking for. It could just be a hunch, but on the other hand, they could hit the jackpot. The pathologist and secondary pathologist Ryan had called in confirmed each other's independent findings. It was disappointing that they hadn't found another vital piece of missing DNA, but it was no more than he had expected.

The financial data had been delivered to him complete with names and dates of transactions.

"Seems like quite a few of the island's gentlemen were donating to the Megan Taylor Charitable Fund," he remarked, scanning the list of names. "Well, look-ee here, Frank."

Phillips looked over, grunted, and then his pug-like face split into a mile-wide grin.

"Our favourite person," he said.

"Now, Phillips, the reverend is a man of the people. A s*hepherd,* if you recall. Perhaps he was concerned for her welfare."

"My arse."

"Get your mind off arses," Ryan said with a grin. "And trot over to see Ingles. I want him questioned under caution as to why he took it upon himself to make regular deposits into Megan's account. Take MacKenzie with you."

Phillips' grin turned into a scowl.

"Now, why would you want to go and spoil my mood like that?"

"Nothing could spoil your mood, after this morning."

Phillips hid his smile with a bout of coughing.

"Better get on with it," he said glumly, eyeing the wind and rain currently battering the windowpanes.

"Take a coat, won't you?" Ryan said cheerfully, checking his watch. "We're meeting the Mathiesons at eleven, sharp. I want you with me."

"Aye," Phillips nodded and walked off to break the good news to MacKenzie.

Ryan turned back to the accounts summary he held in his hand and smiled when he found the other name he had been looking for.

He decided he definitely didn't believe in coincidences and called Phillips back over from where he had been hovering around MacKenzie's back.

"Frank, never mind Ingles for now. Send Lowerson over instead and tell him to bring the reverend back here. We'll get around to questioning him later. You're coming with me."

CHAPTER 24

The vicarage was still in darkness when Jack Lowerson trudged up the pretty gravel path to the wide front door. His dark shoes were still shiny from the polishing he'd given them before work. His white shirt was crisp, his grey suit immaculate, even if it was a bit big across the shoulders.

He had been wearing a conservative navy tie, but that had been appropriated by Phillips, on pain of returning to duty as reader-receiver. Lowerson had taken pity on his DS, who had borne the look of a man who considered himself the protagonist in *The Emperor's New Clothes.*

Chuckling to himself, he came to a standstill on the gravel path leading to the front door of the vicarage.

"That's unusual," he murmured as his eyes fell on the darkened windows. He checked the time. *Eight-thirty.*

Reverend Ingles should have been up for hours, since the island church opened religiously—ha ha—at five-thirty each morning. Shivering slightly, Jack hoped that he wouldn't find another mangled body in the bushes somewhere. The island was getting so that you couldn't turn a corner without finding a pair of dead eyes staring back at you.

Still, he took the job seriously. If there was something to find, he wouldn't shy away from it. He moved to the big oak door with its ornate knocker in the shape of a Celtic key.

He knocked a couple of times in a cheerful rat-a-tat-tat.

No answer.

He leaned closer, listening for sounds of movement inside the house, but heard none.

He knocked again, louder this time.

Still, no answer.

Lowerson took a surreptitious look through the gaps in the curtains on the downstairs windows but could only see a dim house filled with furniture. There were no people, no signs of distress or upheaval.

Shrugging slightly, he started to turn back, then paused, chewing on his bottom lip.

Hadn't Ryan said to check the vicarage first, for signs of Morning Glory? Why would he have said that, Jack thought, if he hadn't suspected that the vicar or his wife was responsible for growing it?

If that was the case, either or both of them could be responsible for killing those people. They could be out there now, killing someone else, Lowerson thought with righteous outrage.

"Bugger that," he muttered, turning to head around the back of the vicarage, skirting the gravel path which bordered the house.

The back of the house bore all the same signs as the front, Lowerson thought. The windows were closed and curtains drawn across them. The patio doors were locked, when he tried them. He knocked once more, for good measure, but received no answer.

The temptation was ripe in his veins to force entry, to have a snoop around the house to see what he would find, but he knew that Ryan would bollock him for entering a suspect's property without the appropriate warrant.

He blew out a disappointed breath and looked out across the lawn at the back of the house. Lovely, he thought, taking in the careful borders with their arrangement of evergreen shrubs and fragrant herbs. There were no flowers, given the time of year, but he imagined that they would bloom in the summer, creating a patchwork of colour. The grass was manicured and touched with frost, leading from the house in a sweep towards the edge of the cliff-face which dropped down to the sea. Partially hidden behind a row of newly-planted conifers stood a large greenhouse and a shed painted dark green. Looking closer, he could see a dark green wire coming from the greenhouse across the edge of the border towards the house.

"Wonder what the hell that's for," he said to himself, then, like a moth he was drawn to the flame. His shoes crinkled the frosty grass as he walked across it, following the line of the wire towards the greenhouse.

He cast glances behind him now and then, but saw nothing. He heard nothing but the sound of his own footsteps and the crash of the sea as it broke against the cliffs.

Stepping around the young conifers, he faced the greenhouse, with its impressive array of tomatoes framing the outward-facing windows. Above the long glass structure, the Priory loomed, visible now through the hedgerow. There was a gate leading through it, to access the Priory graveyard.

Interesting, Lowerson thought.

He coasted around the perimeter of the greenhouse, searching for a clear viewing space since the little door was firmly locked and double-padlocked. That alone was suspicious, he thought. Eventually he found a gap and squatted down to peer through the glass. Every inch of space seemed to be filled with pots and plants, vines trailed across the surfaces and up the glass walls.

Someone in that household was certainly green-fingered, Jack thought.

The glass was foggy with condensation, which made it harder to see clearly. Lowerson squinted and pressed his nose closer, focused entirely on what lay inside. His eyes fell on one of the low wooden benches filled with long troughs of flowers which bloomed a bright, sky blue.

The feeling of success was potent and Lowerson nearly fell backward on his haunches.

Morning Glory, he thought happily. Trays and trays of it.

He stood up, dusted himself off and turned, fumbling for his mobile phone to ring Ryan and tell him the good news. He was preoccupied, worrying about whether he had technically been trespassing, or whether he might be able to argue he had due cause to enter.

He caught a movement in his peripheral vision, but was too late to avoid the swing of the metal garden spade as it crashed against the side of his skull, fracturing several bones in his face.

He was plunged into darkness and the phone fell from his limp hand onto the grass.

* * *

"Any word from Lowerson?" Ryan asked Phillips as they shrugged into their overcoats and prepared to step out into weather which could, at best, be described as inclement.

"Nah, nothing yet. He's probably been held up. Those old biddies love him."

"Must be his boyish good looks."

"I have the same trouble, myself," Phillips said, deadpan.

Ryan looked over and snorted out a laugh as he looked into his sergeant's round, mole-like face.

"We'll chase him up in an hour and hurry him along. Let's go," Ryan yanked open the front door.

Phillips muttered to himself as they left the warmth of the cottage to face the angry wind outside.

"Wait." Ryan came to an abrupt standstill and ran back to the house, called out to one of the female duty officers, who jogged to meet him at the front door.

"Sir?"

"I want Doctor Taylor to be secure at all times, is that understood?"

"Is she under arrest, sir?"

Damn the woman, Ryan thought, for making him sound ridiculous. Maybe it was some sort of female solidarity thing.

"No," he gritted, "She's not under arrest, but she is under protective custody, officer."

If Anna wanted to be stubborn and stay on the island, he would feel a lot better knowing that she was safely housed and barricaded by police. At least until he brought his man into custody, which would be sooner than expected, if all went to plan.

He and Phillips turned back to the road and then Ryan skidded to a halt again on the wet ground and swore.

"Give me a minute."

He turned and jogged back into the cottage and up the stairs, two at a time. He couldn't say which of them was more surprised when he plucked Anna up from where she had been sitting reminding herself of Druid ritual and into his arms for a long, thorough kiss.

"What was that for?" she gulped, when he eventually released her. He was hardly a knight in shining armour, she thought with a smile, judging by his irritated face.

"You didn't have to kiss me goodbye," she said with her tongue in her cheek. "It won't get you any more free dinners."

The tension eased slightly from his shoulders.

"Maybe not," he agreed, "but now you're thinking about it." He smiled and his eyes were bright before he turned away.

"Ryan," she said before he left, "stay safe."

He nodded. "You too, Anna. I've grown used to having you around buying me pizza."

He jogged back down the stairs and left her as she shoved her hands on her hips, ready to come back with a pithy retort about growing used to an old pair of worn boots. He wondered if he would ever get tired of winding her up.

She was a fine sight when she was mad.

Outside, his sergeant rolled back onto the balls of his feet and tried to look nonchalant.

"Forget your gloves, sir?"

"Pipe down, Phillips."

The other man sniggered and was privately relieved to see Ryan looking better than he had in months, despite the circumstances.

"Where to?" he asked.

"The Lindisfarne Inn," Ryan replied shortly.

* * *

Alison Rigby was a meticulous woman. Her hair was ruthlessly styled in an elaborate up-do. With a little help from her hairdresser, she had it coloured every week to make sure that nobody on the island ever saw a grey hair amongst her nest of fine gold curls. She might be carrying a few extra pounds on the hips, but for the most part she was a buxom woman who enjoyed regular yoga sessions with Liz Morgan and Helen Mathieson—poor woman—in Yvonne Walker's front room. After that, they settled down to a nice hour or two of chit-chat, every Saturday morning.

She had two babies to keep her busy: Peter, and the Lindisfarne Inn.

There was nothing that the first wouldn't do for her and there was nothing that she wouldn't do for the second. Both were a source of constant pride.

Alison hummed contentedly as she bustled around the wide drawing room in the old house, lovingly restored over the years from a tired and dated guest house to the gleaming, polished Inn it was today. She stopped to chat with a couple of her guests, both reporters, who huddled together by the window seat. Her neighbours had no time for the press, but she took a different view. People were entitled to know about what happened on their own doorstep, which is why she led the weekly Neighbourhood Watch group and sat on the village council. It was important, she thought, to make sure that things never changed too much.

It was fascinating, really, the things that the media could find. Not that she would know very much about that, she amended. Then again, if she happened to come across some paperwork while she cleaned their rooms, was that really her fault? She couldn't be expected to ignore pertinent information about the people on her island.

Their island, she meant to say.

Her head came up from the mahogany side table she was polishing when the front door chimed.

"Mrs Rigby, may we come in? We have some questions we would like to ask Pete, if he is available."

Alison looked Ryan up and down. *Handsome devil,* she thought and her lip curled. Her Andrew had been a handsome man and look where that had got her. He'd been nothing but a useless layabout with a roving eye, who'd been happy to leave her to tend the Inn and their only child on her own.

Then, he'd died. She couldn't say she'd really mourned the loss, since life went on much as it had when he'd been alive, only now she was better off. Still, looking at the dark good looks of the Chief Inspector, she was reminded of the fool she had been.

"*Peter* is very busy, Chief Inspector," she said regally.

Phillips put a hand on Ryan's arm in silent supplication and stepped forward.

"Mrs Rigby—Alison—we would really be so grateful if you would ask Peter to spare us a few minutes. After all, it concerns his good friend, Lucy."

Ryan watched, dumbfounded, as Alison Rigby's face softened miraculously. If he didn't know better, he would have said the woman was gazing into the beady brown eyes of his DS.

"Of course, Frank, come in out of the rain." She fussed around Phillips, taking his coat and complaining that he wasn't taking good care of his health. She started to lead them into the drawing room, where the reporters waited like spiders.

"Now, Alison, I don't want our wet clothes to damage the furnishings in your lovely drawing room," Phillips said charmingly, taking her elbow to steer a new course. "We would be happy enough just sitting in the kitchen, that is if you don't mind?"

"Why, Frank, it's so thoughtful of you to think of that," Alison gushed. "Of course the kitchen is fine." She shot a disdainful glance in Ryan's direction and noted his grubby boots.

"You can leave those boots by the door, Chief Inspector," she snapped before leading Frank away for a cup of tea in the kitchen.

Ryan didn't bother to mention that Phillips' boots were also covered in mud, but dropped to his haunches to undo the laces.

The kitchen was a gigantic room, equipped with brand new stainless steel units which Alison had installed in preparation for the roaring success of her new restaurant. As far as she was concerned, it would be a success, or nothing.

"This is very, ah, professional," Ryan said lamely.

"Thank you," Alison returned in the same clipped tone. "I'll go and fetch Peter."

Ryan watched her stomp out of the kitchen and looked back at Phillips.

"You dark horse."

Phillips pulled a face.

"It's no laughing matter," he said in a whisper. "She's relentless."

"I always knew you were a cad."

They both sobered instantly when Alison returned with her son in tow. Once again, he looked barely fifteen, dressed in his waiter's uniform of black slacks and a starched white shirt. The odd little beard still looked out of place on his child-like face.

"Peter," Mrs Rigby said in painful condescension, "the police would like to ask you some questions."

"Yes, Mum, I know. They've asked me questions before."

Watching them, both Ryan and Phillips thought of that old Hitchcock movie again.

Alison favoured her son with a look of pure reproach and then patted his arm.

"You're just being testy. Now, I'm sure there's nothing to worry about," she soothed, before turning icy eyes towards Ryan. "Is there?"

"Do I need a lawyer?"

Ryan raised a brow at Pete's question and wondered who he had been talking to.

"That's entirely up to you. We're not questioning you formally, at this time. We merely hope to tie up a few loose ends which you may be able to help us with."

Pete relaxed as far as he could in a room built largely of metal.

"There, now, Peter," Alison smiled.

Ryan eyed the woman with a sprinkling of dislike.

"Pete, would you rather we asked our questions without your mother present?"

Pete flushed and looked uncomfortable, while Alison bristled in her chair, ready to bite.

"What the Chief Inspector means to say is," Phillips hurried to smooth the waters, "Pete might not want to put you in a difficult position, by repeating things about Lucy when you know her mother so well."

Phillips' eyes trained on her wide face, noticed the bright blue eye shadow and tried not to be distracted by it.

"Well," she said indignantly. "I hardly think I would repeat *anything* Peter told me about Lucy, certainly not to Helen."

Ryan was fast losing patience.

"Let me be the deciding factor here, then," he said implacably. "Either we question Pete informally in the comfort of his own home, alone, or I march him through the centre of the village in handcuffs for formal questioning. Which do you prefer?"

He watched the woman's face contort, before she paled again as the full connotations of his threat hit home. Marching Pete through the streets would mean that people would be there to see their humiliation.

She could gossip about others, but couldn't bear to be the butt of it herself.

"Very well," she stood and looked at Ryan with supreme distaste before turning to Pete. "Don't let them bully you, Peter, you know how anxious you get."

With that, she turned and walked from the room.

Left alone, Pete seemed to relax as Ryan had known that he would.

"How have you been, Pete?" Ryan painted a friendly smile on his face and sipped his herbal tea, wishing it was strong black coffee instead.

"Pretty good, all things considered. Busy here at the Inn and over at the pub, same old."

"Life goes on, doesn't it?"

Pete shrugged eloquently.

"How about over at the coastguard station?"

"Been quiet, which is probably a good thing since Alex hasn't, well, you know, since you arrested him—"

"He hasn't what?" Ryan was unperturbed.

"Well, he hasn't been himself," Pete said, feeling like a snitch. "I'm the Deputy, so I'm supposed to handle the station when Alex isn't there. To tell you the truth, I never thought I'd have to."

"You don't like it as much?"

"It's just that I'm stretched a bit thin," Pete said.

Ryan didn't think Pete was speaking literally, but the description was certainly apt.

"Much been happening on the high seas?"

"Couple of tourist cars stranded on the causeway, but we got to those before the tide fully came in, which was lucky." Pete thought back over the last few days. "Group of reporters hired a boat from the harbour and nearly capsized yesterday."

"Where?"

"Over by Pilgrim's Causeway," Pete confirmed, thinking of the stretch of water which covered the old footpath opposite the spot on the beach where Rob Fowler's body had been found.

"Figures," Ryan grunted and lifted his tea, sniffed it, then put it down again. Enough of the pleasantries.

"We've got a couple of things you might be able to help us with, Pete," Ryan said in the same friendly tone, slipping out his notebook. "That okay with you?"

Ryan saw a flicker of unease pass across the man's face but it passed quickly.

"Sure, no problem," Pete adopted a relaxed pose, one arm draped across the back of his chair.

"Tell us again how long you'd known Lucy Mathieson," Ryan began.

"Since we were kids," Pete said. "My mum and hers have been friends for years. We went to nursery school together, then all the way through middle and high school."

"When she left for university, were you sorry to see her leave the island?"

"Sure, it was a shame to see her go, but she'd always wanted somewhere bigger, with opportunities. Nothing changes on Lindisfarne," he added quietly and looked away briefly.

"Didn't you ever consider going to university on the mainland, travelling a bit?" Ryan asked guilelessly.

Pete paused and his eyes darted to the door. His voice lowered.

"I had a place at Edinburgh University to study medicine," he said with a bit of pride. "But I was needed here."

"To help your mother?"

Pete said nothing, but his eyes were dark.

"Do you regret staying?"

"No," Pete denied vehemently. "As I say, I'm needed here."

Ryan glanced at Phillips, who picked up the signal.

"Good looking girl, Lucy," Phillips commented, man-to-man. "I'm surprised you never thought of asking her out."

Pete flushed slightly.

"She was more like a sister," he said defensively.

"Aye, but you're not her brother, are you?" Phillips winked at him.

"Her dad wouldn't have liked it," Pete said, then flushed again.

"Bit protective, was he?"

Pete snorted. "That's putting it mildly. If he ever caught me looking at her twice, he would have strung me up."

"Wonder what he thought about Alex?" Phillips mused.

"I don't know whether he knew or not, but Lucy was kind of rebelling. She said how she didn't care what he thought or what anybody thought."

"What did you think?"

Pete fiddled with his teacup.

"Look, I like Alex a lot. He's a really decent bloke," his boyish face was earnest. "But he's always had a bit of an eye for the ladies. I don't think he would have settled down with Lucy."

They could have asked more, but by tacit agreement Ryan and Phillips left it there.

"Fair enough," Ryan said and switched tracks again. "You and Lucy being close, you would know about the sort of things she believed in, right?"

Pete looked momentarily confused.

"Sure," he shrugged.

"What about Paganism?"

There it was, Ryan thought, as worry skid across the other man's face.

"I wouldn't know about that," Pete lied, eyes darting to the door again.

"Your mother can't hear you from here," Ryan said quietly, pinning the man with his stare which was enough to make Pete gulp. "I want the truth, Pete. You're not in any trouble. Yet."

Pete's lips trembled slightly. His mother was an active member of the church council.

"Look, ah, it was just a bit of a laugh, really," he laughed nervously. "A few of us would meet on the beach, build a bonfire and get drunk, mostly."

"Like the bonfire somebody built for Rob Fowler?"

Ryan's quiet words fell like an axe.

"No, *no,*" Pete held out both hands and his voice jumped. "I'm telling you I have no idea who would do that. Look, I'm just talking about getting pissed on the beach and singing a few songs."

"Ever do anything else?"

"Some people—maybe."

"What and who?" Ryan said flatly.

"Just people from high school, like Lucy and her mates; me and some of the guys from the harbour. Some of them did a bit more than dance, maybe they had sex a few times and stuff like that."

"You didn't?"

Pete's lips clamped shut and Ryan took that for acquiescence. Seemed like Pete never got lucky.

"Okay, so a few of you met on the beach, got jiggy with it, whatever," Ryan shrugged. "What about drugs?"

Pete looked desperately at the door.

"Look, I—"

"Son, we're not going to book you for getting high and we're not going to run and tell your mama," Phillips interjected, ignoring Ryan's fierce look. "We've got bigger fish to fry."

"Okay," Pete swallowed. "Okay. Maybe there were a few things kicking around, once or twice."

"Any of them hallucinogenic?"

"You mean like mushrooms? Yeah, a couple of times, except they were like these little seeds," he said.

"Where'd they come from?" Phillips asked idly, munching on another one of Alison's excellent ginger biscuits.

Pete looked miserable, but another glance at Ryan's granite-like face was enough to keep him talking.

"Lucy brought them," he fidgeted in his seat. "They were in a little red velvet bag."

"That's awfully convenient," Ryan commented dryly. "Easy to point the finger at someone who can't defend themselves, Pete."

"I'm telling you the truth," he argued. "I hate ratting on Lucy like this. Please, please don't tell anyone I told you."

Ryan just looked at him.

"Like I say, she brought them, but she never told me where she got them."

"You sure?"

Pete nodded and his eyes never wavered. Ryan exchanged another glance with Phillips and carried on.

"You ever heard of something called 'camphor', Pete?"

He thought for a moment.

"Sure. Lucy had this book and there was a list of ingredients at the back for performing rituals and stuff like that. I'm pretty sure that was on the list. I don't know what it was for."

"Sounds like Lucy took it all pretty seriously," Ryan said.

"Yeah," Pete said slowly. "I guess she did. She started getting really into it over the summer, wanted to add chants and costumes when we were all just fooling around."

"You know where she kept the book?"

"Dunno—at home?"

"Couple of other things, Pete," Ryan pretended to consult his notebook for a moment while he thought about the next line of questioning. "You ever been inside Megan's apartment?"

Pete fidgeted.

"No-o, not that I remember," he said uncertainly.

Ryan almost smiled.

"Would it help your memory, if I told you that we found your prints all around it?"

"You can't have!"

"Really? Why not?" Ryan leaned forward, fixed Pete with a stare.

"It was ages ago," Pete mumbled. "She must've cleaned them away by now."

Both Ryan and Phillips thought of the unkempt state of Megan's apartment and said nothing.

"Why were you up there, Pete?"

The man flushed again, to the roots of his hair.

"We—she—I—" He stuttered to a stop.

Ryan raised his eyes heavenward and looked across at Phillips, who took the unspoken cue.

"Son, it'll be better for everyone if you just tell us how it was. Look," Phillips said confidentially, "she was a good-looking woman. A bit of a stunner, wasn't she?"

Pete gulped and nodded.

"Must have fancied her a bit?"

"Yeah," Pete admitted.

"Can't blame you," Frank continued. "Did you and she ever, y'know?" To Ryan's fascination, Phillips made some sort of clacking sound with his teeth, paired with a lewd wink.

It worked, because Pete grinned boyishly.

"Yeah, only one time though."

"When?" Ryan asked simply.

"End of October," Pete said without hesitation. The date was etched into his memory, since it was the first and only time he had been with a woman. Not just any woman, either. The most beautiful woman on the island.

Ryan thought back to Megan's diary entry. Pete's timing matched hers.

"So, you two slept together at the end of October," Ryan waited for Pete's nod before continuing. "I need to ask you another question, then, Pete. Why did you transfer one hundred and fifty pounds into Megan's bank account on the twenty-seventh of October?"

Pete looked crestfallen.

"I didn't," he said desperately.

"Pete," Phillips said indulgently. "You have to stop telling fibs."

"Sorry," the young man mumbled. "It's just that I thought—at the time, I thought she was really interested, you know? Then, the next day, she said how she was really low on cash and how if I cared about her I would help her out. I said 'sure, no problem'. As soon as I gave her the money, she barely noticed I was there."

"That must have hurt," Phillips said.

"Yeah, it did," Pete said quietly, "but to be honest, I was just kidding myself with Megan. She had her sights set elsewhere."

"Oh?" Ryan leaned forward again, interested. "Did she ever tell you who she was looking at?"

"It didn't take a genius to figure it out," Pete said caustically

Ryan thought back to the mysterious 'D' that Megan had spoken about and practically rubbed his hands together.

"Looks like I'm not quite a genius, Pete, so you'll have to help me out," Ryan said with a friendly smile.

"Duh," Pete goggled his eyes. "It was *you*."

Phillips just came short of guffawing at the disconsolate look which passed across Ryan's and turned back to Pete.

"The Chief Inspector isn't used to having women fawn over him, Pete," he said. "Not like us."

Pete chuckled, feeling better.

"Nice tiles you've got on the patio," Ryan said conversationally, all business again, casting his eye through the window to where a brand new patio had been laid with tables and chairs. He happened to know that those tiles had recently been purchased. "Local stone, aren't they?"

"Thanks, yeah, they're new. Mum just had it done," Pete said easily. "I thought wooden decking would last longer, but she liked the tiles."

"Know where she got them?"

Pete looked confused but answered easily enough.

"The tiles? Sure, from this builder's yard near Budle called Herbert & Co. I went and picked them up for her."

Ryan listened to the man's quiet admission and thought that they were getting somewhere.

"Must have taken a lot of grunt work," Ryan said, looking at the size of the patio. "Fair amount of lifting."

"Yeah, a fair bit, but Lucy's dad came round to help," Pete answered. "He's got a ride-on lawnmower with this attachment at the back for carrying stuff."

"That's handy," Ryan said blandly.

"Yeah, mum didn't want the lawn trampled by workmen, so that helped a lot."

"Mmm," Ryan agreed. "So, what does he need a ride-on for?"

"Huh? Oh, he does a bit of work for the Heritage. He cuts the lawns for the Priory, the nature reserve, the main square and stuff like that."

"Haven't seen him cutting recently," Phillips remarked, picking up the rhythm. *Nice and easy, nice and slow*, he thought as he stuffed another biscuit in his mouth.

"Yeah, I guess he's been too upset. Grass doesn't grow all that much in the cold weather, anyway," Pete added.

Ryan thought back to the reports on the Mathieson home. It was standard procedure for them to search the premises of the deceased. There had been no opposition from Mr and Mrs Mathieson and the CSIs had been through the entire premises, including the car and the shed in their garden.

He didn't remember seeing anything about a ride-on lawnmower.

"I guess he must keep it up at the Priory, somewhere?" Ryan said.

"Oh, nah, he keeps it here," Pete said simply. "He doesn't have a garage, but we've got a big one around the back. Mum hardly uses it nowadays, so she said he could keep the mower in there."

"How kind of her," Phillips said dutifully.

Ryan sat back and flipped his notebook closed. Pete noticed the action and his face brightened.

"Is that it?" he said hopefully.

Ryan and Phillips stood as if to leave. As they turned to go, Phillips asked,

"Where do you get those little soaps—you know, the ones you put in the bedrooms? Got a nice scent to them."

"You can get them at the Gift Shop, at least that's where we get them from," Pete said helpfully.

"Have you bought any, recently, Pete?"

He stopped to think.

"Yeah, I think I bought a few boxes a couple of weeks back, since we were getting low on stock. Why? You want me to give you some samples?"

"No, we're good. Thanks."

They nodded politely and opened the kitchen door. Ryan was unsurprised to find Alison Rigby fiddling with a flower arrangement on the table nearest the doorway.

"Good morning, Mrs Rigby," he said politely and grinned to himself when her lips pursed waspishly. She helped Phillips into his coat, brushed at the wool for stray fluff and said how she looked forward to seeing him later for dinner.

Frank muttered something non-committal and was relieved to get out of the house, into the fresh air again.

"What are you thinking, boss?"

"I'm thinking that those tiles were quarried sandstone, reddish in colour. Easy enough for a bit to flake off when you're moving them in bulk. I'm thinking that we've been chasing a bag of building sand when we should have been thinking laterally." His jaw twitched. "Frank, I want you to get me a search warrant. Then, I think it's time to pay another house call."

Behind them, Alison stood at the doorway and watched them round the corner towards the village. She noticed that the porch needed sweeping and made a mental note to do it right away.

But, before then, she had a phone call to make.

CHAPTER 25

Half an hour later, after some superior negotiation with the local magistrate which had been expedited in no small part by Phillips' friendship with the court usher, both men found themselves standing outside the garage at the Lindisfarne Inn.

They had already bypassed Mrs Rigby, who had overcome her initial outrage at the sight of a search warrant by the prospect of 'entertaining' a number of young, male police officers. Still, she stayed near the window, where she could keep an eye on Ryan as he assessed the garage.

"Get it open." Ryan instructed one of the officers, who unlocked the hefty double doors and swung them open.

Inside, shining as if it were new, stood an industrial green ride-on lawn mower with a detachable carrier at the back.

"Not a speck of grass on it," Phillips said, annoyed.

"There's always something, Frank," Ryan contradicted, but as he moved closer he could still smell the faint odour of bleach.

"He's cleaned it from top to bottom," Phillips said angrily.

"Yes, or perhaps someone helped him," Ryan lifted stormy grey eyes towards the house and the people within. "That's a possibility."

Phillips popped his gum.

"So, what do we think happened?" Frank started. "Mathieson hides his mower here, doesn't bother mentioning it and gives himself time to clean it all up?"

"Looks like it."

"He must have known we couldn't search the Inn without cause," Frank added.

"He's not a fool," Ryan murmured, edging closer to the mower, but leaving a wide berth so as not to disturb any remaining evidence.

"So, he didn't need to cart her body all the way. He could hitch her on the back of this and drive as far as the fence to the Priory," Frank continued.

"Could have driven all the way up if he wanted to," Ryan said, imagining it, "but he'd already risked making too much noise with this thing." He took out a latex glove, slipped it on and leaned across to start the engine. It roared to life with a smooth purr.

"Not too loud," he commented, "but still noticeable."

"That's the engine noise people heard. One of them said she thought it was a motorboat on the water, coming in late or something," Phillips said.

"Yep," Ryan nodded, "it's plausible and probably the conclusion he hoped anybody would draw if they heard him."

"Boss," Phillips said as he wandered the other side of the mower. "Take a look at this."

Eyes sharp, Ryan carefully walked around the other side.

"Well, now, look at that."

In the corner of the garage stood several stacked boxes marked with the stamp of the Heritage Gift Shop. One had been ripped open to reveal a stash of small, carefully-wrapped soaps. Further along the wall stood a water tap that supplied water to the garden hose outside.

The floor was concrete and like the mower, was sparkling clean.

"He took a risk, bringing her here," Ryan commented. "Somebody must have seen him."

"Nobody says they did."

"It's three streets from here to Mathieson's cottage," he said. "He passed a bunch of houses between here and there."

"Not if he went along the gardens," Phillips said. "There's a long alley which leads behind the row of cottages, with gates off it for access to each garden."

"Back, through the gardens, along the alley behind the row of houses, then he's only risking being seen by the cottages on the end?"

"That's it," Frank nodded.

"Still a massive risk," Ryan concluded.

"Yeah, but he's already killed, so what does he care?"

"Fair point." First rule of murder investigation, Ryan thought, was not to expect the perp to think like a normal person. "Let Faulkner's team in, I want this place going over inch-by-inch. There would have been sandy residue in that carrier, chipped off from the big pile of tiles he transported for Mrs Rigby," he added. "If he dumped Lucy in there to transport, maybe he didn't realise she was still alive when he took her up to the Priory."

"Still alive?" Phillips turned horrified eyes to his SIO.

"You didn't connect the dots?" Ryan wasn't known for his patience. "Of course, she was. Pathologist confirmed the blow to the head was received ante-mortem. I see it like this," he spread his hands. "He gets angry when she rolls in late, gets jealous and finally snaps, since he's a little bit loco." Ryan made a circular motion with one finger near his temple.

"He finds his hands round her throat, squeezes tight enough to make her pass out, but he thinks he's killed her so he panics. He carries her out through the garden, along the alley, over here. For whatever reason, he doesn't want to clean her up at home, maybe he's afraid his wife will wake up and find him. Anyway, he's got some funky ideas about ritual burial, so he cleans her up, makes her pretty for the afterlife. Uses the hose, the soap. The camphor?" Ryan paused. "Maybe he grabbed that as he left, had to have done, because Lucy bought the stuff. Maybe he thinks it's poetic that he's using something she bought herself." Ryan shrugged.

"Then he dumps her on there," Phillips jerked a thumb at the carrier. "Doesn't realise she's hit her head. Drives up to the Priory, keeps it slow and steady even if he wanted to rush."

"Yep, he had to have been sweating like a pig on market day," Ryan muttered, thinking of it. "Must have wanted to punch the engine up there, but couldn't risk the noise."

"So he parks, carries her up the rest of the way?"

"Yeah," Ryan nodded, stepping back out into the misty air. "Sets her up, maybe he's praying for her immortal soul or dancing butt naked when she starts to come round, who knows. He craps himself and tries again, finishes the job this time."

"Aye, sounds right," Phillips agreed. "What about the others?"

"Megan noted down a 'D' in her diary, an older man, possibly married, pillar of the community who was involved in some sort of ritualised ceremonies on the side. CSIs didn't find anything to do with ritual when they swept the house, which is weird since Lucy was into it herself. Like father, like daughter?" Ryan mused. "Anyway, he's just a man, with a man's needs, isn't he? Scuttled off to see Megan behind his wife's back, he made two bank transfers to Megan's account, one four months ago, the other eight months ago. Stupid of him to leave a trail."

" 'D' for 'Daniel'?" Phillips enquired.

"Looks like it," Ryan said.

"Maybe he didn't expect it to come to this," Phillips shrugged. "Never expected us to check her bank account."

"Maybe. Sounds like Megan pushed him into a corner, gave him an ultimatum or as near as," Ryan said. "Any word from Lowerson?"

"Not yet," Phillips shook his head. "I can chase them up. In his statement, Mathieson said he was with his wife when Megan bought it and Helen confirmed that."

"Megan was drugged. Easy enough for him to give his wife something to wipe her out for a few hours while he ran his errands. Could have slipped out of the house while his wife slept off the stress and strain." Ryan shifted feet. "He got lucky again when he wasn't seen around the pub," Ryan said. "Then again, people don't notice everyday things, everyday people, do they?"

"Aye," Phillips pursed his lips. "We need to talk to the vicar, find out where he fits into this. He must've supplied the drugs."

Ryan nodded, thinking through the processes.

"What about Fowler?"

Ryan's jaw tightened.

"Can't see the motive," he looked out across the lawns of the Inn as he spoke in an undertone. "Had to be something personal—maybe Rob saw something? Still doesn't explain how he came to be on the beach."

He thought of the call logs at the coastguard station. There had been nothing untoward.

"Could be retribution," Phillips said, wishing for a drag of nicotine. All this was making him edgy.

"For...?"

"We've got a jealous guy with a whack of unnatural feelings towards his daughter," Phillips started. "He might have found out about her relationship with Walker, saw red—or green—and decided to pin the murder on him as an afterthought. So, he dumps the clothes in Walker's fishing hut, thinking that we'll get around to it eventually and he'll have a handy scapegoat."

"Go on," Ryan nodded.

"Problem is, we're not charging him right away and he starts to panic again. Added to that, he's still a crazy bastard."

"Indubitably," Ryan said.

"He might have got a taste for killing after the first two," Phillips shrugged. "A lot of them do. Maybe he knows about Alex and Rob, thinks Walker's been having his cake and eating it too—with his daughter—which pisses him off."

"It would do, since he never—ah—got a slice of the cake."

"That was borderline."

"I know. Carry on," Ryan flashed a quick grin and took a stick of the gum Phillips offered.

"So, he decides to hurt Walker some more."

"It's vicious," Ryan said.

"All three of them were. Reckon we'll just have to ask him," Phillips ducked his hands into his pockets and looked across at Ryan. He didn't look satisfied. "What you thinking?"

"Mostly sounds right," Ryan said slowly. "It fits the evidence and if Faulkner comes up with anything from the mower, we'll have Mathieson tied up in such a pretty bow he'll break like a twig in questioning, lawyer or no lawyer."

"But...?"

Ryan shook his head distractedly.

"Something still feels off."

"That's as maybe," Phillips said, scratching his balding head, "but I think I've just found another missing link."

Ryan walked over to where Phillips was bending down between two large crates of restaurant supplies.

"What have you got?"

In his gloved hand, Phillips held a single key, with a chain displaying a 'Newcastle University' emblem.

CHAPTER 26

Daniel Mathieson took his time over his appearance. The police would know by now, since they'd found out about the lawnmower, but that was alright. He had been given his instructions. He was comforted by the knowledge that, for those whose opinion mattered to him, he wouldn't be a murderer. He would be a martyr.

He brushed his greying hair back carefully, selected a pair of smart slacks and a shirt, added cuff links which had been a gift from Lucy for his fiftieth birthday a couple of years earlier.

"Dan!" his wife called up the stairs. "Can you come down? The police are here, I think they must be ready for the press statement now."

That was what the police had told them last night. It had been a good idea, Daniel thought, to tell them to prepare to make an on-air appeal to Lucy's killer. It had put him at ease, safe and secure in the knowledge that they couldn't suspect her own father. He had been almost giddy with relief at the thought. For the first time in days, he slept soundly, snuggled against his wife. Perhaps, he had thought, in time, they could put Lucy's death behind them.

He knew now that he had been dreaming.

"Coming, dear," he called down. He checked his face in the bathroom mirror, straightened the ceramic pots on the shelf above the sink. For a second, he considered killing himself, just putting an end to it all without having to suffer the indignity of police custody, but was saddened to realise that he was just too much of a coward.

Besides, he had his orders.

He walked downstairs and into the sitting room where Ryan and Phillips waited.

"Mr Mathieson," Ryan greeted him evenly, eyes searching.

"Dan, they say they might not need us to make an appeal after all, isn't that right Chief Inspector?" Her eyes were hopeful. "That means you must already have an idea of who—who did this terrible thing to Lucy."

She reached for Daniel's hand and as her fingers clasped his, he almost wept.

"Helen," he said quietly, "why don't you let me deal with this?"

"What? No! If the police have found him, I want to know about it, I want to be here," she said defiantly.

Daniel raised his eyes to Ryan's, sent a silent plea.

"Mrs Mathieson, there are some things which we need to ask your husband which might be best said in private."

Helen shook her head in confusion. "Mr Ryan—I mean, Chief Inspector—if you have something to ask Dan, you can ask me too. We both lost Lucy and we both want to find the person responsible."

Ryan glanced at Phillips, who read the look and nodded, stepped outside and found MacKenzie, who was waiting outside the house with some others.

"I'm sorry, Mrs Mathieson, I think it would be best if we questioned your husband formally. Phillips," Ryan gestured to Frank, who stepped back into the room.

"Daniel Mathieson, you are under arrest on suspicion of the murder of Lucy Mathieson, Megan Taylor and Robert Fowler. You do not have to say anything, but it may harm your defence if you do not mention when questioned something which you later rely on in court. Anything you do say may be given in evidence. Do you understand?"

"I understand," Mathieson said laconically, untwining his fingers from his wife, who looked as if she had been punched in the stomach.

"What—what's happening here?" Wide blue eyes swept the faces of the three men and tears leaked from the corners. "Dan?"

Mathieson stared ahead and couldn't look at her. Ryan watched him carefully.

"Your husband will accompany us into custody, where he will be questioned formally, Mrs Mathieson." Ryan hardened himself against the look in her eye, the pain he knew he was causing her, the grief piling on top of grief.

Right on time, MacKenzie came forward.

"Helen, this is Detective Inspector Denise MacKenzie. She'll stay with you and make sure that you have all that you need while your husband comes with us."

Helen turned fierce.

"I don't need anyone! I just need an explanation. You should be ashamed," her voice hitched pathetically as she swung around again, "instead of finding the person who killed Lucy, you're picking on Dan, her own *father!*"

Mathieson's eyelids drooped wearily. He couldn't stand much more.

"Phillips," Ryan gave a jerk of his head and watched Frank lead the man from the room without any objections. At least he was pliant. It was his wife who seemed to feel outraged, but then that was blind faith.

"Helen," Ryan kept his voice low. "We wouldn't be questioning Daniel unless we had good reason to do so." He was quiet a moment, let the words penetrate.

"Here now," MacKenzie murmured, easing the woman into a chair.

"You think he killed her," Helen said, raising disbelieving eyes to his face. "But you're wrong. I told you, he was with me all night."

"Can you be sure about that?"

He hated this, Ryan thought, hated himself, but there was no other way.

"Of course! I went to bed and he came half an hour later. We slept right through until morning. I would have *known* if he had left, if anything had happened," she said earnestly.

"Are you a light sleeper, Helen?"

She just looked at him. "No, well, I suppose not. I've been on some sleeping tablets for the past few months as I was having trouble dropping off, but still—"

"Helen," he said gently. "You asked me to find the person responsible for killing your daughter. I promised that I would give you justice, but sometimes, justice comes at a high price."

Tears leaked from her eyes again, but he watched in admiration as she drew herself up in the chair, stood to face him.

"You did promise me that. I still believe that you will. I believe that you've made a mistake in arresting my husband, but then I'm sure that will become clear once he answers all your questions." Her voice wobbled, but she firmed her lips. "Either way, Chief Inspector, I'll take whatever justice you have to offer me and if there's a price to pay, I'll pay it for Lucy."

"Thank you, Mrs Mathieson," he took her hand briefly, felt her squeeze it before letting go.

Looking down into her face, he saw resolve and the stirrings of anger. He saw a mother who would fight for the rights of her child, even when that child had died. Unconditional love, he thought, and was reminded of his own mother. She had come to him, after Natalie's death, had tried to draw him to her, to comfort him. He had pushed her away because he couldn't face her or the condemnation he was sure he would find in her eyes.

Had he been wrong?

He turned and left Helen Mathieson in MacKenzie's capable hands.

* * *

It was an exodus, Ryan thought as he walked the beach pathway home. Police officers and detectives quitted Lindisfarne and the tide remained biblically parted to allow their departure. Within earshot of several police detectives including himself and Phillips—and whilst under caution and aware of his rights—Daniel Mathieson had confessed to the murders of three people. If he was taken aback by the easy, docile manner in which Mathieson allowed himself to be arrested, Ryan said nothing at present. After all, the evidence fit and the man had confessed.

There was a saying somewhere about never looking a gift horse in the mouth.

Her duty with Helen Mathieson complete, MacKenzie was accompanying Phillips as they transported Daniel Mathieson off the island to headquarters in Morpeth for formal questioning.

The CSI team had spent three hours in the garage at the Lindisfarne Inn and a skeleton team still remained long after the initial findings had been logged. Faulkner was working at the lab in Morpeth to get the results pushed through but already it wasn't looking good for Daniel Mathieson.

Mathieson had been thorough—splashing bleach around like it was going out of fashion—but just not thorough enough. Trace samples of Lucy Mathieson's DNA had been found on the inside of the lawnmower carrier, as well as some strands of her hair on the garage floor. It was circumstantial but it carried weight.

The pathologist had signed the release order for the bodies of the deceased to be returned to their families for burial.

Some idiot had informed the press that they had taken a man into custody and that, therefore, the 'Lindisfarne Ripper' had been captured. He would chase down the loud-mouthed officer responsible and reprimand him, but that could wait.

Before then, Ryan had some matters to attend to. Opening the door to his cottage, he found the scattered remains of police debris throughout the living space. Bits of tape, crumpled scraps of paper, snack wrappers. Muffled laughter came from the direction of the kitchen and he opened the door to find Anna sitting cosily with his superintendent enjoying a cup of bad coffee and some mini-cakes.

"Arthur, just let me know when you'd like your godson to come for a tour," she was saying. "I'm always happy to show off the university."

"That's kind of you, Anna," Gregson returned, sipping daintily at his mug of coffee. "I know that Harry will be over the moon." His eyes shifted to where Ryan stood transfixed in the doorway.

"Ah, Ryan," he said smoothly, gesturing for him to come closer. "We were just talking about you."

"You were?" he realised that sounded guilty, so he cleared his throat and made a point of never making eye contact with Anna.

"Mmm," Gregson watched the discomfort on his DCI's face and smiled into his coffee. "Just saying how it was a good idea, you bringing Dr Taylor to stay with you here. Under protective custody, that is," he added after a slight pause and fixed Ryan with a penetrating stare.

"Ah—"

"Always better to be safe, than sorry," Gregson carried on, smiling broadly at Anna. Yes, he thought, he could understand well enough what had happened here.

"You've found your man now, haven't you?" Anna smiled up at Ryan and he turned to her finally.

"Well—"

"Excellent work, there, Ryan," Gregson cut across him, setting down his mug. "You'll be heading across to begin the questioning?"

"Yes, sir," Ryan confirmed. "I wanted to check in here, first."

"Team's already packed up here. Needed all hands on deck to handle the crowds, the causeway and the on-site work."

"Yes, sir, that's right but—"

"You'll be releasing Dr Taylor from protective custody, I imagine?" Gregson added and Ryan admired the man's slippery skills, not for the first time.

"Well, since we haven't charged the suspect formally, I'm reticent to remove the officers currently detailed to guard Dr Taylor," Ryan said firmly.

They still didn't know who sent the amulet.

"Ryan," Gregson adopted a firmer tone to his voice and stood up to match his height to Ryan's. "I understand that you're feeling *protective,* given what's happened. Still, you have to look at the practicalities." His voice told Ryan to put his personal feelings to one side and think clearly.

"I can put Lowerson on her," Ryan said stubbornly, forgetting that Anna was sitting next to him. *When I find Lowerson,* Ryan added to himself, slightly concerned.

"I'm sure Lowerson is busy," Gregson contradicted, "as are all of the officers assigned to this investigation."

"I—" Ryan started but was cut off again, this time by Dr Taylor herself.

"I think I should have some say in this," she said coolly, setting down her cup.

"Not really," Ryan said abruptly and earned himself a frigid stare in return.

Gregson opened his mouth and then closed it again. He knew when to retreat from the battlefield.

"Ryan, I agreed to remain under protective custody until you found your man. You've found him. Therefore, there's no need for me to remain under lock and key."

"Unless, of course, you feel the arrest was incorrectly made?" Gregson's brows drew together.

"No, sir, I don't think the arrest was made incorrectly, but I have some doubt about whether Mathieson is responsible for all three deaths, or at least whether he was solely responsible."

"Then, I suggest that you hurry up and question the man, to find your answers," Gregson barked, polishing off his drink and preparing to leave. "I'm heading over myself, I'll give you a lift."

"Thank you, sir, but I have one or two things to do here before I drive across," his eyes narrowed on Anna. "I won't be far behind you.

Phillips will take care of the preliminaries, walk Mathieson through holding beforehand."

"Good enough," Gregson nodded, then leaned over and gave Anna a firm handshake. "Lovely to meet you, Anna and put a face to a name."

"Same goes, Arthur."

When Gregson took his leave, they remained facing one another in the kitchen. Ryan was the first to break the silence.

"Anna, please, trust me a bit longer. I wouldn't ask you if it wasn't important."

She huffed out a breath and found herself neatly boxed in.

"That's quite a clever trick, Ryan," she said irritably. "You must know that it's nearly impossible for me to turn down a strong man who humbles himself."

He carried on looking at her with appealing eyes.

"I must be soft in the head," she complained.

He waited.

"Oh, for God's sake! Fine, fine. I'll carry on climbing these four walls until you tell me otherwise." He started to smile and she pointed a finger at him. "Don't start crowing too soon. My obedience comes with a condition. Bill's holding a wake this evening, at the pub. It's for the dead, for their loved ones, for the island people to remember the best in those they've lost."

Ryan sighed. He could see where this was going, he'd heard about the wake and selfishly, he had hoped news of it hadn't reached Anna. He knew that the islanders and many of his colleagues, even his superior, felt that the case was almost closed. Until he'd spoken with Mathieson, located Lowerson and Ingles, he wasn't ready to celebrate an end to it.

"You can't ask me to miss it," she added into the silence.

He paced away and then back again.

"I plan to be back on the island by the time it starts," he said eventually, trying to be reasonable. "I'll take you myself. If I'm not, I don't want you going anywhere unless there's an officer with you."

"I can live with that," she agreed.

"I've been trying to get hold of Lowerson," he frowned at his mobile phone. "No word from him yet. I want to do a run by the vicarage—he was supposed to be there this morning." He checked his watch as he spoke. *Nearly one-thirty.*

Anna's brows raised.

"You suspect Ingles?"

"Or perhaps his wife."

"Wow," she concluded. "You think they worked with Mathieson?"

"No real motive to kill," he shook his head, "I pegged them for the narcotics but people can surprise you.

"Give me a minute," he murmured, distracted. He dialled a number. "Ops team? Yeah, this is DCI Ryan, badge number 4007852. I need a trace on a phone. No, he's one of ours, Detective Jack Lowerson, I don't have his badge number, but the phone number is 07849684756." There was a pause. "I need this marked Code 1, there's a risk to life."

He rang off and scanned Anna's pale face.

"You think something's happened to Lowerson?" She thought of the young man with the smiley face, always eager to please.

Ryan passed his phone from hand to hand.

"I hope not but I don't have a good feeling," he said. "I've asked them to trace his phone. The mobile's a work issue so we don't have to waste time tracing the phone provider. They're running it now, should be able to triangulate the location fairly quickly."

Ryan looked unseeingly out at the sea through the kitchen window, where he'd stood contemplating the water so many times before. He thought of a young man filled with ambition and the thrill of being part of the team hunting a killer. There was a draw to it, Ryan understood that, had felt it in the early days himself.

Hell, he still felt it.

But Lowerson should have known better than to go over there alone. Basic training told you never to enter the premises of a suspect without a partner. Lowerson knew that, Ryan told himself, could have taken any one of the officers on duty, but he hadn't.

Maybe that's because he hadn't gone to the vicarage, after all. Maybe he had prioritised the other work.

Maybe pigs could fly, Ryan thought, worry rolling through him again in swift waves. There were no available officers on the island aside from him, so he made a decision. He would have to take Anna with him.

"Anna, I need to check the vicarage, start a search for Lowerson—"

His phone rang, mid-sentence and he snatched it up.

"Ryan." He listened for a moment. "That was quick. Thanks. Yes, I know that location. I need an air ambulance over here immediately, suspected accident or injury. Thanks."

Anna was on her feet, pulling on a jacket when he rang off.

"The vicarage?" she said shortly. "I'll ring Doctor Walker and ask him to meet us there."

Ryan nodded, appreciating her foresight.

"Let's go," he said, pausing only to unlock a small metal tin from one of the topmost cupboards. Anna didn't say a word when he drew out a small handgun from the locked tin, checked it for ammunition and tucked it into the back of his jeans, pulling his jacket over it. If she had asked him, Ryan would have told her that he had specialist firearms authorisation, as did certain members of his team, but his eyes were hard when they turned back to her, signalling that there was no time for small talk.

They left the cottage at a run.

* * *

Lowerson lay where he had fallen, his battered body exposed to the elements for nearly five hours. Ryan had known real panic as he circumvented the vicarage, seen the darkened windows and locked doors. In a move which came naturally to him, he urged Anna behind him as he stalked the outskirts, using his body to shield her if need be. He had considered breaking a window, forcing his way inside, until common sense had kicked in. Lowerson would have followed his instinct and it would have led him exactly where it had led Ryan and Phillips the day before.

The greenhouse.

Ryan sprinted across the lawn and Anna was just behind him all the way. Later, he would add to his list of things to love about Anna and include the fact that she wasn't a simpering, insipid woman he had to lead by the nose. She matched him and, in many ways, exceeded him. That was something to think about.

Not now, though, not while one of his junior detectives lay broken and bleeding in a crumpled heap on the cold ground.

Lowerson's skin was very, very pale. Almost blue, Ryan thought frantically, desperate for a paramedic. He dropped to his knees and brought his face up close to Lowerson's, waited to feel a breath against his skin while his fingers struggled to find a pulse.

He waited, for what seemed like an eternity, but there it was. Thin, thready, but a pulse nonetheless.

"Thank Christ," Ryan said, yanking off his coat and laying it over the other man. Anna did the same, covering Lowerson's legs. Close up, they could see the ugly indentation of a sharp implement on the side of his head and face. Blood congealed and crusted around a large gash and Ryan prayed there wouldn't be permanent brain damage, but the force of the blow made that an outside chance.

Anna laid a gentle hand on his arm, understanding that he would feel responsible for this.

After endless moments, they heard Steve Walker shouting and Anna stood up, waved him over.

The man came at a run, bag in hand.

"What's happen—" Walker broke off, taking in the scene immediately. "Move back, please."

Ryan stood a few metres away and watched the doctor work with nimble, gentle hands on Lowerson's injury, checking for vital signs, covering him with another thick blanket. Anna went back to the front of the house to wait for the ambulance.

"What are his chances?" Ryan asked eventually, when there was nothing more that Walker could do.

The older man passed a hand across his forehead and turned to him with sad eyes.

"Frankly, it's a miracle he's still alive," he said quietly and Ryan realised that was his way of trying to prepare him for the worst.

"He's come this far," Ryan said stubbornly.

"We've done all we can," the doctor said, understanding. "It's up to the specialists now."

It seemed like an eternity from the time they first heard the helicopter until they finally saw the neon jackets of the paramedics racing across the lawn. Still, they waited while Lowerson was moved, painstakingly slowly so as not to jar his spine, onto a board and strapped down. They watched him until the helicopter lifted into the sky, seemed to sway against the winds for a nauseating moment before moving off.

They all prayed, whether they believed in a God or not.

"Thank you for everything, doctor," Ryan said, feeling inadequate. "I'm going to follow in my car, contact his parents so they can get down to the hospital. Anna—"

"Don't worry about me," she said, anticipating him.

"Come with me," he said, but thought of the tasks which lay ahead, clouding his mind.

"No," she shook her head. "I'll be here for you when you come back. Do what you need to do, Ryan."

He reached for her hand and brought it to his lips.

"Thank you," he said softly.

CHAPTER 27

Two hours later, Ryan left the clinical, whitewashed walls of the intensive care unit at the county hospital for the clinical, whitewashed walls of CID headquarters.

Everything was familiar; the ugly décor, the worn, industrial-grey linoleum floors, the unique mixed smell of stale body odour, lemon-scented floor cleaner and cheap coffee. When he walked into the Criminal Investigation Department, which consisted of a large, open-plan office filled with noise and clutter, it was like coming home. He stood for a moment, just taking it in. Most of the men and women sitting at desks or mouthing off down the phones had been assigned to Operation Lindisfarne and had been in and out of his cottage on the island. Still, it was different, seeing them here in their natural habitat.

It felt right, again. Not like the last time he'd walked out of the office, head bent and soul weary, ready to pack it all in. He belonged here, along with the rest of them who spent their lives seeking justice for the dead.

He spotted Phillips at his desk in the corner, sporting a fresh tie decorated with tiny palm trees against a banana yellow background. Frank was nothing if not original.

"Phillips? What's the word on Mathieson?" Ryan exchanged a few handshakes as he walked towards Frank's desk.

The man himself swung around in his olive green desk chair.

"He's in conference with his solicitor. Been easy-going so far, lots of 'please' and 'thank you'. It's a bit creepy, to be honest." Phillips pulled an expressive face and then glanced at the big clock on the far wall. *Four-thirty.* "Haven't got much time left with him, before his lawyer'll start complaining. The wife—Helen—she's sitting in the family waiting room with Yvonne Walker who drove her across."

Ryan nodded, thinking of the doctor's wife.

"He got himself a lawyer pretty quick."

"He has to know that he's in deep shit," Phillips shrugged. "Heard from Faulkner—the results are looking good for us, bad for him.

Found blood traces on the far edge of the carrier attachment, Lucy's hairs on the inside of that and on the floor of the garage. Camphor residue on the floor, too."

"Nice work," Ryan said.

"How's Lowerson doing?" Phillips' face crinkled into lines of concern.

"Touch and go," Ryan said and his lips flattened into an angry line as he thought of Jack Lowerson lying on his hospital bed, surrounded by tubes. He'd looked so young, only serving to remind Ryan that he'd been responsible for him. Lowerson was one of his.

"They've operated on the head wound, put splints into his face. They're not sure if there'll be permanent damage, he's still in a coma." He faltered. "I should have been quicker."

"Don't start that," Phillips said in a surprisingly firm voice that brought Ryan's head around. "Not your fault, nobody's fault except the person who did that to him."

Ryan said nothing.

"No sign of the vicar or his wife," Phillips continued in a business-like tone. "We put out an APW for them."

Ryan nodded, thinking that an all-ports warning should prevent Mike and Jennifer Ingles, or persons matching their description, from leaving the country. If they had been responsible for putting Lowerson in that hospital bed, he would personally hunt Ingles and his wife to the ends of the earth.

"You ready to hit Mathieson now?"

"More than ready," Ryan replied, thinking of the people—and one in particular—he had left back on the island and the unshakeable feeling of unease which increased by the minute. "Let's do this."

* * *

Daniel Mathieson sat in Interview Room A with his hands folded and his face expressionless. To the casual observer, he looked exactly what he was; a retired schoolteacher with thinning hair, average features and a penchant for beige slacks. His solicitor was of a similar type: a middle-aged man in a poorly-fitting suit, nearing the end of his unremarkable career and hoping to avoid too many dramas between now and then.

"Standard procedure, Frank," Ryan murmured as they stood watching the couple through the two-way glass.

"Aw, now, you always get to play bad cop," Phillips complained, chewing steadily on his nicotine replacement gum.

"It comes naturally to me," Ryan said with a tigerish smile.

"I could be a bad cop." Phillips assumed what he thought of as an uncompromising stance, put on his meanest face. Unfortunately, he just managed to look constipated.

"Keep trying." With that, Ryan pushed open the door and walked directly to the table. He made the introductions for the sake of the tape recording, stated the names of those present along with the time, the date and other formalities. He repeated the standard caution and asked if Mathieson understood everything that had been said.

"I understand," he said placidly.

"Mr Mathieson, I have here copies of three signed statements which you provided to the police. The first is dated 21st December and was taken shortly after you were informed that your daughter, Lucy Mathieson, had been found dead at Lindisfarne Priory. Is that your signature?"

"Yes."

"Do you wish to re-read your statement?"

"No, I remember what I said."

Ryan flicked a glance at the lawyer, whose jaw was clenched tight.

"Very well. In that statement, you told the police that the last time you saw your daughter was at roughly ten past six on the evening of 20th December. Do you remember saying that?"

"Yes."

"Before we go any further, is there anything you wish to add?"

"I killed my daughter, Chief Inspector."

They could have heard a pin drop in the room during the heavy silence which followed Mathieson's bald statement. The lawyer practically dropped his head in his hands.

"Might I have a moment to confer with my client?"

"You've just had two hours to confer," Ryan pointed out, reasonably, before turning to Mathieson again.

"To confirm, you are admitting to having killed your daughter, Mr Mathieson?"

There wasn't a flicker in the other man's eyes, just the same, slightly vacant expression accompanied by a calm monotone. Ryan tried not to feel disappointed that his legendary 'bad cop' routine appeared to be unnecessary after all.

"Yes, Chief Inspector, that's right."

"Would you like to tell us how it happened?" Ryan poured the other man a glass of water, held it out.

"Of course," Daniel took a sip of the water, set the glass back down gently in the same controlled manner. "Lucy left for the pub around ten past six, as I said…"

He stopped abruptly and his eyes flickered.

"I should go back further than that, so that you understand why—why I felt I needed to—to do it."

"Alright, Daniel, take your time," Phillips said quietly.

They waited while he straightened in his chair, refused further advice from his solicitor.

"I worked as a teacher for twelve years. I taught music to boys and girls of high school age in Newcastle. I was told to take early retirement or be sacked."

"Why was that?" Ryan prompted him.

"Apparently, I was deemed to have developed an unhealthy relationship with some of my students." This was said with a tinge of defiance, Ryan noted.

"You didn't agree?"

"Some of the girls—it's natural for teenage girls to become…*intrigued* by mature members of staff."

"You're saying they flirted with you?" Phillips asked.

"Of course they did," Mathieson said unflinchingly. They could see where this was going. "Still, rather than risk a scandal, the school offered me early retirement. Naturally, I could have stayed to argue my case."

"Naturally," Ryan murmured. If he needed to find out any details, he could contact the school, the parents or the children, since that's what they had been.

Children.

"For the sake of Helen, for my family, I felt it was easier if I took what they offered me."

Neither Ryan nor Phillips said anything, so he continued.

"Lucy was just like any other teenage girl," Mathieson continued. "She had always been a well-behaved child, no trouble at all really, but just recently she became very rebellious."

"In what way?"

"Seeing all kinds of men, staying out all hours; that sort of thing."

"You disapproved of her relationships with other men?"

Ryan could see the moment when Mathieson's careful mask began to slip. It was there, when he was forced to think of Lucy with other men.

"She never really had other *relationships*, as such."

"What about Alex Walker?"

There, Ryan thought, *there's the trigger.*

"He was entirely unsuitable for Lucy." Mathieson took several deep breaths as he said this and reached for his water again, took a long gulp.

"You mean, because of his reputation with other women, or because he wasn't you?"

A muscle jerked near Mathieson's left eye and Ryan wondered if he had pushed too hard.

"Both."

That was quite an admission, Ryan thought, and had probably been more difficult than admitting to her murder.

"Your feelings for Lucy went beyond father-daughter?" Ryan concentrated on keeping the disgust out of his voice, so it came out more clipped than he intended.

"I felt that Lucy *belonged* to me, Chief Inspector, not simply because I fathered her. I don't expect you to understand. Most people are constrained by ordinary societal values."

Ryan paused, made sure he was calm before continuing.

"Lucy didn't feel the same?"

"She used to," Mathieson said, swallowing sudden tears.

Phillips and Ryan remained silent, unwilling to think too hard about what Lucy Mathieson's childhood might have been like. They would question Helen again, if only to determine whether she was aware of all that had happened under her roof, but for now they needed to stay focused.

"To summarise," Ryan said, "would it be fair to say that you felt frustrated by Lucy's independence, her rebellion, as you called it?"

"Yes."

"Getting back to the evening of 20th December, then, can you describe your movements?"

"After she'd gone to the pub, wearing a red top which left everything on show," Mathieson sneered at the memory, ran shaky hands through his wispy hair, "I had dinner with Helen, we watched some TV. It got quite late and Helen was tired, so she went to bed around half past ten, I think."

"What did you do?"

"I made sure she took her sleeping tablets, put her to bed. I came to bed a bit later, but couldn't sleep. I got up again and tried to call Lucy, to see when she would be home. She didn't answer. I thought about going down there and dragging her home. I was about to, when she finally came in just before midnight."

"Your wife was upstairs, in bed?"

"Yes, she was fast asleep. She sleeps quite heavily when she's on those tablets."

"What happened when Lucy came home?"

Mathieson paused, remembering.

"She came into the kitchen, quite drunk," he said disapprovingly. "She called me several names, said some unpardonable things and we argued."

"What sort of things?"

Mathieson's hands shook again and he clutched them together.

"She called me a 'sick old man' or words to that effect."

"How did that make you feel?"

"How do you think I felt?" he exploded, then quickly contained himself. "The anger—it just—just—overwhelmed me. I wanted to remind her of who she really was, how she used to feel about me, what we were to each other." His myopic eyes appealed to both of them to understand. "I reached for her, tried to embrace her."

"Embrace her?" Phillips prodded.

"I wanted to kiss her."

"She didn't return the feeling?"

Mathieson raised a hand to his temple, rubbed at an invisible ache there.

"It—it gets a bit hazy. It was all over so quickly. I tried to draw her into my arms but she struggled, tried to push me away. I think I was holding her arms. She kicked my leg with one of her boots," he said dreamily, rubbing absently at the bruise beneath his trousers. "Somehow, we were on the kitchen floor. She was struggling, threatening to scream for Helen. I think she meant it."

"What did you do?"

"I had to quieten her," Mathieson said softly. "I just wanted her to be quiet for a moment, to listen to me. I wanted us to be together again."

"How did you 'quieten her', Daniel?"

Mathieson's voice shook now and his hands were trembling badly. He was staring at them as if they belonged to someone else.

"I—I—I..." he gulped. "I had my hands around her neck—" He raised his hands and repeated the motion as tears began to trickle down his face. "And suddenly, she wasn't struggling anymore."

There was a moment's silence and Ryan re-filled their water glasses.

"You've come this far, Daniel, you might as well tell us the rest."

Ryan sat back, silver eyes hardened to a flinty grey as he listened to the man describe how he had carried his daughter out into the night and along to the garage at the Lindisfarne Inn, only a couple of streets away.

"Why did you take Lucy up to the Priory, Daniel? Why did you clean her? Why the ritual?"

"It was only proper." The calm tone was back, now that the worst part was over.

"*Proper?*"

"According to our beliefs, the body of a loved one must be cleaned thoroughly, Chief Inspector, as a mark of respect. It was right that I tended her body and removed her to holy, consecrated ground."

There were so many questions to ask, Ryan barely knew where to begin.

"You say 'our' beliefs? Whose beliefs would they be?"

For the first time, Mathieson hesitated, his answers more measured.

"Mine and Lucy's, of course."

"Paganism?"

Again, a tiny pause.

"Yes, that's right." Little or no eye contact, Ryan noted, which usually denoted a lie.

"Where did you get the camphor, Daniel?"

"Lucy had some, in her room."

"Surely, if she followed Pagan ritual, Lucy would have kept some Pagan items in her room. Yet, we found none when we performed a search. Did you remove them, Daniel?"

"No comment."

Both detectives raised their eyebrows.

"Why be uncommunicative now, when you've been so helpful? We're just trying to understand your beliefs."

"No comment."

"Very well," Ryan fought back frustration. "You cleaned Lucy up at the garage. We found her DNA all over it," he added casually, so there could be no mistake. "You used camphor. What else?"

"I used some of the soap they keep in boxes there," Mathieson piped up again, seemingly happy to discuss this part. "Some turps and bleach, too."

"Must have been hard, transporting her to the Priory, worrying if anyone would see you. Then, carrying her up the steep side of the hill," Phillips said sympathetically.

"It was difficult, yes. I nearly lost my resolve," Mathieson added, as if he were reminiscing about old times. "But I got there in the end."

* * *

Ryan and Phillips spent another hour going over Mathieson's story, picking it apart, tugging at the different directions again. He was happy to discuss, ad nauseam, how he had killed his own daughter. He was happy to describe how he had prepared an altar for her, smoothed her hair and said prayers over her body before leaving her. He confessed to cleaning the lawnmower and the garage floor later the same night and even admitted that he had planted Lucy's clothes in Alex Walker's fishing hut in a childishly spiteful act. Remarkably, he was unrepentant about it, claiming that Walker deserved all he got.

Jealousy came in many forms, Ryan decided, and every one of them was ugly.

What Mathieson refused to talk about was his religious beliefs. No amount of cajoling, flattery or threats could induce him to discuss it.

Only once did his resolve falter, on the topic of Megan.

"We found several bank transfers in your name, deposited into Megan Taylor's account. Can you explain that, Daniel?"

"I slept with Megan several times over the course of last year," he answered without any qualm. "She seemed to expect a payment, which didn't surprise me since I went to her with the expectation that she would prostitute herself."

The coldness of that statement, Ryan thought, the detachment. He didn't bother to ask if his wife had known about the association. He was betting not.

"Were you aware that Megan kept a diary, Daniel?"

No comment, but curiosity peaked in the older man's face.

"She did," Ryan affirmed, "discussing her appointments and so forth. She described someone called, 'D', along with her attendance at several ritual 'circles'. Do you know anything about that?"

"No comment," was the expected answer, but there was a knowing look.

"Did you kill Megan, Daniel?"

"No comment," he said in the same pleasant tone.

Ryan and Phillips stared for a moment.

"Earlier this afternoon, as we were leaving Lindisfarne, you confessed to the murders of Megan Taylor and Robert Fowler," Ryan said in patient tones. "Are you now retracting your confession?"

Mathieson folded his lips.

"Look," Ryan said, beginning to lose patience. "DS Phillips and I are reasonable men. We understand what you've told us about Lucy, we're even willing to accept that there was no premeditation there. I'm sure you can argue it down from murder to manslaughter in court," the words stuck in Ryan's throat, but he knew it was the truth. "But Megan and Rob, that took planning. It wasn't the heat of the moment there. It's going to be very hard to argue those ones down, Daniel, unless you give us a reason to believe that it wasn't you."

Silence, punctuated only by the sound of Mathieson's heavy breathing.

"You made transfers into Megan's account. Was she going to expose you, Daniel? Was she going to tell Helen?"

"Megan served her purpose, as did Rob," Daniel hissed, sending small drops of spittle across the table.

"What do you mean, 'their purpose'?"

Mathieson would say no more.

Ryan stared at him for a few long moments and then called a break, since it was nearly half past six. Outside, he turned to Phillips.

"Anything to do with the ritual, anything to do with Megan or Rob and he clams up. Why? He's practically singing about Lucy."

"I can't understand it," Phillips agreed. "He's almost proud of himself when he's telling us about killing his daughter."

"He thinks that he's atoned for his crime by giving her a 'proper' burial," Ryan said.

Phillips watched while his SIO paced to the coffee machine, watched it percolate, then swallowed the greasy liquid from one of the little polystyrene cups.

"What you thinking?"

Ryan finished swallowing and lobbed the cup across the room where it fell perfectly in the centre of the open bin. Then he turned back.

"I'm thinking that if I go back in there and question him again, he'll tell us absolutely nothing about Megan or Rob. I'm thinking he's been stringing us along about those two. He was under surveillance when Lowerson was hit, so we know it wasn't him. I was betting on Ingles for that but now I'm not so sure."

"He had an accomplice?"

Ryan looked out of the boxy window, but instead of seeing the police car park below, he saw in his mind's eye the map of Lindisfarne he had taped on the wall of his cottage. He saw the little red flags which marked where each body had been found: Lucy on the south of the island, at the Priory. Rob on the west of the island, on the causeway beach. Megan in the centre, on the roof of the pub, but the weather vane had been fixed to point north.

They served their purpose.

"Frank, what was it you said about pagans attaching meaning to the four points—north, south, east and west?"

Phillips scratched his head. "Ah, just that it's a big part of their ritual, boss. Each point, or watchtower, or guardian or whatever they like to call it, means a different element."

"Earth, air, fire and water?"

"Yeah, that's it. Why?"

"He's not finished."

"Mathieson?"

"No," Ryan spun around again and his eyes were fierce. "Mathieson was finished after Lucy. It's been staring us in the fucking face. Why would he practically turn himself in when he hasn't made his sacrifice to the east? It makes no sense for Mathieson to confess now, if he was responsible for all three. There's still one to go."

"Ah—"

"The victims—I thought there should be a pattern—there isn't, or not in the usual sense," Ryan carried on, the words tumbling out in a stream of consciousness. "I was thinking of it yesterday, of how psychopaths are goal-driven. There's always a meaning behind everything they do, something to gain. This isn't some bloke gone cuckoo, dancing around a wicker man and it isn't about some perverted old man who finally flipped and killed his own daughter. The man we're after had a reason, a very specific reason, to kill Megan and Rob. It fits, why the bodies were treated differently, marked differently."

"Who?" Phillips said urgently.

"The same man who didn't want Megan mouthing off to his wife about their affair. A man she calls 'D', the pillar of their community. The same man who didn't want to see Alex Walker jailed for a murder he didn't commit, so arranged for another one to happen, so that we could be sure that Walker didn't do the first. Side benefit was killing off Rob Fowler, who maybe knew too much and was, as this man viewed him, undesirable. Who fits the bill?"

"Christ," Phillips breathed as he felt it all click into place.

"So simple," Ryan shook his head, ran fingers restlessly through the heavy black hair. "We have to get back."

"Mathieson—" Phillips trotted behind Ryan to keep up with the long strides as they powered along the corridor towards the exit.

"Get MacKenzie to finish going over his story, try again to get him to tell us who 'D' is, because he knows, all right. He knows and he's feeling pretty fucking smug about it," Ryan snapped out. "Threaten him with exposure, if necessary. Mathieson feels loyal to this prick and he's acting on orders; that's why he doesn't want to give him away. Break that loyalty, tell him we'll let it be known that he sang like a canary, unless he tells us and we'll charge him for one murder rather than three. He's frightened of him, so he won't like that."

"On it now," Phillips huffed. "Where will you be?"

The clock read *six forty-five* and the tides were due to roll in just before eight. The island was an hour and a half's drive away, on a good day.

"I'm going to be on the island." *He hoped he would be on the island.* "Get a team together. We're looking for somewhere that suits his ego, somewhere big enough. It has to be the castle. That's where I'll be."

"We'll be right behind you."

Ryan looked into the steady brown eyes of his DI and nodded before heading out into the wind.

CHAPTER 28

The Jolly Anchor was brimming with rekindled Christmas cheer when Anna eventually gave up waiting for Ryan and headed along to the wake by herself. Multi-coloured lights hung from the pillars of the bar and holly sprigs had been tacked to the walls and around the big fireplace, which was blazing. The warmth of the room, filled with so many recognisable faces, helped Anna to shake off the remaining anxiety which had filled her as she'd watched Ryan drive away.

It was pathetic to feel so needy. He had left Lindisfarne so that he could question and presumably charge the man responsible for killing three people. That was a reason to be thankful, she reminded herself, not to feel lonely and bereft. She had lived alone for years, had been the mistress of her own destiny. Why should that change after only a few days spent with Ryan?

Anna reached into her bag to check her mobile phone again before she remembered there was barely any reception on this part of the island. Still, it didn't matter too much. Ryan knew where she would be if he wanted to find her.

She saw Mark heading towards her wearing a thick Christmas jumper decorated with white bobbly snowflakes and was compelled to smile. Tonight was meant to be a celebration of the lives of those they had lost, a salve for the hurt they had all felt in varying degrees over the past few life-altering days. She owed it to Megan to get into the spirit of the occasion, so she took the offered glass of mead.

"It's good to see you here, Anna," Bowers said, noting the shadows under her eyes and the way the firelight danced across her face.

"It's good to be here," she replied, waving across to Bill Tilson, who was manning the bar with Pete. "I wasn't sure if I would come."

"No Ryan tonight?" Mark asked.

"He's across on the mainland…"

"Oh, of course, questioning Dan Mathieson. That came as a bit of a shock to us all."

"I know," Anna said, "it was always going to be a shock, because it was almost certain that we would know the person responsible. Let's hope that's an end to it."

Bowers nodded reflectively and swirled the brandy in his hand.

"Let's hope Mathieson does the right thing," he said. When Anna turned with a questioning look, he added, "Confesses to his crimes."

"Oh! Yes, that would make Ryan's job much easier. There's so much evidence, apparently, down at the Rigby garage, it seems to be all tied up."

"That's very good," Mark said. "Here's to the end of a nasty interlude, then."

Anna raised her glass to clink with his and, since the mead was beginning to make her head slightly fuzzy, she asked a personal question.

"Do you ever feel lonely around Christmas, Mark? It never used to bother me, but just lately, I've realised my outlook might have changed."

Bowers looked down into his glass, watched the amber liquid for a long moment.

"I used to feel lonely. Life passed me by, really, because I got caught up with work. I never made time for a 'Mrs Bowers'," He turned to look at her briefly, just once and then turned back to the room.

"You don't feel that way, anymore?"

Bowers glanced around the room, a wide sweep of intelligent eyes.

"Not as much. We find other things, other people to occupy us."

"Well, nobody could say that you're a layabout, Mark," Anna chuckled, thinking of all the good work he did for the island.

"I like to keep busy," he shrugged it off. "But don't make my mistake, Anna. Grasp life and everything it has to offer you, because otherwise you'll wake up one morning, much older, lamenting the fact that you squandered your opportunities. Ryan's a good man."

He drank more and thought of their absent friend.

"How do you—" Anna broke off, embarrassed.

Mark turned to her with a smile.

"I was going to say, 'how do you know when you've found the right person?' "

Bowers turned fully towards her and reached out, touched the ends of her hair briefly before pulling back.

"I used to love a woman, Anna. She was the most beautiful person I'd ever known, inside and out. I adored her, but now she's gone."

"I'm sorry, Mark," Anna said deeply. "I never knew."

"How could you? I never told you." *And still, you don't understand,* he thought.

"Why didn't it work out?" She should probably stop being so nosy, Anna thought, but Mark was the closest thing she had to family now.

He shook his head.

"She belonged to someone else."

* * *

The roar of the engine was a shock to the quiet coastline as Ryan's car sped along the winding road towards Lindisfarne. He punched in Anna's number on the hands-free phone again.

It rang out, again.

He punched the number for Phillips and swerved to avoid a rabbit as it leaped out into the lane ahead.

"Ryan?" Phillips' comforting voice filled the confines of the car.

"You've got the team together? Good. I want Group A to man the exits. Group B crowd control. Group C with me, that's you and MacKenzie if she's finished in interview, bring a couple of officers, I need experienced people."

"Understood," Phillips said simply.

Countryside passed by in a haze until the car pulled up sharply at the entrance to the causeway, sending sand flying in a misty arc across the tarmac. Over the water, lights flickered on the little island. Ryan swore, long and hard.

The tide had beaten him to it, concealing the causeway underneath a blanket of dark, choppy water.

"I didn't make it, Frank," he bit out, considering his options. The seas were rough, signalling the onset of a storm. It was no surprise, he thought grimly, since the weather had been grey and foggy, the winds running high for the past few days.

"Requisition a helicopter, get the team down to the RAF site and tell them to get across to the island as soon as it's safe, but not before. I won't risk any more lives."

"What will you do?" Phillips asked.

"Whatever I have to do, Frank."

* * *

Anna shared another drink with Mark, talking over old times, before he gave her a brief kiss and bade her goodnight. He had an early start in the morning, as he was planning to visit his sister's family on the mainland for Christmas Day. The crowd in the pub had thinned slightly, those with younger families having gone home already, but a fair few remained. It was just as well, because Anna wasn't ready to head back to a solitary house.

Outside, the wind cracked against the windows like a whip, rattling the wooden frames. The walk home would be brutal and Anna wished she had foregone the mead in favour of bringing her car.

"Anna? How are you keeping, girl?" Bill ambled over to her, his reddish face glowing after sampling some of his own produce.

"Better than expected, Bill. And you?"

He took another slug of beer and looked across at her with slightly unfocused eyes.

"Funny how life turns out, isn't it?"

"I suppose so," Anna agreed, wondering where he was going with the conversation. It wasn't like Bill to come over all deep and meaningful, but then it was an emotional occasion. She followed his gaze and looked across at three large picture frames which he'd fixed above the fireplace—one for each of the victims. Her eye was drawn to Megan, her beauty and vitality shining through the grainy photograph of her sitting cross-legged and relaxed on the beach.

"Where was that one taken, Bill?"

"That was last year, down on Bamburgh beach," he thought back to a perfect summer's day on the wide, golden sands which spread out beneath Bamburgh Castle and the jutting rock it rested upon.

"She looks happy," Anna said, with a touch of wonder. She couldn't remember seeing Megan truly happy.

"I think—I think she was," Bill said uncertainly.

Anna looked at him closely.

"Bill," she said softly, "you took the picture?"

He managed a nod.

"I'm sorry, I didn't realise."

"No reason you should," he said briskly, knuckling away a stray tear which had leaked onto his cheek. "Didn't realise myself, for a long time. She was like a butterfly, wasn't she? A beautiful, colourful butterfly, but if you get too close to her wings, she would break. She didn't like to be stifled."

"That's a good way of describing her, Bill, she would have appreciated it."

He nodded.

"She was proud of you, Anna," he said suddenly, deciding that there were things she should know.

Anna turned to him patiently, ready to nod and smile.

"I know you won't believe me if I tell you that she ordered a copy of your book," Bill was smiling now, thinking of how Megan had looked when he'd caught her opening the delivery parcel.

"She did?" Anna looked at him blankly.

"Aye, she made some excuse about it being a delivery error, then how she had a right to read about local history and all that, but the truth is that she bought it to have something of you."

Anna forced back tears and turned to look at her sister again, fully.

"I've been a fool," she said thickly.

"We've all been fools," he said and polished off his beer.

* * *

As the storm began to rage in earnest, Ryan gave up trying to get through to Anna and refused to think the worst. There could be an explanation, he reasoned, she could be at the pub and unable to hear the sound of her phone above the din.

He was worried sick.

Single-mindedly, he drove through the night, along dark roads bereft of light apart from the flickering beam of the headlights of his car. Twice, he lost the route and took a wrong turn, ending up along an unmarked country lane which laughed in the face of satellite navigation. Twice, he almost cried out with frustration.

Eventually, he saw the signpost marked 'Budle' and swung through the lively streets, filled with local revellers toasting the night before Christmas.

He made directly for the harbour, the only place where he could get a boat across to Lindisfarne.

* * *

Anna was starting to enjoy herself. The mead was definitely doing its job, she thought with a schoolgirl giggle. Frankie Goes to Hollywood was singing across the bar speakers about the power of love and she felt abruptly tearful as she slumped in one of the leather armchairs near the fire.

What was the matter with her? She tried to shake the fuzziness from her head and thought about wandering back over to the bar to ask for a cup of coffee, or some water, but it was so warm and cosy by the fire.

Her muddled gaze swept around the room, met the eyes of old friends and neighbours. Pete smiled at her as he pulled pints behind the bar. Bill was talking with Steve Walker and some others. Alison Rigby held court amongst a group of women but, spotting Anna alone, she made her excuses and headed towards her.

"Oh, bugger it," Anna mumbled to herself, tried to get up with some thought of escape, but slumped back and giggled again. Her throat suddenly very dry, she took another sip of the mead.

"How are you, my dear?" Alison bustled across the room in a stiff black satin dress which was at least a size too small, bringing a strong odour of hairspray with her.

"I'm fine, thank you Mrs Rigby, just a little tired." Anna found she had to work hard to enunciate each word.

"It's been a terrible time, hasn't it?" Alison clucked, urging Anna to sit back and be comfortable as she settled herself on the chair opposite.

"Mmm hmm," Anna agreed sleepily.

"All this death, it's reminded me so much of when my Andrew passed away," Alison remarked, but there was no sign that she was unhappy about it. Rather, her eyes gleamed as she looked around the room. She was a woman who fed off other people's dramas.

"Sorry 'bout that," Anna mumbled politely, trying to remember what Andrew Rigby had looked like.

"No need, dear. In all honesty, Andrew's passing was a blessing in disguise. He really was the limit, sometimes," she flicked a speck of lint from her skirt and smoothed manicured hands over it. She looked at Anna closely and decided there was no harm in them having a little chit-chat. "You must have known, dear, about Andrew and your sister. Surely, you heard the rumours?"

Anna frowned, trying to piece together what Alison had said.

"My—my sister?"

"Yes, of course, your sister," Alison said sharply, then quickly lowered her tone. "Who else? Quite the alluring little lady, Megan Taylor."

"I—I don't understand," Anna said.

"It's very simple, really. Your sister lured my husband away from his home and family, made him forget his responsibilities."

"She wasn't like that," Anna's foggy brain managed that much.

"Well, of course you *would* say that," Alison leaned across and patted Anna's hand in a mockery of affection. "It's amazing, isn't it, how the apple doesn't fall very far from the tree? Megan was very like your mother in that way. She could wind men around her finger at fifty paces."

"Who?"

Alison huffed out a laugh which shook her beehive hair.

"Your mother, dear. Sara Taylor was a fine-looking woman, I'll give her that. Especially with all she had to put up with, living with your father. I wouldn't have put up with it. I *didn't* put up with it," she laughed a hard laugh. "All's well that ends well, though, isn't it?"

Anna stared at the other woman with confusion and horror, tried to lever herself up but couldn't quite manage it.

"There now, don't fret. You just stay where you are, it'll all be over soon enough."

With that, Alison picked up the glass of mead sitting on the table beside Anna and urged it into her hand, brought it firmly to Anna's lips.

"Keep drinking, there's a good girl. You'll feel better soon enough."

With that, she got up, made a subtle gesture to a man standing across the room and then went back to her ladies.

* * *

Ryan had sailed before, in his childhood. He had spent several pleasant summers on the south coast at his grandmother's house in Devon, where he could remember her teaching him and his sister the basics of sailing. The skies had always been blue, the water placid and the warm wind just strong enough to fill the sails.

The reality of the present was a world away from those comfortable memories of the past. He'd argued and then threatened the harbourmaster in Budle to let him have a boat and when that had failed, he'd tried to bribe one of the fishermen to sail him across in one of their scarred-looking vessels. Even large wads of cash paired with a police warrant card couldn't tempt the locals to brave the North Sea conditions. In other circumstances, he would applaud their good sense.

Instead, he'd unrigged one of those vessels and commandeered it.

Now, he found himself questioning his own sanity as he chugged across the rolling waters, felt his stomach heave and somersault inside his body as the boat rocked like a feather in the wind. Water seeped through his supposedly 'all-weather' jacket, dripped from his hair in a slick black cap as the sea sprayed over the boat. He knew a bit about the waters around Lindisfarne, knew they could be deadly and that he took the biggest risk of his life by setting out alone, in the dark. He hoped that his memory of the terrain would serve him well as he urged the engine onwards, fighting the power of the waves, skirting around the darker waters where sharp-toothed rocks lay hidden.

The going was painfully slow, but when he rounded the headland and hit the current from the ocean which ranged before him, he knew real fear. Teeth gritted, jaw tensed, he pulled the hood back over his head to keep the worst of the salty spray from his eyes and focused on the dim glimmer of light which seemed to rise from the sea a little further down the coast.

Lindisfarne.

He gunned the boat's engine and thought of Anna.

* * *

Anna felt sick and her head was pounding. Faces swam in front of her like ghosts as she fought to stay lucid. She was struggling to sit up, when a gentle hand gripped her arm.

"Can I help you, Anna?"

"Bill," she said gratefully. "I feel—I feel unwell."

He tutted as he noted her pallor and over-bright eyes with their contracted pupils.

"It looks like you might have had a bit too much to drink," he said, pursing his lips and helping her to stand. "Come on, I'll walk you home. Pete can handle the bar."

"I—I don't usually," Anna took several panting breaths as she leaned against his warm bulk and let him put an arm around her. Over her head, Bill made a funny gesture about having too much to drink, for the benefit of those who watched.

"There, now, one foot in front of the other," his soothing voice urged her onwards.

"Will you call Ryan, please?" she asked.

"Now, now, you don't need Ryan," he said affectionately, holding her hard against him as they headed out into the night.

Anna felt the cold air like a slap in the face and for a moment it was sobering.

"I—I think I need to lie down."

"Good idea," Bill agreed, giving her arm a friendly rub. "Probably best if we don't walk after all. Let's just use my car."

"Okay," she nodded weakly, feeling like she was floating now. Distantly, she let him strap her into the passenger seat and rested her heavy head against the cold window.

"Nearly there," Bill said as they drove along the long road which led from the village eastward towards the castle.

Anna lifted herself enough to notice the surroundings.

"No, Bill, I should have said. I'm not staying at my cottage anymore; I'm on the other side of the island, staying with Ryan."

"I know that, Anna," he said quietly.

"But—but you're going the wrong way," she said logically and heard him sigh deeply.

"This hurts me, Anna, it really does. I've always cared about you, same as I cared about Megan."

Anna could make no sense of it.

"Shall we have some music on?" he said, suddenly cheerful again. He turned on the radio and fiddled with it until Bing Crosby's rich voice sang out, dreaming about a white Christmas.

"You probably don't understand any of this," he assured her. "But the High Priest will explain it to you, so that you can appreciate how important you are to our circle. Without you, there would be no offering."

Anna put her head between her legs and vomited.

* * *

Ryan could sense he was getting closer, although every metre across the sea was hard won. The problem was negotiating the harbour, once he got there. He thought he could find his way to the little inlet, around to the east just before the fortress which overlooked the vast expanse of ocean, but before then he had to avoid the rocks which lay like land mines guarding the entrance. He was going to need help.

He reached for the radio he had switched off, fired it to life again. Appearances could be deceptive. Here, on the tin-bucket boat, her owner had installed a state-of-the-art radio system complete with digital selective calling.

After another hideous moment where Ryan couldn't immediately recall the marine identity number for the Lindisfarne Coastguard, he realised the number had been pre-programmed like a speed-dial and marked helpfully on the dashboard.

He pushed '16' and waited for someone to answer.

There was a crackle across the line which was music to his ears.

"HM Coastguard Lindisfarne, receiving. Please identify. Out."

Ryan recognised the voice.

"Alex, this is Ryan. I'm in a fishing vessel, approaching the south-eastern edge of Lindisfarne from the direction of Budle. Require assistance to negotiate harbour entry. Out."

"Ryan, you crazy fuck. Conditions too severe for harbour entry. Turn your boat around. Repeat. Turn your boat around. Out."

"Negative. Maintaining present course. Out."

There was a momentary crackle on the line. At his desk in the coastguard hut, Alex rubbed a sweaty hand across his face and looked out at the storm which raged beyond his window. Then, back at the radar which beeped to indicate Ryan's position. He was bobbing precariously between two long stretches of rock which had lain boats and their skippers to waste for hundreds of years.

"Drop anchor. Coastguard will meet you. Confirm. Out."

"Negative. Not enough time and too risky for you. Guide me in. Out."

Alex swore. Stubborn bastard!

"Have it your way. Adjust fifteen degrees starboard, then maintain course."

CHAPTER 29

Anna was dimly aware of being in Bill's car as it struggled up the steep, curving road which led up to the island fortress atop its mount. She knew it to be a spectacular spot; on a clear day, you could see out across the sea for miles if you climbed the stone tower, the tallest structure on the island.

Eventually, his car reached the top and wound through the curved stone entrance flanked with lanterns that had been freshly lit in welcome. Bill pulled up in front of the wide doors, which stood open.

"Here we are," he said in the same maddening voice, as he hauled her up and out of the car. Anna's legs buckled beneath her and her head still swam, so he lifted her easily and carried her like a baby through the doorway.

Inside, the fortress was surprisingly warm in comparison with the howling gales outside. Fires were laid in every grate to provide heat and light. Bill seemed to know where he was going because he didn't pause in the long entrance hall but rather carried on up the stone stairwell, his boots thumping with the effort.

"Bill," Anna plucked at his sleeve desperately, but couldn't seem to grasp the material. "Please."

"Hush," he said quietly. His course was already decided and he was unwilling to alter it.

At the top of the stairs, he took a left along the passageway until he came to a large hexagonal room at the end. The circle stood ready, dressed in long black robes, anonymous beneath their animal masks. Windows afforded a panoramic view of the sea and land beneath and a fire warmed the wood and stone interior, casting shadows over the old framed paintings of men and women long dead.

In the centre stood a man. He wore a long fur pelt which draped over his shoulders and down his back to brush the floor. He moved around a low wooden table which had been draped in red cloth.

"Our brother and Anna. Welcome."

Bill dipped his head briefly in a mark of respect and then moved to deposit Anna on the table.

Tears leaked from her eyes as Anna struggled to move. Black spots swam in front of them as she tried to focus, to move her limbs.

The High Priest moved towards her and his horned mask swam in front of her eyes, the lines between reality and unreality blurring so that, for a moment, man and beast merged as one.

"The seeds are working," he said quietly and her eyes flew open again, horror mirrored clearly in them.

He noticed it and smiled. It was always sweet, that moment of recognition, the prelude to the crippling fear which would follow.

"Yes, you know me, don't you Anna?"

She said nothing, simply stared at him, her chest heaving.

He smiled through the hole in his mask, straight white teeth stretching across an attractive face.

He straightened and turned to his followers, told himself to be patient and complete the ritual. It was necessary, he understood that now. He lifted the dagger he held in his hand and cast a circle in the air, called to the Master.

Emperor Lucifer, master of all the rebel spirits,

We beg you to favour us in the call that we make to you.

O, Count Astarot!

Be favourable to us and make it so this night you appear to us in human form.

Accord to us, by the pact that we make with you, all the riches we need.

Ave Satani!

Anna heard the words and struggled again, retching. Her arms and feet were pinned, strapped to the table with two long strands of rope which wrapped fully around and underneath the wood to cover her chest, then underneath again to cross over her legs and ankles. The rough material rubbed against the skin on her ankles and wrists hard enough to draw blood but she didn't feel it.

Above and around her, they chanted.

Turning her head, Anna watched them with a growing sense of finality. Faces merged into nightmarish effigies of mythical creatures.

* * *

When Ryan steered the tired fishing boat into Lindisfarne's tiny harbour, any relief he felt was outweighed by gratitude towards the coastguard who had ensured he got there in one piece.

Alex Walker ran along the slippery wooden jetty, feet skidding, to meet him off the boat. He offered a calloused hand, which Ryan took.

"What's going on? What the hell's going on?"

Ryan looked into the other man's weary face and decided to trust him. Sometimes, the apple fell far, far away from the tree.

"I need to get up to the castle. I think they've got Anna up there."

"They?"

"There's a circle of people on the island, you know that."

Alex didn't bother to deny it.

"My father's part of that circle and he's a healer, Ryan. He isn't violent, believe me."

Ryan felt the stirrings of pity.

"I'm going up there with or without your help."

"Have you tried calling Anna?" Alex said desperately. "She's probably just down at the Anchor, having a drink with the others. Here, use my phone—"

"Already tried calling her. No answer. I've tried the pub too and Pete tells me the place is mostly cleared out and that Bill took Anna home, which is funny because there's no answer there, either." Ryan muscled past him to run down the jetty, out onto the road leading up to the castle.

"Any cars been past here?"

"A couple, I think, but that was probably just Mark, going up to the castle to make sure the place is locked up—"

"I need your jeep." Ryan held out a hand for the keys, looked at Alex square in the face.

Walker closed a fist around the keys in his pocket.

"I'll drive you, I know the road."

* * *

Anna watched as the man threw his arms above his head, called to his Master and instructed the others to do the same. Around the room, men and women she had known since childhood watched her with vacant, drugged expressions devoid of compassion. To them, she was no longer Anna; she was their offering in exchange for riches, whatever they may be.

To the man in the centre, she was his drug, another means by which he could get a taste of the heady power which flowed from killing. His body quivered as he thought of how her blood would feel as it poured over his hands, as he imagined the taste of it on his tongue.

Satisfied that the ritual was complete, he moved back to her, his bare feet sticking slightly on the plastic-covered floor.

He realised he wanted her mind to be clear, so that she would recognise him and respect him.

"Anna," he gave her a couple of hard slaps across the face, watched her eyes register again. He smiled.

"Doctor Walker," she croaked.

"I am so much more than that now. You need to understand that, to understand why you're so important, Anna. Without you, we would have nothing to offer."

"You've gone mad," she said without thinking and watched him snarl, watched his fist clench and unclench.

"Ignorant bitch," he hissed. "Just like your mother."

Her mother?

Anna watched him as he circled the table like a hungry lion, ready to pounce. She started to feel the clouds in her mind part and told herself to keep talking, keep him talking. He wanted to tell his story; that much was clear. He wanted to brag.

"My mother died," she said quietly.

"Nothing so simple," he demurred. "Your mother was my first offering."

Anna stared at him and pain stabbed her like a knife, followed quickly by white hot anger.

"Yes," he saw comprehension dawn. "Unfortunately, there was no time for a complete ceremony. I had to make do."

He thought back a moment to Sara Taylor's face as she had fallen, suspended in mid-air, her arms flailing around for something to hold onto. He smiled in remembrance.

"A great beauty, your mother," he said conversationally. "You have the look of her."

"Megan. You killed Megan."

"She was different again," he ran a tongue over his teeth. "A delicious sin, but as with many other things we know are bad for us, the moment comes when we have to step away. She was willing. She was willing to offer herself because she understood our circle, our worship."

"She didn't agree to die."

"Oh, yes she did," he tutted and flicked a finger across her nose in an old gesture she remembered from when she had been a teenager having dinner at his home. "Megan understood that the wheels of nature keep turning, that there must be a fair exchange between us and the forces. She was part of that exchange."

"You're nothing but a murderer. You'll burn in hell," Anna snarled.

He laughed, throwing his head back so the furry pelt rolled and swept the floor dramatically.

"Do you think I am afraid of hell? Who is it that you think we worship?" he leaned closer again in a sudden motion which caused her to take in a rasping breath, fearing what would come next.

"I *am* hell," he whispered, so close now that she could feel his breath on her face. She looked at his eyes, glinting with madness behind the plastic mask and forced herself to focus, to remain conscious, and not to give in just yet.

Where was Ryan?

"You killed Rob too."

"Talkative, all of a sudden, aren't you?" he said with a chuckle. "Well, I suppose I can oblige you. It isn't as if your lover will be able to save you, is it? The tides are in, Anna, and only a madman would try to cross by sea. Besides, Daniel has already agreed to pay the price society demands for our sacrifices."

A single tear leaked from her eyes, but her mouth remained closed.

"Very well," Walker continued, but he lifted the dagger. The blade shone silver-white in the light of the fire and Anna told herself to breathe, even when her stomach rolled and her bowels wanted to loosen. She stared up at the old ceiling, refused to look at him as he started to nick the blade over her clothes, cutting away the cloth of her top.

"Rob was weak," Walker continued. "He didn't appreciate the great sacrifice Daniel made for us by killing his own daughter. I love the irony, don't you? Very much like Abraham and Isaac, but of course our Gods are vastly different to the one they sing to every Sunday."

Anna wondered how he could venerate a paedophile, who had subjected his own daughter to untold years of torment before eventually killing her, but focused on questions he could answer.

"Rob wanted to go to the police?" Her breath came through her teeth as she felt him nick the last scrap of material, baring her torso.

"Indeed," Walker growled. "But as I said, he was really very weak. Imagine, telling me that he had seen Mathieson that night. He must have known that we can risk no traitors in our circle."

"You punished him," Anna said.

"He needed to be made an example of," Walker agreed. "First, for his disobedience. Second, for his lack of faith. Third, for his *audacity* in attempting to lead my son along an unclean path. In the end, like Megan, he came to me of his own free will."

Conveniently, he overlooked the part where he had drugged and tied the man down before setting him alight, Anna thought.

"Alex is one of you?" She whispered the question and dreaded the answer, chose not to look around the room in case she recognised another old friend.

"When he is ready, he will be welcomed as one of us. He has been a disappointment in many ways, I'm sad to say," Walker's voice dipped and fell for a moment, before it rose again.

"Rob had been initiated. Did he think I didn't know that he was sleeping with my son?" Steve was nearly shouting, his lips peeling back over his teeth.

Anna said nothing, couldn't risk it.

"Of course, the timing was ideal. I had planned to use Jennifer Ingles," he mused, tracing little circles over Anna's skin, scratching here and there. "She supplies us with our life force, the means by which our followers see the true path, but she and her fool of a husband are beginning to become tiresome."

He thought of Ingles for a moment and tapped the blade against his hand in an angry gesture. The man and his wife had run from him but they couldn't hide. He would find them and punish them for their betrayal. That pleasure would be for another day.

"She supplies you with drugs, you mean."

"So prosaic, so narrow-minded," he chided her. "Surely, now that you've sampled the effects yourself, you can attest to the wonderfully liberating effect they have on the human psyche."

"The drugs help to brainwash people," she said flatly. "Reducing their faculties, giving them a false sense of invincibility."

"I never expected you to believe," he said sadly. "But I did expect you to understand."

"I understand completely."

He leaned over her so that they were eye to eye.

"No, my dear, but you will."

* * *

Phillips was an ordinary man with ordinary tastes. Those tastes did not include donning a bullet-proof vest and flying through a storm in the middle of winter, across treacherous waters, with only a tin-pot helicopter between him and certain death.

Not that he would admit that he was afraid of heights or that he couldn't swim; not when Denise MacKenzie sat across from him looking like a cross between G.I. Jane and Miss Ireland. Her red hair was caught up in a black helmet, tendrils escaping around her ears. She wore dark protective clothing, as he did, but where his tended to cling a bit across the stomach region, hers skimmed her body like a second skin. He told himself to keep his mind on the job.

He was their commander, after all.

"Aye, right, you all know the drill," he shouted above the sound of the propeller, trying to ignore the roll of his stomach as the helicopter swayed sickeningly in the wind.

"We land beside the nature reserve, on the north of the island. Team A, I want you manning the exits to the castle. Team B, head to the village, crowd control. Team C, you're with me. We'll split up. Yates and Jennings, sweep downstairs. MacKenzie, we'll take upstairs."

He cleared his throat.

"Suspect is Steve Walker, aged fifty-eight. He's the island doctor but he's a man we suspect of being responsible for two deaths, potential third in progress. He may have accomplices in a group of local men and women, who refer to themselves as a 'circle', acting under his direction. They may be armed and should be considered dangerous. DCI Ryan may be in the vicinity attempting to recover the victim, identified as Anna Taylor, sister of one of the deceased. Any questions?"

There were no questions.

The helicopter started to lurch in what Phillips considered an unnecessary nose dive towards the island and he clipped on the side of his helmet.

"Let's go, boys and girls. One of ours is down there and he needs a helping hand."

* * *

Anna lay naked on the wooden table but for her underwear. She shivered, small jerks of her body as Walker circled around, peeling away her dignity piece by piece.

"Why are you doing this?" she asked the question through lips that were dry as parchment and wished desperately for a sip of water.

"I am compelled," he answered easily. "Our Master demands it." He remembered the circle standing around him, realised he had forgotten their existence and spoke up. "He compels *all of us* to make offerings and, in return, he showers us with fortune. I am the Master in human form."

Anna laughed, she couldn't help it. It came out long and loud, slightly hysterical, but she was past caring.

"Who do you think you're kidding? You think that killing people makes you a god—or that it makes you invincible?" Her voice was scathing. "The police will know you've done this, done all of this. You're nothing but a common psychopath. They're two-a-penny down at the max security wards in Broadmoor, I'm sure you'll fit right in."

He stood perfectly still, then something finally snapped. With an animal-like howl, he straddled her on the table. The action dislodged the mask and it clattered to the floor, leaving his face bared to her. Eyes feral, teeth bared, he clutched the dagger in both hands and prepared to plunge it deep into her chest.

The circle stood, watching.

Anna looked up, up at the face of a man who believed himself to be a god, who held her life in his hands. In that moment, she thought of Ryan and all they had shared so quickly. If she had known, if she had thought that there wouldn't be any more time, she would have told him how much he had enriched her life.

She would have told him that she loved him and screw the fact that it had only been a few days. She would have enjoyed watching that awkward look on his face while he fumbled to find an appropriate reply.

She smiled, thinking of it.

* * *

Alex was true to his word. The jeep made record time as it flew up the hilly road to the castle, sending small rocks and gravel flying over the cliff edge as it went. Ryan was out of the car before it came to a stop, already reaching for the clutch-piece which still lay tucked into his jeans.

"Wait! I'm coming with you," Alex stopped to pick up a flare gun—it was the best he could do—and ran into the stone fortress after him.

It was pure instinct which led Ryan to the stairs. That *feeling* again, guiding him. He took the stairs, two at a time, his tread light. He moved like a shadow, blending with the darkened hallway. He heard Alex moving behind him cautiously, which was good.

"Keep behind," he murmured, but didn't wait for an answer. He heard the chanting, a low drone coming from the end of the corridor and followed the sound.

His heart stopped as he took in the scene. He was vaguely aware of the people swaying and mumbling in a circle, but his eyes flew to the centre, where Anna lay roped and bound. Above her, Walker was poised, resting on his haunches either side of her.

"Police! Drop your weapon!"

Walker looked across when he heard them in the doorway and gave Ryan and his son a wide smile. He raised his arms higher, preparing to sink the blade into Anna's chest.

Ryan pulled the trigger and at the same time a stream of red light whistled past his ear. Walker let out a long howl before his body crumpled to the floor, writhing in agony as one bullet speared his shoulder and the hot flare grazed his right cheek.

Ryan turned to Alex, who stood just behind him with the flare gun raised and still smoking. He was breathing hard, tears glistened but they didn't fall. Gently, Ryan pushed the gun to face the floor.

"For Rob," Alex said in a low voice.

Ryan nodded.

"Watch the others."

He ran to Anna, felt the tightness in his chest ease slightly when he saw her alive, breathing, looking at him.

"Get me out of here, for God's sake," she muttered and he sobbed out a laugh, began unravelling the heavy rope. He helped her up, wrapped his jacket around her.

They heard the sound of footsteps—one light and one distinctly heavier—just before Phillips and MacKenzie burst into the room. Ryan was amused to note that Frank had elected to swing low as Denise swung high, looking like a Northumbrian version of Starsky and Hutch.

Still, he was damn happy to see them.

"Took you long enough," he said, then turned to the figures huddled on the floor, hands behind their heads. "Let's shine some light on this."

They switched on the overhead lights and systematically unmasked the circle of locals. There were fishermen that Ryan recognised, the receptionist from Walker's surgery, but among them were Alison Rigby and Bill Tilson.

"She said that my sister had stolen her husband," Anna said dispassionately as she looked down on the woman who lay weeping on the floor.

"Whores! Every last one of you!" Alison screamed, her mascara running in black tracks down her face.

"Now, let's not have any of that language," Phillips said mildly, then rested a heavy boot on her back as she struggled on the floor, trying to claw at him. "I suppose there'll be no more cake for me," he said.

"Bill." Anna looked at him as she would a stranger. "You were like a brother to me but you betrayed Megan and now you're nothing. You've made yourself nothing."

He held his head in his hands and wept.

CHAPTER 30

December 25ᵗʰ

If she wasn't so tired, Anna might have found it sentimental that Ryan hadn't once moved from her side since he had burst back into her life in spectacular fashion.

"How are you feeling?" he asked her for the fiftieth time as he helped her into the coastguard's jeep, dressed in the baggy khaki trousers and spare red jumper Alex had lent her.

"Stop fussing, for God's sake," she muttered.

"What's that?"

"I said, I'm feeling much better," she amended sweetly.

"You need to take it easy," Ryan continued to fret, checking her pupils one more time. "The doctor will be along after he's finished patching up Walker."

Anna was silent.

"I know what you're thinking," Ryan said.

"No, you don't."

"You're wondering whether my aim was off."

Damn the man, she thought, for being such a know-it-all.

"Well?" she said testily. "Was it?"

His lips twitched.

"I hit the target I aimed for," Ryan said quietly. "I want him to spend the rest of his life behind bars, although he'll probably try to argue diminished responsibility, play up the god complex."

His fingers tapped against his knee, the only outward sign that he was irritated by the prospect.

"Either way, it's hard on Alex," she said.

"Yeah," Ryan looked out of the window at the coastguard, who stood beside Phillips and watched as they hoisted his father onto a police medical gurney. They would patch him up and transport him to the hospital in Alnwick but Steve Walker would be restrained at the ankles and wrists, as Rob had been. Alex never moved to bid him farewell, or to offer support in any way. He watched and ran a weary hand through his blonde hair. He thought of how he would tell his mother that her beloved husband, the man she shared a bed with every night, was a killer.

"We'll re-open the files relating to your mother and father's death," Ryan spoke quietly, watching her profile.

Anna swallowed.

"Yes. They both deserve the truth to be known. My father may have been a cruel bastard, but perhaps we can acquit him of murdering my mother."

"You said Walker confessed to that?"

"He boasted about how she had been his first 'offering'," Anna said dully.

Ryan brushed his fingers across hers in a gesture of quiet sympathy.

"Alison, Bill and the others will be charged as accessories to murder," he supplied, thinking of all the paperwork.

Luckily, Phillips was a sucker for paperwork.

"What about Pete and Alex?"

"It's looking like Pete was in the dark but we'll check it out. Alex claims he knew there was some sort of Pagan cult developing and that his father was involved, but he didn't know that their practices had turned violent. I need to drill down into that a bit further."

"Doctor Walker said that his son hadn't been initiated and that he was a disappointment. Maybe Alex knew his father was mixed up in something, but didn't want any part of it so he turned a blind eye."

"I could charge him with obstruction, accessory at a push."

"But?"

Ryan smiled.

"Without him, I wouldn't have been able to get up to the castle in time. Or to get into the harbour at all. He went against the grain, against every natural instinct he held towards his father. In this case, blood wasn't thicker than water and I'm beholden to him. If it weren't for Alex Walker, I wouldn't be sitting here with you in my arms."

Justice was often black and white but there were so many shades of grey in between.

"I'm grateful to him, too." Then, she turned to look at him fully. "What do you mean, 'getting into the harbour'?"

Ryan shifted in his seat.

"Oh, just a bit of boat trouble."

Anna looked into his bland face and decided that she could find out the details later. Presently, there was a band of kangaroos hopping merrily around the inside of her head.

"What about Mr and Mrs Ingles?" she asked, sighing deeply when Ryan lifted a hand to knead her shoulders and the base of her neck.

"There's an APW out for them but there's no word yet. We've passed their details to Interpol, so they'll pop up on the system at any port they try to leave."

"Walker said that Jennifer Ingles supplied the drugs to their circle. You think they were responsible for Lowerson?"

"That was my first thought but on reflection Ingles doesn't strike me as the violent type. Snivelling, bigoted, egoistic, but not violent. His wife was the brains behind the drug operation; she had previous, under a different name. If I've said it once, I've said it a thousand times: it's always the quiet ones you need to watch."

Anna flashed a quick smile, which died as she thought of the young man lying in a hospital bed over on the mainland.

"So who are you looking at for Lowerson?"

"If Walker doesn't hold his hands up to it, then we won't know for sure unless Jack comes round. I rang the hospital and they say he's in a stable condition, but no change."

"I'm sorry."

Ryan looked down at his hands briefly, then back up again.

"He was on my watch. I may not have swung the shovel, but I sent him out there."

"He's a grown man, with police training. He took the decision to go in there alone."

Ryan heard her but all he thought of was a young detective with stars in his eyes. He would have Jack Lowerson on his conscience until he recovered; if he recovered.

"Come on," he said suddenly. "Let's get you home."

Anna turned to him as he fired the engine and wondered if he realised that he had called the little white cottage 'home'.

* * *

Phillips oversaw the transfer of Walker along with his circle of accomplices for formal charge. He hadn't bothered changing out of the riot gear since he was inclined to think it lent him a roguish air. Briefly, he considered a move away from silk ties towards leather accessories, but dismissed it as something he could look forward to during his mid-life crisis.

Thinking himself alone, he glanced around and then fished underneath the bulletproof vest until he found the cigarette he'd hidden there. He looked at it a moment, ran it under his nose to smell that sweet nicotine smell.

What was the harm? he thought, standing looking across the sea. He fished out a lighter.

The cigarette was snatched from his lips by pale, elegant fingers tipped with bright polish. In his peripheral vision, Frank saw the glint of copper hair shining in the morning breeze.

"Didn't know you cared so much about my health, MacKenzie," he began testily, gearing up for the inevitable argument.

Her fingers framed his face, yanked it towards her in a lightning move.

"You haven't got a bloody clue, have you Frank?" she said in her creamy, Irish burr before giving him a smacking kiss.

"Now," she said, pleased with herself. "Are you going to ask me out or not?"

Phillips grinned like a puppy.

* * *

Ryan watched them both from the window and then turned to the woman who lay sleeping on his sofa, covered with a thick tartan blanket. Her chest, scratched and probably still sore, had been tended by the police doctor. He'd given her painkillers for the aftereffects of the LSA and she'd mostly slept it off. They had probably ground down some seeds and spiked her drinks last night, he thought. He would ask her about it, but that could wait.

He watched her quiet breathing and thought about how he'd come so close to losing her. He was a good policeman, he thought honestly. He would have done his best for any victim, living or dead, but last night had gone beyond that. The threat of harm to this woman had sliced at his heart.

She had decorated the cottage, he thought inanely. A tree stood in the corner of the room, decked in red and gold baubles and a string of white lights which flicked on and off. Sprigs of foliage rested on the mantelpiece alongside pine-scented candles. A small box stood underneath the tree, which he had added himself.

He needed her in his life, on a permanent basis. The problem was convincing her that it was a good idea to stay with him. His work was unpredictable; *he* could be unpredictable. She was used to her independence, managing on her own.

Would it work?

He was watching her, thoughts and emotions swirling, when her eyes flickered open. When his face came into focus, she smiled.

"I had the most awful dream," she said, yawning.

"So did I, but luckily it's over."

She lifted her arms and drew him in, explored the taste of him, ran her fingers through his thick hair. Neither of them noticed the snow begin to fall outside.

Eventually, they pulled apart and her eye rested on the package underneath the tree.

"Ooh…" she gestured to it. "Is that for me? Gimme."

He laughed and pushed her back onto the sofa, reached for the box.

As she looked at the little box, her expression was easy to read. He laughed again, louder this time.

"Don't get ahead of yourself," he said, watching her face light up as she pulled out a pair of exquisitely carved silver earrings.

"They're beautiful, thank you," she said, putting them on.

"I saw them the other day," he said, slightly embarrassed as he remembered his surreptitious trip to the Gift Shop. "I thought you might like them."

"I love them," she corrected, then looked shifty. "I got you a present—of sorts."

"Where is it?" He raised his eyebrows.

"Ah—" She broke off as there was a well-timed knock at the door. "That should be it now."

Intrigued, wondering if Anna had arranged a delivery of some kind, he moved to the hallway and opened the door.

He stood speechless for a moment, throat clogged. His mother and father stood on the doorstep, bundled into winter coats and wielding heavy bags full of food and presents. His father was an older version of himself; tall and well-built with a shock of white-grey hair which had been jet black in his formative years. His mother was a petite woman with a cap of dark hair styled around an elfin face dominated by the intelligent grey eyes she had passed on to him.

"Well?" Eve Finley-Ryan cocked her head at her son. "Aren't you going to let some weary travellers in out of the cold?"

He said nothing, but stepped forward and enfolded her in his arms, took in the scent of her, the feel of her.

"Mum."

"There," she soothed him, running gentle hands over his broad back.

He stepped back eventually, gave his father a dose of the same and then gestured them both inside.

"There's someone I'd like you to meet," he managed.

Eve rubbed her cold hands together and thought of the telephone call she'd had with Anna the previous day. She was looking forward to meeting the woman responsible for bringing her son back to life.

EPILOGUE

Christmassy music played on an invisible stereo hidden somewhere on the packed bookshelves and a fire crackled in the hearth. Outside, the island was white-washed, heralding new beginnings.

The air smelled appealingly of cigar smoke and musty books.

"I can't stay long," Gregson said, settling into a soft leather armchair. "I just wanted to stop by to give you the good news."

"What news would that be?"

"The circle has chosen you as its next High Priest," Arthur replied, offering the other man a cigar.

Mark leaned forward slightly, took the offered cigar and felt a thrill rush through his body.

"It's too risky," he said, but his eyes shone.

Gregson waved a wide hand.

"It's a shame about Steve, but he got carried away. There was only supposed to be one offering."

"Mathieson was the first failure," Mark reflected.

"He was a definite bore," Gregson barked out a laugh. "Bloody old pervert, it was only a matter of time before he did something stupid. Still, we've got nothing to worry about there. He knows what's best for him."

"Three High Priests in as many decades? It's unheard of."

"It happens," Arthur shrugged, took another puff of his cigar and enjoyed the aroma. "Andy was a bad choice; I can see that now. Too unpredictable. Steve—well, God, we all thought he was a safe bet, but he had his own ideas."

Mark smiled to himself as he thought of Walker. There had been no religious sacrifice there; the man was just a pure born killer.

"He intended Anna as an offering?" he said, already knowing the answer.

"That was the plan. Never told me he'd had eyes for the mother and that he was shagging the sister. I wouldn't have brought Anna across if I'd known. Far too risky."

"She wasn't Steve's to offer. She has always been mine."

Gregson didn't argue. There was a pecking order, in all things.

"I was surprised at your choice in Ryan," Mark added with a touch of menace.

Gregson spread both of his hands.

"The man was an emotional wreck the last time I saw him. I thought he would have cracked long before now. Instead, he seems to have stepped up." There was a hint of admiration in Gregson's tone that Mark didn't like.

"He can be disposed of," he bit out, leaning forward to emphasize his point.

"Not necessary," Arthur said easily, as if they discussed these matters daily. "He'll be reassigned somewhere else. Keep him out of the way."

Mark sat back again, took a drag of his cigar and thought of when Anna had been sitting in the chair Gregson now occupied. Further across the room stood a glass cabinet where a small onyx amulet had once lain.

"She will return to Durham and he will probably follow her," he said.

He battled with himself. Anna had already made her choice in Ryan. Walker had failed to make her his offering; perhaps it was a sign to let sleeping dogs lie.

He flicked the remains of his cigar into the fire.

"What now?" he asked.

"You must make your first offering, as High Priest."

"Very well," Mark agreed.

"You have someone in mind?"

Mark thought of a night many years ago, when he had made his first offering of Andy Taylor. He'd made sure the man was blind drunk and Alison Rigby had offered her services that night to make sure their High Priest was sated on women too. Then, he'd led Taylor up to the bluff and hurled him over the edge.

He had told himself it was justice, necessary action, but really it had been for himself. Simple pleasures.

"I have two people in mind, actually," Mark said with a slight smile. "They require punishment."

"Ah, excellent," Gregson clapped his hands together, already aware of the chosen two. "That will tie up loose ends. You know we will protect you, as always. For now, I'd better be getting back to the office to keep up appearances."

"It was necessary to disable the younger detective," Mark began.

"I know that," Gregson pulled a face. "Shame about that, he's a decent lad. Still, never fear, if he shows signs of coming round we'll take care of him."

Mark nodded then bade him farewell, raised a hand to his friend and follower. On his wrist, a dull gold watch glinted beneath the cuff of his linen shirt. For a moment he smiled, remembering the times he had spent with Megan, as if remembering a pleasant holiday long ago. Eventually, all holidays must come to an end.

He enjoyed the crisp wintry air for a moment longer, then walked back inside the house, removed the long ceremonial sword from its position on the wall of his study and felt the weight of it. He paused along the corridor to don a long, weatherproof jacket which covered him to mid-shin, before he opened the door to his cellar.

Below, in the darkness, Mike and Jennifer Ingles lay restrained by thick fishing rope, duct tape spread across their mouths. Both started to moan again as he flicked the overhead light on and walked down the stone steps towards them, their wails having died down to whimpers after the first twenty-four hours.

He used the edge of the sword to tip the vicar's chin up, saw the signs of terror, dehydration and pleading amongst the fading bruises on his face.

He consecrated a circle in the dank cellar and turned deaf ears to the increasingly desperate sobbing beside him.

Afterwards, he stood for a moment surveying his handiwork, took a rag and cleaned off the sword before mounting the stairs.

The cycle began again.

ABOUT THE AUTHOR

Born in Newcastle-upon-Tyne, LJ Ross moved to London where she graduated from King's College London with undergraduate and postgraduate degrees in Law. After working in the City as a regulatory lawyer for a number of years, she realised it was high time for a change. The catalyst was the birth of her son, which forced her to take a break from the legal world and find time for some of the detective stories which had been percolating for a while and finally demanded to be written.

She lives with her husband and young son in the south of England, but will always be a northern girl at heart.

If you enjoyed *Holy Island*, please consider leaving a review:

* www.amazon.co.uk

* www.amazon.com

* www.goodreads.com

Connect with LJ Ross online:

* Twitter: https://twitter.com/ljross_author

* Facebook: https://www.facebook.com/LJRossAuthor

* Blog: https://lovesuspense.com

* LJ Ross website: https://www.ljrossauthor.com

AUTHOR'S NOTE

Although this book is very much a work of fiction, Holy Island is a real place and is located in a spectacular setting off the coast of Northumberland. Twice a day, it is separated from the mainland by a tidal causeway which lends itself to all manner of potential Agatha Christie-style mysteries. Beyond that genre, the local geography has provided the inspiration for numerous fantasy epics and it is steeped in a history which spans over a thousand years.

Nowadays, the island is inhabited by a warm and friendly community for whom the beauty of the landscape never gets old. It is worth mentioning that I have made liberal use of artistic licence and both names and places have been changed to enhance the pace of the story. As the saying goes, all characters appearing in this book are fictitious. Any resemblance to real persons, living or dead, is purely coincidental.

The cover image is based on a photograph of the castle on Holy Island, the setting for the climactic scene of the story.

ACKNOWLEDGMENTS

As with all the best things in life, they are never to be enjoyed alone. That is very true of the making of *Holy Island* which, from the start, has been a fun and collaborative process and I am grateful to all of my friends and family for their input along the way. Particular mention must be made of Kirsty, Kirsten, Kate and Tallulah, four Northern Lasses who have offered their enthusiasm, expertise and unstinting support throughout the writing of this novel. Special thanks to my lovely sister Rachael and my stepfather, Jim for their wit and levity along the way. To my mother, Susan, a true woman of substance whose love and guidance over the years has given me the confidence to chase my dreams and grasp life with both hands. Lastly but by no means least, to my husband James, that wonderful man who stands shoulder-to-shoulder with me as we walk through life together and without whom none of this would be worth doing.

Printed in Great Britain
by Amazon